PENDLE FICTION RESERVE

SEP 1989

SKELMERSDALE

FICTION RESERVE STOCK LL 60

AUTHOR	CLASS
CLINE, C.T. Jr	
TITLE	No
Damon G	1790 5131

Lancashire
County
Council

This book should be returned on
or before the latest date shown above
to the library from which it was borrowed

LIBRARY HEADQUARTERS
143, CORPORATION ST. PRESTON PR1 2TB

30118

D1334547

BOOK

DAMON

C. Terry Cline Jr.

Weidenfeld and Nicolson
London

00197830

Copyright © 1975 by C. Terry Cline, Jr.

First published in Great Britain by
Weidenfeld and Nicolson
11 St John's Hill London SW11

All rights reserved. No part of this
publication may be reproduced, stored in
a retrieval system, or transmitted, in
any form or by any means, electronic,
mechanical, photocopying, recording or
otherwise, without the prior permission
of the copyright owner.

Poems on page 314 from "Look not in my eyes, for fear"
from "A Shropshire Lad"—Authorised edition— from *The
Collected Poems of A. E. Housman*. Copyright 1939,
1940, © 1965 by Holt, Rinehart and Winston, Inc.
Copyright © 1967, 1968 by Robert E. Symons. Reprinted
by permission of Holt, Rinehart and Winston, Inc., and
the Society of Authors as the literary representative of the
Estate of A. E. Housman; and Jonothan Cape Ltd.,
publishers of A. E. Housman's *Collected Poems*.

ISBN 0 297 77016 0

Printed in Great Britain by
Redwood Burn Limited
Trowbridge & Esher

17905131

SL 7/86	SL-P ...
SA	SO Jun80
SB	SP ......
SK	SY ......

DEDICATED TO:

R. N. Jones
James M. Smyth
J. T. McGouirk
Charles T. Cline, Sr.
molders of men

CHAPTER 1

His MOTHER stood at the kitchen window, watching; the boy was in the backyard, motionless, like a deer alert to every movement. He held his chin up, as though sniffing the air. His small, frail hands were at his sides, but the fingers were stiff, separated. Did he hear something? She held a plate and dishtowel, herself motionless, watching. It frightened her when he took on one of these spells, the four-year-old struck to stone-still posture, eyes slightly glazed.

She knew from past experience, at this moment she

7

could scream his name and it would leave him unmoved. She had once rushed up to him in anger because he had not responded to her call. The memory of that experience stayed any repetition of such action. The boy had sucked air between clenched teeth, his eyes rolled back into his head, and he shuddered beneath her hands. When, finally, he looked her in the eyes, she was stunned with the malevolent fire in his expression.

"Never do that again, Mother," he had said. His voice was deep, astonishingly bass for a child so young.

Now, at the window, she watched the frightening metamorphosis as her son stood transfixed. He had not moved for fully ten minutes. Then, slowly, like thawing sinew and bone, he visibly relaxed, the fingers of his small hands flexing slowly as though they had been cramped.

She had been debating the feasibility of taking him to a doctor. She had discussed it with her husband several times. His reaction was a fatherly scoff, "He's just being a boy, Melba. Stop worrying about him. Boys play games with themselves; that's all Damon is doing, playing a game."

But this morning was different. This was the day that galvanized her to action. Damon had been acting strangely since breakfast. He refused oatmeal, protesting it was cold although she had just that moment scooped it from a steaming pot atop the stove. Melba was in no mood to pamper his idiosyncrasies this day and irately she snatched the bowl from the table admonishing, "Then, do without, Damon!"

"I'm cold, Mommy," Damon had said. She felt his forehead and the calf of his leg. His temperature seemed normal. Nonetheless, she bundled him into a sweater despite the warm sunshine of this lovely spring day. She let him out the back door, instructing, "Don't leave the yard, Damon." Off and on, she had been making it a point to check on the lad. He was still there, standing alone, not playing, just there in that frozen posture she had come to dread. Then, finally, he relaxed.

8

Sometimes when Damon came out of these spells, he instantly returned to playing as though nothing had happened. Today, he seemed to linger in the effects of that frigid moment. Slowly, he walked to the lane which sloped gently toward the barn. Grandpa owned the barn, his property abutted theirs. Damon was not allowed to go down there during milking hours, or without the express permission of Grandpa Daniels.

The lane was narrow, hard-packed clay. On either side grew magnificent tangles of roses, the climbing kind, with thorned branches falling groundward, bowed by their length and weight. It was a seventy-yard stretch of red and pink flowers. The hedge was one of Grandpa's joys. He had planted it nearly fifty years ago when he first came here with his new bride. He tended the lane and flowers as carefully as any growing thing on his two-hundred-acre farm.

Damon strolled toward the barn and his mother was about to go to the screened door and call him back when it happened. He was walking with his arms extended, somewhat as a child extends a stick in passing a picket fence. His hand was brushing the shrubs and he began to run, his fingers tracing the leaves and bumping the roses. He raced downhill and for an instant it appeared he might disobey his instructions and go beyond the fence into the barnyard. Suddenly he snatched his hand away from the shrubs, sucking his finger.

A jagged tear in his skin fell open where a thorn had snagged tender flesh. Damon stood looking at the injured finger, watching blood slowly well up in the wound, bulging above the pricked area in a shimmering orb. He sucked away the blood and repeated the process, watching new blood rising on his finger.

Even from her window, his mother could see he was disturbed by the unexpected hurt he had sustained from the bank of roses. He looked up at the shrubs, towering far over his head and extending all the way to his own yard. Then, deliberately, slowly, he walked toward the house, his arm extended again, touching flowers and rich green leaves as he moved. He was no longer playing, this was evident. He strode methodically, with purpose, one hand brushing along the hedge. His mother still stood, plate in hand, observing.

Upon reaching the yard, Damon turned full circle and looked back down the lane. Expectantly, it seemed, he watched. His mother's eyes were on her son. She was held by his exaggerated posturing, back arched, chin tucked into the chest, looking through his eyebrows in the direction of the barn. Another spell? He was unmoving.

"Oh, my God," Melba Daniels whispered. The plate dropped to the floor unnoticed. Her attention was drawn to the hedge, to Grandpa's roses. She drew air into her lungs in short movements, her body trembling. "Oh, God," she said aloud.

The roses, the beautiful budding roses, were wilting. Blossoms showered down in a silent fall that covered the lane in red and hues of pink, and Damon stood looking at the phenomenon in a strange, almost terrifying posture.

"Oh, God, no—" She raced to the telephone and dialed her husband's office in Decatur.

She was so excited she had to repeat everything before he grasped the meaning of her words. She babbled into the receiver and cried as she spoke. When her husband promised to rush home immediately, then and only then would she hang up the telephone. She turned and gasped. Damon stood in the doorway. Had he heard? He was innocently observing her. She clutched her apron and stared at him.

"I'm hungry, Mommy," Damon said. "May I have a peanut butter sandwich?"

Dr. Kyle Anderson Burnette matriculated at Emory University of Atlanta, where he received a doctorate in psychiatry. He interned at Emory University Hospital, later at Milledgeville State Mental Institution, and took a fellowship to continue his studies at Mayo Clinic for

10

another eighteen months. He was psychiatrist and chief medical officer for the First Infantry in Vietnam for two years. When he returned to begin private practice in Atlanta, he'd been fortunate in choosing his associates. His partner was a noted neurosurgeon specializing in organic psychiatry. Their four years of practice had been financially rewarding and now there were four junior-level psychiatrists in the same clinic.

Dr. Kyle Burnette took the case because it had come to him through a former fraternity brother who frankly professed, "There's absolutely nothing wrong with the boy organically, Kyle. He's in excellent physical condition. He appears to have a high IQ, a good family situation, and yet he's obviously under duress. His father is a moderately well-to-do attorney—a damn good tax man too, by the way. The boy has a rural background; the family lives on ten acres adjoining the child's paternal grandfather's dairy farm. The place is in a community called Panthersville, about fifteen miles out of Decatur. As for the grandfather, he still holds two hundred acres of land valued at close to ten thousand an acre. He sold twice that much a few years back for the same amount, so money is no problem. Jesus, I wish I'd bought some of that land fifteen years ago. Who would've thought it'd ever be so valuable stuck out there in the boondocks, eh?"

"Tell the Danielses to bring the boy in next Thursday for a preliminary examination," Kyle had agreed. "It won't be necessary for both parents to be here, but if they can make it, all the better."

"Okay, Kyle, Thanks."

"Oh, Bob!" Kyle said abruptly. "Send along the medical records, will you? No need going over the same ground twice at needless expense to the family."

"Right, Kyle. Will do."

Kyle Burnette thought no more about it until the day he met Damon Daniels for the first time. Mrs. Daniels was modestly attired, simple clothing, simple cut, but the texture and accessories indicated she had money. Her

11

husband, Edward A. Daniels, was in court, she explained. If necessary, he would make arrangements to come by the doctor's office on the next visit.

As was his custom when children were involved, Kyle spent the first half hour with both parent and child. His questions were of a general nature concerning family background, childhood diseases, the purpose being to break the ice, so to speak. Then he asked Mrs. Daniels to allow him a few minutes alone with Damon.

Children do not like to be pinned with an overt stare. Nor do they appreciate being questioned uncomfortably. The most advantageous approach is a subtle one. Preferably, let the child think he is bringing up the questions and providing answers of his own free will.

"What is your favorite animal on the farm?" Kyle asked idly.

Damon shrugged one shoulder and sat, hands clasped, his feet not quite touching the floor. His knees were knobby and scrubbed red where his mother had attempted to cleanse the ground-in dirt accumulated from play.

"You don't have a favorite animal?"

"The goat."

"The goat?"

"Yes." Pause. "Sir."

"I always wanted to live on a farm," Kyle noted.

"It's all right."

"I should think it would be fun."

"No," Damon said, seriously, "not always."

"What about it is no fun?"

The child's eyes followed the psychiatrist's movements, broken only by long, lingering blinks, quite like an owl. He had huge brown eyes, obviously taken from his father since the mother's eyes were blue.

"Don't be condescending with me, please," Damon said.

The unexpected vocabulary brought Kyle up short. "I'm sorry, Damon. I didn't mean to be."

"It's all right." If it doesn't happen again, the tone clearly indicated.

12

A mental shifting of gears and Kyle took a different approach. "Your mother seems worried about you, Damon."

"I know."

"What do you think is worrying her?"

"She doesn't understand me."

"What is it she doesn't understand?"

"My visions."

"Your visions? What type visions do you have?"

"I don't know."

"You don't want to tell me?"

"No." Pause. "Sir."

"Very well, let's talk about whatever pleases you. Is there anything about the visions that pleases you?"

"Oh, yes. I like the feeling it gives me, sometimes. Not always, but sometimes."

"What kind of feeling is it?"

"It makes me tingle all over; my tongue tingles, even. I feel it in my legs and stomach and it makes me start trembling inside. It feels warm. Sometimes it makes shivers go all down my back and arms. It feels good."

"What else happens, Damon?"

"I make a mess."

"What kind of mess?"

"You know—a mess."

"You mean, like you have to go to the bathroom?"

"No. Yes. I mean—almost."

"I don't understand exactly. Can you describe it to me?"

"I make a sticky mess. Like I have to go peepee, but it isn't really peepeeing. I don't know how to tell you."

For the first time, the child showed the slightest signs of discomfort. Kyle veered from the subject. "Do you like living in the country?"

"It's all right."

"Would you rather live in the city?"

"No. It doesn't matter."

"Why not? Wouldn't you rather live where there are children next door with whom to play?"

13

"No." The reply was adamant.

"Do you have friends with whom you play now?"

Damon shook his head. "It doesn't matter."

"With whom do you play, then?"

"Myself."

"What kind of games do you play with yourself?"

Damon's eyes changed subtly. It was an expression Kyle could not read. Not anger, or wariness, not displeasure even. More like an alertness, a keener perception, suddenly. The boy almost smiled. "I play a game nobody would understand."

"Perhaps I would understand."

"Not yet."

"What do you mean, not yet? Do you think I would understand it in time?"

"Oh, yes, someday."

"Try me, then," Kyle suggested. "Tell me about the game and let me see if I understand."

"Not yet," Damon said softly.

"All right," Kyle concluded amiably. He jotted a note on his calendar pad and tore off the leaf. "You and I are going to be seeing one another for a while, Damon," Kyle said, smiling. "I hope we can become very good friends. I want you to be able to talk to me. Everybody needs a friend. I hope to be your friend, somebody you can tell the deepest darkest secrets of your mind and they'll be our secrets. That's what friends are for, you know—sharing secrets."

"Then," Damon said soberly, "I look forward to hearing yours."

Kyle was still thinking about Damon that evening as the patients began to thin out and the secretaries were repairing their makeup, preparatory to closing shop for the day. He sat at his desk, smoking, the bottom drawer pulled out revealing a miniature bar, although he had not as yet poured himself a drink. Ted Drinkwater, his associate, entered and collapsed in his favorite chair.

"My God, what a day!" Ted exhaled. "I have a neurophonia case that's giving me the hives."

"Drink?" Kyle asked.

"Two fingers," Ted instructed. Ted was not married. "My wife is," Ted was fond of saying, "but not me." As for Kyle, he had no wife and had never had.

"This guy from Kentucky," Ted continued, "the neurophonia deal; he barks. Have you heard him?"

"No."

"Sonofabitch barks, I tell you! It's the most acute case of *aboiement* I've ever witnessed." He took a slug of the Scotch, winced, and opened his mouth in silent protest as the liquor seared its way to his belly. "Sounds like a Pekingese. Yip! Yip! You say something funny and the poor bastard barks at you. Of course, there's nothing funny about neurophonia."

"There's a fair movie at the Fox. Want to have a bite and go with me?" Kyle asked.

"Sorry, I'm horny. Tonight is my Oriental night. I wouldn't miss that for all the tee-hees in China."

"I had an interesting case today," Kyle said, as they walked around the office checking to see that the doors and windows were secured. They still carried their drinks.

"Really?" Ted questioned, not the least bit interested.

"Four-year-old boy," Kyle said. "His mother attributes supernatural powers to him. She says he can kill bushes by touching them."

"If he works on weeds, send him to my house," Ted said.

"I haven't tested his intelligence yet," Kyle continued, "but it's apparently above normal. Anyway, he gave me a description of a condition, a feeling he has. I'd like your opinion on it."

"So, shoot."

Kyle recounted Damon's version of the "feeling" which he experienced. "It makes him tingle all over, even to his tongue, he says. It begins in his legs and stomach and evidently wells up inside, making him tremble internally.

He says it makes him feel warm, not unpleasant. He said it makes shivers go over his back and arms and that it felt good."

"Sounds like orgasm," Ted said, draining his Scotch.

"That's what I thought."

"Is he showing signs of attaining puberty?"

"I don't know. I was wondering if you'd mind giving him an examination."

"No problem. Well, enjoyed the drink. Can't keep my lotus blossom waiting. See you tomorrow—no, this is Friday. See you Monday."

"Okay, Ted. Good night."

Ted Drinkwater's examination was summed up tersely: "No hyperfunction apparent. Checked dentition, gonads, and body hair. Everything normal so far as I can ascertain. (signed) Ted."

The second meeting between psychiatrist and patient started smoothly. Damon entered the office, eyes bright, smiling, took a seat in the same chair he had occupied the week before.

"How are you today, Damon?"

"Okay."

"Did you have a nice weekend?"

"It was okay."

"It doesn't sound as though you had much fun."

"No. Not much."

"Do you ever have much fun?"

The boy met Kyle's eyes squarely. "Not really."

"Are you unhappy, Damon?"

"Not now."

"Were you unhappy shortly before now?"

"Until I got here, I was. I like coming here."

Well, that was good, anyway. "I'm happy to hear that," Kyle noted. "What makes you happy about coming here?"

"I've been waiting a long time to meet you."

"To meet me?"

"Yes."

"You thought you were going to meet me?"

"I knew I would meet you. I even knew what you looked like. As soon as you relax, we can become better friends."

Kyle studied the slightly bemused expression. "Damon, I have some games—some tests, actually."

"I know."

"Do you know? How do you know?"

"I just know, that's all."

"Very well," Kyle said, "let's do play a game. I'm going to think of a color and you tell me what color."

Instantly, "Red."

"Very good. Now, I'll think of another—"

"Yellow."

Kyle's heart picked up a beat. He turned his mind to colors in rapid succession and as quickly as he did so, Damon named them, "Purple, green, black, blue!"

Without speaking a word, Kyle switched to fruits and listened enthralled as Damon recited, "Apple, orange, lemon, pear, grapefruit—"

"That's extremely good," Kyle said calmly. "Do you want to know how well you scored?"

"I got them all," Damon laughed.

"Yes," Kyle said softly. "So you did."

CHAPTER 2

WITH DAMON'S medical history before him, Kyle Burnette sat at his desk speaking to the boy's parents. "Damon is a very unusual child," Kyle said. "He is extremely intelligent, apparently a genius. Our tests score him close to two hundred."

"How does that compare to an average child?" Edward Daniels asked. "I've never quite trusted IQ tests."

"Nor do I," Kyle stated. "Actually, it's merely a tool for the psychologist. We define a person's intelligence quotient by dividing the mental age by the chronological age and

19

multiplying by one hundred. After age fifteen, IQ is really only a standard score which places an individual in reference to the scores of others within his age group. For the purpose of planning a child's education, for example, an IQ test can be invaluable. With your son, there are certain mitigating factors which must be considered. This is part of what I wish to discuss with you."

Mrs. Daniels had a distinctly frightened expression in her eyes, a dread of what she feared to know. Mr. Daniels, an attorney through and through, deliberately masked his emotions.

"With most children," Kyle explained, "or adults for that matter, a proper IQ test is a series of graded questions. The farther one can go, the more intelligent he proves to be. Therefore, if a four-year-old child is capable of working algebra, we would say he is a genius. By all logic, a child that age shouldn't be capable of performing such a mathematical function."

"Can Damon do algebra?" Melba Daniels asked.

"No, but as I said, there are certain factors involved here. Damon does extremely well on an intelligence test because he can read minds."

"What?" Mr. Daniels snorted.

"That's correct, Mr. Daniels. Damon has the most highly developed ability to utilize mental telepathy I've ever heard of. He is capable of correctly identifying any symbol or word you choose mentally."

"I can't believe that," Mr. Daniels said.

"I believe it," Mrs. Daniels said, her lips compressed.

Kyle continued, "I've tested him thoroughly. We began by guessing colors, then fruit, then objects, and finally abstracts. He correctly listed every thought I registered. There is no doubt of his ability."

"Fantastic," Edward Daniels whispered.

"Yes, it is," Kyle agreed. "However, this ability makes it virtually impossible to test his intelligence. As long as the testing is performed by someone who knows the answers,

20

Damon has no trouble reading these thoughts. It's a moot point. That his intelligence is very high is beyond dispute. The only question is, how numerically high?"

"I can't believe this," Mr. Daniels said.

It was obvious, from his wife's strained appearance, Melba Daniels not only believed, but was frightened by this confirmation of Damon's ability.

"What about the spells?" Mrs. Daniels queried. "When he freezes and stands so motionless?"

"We aren't sure about that, yet," Kyle admitted. "It could be a fantasy, a game as your husband calls it. It could be something else. We are investigating various possibilities."

"Can you give any probable cause for such a thing?" Melba Daniels persisted.

"There are several things which could cause such a reaction. It's pointless for us to speculate, however."

"Just one example," Mrs. Daniels pleaded.

"It could be a form of tetany," Kyle said. "I doubt it, but it might be. Tetany is usually experienced by babies during breast feeding, but it happens to adults, too. It's a nervous affectation. In Damon's case, it could be caused by a deficiency of calcium, vitamin D deficiency, perhaps. It produces a tingling sensation in the extremities, muscular spasms, and is sometimes associated with thyroid problems."

"Is it serious?"

"Not necessarily. Once we determine the problem, the cause, we can pursue a cure. As I said, tetany is merely one of many things we're investigating. We do know Damon has an emotional problem. Now, we must find out why. I don't want to indulge in conjecture. Such postulating is disturbing and frightening and probably wrong. I'm trying to point out, however, there are some bright and encouraging things which you have not known. Damon's unique ability is foremost in our consideration at the moment."

"What do you want us to do?" Melba Daniels asked.

"What I'm about to suggest is going to take concerted effort," Kyle said. "But it is imperative that you never lie to Damon about anything."

"We don't lie to the child now!" Mr. Daniels snapped.

"Not overtly, about serious things," Kyle agreed. "But, when he asks you how you feel, don't automatically respond 'fine' unless it is the absolute truth. If you two have an argument and you're angry, when Damon asks you not to be angry with one another, don't retaliate with that age-old reply, 'We're *not* angry, we're merely having a discussion.'"

"I see," Mr. Daniels said.

"The most trivial untruth is a flagrant lie to Damon. He sees through it instantly. He knows the answer before you respond. He's keenly perceptive to your thoughts. If you are troubled, it may well be that Damon is taking your problems on his shoulders, too. Whereas most children sense family dissensions, Damon actually hears and sees them through your minds."

"That's a big order," Mr. Daniels confessed.

"I said it was," Kyle agreed. "The next thing is no easier. You should do your utmost to avoid patronizing the boy. He bitterly resents it. Damon says his mother doesn't understand him. I suspect he feels the same about everybody else. Talk to him as you would an adult, not a child. Remember, he has the same emotions as a child, but the mental capabilities of a young man. He still requires guidance and discipline backed with love, don't misunderstand me. But you must live a very open life in the presence of your son. Keep telling yourself that you are incapable of hiding anything from Damon. With his exceptional ability, he sees through maneuvers to deceive him and it lowers his respect for anyone who tries."

"My Lord," Mrs. Daniels said. "All this time he's been in my head. He knows how I feel about his spells, everything!"

"Yes, undoubtably he does," Kyle said.

"I'm going to have to see this 'ability' before I can believe

22

it," Mr. Daniels said. "No offense, Doc, but this is pretty difficult to take, you know."

"I think we can demonstrate it very quickly," Kyle stated. "However, let me caution you not to be overly impressed with Damon's exceptional perception. Don't make an issue of it, or make him keep proving it to you. Above all, never ask him to display his talents to anyone. Making Damon a curiosity would be damaging to him, in my opinion. The newspapers would have a field day with this. The last thing we want, right now, is to make Damon feel different. We want him to live a normal life. Making him a freak attraction would be a catastrophe. At first, I was tempted to call the parapsychology department at Duke University and report the entire case. But, as I thought about it, thought about Damon, I decided that was the worst possible decision I could make."

"I agree," Mrs. Daniels nodded.

"You say you can demonstrate for me?" Mr. Daniels questioned.

"I think so," Kyle said. "I'll ask Damon to come in now. When he does, you say nothing. Think of colors, first, then think of fruit. We'll see if Damon can name them for us."

Kyle spoke into the intercom on his desk, "Send in Damon Daniels."

Damon entered the office, carefully closing the door behind him. He turned and faced Dr. Burnette hesitantly. "Black," Damon said. "Blue; red; green; yellow." He laughed. "Apples from Daddy. Mommy is thinking purple. Bananas from Daddy, Mommy is thinking apples." Damon laughed with obvious relish. "I hear you, Dr. Burnette!"

The parents laughed nervously, and suddenly Damon ran into his mother's arms. "I love you, Mommy!"

She held him tightly, her tears dropping on the shoulder of his new sports coat, staining the blue material a darker shade with each spatter.

"I can't help it, Mommy," Damon said softly. "I didn't mean to scare you. I can't help it. I'm sorry."

"It's all right now, my baby."

23

Mr. Daniels reached out, touched the boy's shoulder, and was pulled into the arms of his wife and son. Kyle Burnette watched the emotional scene with satisfaction. Carefully keeping his thoughts neutral, he realized he too had tears in his eyes. Helluva professional reaction!

"How'd it go?" Ted Drinkwater inquired, throwing himself in a chair, waiting for his drink to be poured.

"Very well, I thought," Kyle noted.

"Fantastic kid," Ted said. "You know, it takes willpower not to keep trying him out just to see if he's real."

"I know." Kyle pushed the glass of Scotch across his desk. He lifted his own drink as an unspoken toast.

"I needed that," Ted stated. "I've given myself doctor's orders to take the weekend off. Going up to Lake Allatoona for a bit of angling. Care to join me?"

"Sure," Kyle said. "I'll have to buy a fishing license."

"No sweat," Ted said. "Meet at my place tomorrow morning at seven."

"Will do."

Kyle continued sitting at his desk, listening to Ted humming down the hall. The neurosurgeon let himself out a side exit and after a few moments came back to rattle the door, double-checking to be sure it had closed securely. Kyle put his feet atop the desk, smoking a cigarette, sipping his drink. He didn't like weekends. Saturday and Sunday were rude intrusions on a work week. He debated calling a couple of women he sometimes dated, then decided it wasn't worth the effort to be amiable. He stabbed his cigarette into an otherwise clean ashtray, took the glasses, rinsed them, and returned them to his bottom desk drawer. He walked around the offices putting out lights, checking to be sure the doors were all locked. He positioned the air conditioner to the night setting and let himself out the side exit.

Like most psychiatrists, Kyle Burnette's most enduring case was himself. He studied his own id, ego, and superego far more and far longer than any other. In his life there were

24

really very few accomplishments about which he felt a great pride. As a child, growing up in south Georgia, he had once won a Future Farmers of America award for raising the best New Zealand white rabbits in the county; that had pleased him. That childhood accolade was surpassed only by the sense of accomplishment he experienced upon receiving his doctorate and then his diploma from the American Board of Psychiatry and Neurology, which placed him with the elite ten thousand practicing psychiatrists in the United States. Later, he published several papers dealing with the psychological ramifications of certain organic disorders. In fact, it was his series of papers that had drawn Ted Drinkwater and him together. Drinkwater was absolutely brilliant, probably the world's foremost authority in his highly specialized field of neuropsychiatry.

Kyle did not permit himself many excesses in life. His automobile was the most flagrant of the few he did allow. He had debated for months, read hundreds of automotive magazines, talked to dozens of auto buffs and mechanics. Finally, he made his decision and invested $29,000 in a Lamborghini Miura-S model, two-seat coupe with a mid-engine V-12 motor. The vehicle had a custom lacquer finish, metal flake blue, and was the only one in Atlanta and only one of four in the South, to his knowledge. For his one and only real test of the automobile, Kyle had driven it to Daytona Beach speedway, where it was timed at 174.335 mph. Slightly less than the manufacturer's claim of a top end speed of 179 mph, but fast enough to satisfy Kyle.

Immediately after settling himself inside the car, Kyle spent a few moments dusting the interior with a chamois cloth prior to snapping his seat belt and starting the motor. What he drew from this vehicle was almost sensuous. He had once described the sensation as a "motorized orgasm of indefinite duration."

He drove south on Peachtree toward the downtown area, not consciously going to any particular destination, simply enjoying the feel of the machine under his control. Had someone asked him tomorrow how he spent his evening, he would be hard put to reply. Fridays were an automatic response period for him. Hunger sent him mechanically to Mammy's Shanty for food; boredom and lack of purpose drove him home. He took a hot bath, turned on the TV, and promptly fell asleep sitting before the set.

The telephone roused him. He stumbled across the room in the half-light from the crackling television set and grabbed the receiver.

"Dr. Burnette?"

"Yes."

"This is Edward Daniels, Damon's father."

"Yes, Mr. Daniels."

"I'm sorry to disturb you at this hour, Doctor, but something is happening to Damon."

"What is it, Mr. Daniels?"

"I'm not sure. He seems to be hallucinating. After we arrived home from your office, we spent a pleasant evening of open discussions about our individual failings. We ate an early supper and afterward we enjoyed the most relaxed evening we've had as a family in months. About nine-thirty, Damon said he was sleepy and went to bed. That isn't unusual for him. Around midnight, Melba and I retired. A few minutes ago we were awakened by strange sounds from Damon's room. He was sitting up in his bed, eyes open, apparently wide awake. He doesn't respond to his name. He—he's also very stiff, physically. Melba says this happens sometimes when he's out playing, but it has never happened in his sleep before. She's afraid for me to touch him, to shake him. It's really quite alarming to see. Should I call our family physician?"

"I'll be there as soon as possible," Kyle said. "Give me directions to your place."

He paused only to brush his teeth, comb his hair, and dress casually. Less than an hour had elapsed when Kyle pulled into the Daniels's drive; the house was brilliant, every light burning. Mrs. Daniels led him down a richly carpeted hallway past two large bedrooms and a spacious tiled bath, to Damon's room.

26

The appearance of the child was stunning. He sat ramrod straight in the center of his bed, arms at his sides, legs together, dressed in nothing but BVD shorts. Damon's eyes were the only movement in an otherwise immobile being. Those dark, liquid eyes flitted wildly from side to side, pupils dilated, giving the normally placid face a sense of urgency, possibly fear. Kyle took the boy's wrist and was shocked at the inflexibility of the arm, although Damon did not appear to be resisting. Kyle counted the firm beats and each distinctly separate surge of pulse indicated a slightly slower than normal heartbeat. His breathing was shallow, long pauses between inhalation and exhalation. In no way did the child give the impression of hyperactivity. Yet, his eyes were darting about as though the real boy was trapped inside this alien body of stone.

"Damon, can you hear me?" Kyle asked. No evidence that he could. Turning to the boy's father, Kyle said, "I have a small medical bag on the seat of my automobile. Get it for me, will you?"

He began a systematic examination of the child. He ran his fingers down Damon's back. He kneaded the muscles of the boy's calves, thighs, and shoulders. The muscles were firm, but not tensed. Kyle tried to flex Damon's toes and they yielded in precisely the same manner as a corpse in the final stages of rigor mortis, slowly, stiffly.

Mr. Daniels returned with the medical bag and Kyle listened to Damon's heart, moving the stethoscope over the boy's chest and back. He positioned himself as nearly in front of the child as possible and peered into Damon's eyes with an ophthalmoscope. No sign of pressure there.

"How long has he been like this?" Kyle asked.

"About two hours now," Edward Daniels said.

"Has he spoken at all?"

"He was making sounds," Mrs. Daniels said, her voice trembling. "Not really words, but sounds."

Kyle gently turned Damon on his side, the boy in the same position as when he was sitting, legs at right angles to the torso. He inserted a thermometer in Damon's rectum.

27

"What type sounds?" Kyle asked.

"I don't agree with Melba," Edward Daniels said. "Damon was saying words, or at least, the sounds were like words."

"What did he seem to be saying?" Kyle persisted.

"It was foreign, like another language," Mr. Daniels said. "Maybe they weren't words, but they had the flow and inflections of words."

"Could you decipher any of them?" Kyle questioned.

"No," Mr. Daniels admitted. "Not really. It sounded as though Damon were saying 'seven' several times."

"Was he mumbling, were the sounds slurred?"

"No, they were distinct, but unintelligible," Mr. Daniels said.

"Did the tone of his voice sound normal?"

"He was speaking in a normal tone, if that's what you mean. He wasn't shouting or whispering."

Kyle withdrew the thermometer. Normal. He placed his paraphernalia back into the seldom used medical bag and zippered it shut.

"Would you like a cup of coffee, Doctor?" Melba Daniels asked.

"Yes, please. Cream and sugar if you have it."

With his wife out of the room, Mr. Daniels said, "It's bad, isn't it, Doctor?"

"I know you think it looks bad," Kyle said. "But then, so does an epileptic seizure, Mr. Daniels. Damon's heart, breathing, and temperature are normal. His muscles aren't fibrillating. Medically, he seems to be all right. I'm inclined to attribute this more to an emotional seizure than one from physical causes."

Kyle pushed back Damon's lips. The gums were a healthy color. "I don't know what it is," Kyle confessed.

Mr. Daniels sighed heavily. "All I ever asked out of marriage was a son, Dr. Burnette. When this boy was born, it was when life began for Melba and me. We swore we'd give him all the love and happiness a child could want. Then—this—"

28

Kyle sat with one hand on the boy's shoulder, the oddly postured body still bent, Damon's eyes still open and darting. Mr. Daniels had paused to compose himself.

"We never had but this one child," Daniels continued. "Melba and I thought we could give one child so much more by not dividing ourselves between several children. He has the whole world in front of him. I wanted him to attend the best schools, the best colleges—"

"He will," Kyle said firmly. "We'll solve the problems, Mr. Daniels. At the expense of sounding Pollyannaish, consider yourself lucky. If this were organic, rather than emotional, it could spell far more serious consequences. With emotional problems, it takes time. Time is the best medicine available to us. Time, research, and more time, that's what we need."

"Here's the coffee, Doctor." Melba Daniels stood in the doorway with a small tray. Knowing the doctor was coming, she had dressed and brushed her hair. It appeared she'd never been to bed.

"Thank you," Kyle said. He moved from Damon's side to a rocking chair. "I'm going to sit here until this is past," he said. "May I suggest that you folks go ahead and retire, if you can. Be as quiet as possible until this is over."

"I don't really want to leave," Mrs. Daniels said.

"I think it might be best," Kyle stated. "I'll call if anything changes. When Damon appears to be all right, I'll let myself out and go home."

"I really want to stay," Mrs. Daniels insisted, her lower lip twisting.

"Come now, Melba," Mr. Daniels urged gently. "We'll be across the hall if you need us, Doctor."

Kyle rocked slowly, sipping strong coffee, watching the boy. He glanced at his watch. Past three-thirty. He reached for a cigarette and mentally cursed himself for leaving them back at the apartment.

Shortly before dawn, Damon began to move. His hands were first to flex, stretching, fingers widely separated, then slowly curling, relaxing. A few minutes later, the same

29

reaction with his toes. As though life were returning to his extremities, the next movement was at the wrists and ankles. Kyle had been turning the small body every twenty minutes to ensure proper circulation. At this moment, Damon was lying with his back to the doctor, legs extended across the bed to the far side. Kyle could see the muscles in Damon's forearms and calves stretching, relaxing. He stood at the foot of the bed, where he could see Damon's face. The boy's lips were compressed, nostrils flared, and for the first time during the ordeal, his eyes were closed. But behind the thin eyelids, Damon's pupils were still flitting. Eerily, even the child's scalp moved backward, then forward. The hair at the base of Damon's neck rose like the hackles of a chicken. The stretching, flexing, relaxing activities progressed from fingers to wrists to arms and shoulders; his toes then ankles, calves, knees, and hips moved. Finally, as though with great effort, the legs moved, knees together, in line with Damon's body and he turned on his back. His breathing came in long, deep drafts.

Kyle took the boy's hand and it was limp. The pulse was slightly stronger, but still slow. Damon's arm now yielded easily as Kyle tested the suppleness of the appendage. He leaned across the child and studied the boy's face. The lips were now parted; delicate blue and red veins etched pink flesh and beneath the closed eyelids there was no longer perceptible movement. Damon was asleep.

Kyle reached the front door, where Mr. Daniels stopped him. "Is he all right, now?" the father asked.

"I think so. He's asleep."

"What is your opinion, Doctor?"

"I don't know, Mr. Daniels. I want to see Damon Monday morning. I want Dr. Drinkwater to reexamine the boy."

"Thank you for coming Doctor."

Kyle nodded. "If you need me, I'll be at my home or office. You may call at any hour."

Sixty minutes later, Kyle drove into Ted Drinkwater's backyard and halted beneath a towering magnolia tree which shaded a tiled patio area. Ted was sitting at a glass-top table sipping orange juice from a tall glass, dressed in baggy fishing attire.

"Thought you weren't going to make it," Ted said.

"I can't go, Ted," Kyle replied. "It's the Daniels boy, Damon. I've been over there all night."

"Let's have some coffee," Ted suggested. "Tell me about it."

Kyle described the events as they had transpired.

"How long would you say it lasted?" Ted asked.

"Over five hours."

Ted took a long pull on his coffee and sat with elbows on the table staring into space. "Could be a tumor."

"I want you to check it out, Ted. The boy's coming Monday morning."

"Has anybody run an EEG on the kid?"

"Yes, Dr. Robert Ingalis, the family physician who referred him to us. But let's run another, just to be sure."

"All right." Ted reached out and absently patted his wife's posterior as she poured more coffee.

"Good morning, Kyle."

"Hello, Elise." Goddamn she was beautiful. Even at this hour, her blond hair was in place, cosmetics sparsely and artfully placed, green eyes that could drown a man with a glance.

"You'll ruin those clothes fishing in them," Elise warned.

"We're not going," Ted said. "We have to go to the office."

"You don't have to do that, Ted," Kyle protested. "I told them to bring the boy in Monday."

"No," Ted said flatly. "I want to study everything that's been done. Maybe we overlooked something."

"I doubt it," Kyle insisted.

"I doubt it, too," Ted agreed. "But if we didn't miss something, that doesn't leave us much room to wiggle, does it?"

"Unfortunately," Kyle said.

Ted stood and drained his cup. "Give me a minute to change duds and I'll be right down. Have you had breakfast?"

"No."

"Feed the man, Elise," Ted said over his shoulder, disappearing into the house.

"What's wrong with this child?" Elise asked.

Kyle rubbed his forehead with the tips of his fingers, kneading away the first dull throbs of an oncoming brain-splitter. "I don't know," he admitted. "By God, I just don't know."

CHAPTER 3

TED DRINKWATER and Kyle Burnette complemented each other. Ted the inventive scientist and Kyle the plodding systematic investigator. Together, they examined each page of Damon Daniels's medical records, intelligence tests, statements from his family physician and family members. They scrutinized the various tests administered at Georgia Baptist Hospital, where he had been kept for five days of examinations by Dr. Ingalis. It was now past nine o'clock in the evening, both were tired, and neither man had changed his mind about the case.

"How'd you look on the business of killing the roses?" Ted asked.

"Hysterical response to a natural phenomenon," Kyle replied.

"Agreed," Ted concluded. "Then we have to arrive at one of two conclusions, don't we? The boy is either the best actor in the world, and this is all a play for attention, or he is truly ill."

"I think he's ill."

"So do I. But if that is so, what is the basis of his problem?" Ted pondered.

"I suspect he's suffering advanced, but strong symptoms of schizophrenic catatonia."

"Functional or organic?" Ted persisted.

"I'm not sure, yet."

"I'm inclined to think it's organic," Ted stated.

"Perhaps you're right."

Ted placed both hands on his desk, palms down, as though holding the furniture to the floor. "If I were to hazard a wild guess," he said, "I'd have to suspect a pituitary or thyroid tumor."

"I'm not sure yet," Kyle repeated.

"Who the hell ever heard of a five-hour catatonic reaction in a child four years old?" Ted asked.

"I know."

"I think we should go at this thing from the thyroid angle," Ted insisted.

"I think we should investigate it, surely," Kyle said. "But, I'm considering narcosynthesis."

"Christ, Kyle, the kid is four years old!"

"At the risk of sounding antediluvian, I think this boy might be a textbook case. He's capable of telepathy, we both know that. He has phenomenal intelligence. That experience last night, watching him go through what he went through, those eyes were wild, by God. I think we have something—different."

"If his father agrees to narcotherapy, I'll be surprised."

"I'm going to recommend it, nonetheless."

34

"Okay," Ted sighed, "you're the doctor. But I intend to pursue the theory that the whole thing is organic in origin and the situation is critical. If I'm right, and God knows let's hope not, it might be the cause of everything."

"Frankly, I hope you're right," Kyle said sincerely. "It's probably better than my half-ass theory."

"Narcosynthesis is psychotherapy utilizing drugs," Kyle explained. Edward Daniels and his wife sat before him, their faces drawn.

"Is it dangerous?" Mrs. Daniels asked.

"No," Kyle said. "It's a form of therapy that came into practice during World War Two. The patient is given a light dose of a drug; I'll use sodium amytal or Pentothal. This places the patient in a sleepy twilight state, releasing his natural inhibitions to communicate so he will talk freely."

"It was used during World War Two," Mr. Daniels questioned, "for what purpose?"

"Usually as a method of coming to grips with neuroses of combat origin. For example, if a soldier became despondent and incapable of adjusting to civilian life and it had reached a point where it hindered his normal living functions, then a doctor might use narcosynthesis. It clears the hurdle thrown up by the conscious mind and lets us get to the subconscious. It's completely safe and there is no physical impairment to the patient. The facts that are revealed during these sessions will then be discussed by Damon and me when he is fully awake."

"It seems a little drastic to me," Mr. Daniels protested.

"The purpose of psychiatry is twofold, Mr. Daniels," Kyle explained. "First, I am an investigator, listener, confidant. Then, my job is to make it possible for a patient to see his own problems and the causes so he can make adjustments accordingly. A psychiatrist does not cure a patient. He helps the patient cure himself. With Damon, whatever is wrong, it is so deep and causing him such turmoil that I am recommending an accelerated course, the narcosynthesis. Under normal circumstances we try to methodically trace the problem of a patient, letting him set his own pace more or less. I don't think this is wise with Damon. Therefore, after considering it carefully, I do recommend this."

"Do you think he's—" Mr. Daniels cleared his throat and began again. "You think it's serious, then. Whatever is wrong with Damon, it's serious then?"

"Frankly," Kyle admitted, "it is perplexing to be faced with a child this age who experiences catatonic reaction of such duration. During such times, it's important that someone remain with Damon. He must be turned periodically to keep his circulation active. Also, we wouldn't want this to happen while he's climbing a tree or swimming. However, the point is this: the catatonic state Damon experienced was enough of a symptom to warrant a more forceful approach."

Mrs. Daniels gripped her husband's arm, her other hand clenched so tightly the knuckles were white. "Let's do whatever is necessary," she said intensely.

"Yes," Mr. Daniels agreed.

"I would like to keep Damon here in the clinic for several days under observation and for a battery of physical examinations we have scheduled."

"Then you do think it is something physical, not mental?" Mr. Daniels asked.

"We don't know," Kyle said. "Dr. Drinkwater is pursuing a theory that it might be a pituitary or thyroid condition."

"Pituitary could cause this?" Melba Daniels asked.

"Possibly," Kyle stated. "Science does not fully understand the complexities of that gland. It is a pea-sized lump on a tiny stem under the brain. It weighs about one-fiftieth of an ounce in an adult and eighty percent of that is water. The pituitary serves an extremely complicated function for the body. When healthy, it is the producer of hormones which determine your size, sexual activities, and aging process. Actually, the pituitary monitors other glandular functions. If the pituitary goes awry, it affects a patient in ways that can be quite bizarre. Until the advent of modern chemistry, we had absolutely no idea what the pituitary did. From the pituitary flow commands to the thyroid gland in the neck. The thyroid, when unbalanced, may cause a person to eat ravenously and remain skin and bones. Yet, the same gland might cause a patient to become sluggish, dimwitted, and obese."

"If it is the pituitary?" Mr. Daniels questioned. "What can you do?"

"That remains to be seen," Kyle said. "A system of medication might be required. It could call for an operation. It may be something that time will cure if we only nurse Damon through this difficult period. At any rate, this is what Dr. Drinkwater is researching. The tests include an electrocardiogram. We don't think Damon has heart trouble, but even though it is remote, we'll investigate. We're also running an electroencephalogram and dozens of other tests. Some of these were already done by your family doctor, but now and then a later test can be compared to the first and any deviation can be noted as a clue."

"You will be completely honest with us, won't you?" Mrs. Daniels asked. "No nonsense, no hiding anything from us."

"On that I give you my word," Kyle promised. "You will know the results as quickly and honestly as I can get them to you. I am being honest with you now when I say we simply don't know the source of Damon's troubles."

"When do you want Damon to come in?" Mrs. Daniels questioned.

"Today, Mrs. Daniels."

"He doesn't have fresh clothing, no pajamas—"

"You can bring them later," Kyle reassured her.

"Doctor"—Mrs. Daniels's lips were now darkly discolored, twisting as tears rose in her eyes—"is my boy going to be all right?"

"I'm sure he will be," Kyle said emphatically. He stood now, to end the interview. "Perhaps after these next few days of tests we'll be in a better position to evaluate the situation. In the meantime, try not to let your imagination run away with you and avoid conjuring up bad thoughts. Be positive in your thinking. Remember, our thoughts are all quite apparent to Damon."

Mrs. Daniels composed herself and held back a moment until she could bring a smile to her face. As they walked out of the office, Kyle stood in the door looking at Damon. The boy sat in a far corner of the waiting room, huge brown eyes sober, unsmiling.

"I'll see you later, my darling," Mrs. Daniels said, kissing the child.

"I'm staying here alone?" Damon asked. He did not sound disturbed with the prospect.

"For a while," his mother replied. "I'll be back with some pajamas and clothing later, so I'll see you then."

"Okay, Mommy."

"I love you, son."

He looked tiny beside the adults. "I love you, Mommy."

Bravely, Damon turned from his parents and walked toward Kyle. "Good morning, Dr. Burnette."

"Good morning, Damon."

"You're worried about me?" Damon asked flatly.

"A bit," Kyle admitted.

"You think I have a tumor?"

"There's a possibility of that," Kyle said. It still took him by surprise to be met so overtly.

"I don't," Damon said.

"What makes you so sure?"

"I just know I don't."

Kyle sat behind his desk, hands clasped in his lap, chair tilted back, observing the child. "I have something I want to try with you," Kyle began.

"I know."

"Do you? Do you know how it works?"

"I think so. You make me sleepy so I'll talk."

"Yes. Does that bother you in any way?"

"I suppose not."

"It's perfectly harmless," Kyle said, smiling. "In fact, it feels pretty good, I understand."

Damon nodded. He seemed tense.

"Are you worried about it?" Kyle asked.

"A little."

"You'll be staying here a few days until we complete some tests which Dr. Drinkwater will run on you, Damon."

"Even at night?"

"Yes. But there'll be a nurse here with you. You won't be alone."

Damon laughed unexpectedly. "I'm not afraid to be alone."

"Good. I'll try to get you a pretty nurse."

Damon's head jerked slightly to one side and he cut his eyes at Kyle. He was almost smiling. "How does it feel to make love?" Damon asked.

Kyle felt his face flushing. His mind had turned to Betty Snider, a nurse with whom he had enjoyed a long, but not particularly feverish affair.

"It feels good with some people," Kyle replied, evenly. "It feels better with others. It depends on the partners involved."

Damon's eyes narrowed and the boy's expression disturbed Kyle in a way he could not readily identify. Damon threw back his head and laughed.

"Now you have one of my secrets," Kyle admitted.

"Yes I do," Damon agreed.

Betty Snider sat at her vanity table nude, face contorted, snatching tangles from her hair with a comb. She hated her goddamned hair. It was thick, coarse, cropped short for the sake of care, and still unmanageable. In her mouth she held several bobby pins.

"Dammit!" she snapped at her image, seizing the hair in one hand to lessen the pull of the comb by the other hand. Finally, exasperated, she spit the bobby pins on the dresser and sat glaring at her reflection. Her eyes fell to her breasts, small, still firm and tight, well placed. She worked hard as hell to keep her figure and, even if she did say so herself, she looked fairly good for a woman pushing thirty-one. She

39

stood, sucking in her belly and turning to one side for a closer assessment of herself. Fanny well rounded, prominent, but not hippy. It was a nice rump as rumps go. Her legs were smooth, tanned, long and shapely. Despite the thousands of miles she had walked in hospital corridors, the veins were not breaking in the ankles and behind the knees like they did with some nurses her age. But her hair! That ungodly tangle of ratty matted matter, for Christ's sake! She dropped back down on the stool and sat, frowning at her own face. Was that a wrinkle? She was nose to nose with the image before her, stretching the skin under one eye and releasing it to see the fall of the folds.

"It would help," she said aloud, "if you fixed yourself up more often."

She lit a cigarette, reciting the surgeon general's warning from the package as she inhaled the first deep puff. The macabre admonishment that "smoking is dangerous to your health" did not diminish her enjoyment of tobacco. It merely made her feel a bit reckless to repeat it to herself as she flagrantly disobeyed the advice. She lifted her chin, eyebrows raised, and looked at her reflection. Then, resigned, she began to comb again, the cigarette dangling between her lips.

"Can you spend a few nights at the clinic?" Kyle had asked.

"Let me check my schedule," Betty had responded, knowing damn good and well that he knew damn good and well she could. After a pregnant pause, she said, "What hours, Kyle?"

"About five-thirty afternoon to eight-thirty next day," Kyle had said.

"The pay?"

"You name it."

She softened her voice. "Any fringe benefits, you bastard?"

Kyle laughed. "I'm sure we can work that out, too."

"I once thought all you wanted was my body," Betty said, "but I know better now."

"Listen, woman," Kyle protested, "I'm on the office phone!"

So, all right, she had agreed. Since leaving Oglethorpe Hospital as a staff RN, she had been taking special nursing assignments only. A little old lady here, an ambulatory senility case there; it had been a drag of the first magnitude. Whoever said the way to meet a man was as a nurse? She'd like to find that misinformed bastard and feed him vegetable soup from a bedpan. So far, after nearly ten years in this profession, she had less prospect of matrimony than a PBX operator in a convent. Let's see, she had met a number of hypochondriacs with a mother complex; she couldn't remember the names of any of them. There was Mr. Hives, Mr. Psoriasis, Joe Prostatotomy, and Otto Osteitis. A great way to spend your life! The most romantic connection she'd ever had was with Kyle Burnette and today was the first time she'd heard from him in four months.

She dressed, sipping cold coffee as she pinned on her RN symbols, tacked down her cap and with a final, furtive glance at her hair, left for Burnette's clinic. She arrived promptly at five, as Kyle had requested. He was waiting for her in his office.

"This is an unusual case," Kyle began. "Anything you observe here, I want held in the strictest confidence."

"Is the boy a king or something?"

"No," Kyle said, seriously. "But I don't want this child to become the subject of publicity."

"Okay," Betty agreed lightly, "mum's the word."

"There are some things you need to know," Kyle said. "This boy is capable of mental telepathy."

"You're putting me on!"

"I'm not, as you will soon see," Kyle replied. "His ability demands an open, frank approach. You must control your mind and be conscious of your thoughts at all times. What you think he knows. He knows you and I have indulged in accubation."

Accubation. For God's sake! Kyle Burnette was the only

41

man in the world who would describe his urge for sex as being "keratose," a medical term defined as "horny."

"So, I have to have clean thoughts," Betty said.

"Your amusement may not last," Kyle warned, "when that child jumps inside your skull. The most fleeting thought apparently comes through to him. However, knowing this, if he confronts you with it, it is imperative that you be open, frank, and truthful in your verbal response."

"Well," Betty laughed, "at least it sounds interesting."

"The hours are long," Kyle explained, "because I don't want to trust this matter to any more people than I must. I hope you don't mind."

"What is the nature of the problem?" Betty asked.

"We aren't sure, yet. However, he definitely has psychosomatic problems. He's prone to catatonic seizures."

Briefly, he gave Betty the background of the case and instructions on the necessity of keeping the boy's body turned if such a spell occurred in her presence. Then, as the office staff departed, he led Betty to the inpatient area of the clinic.

It was an antiseptic tiled room which, despite colorful curtains and carpeting, had the feel and smell of a ward. There were two beds, one a standard, adjustable hospital type which was pushed against a far wall, the other a firm, low single bed such as one found in a residence. A color TV had been installed and the background music was muted for the lone, small guest.

"Dinner will be delivered by a caterer," Kyle said. "You know where the kitchenette is, if you want coffee or milk. I had some cookies sent in. If you need anything, call and get it delivered. However, I do not want either of you to leave the clinic during the night."

"Yes, sir," Betty said, professionally. Her attitude changed as they stepped through the door and she met Damon Daniels. He was a relaxed child, apparently at ease with his surroundings. His liquid brown eyes were expressive, yet reserved. He extended a delicate hand to greet Betty and soberly acknowledged the introduction.

"I'll see you two in the morning," Kyle commented, departing.

Alone with Damon, Betty sat in a stationary rocker beside the bed, looking at the boy, he in turn studying her. Despite herself, she thought back to her conversation with Kyle a moment ago.

"What does 'accubation' mean?" Damon inquired.

"It means 'the act of taking to one's bed, or lying in bed with another person,'" Betty replied without hesitation.

Damon nodded. He smiled warmly. "I like you," he said.

"I'm a likable person." Betty grinned.

Damon laughed. He scooted off the foot of the bed to the television set. "What's your favorite program, *Hogan's Heroes*, which is a rerun, or *Felony Squad?*"

"*Hogan's Heroes*," Betty said. She felt her muscles relaxing. This was going to be all right. She watched Damon adjust the set, deftly turning the dials, tuning the color. When he was back on his bed, Betty said, "Hey! I nearly forgot. I like you too."

Damon's eyes sparkled. "I know," he said.

CHAPTER 4

"How LONG did it last?" Kyle queried.

"Approximately two hours," Betty said. "First he fell asleep and for the better part of four hours everything was normal." She glanced at her notebook. "At one-seventeen he sat up in bed, his eyes wide open, and looked at me. I said, 'What do you need, Damon?' and he didn't answer. I realized then that he was going catatonic and I began making preparations for it. At this point he was flexible. He began a rocking motion, back and forth, and his fingers curled at the tips, the first joint of the finger bent. At one-thirty-three he began to get stiff; unpliable would be a more accurate description. His muscles were firm, but not tense. His eyes began darting horizontally, the pupils dilated. He commenced chanting—we really should tape this, however, for better analysis."

Betty self-consciously adjusted a pair of reading glasses and studied her notes. "It sounded as though he was saying, 'seven . . . seven . . . see in seven' and then it became a jumble of sounds, incoherent and not sufficiently enunciated to allow me a phonetic interpretation. I repositioned him every fifteen minutes, gently massaging his back, legs and arms to ensure proper circulation. I noticed, by the way, that pressing his flesh left a white spot which was slow to recover natural coloration. At the beginning, his heartbeat stepped up to one hundred twenty. Once he was fully catatonic, it slowed to a steady eighty count, strong beats. His blood pressure was normal. Temperature normal throughout. When he began to come out of it, his temperature rose drastically to one hundred three, but there was no perspiration even after it dropped, so I don't think it was a fever as such."

Ted Drinkwater and Kyle listened without interruption. Betty's notes took the better part of half an hour to cover and she had obviously done an excellent job of monitoring the boy's vital functions. As he had done with Kyle watching him, Damon emerged from the spell into a deep sleep.

"Appetite good; reactions good; no evidence of lingering locomotor effects upon awakening this morning," Betty continued. "If he had not read my mind, I don't believe he would've known what happened during the night. He asked me about it and I told him what had transpired. He made no comment, except to appear slightly embarrassed."

"Very good, Betty," Kyle said. "I know you're tired, so you may go home if you wish."

Betty rose and closed her notebook. "I'll have these typed by this afternoon," she said. She paused at the door. "There was one other thing, Kyle."

"What's that?"

"He gained an erection during this thing and ejaculated several times during the course of my turning him over. I left the towel in the kitchenette if you want to see it. It's semen."

Ted Drinkwater laughed. "How can you tell without an analysis?"

"It's sticky," Betty said. "It has the consistency, odor, and texture of semen."

"Oh well." Ted waved one hand, dismissing this unscientific conclusion.

"Curiosity got the better of me," Betty admitted. "I'm willing to bet it's semen. I tasted it."

Speechless, the two men watched her smile airily and close the office door behind her.

"Well, my goodness," Ted wheezed. "I'm going to have to explore her research capabilities for myself."

"Not until this case is over," Kyle said. "With Damon reading everybody's mind around here, let's not treat him to an orgy."

"I don't want Damon eating anything after eight tonight," Ted said, turning serious. "Tell the nurse to keep his liquid intake at a minimum. Also, have her give him a deep enema before nine in the morning. I've made appointments for an intestinal X-ray at the hospital for ten tomorrow morning."

"All right."

"I'm growing stronger on this theory of the pituitary being the cause of all this," Ted noted. "Have you examined his pubic area lately?"

"No."

"He shows signs of maturity. You might want to check it out."

"I will, this morning."

"Okeedoakee," Ted said, dropping both hands to his knees. "I've got my barking patient coming in this morning. Have you seen him, yet?"

"No."

"Just like a Pekingese," Ted said. "If you could see that big guy barking, I swear, you'd fall out! He must weigh two hundred pounds. Looks like he's ruff, ruff, but no, it's a yip, yip!"

"Get out of here," Kyle said kindly. "I have work to do."

"Do you have any questions you'd like to ask first?" Kyle inquired.

"I don't guess so," Damon replied. The boy was on his back atop the sloping black couch in Kyle's office. The nurse was drawing sodium amytal and preparing for the injection.

"All you have to do is relax," Kyle said. He sat on a stool beside the couch and cleansed Damon's arm with an alcohol swab.

"Will it hurt?"

"Just a little prick," Kyle said. He gently thrust the needle into flesh and felt Damon's arm quiver with the admission of the instrument. The vein was full and easily found. Kyle secured the needle in place with adhesive tape so the syringe could be changed, if necessary. Slowly, expertly, he sent a portion of the drug into Damon's system. The nurse sat across the couch, on the far side, monitoring the boy's heartbeat, blood pressure, and breathing. Damon's eyes fluttered, closed, slowly reopened, and fluttered again.

"You're getting sleepy now, Damon," Kyle said, his tone reassuring. "It's all right, you're getting sleepy, but you aren't going to sleep. You're going to float on a cloud, now. Float along and be comfortable."

"Will I fall?"

"Fall?" Kyle repeated. "No, that won't happen. This is a very large cloud that fills the entire sky, so you can't fall. Besides, I'm here to hold you and look after you. You are completely safe and everything is wonderful, warm, and pleasant. Close your eyes now, and relax."

The nurse nodded and Kyle sat waiting for the drug to take complete effect. The nurse held Damon's wrist, her eyes constantly on her watch.

"Damon, do you hear me?"

"Yes, sir." His voice was tremulous.

48

"You are warm and comfortable now, Damon. How do you feel?"

"Fine."

"How do you like Nurse Snider?"

"Who?"

"The lady who stayed with you last night—Betty Snider. How do you like her?"

The boy's lips parted in a smile and he chuckled. "I like her."

"Do you remember going to bed last night, Damon?"

"Yes."

"Did you sleep well?"

"Yes. I slept—"

"Did you awaken during the night?"

"No. Yes. Well, no."

"You don't seem sure," Kyle persisted. "Did you awaken during the night?"

"No." Adamantly.

"You sat up during the night, Damon. Did you know that?"

"It was my seven."

"Your seven?" Kyle said.

"Not seven," Damon snapped, "*seven!*"

"What is your seven?"

The boy's face twisted and his eyes opened wide, staring at the ceiling. "Not seven," he said emphatically. "Seven."

"You mean like one, two, three, four, five, six, seven?"

"No."

"What is it you do mean then?" Kyle questioned.

"My seven—" Damon's eyes closed again.

"What is this thing, what does it do, this seven?"

Abruptly, Damon's lips curled back exposing his teeth and his eyes flared open, then narrowed. He turned his head slowly to fully face Kyle. The nurse involuntarily dropped Damon's arm. Kyle felt a rash of goosebumps rise on his shoulders and it was all he could do to hold onto the lad's arm with the needle still injected and hypodermic in place.

"What are you doing, Doctor?" The depth and tone of the child's voice stunned Kyle and he stared unbelieving at the

49

transformation taking place before his eyes. The thin lips curled, teeth bared, eyebrows arched with the outer corners high, Damon's expression was almost demonic.

"Do your homework, Doctor." The timbre of the rich baritone held physician and nurse motionless. "The child is saying, 'sweven,'" the voice said, enunciating the letter w clearly.

"It's all right," Kyle said. "Lie back now, Damon. Lie back and rest."

. The heinous mask melted and the nurse stared at Dr. Burnette in amazement. Kyle nodded at the boy's arm and she hesitantly took Damon's wrist again, feeling for a pulse, consulting her watch. The arched eyebrows slowly settled into a childlike configuration again, the lips unfurled and relaxed, eyes fluttered and closed, opened, fluttered and closed.

"What happened then, Damon?" Kyle asked.

"I don't know."

"Was that you?"

"No."

"Who was it, then?"

"My sweven."

"Who is your 'sweven,' Damon?"

"My father."

"Mr. Daniels, your father?"

"No. That's enough." Angrily almost, the voice ranged somewhere between the normal childish tenor and the guttural baritone of a moment ago.

"Last night," Kyle pressed, "was it your sweven who made you sit up?"

"Yes."

"Why does he do that?"

"He comes to visit me."

"What does he want?"

"He wants to know what I've learned."

"Learned about what?"

"About—things."

"What kind of things?"

"That's enough!" Damon's arms stiffened and the eyebrows began to arch.

"Relax, Damon, easy, relax." Kyle injected a bit more of the fluid from the hypodermic and waited for effect.

"Damon?"

"What?" Testily, now.

"When you say the sweven is your father, you don't mean Mr. Daniels, Edward Daniels?"

"No. He is not my father."

"Who is your father then? What is his name?"

The boy suddenly snorted and the eyes opened again. "Goddamn it, that's enough!"

"Relax, Damon, lie back and close your eyes."

Another snorting sound, the nostrils splayed, eyes intense.

"One more question, Damon," Kyle said softly.

"What is it?"

"Would you like to make love to Nurse Snider?"

"I already have," Damon said. Then he laughed, the tinkling falsetto suddenly dropping to a coarse bass, the room vibrating with the sound. It had a dirty tinge to it, like the snicker of boys behind their hands when the town's naughty girl passes on the street. Kyle withdrew the needle, daubed the arm, and taped cotton atop the reddened puncture point.

"This is all confidential," Kyle reminded the nurse.

"Of course, Doctor."

"Not even between nurses or with another doctor," Kyle stated.

"Yes, sir."

"Thank you, Nurse."

She glanced apprehensively at the child. "Do you want help moving him?"

"I don't want to move him for a while. I'll call when I do."

"Yes sir." Under her breath as she left, Kyle heard her say, "Jesus!"

51

Kyle entered Dr. Drinkwater's office unannounced. Ted looked up through his eyelashes, his finger marking a place in a book he was consulting.

"Have you ever heard the word 's-w-e-v-e-n'?" Kyle asked.

"No, what does it mean?"

"I had some difficulty looking it up. It's found only in an unabridged dictionary. It's archaic, probably Icelandic or Latin in origin. It means a 'vision' or 'dream.'"

"So?"

"You know I mentioned that Damon's parents said he kept repeating the word 'seven.' Actually, he was saying 'sweven.'"

Ted Drinkwater closed his book, marking it with a Kleenex tissue to keep his place. "A dream or vision?"

"Right. Just a while ago, during narcosynthesis, Damon's voice took a drastic change and he spoke of his 'father,' whom he seems to attach to the term 'sweven' in some way. He displayed a remarkable alteration of facial contours, mannerisms, and attitude. I'm so goddamned excited I can hardly speak!"

"Well, so am I, man, keep talking!"

"I think we might have a classic example of dual personality, Ted. I mean genuine, bona fide case! You'll have to see it to really appreciate what we've just been through. Damon's alter ego is a grown man, a lascivious man at that. I asked him if he wanted to make love to Betty Snider and he informed me that he already had."

"My God!" Ted exclaimed. "Go on—"

"This alter ego is a husky, strong, masculine force. My first thought was, perhaps a father image for his real-life parent. I asked him if he meant Mr. Daniels when he spoke of his 'father' in reference to the sweven. He abruptly corrected me that this was not so. By God, Ted, it was amazing."

"This would certainly be the youngest case, that's for sure," Ted said, his mind already reaping the rewards of recognition that would come to the clinic from a case of this nature.

"Tonight," Kyle said, "I want a tape recorder in that room with Betty and Damon. She should tape every sound made if he experiences another catatonic seizure. Damon says, during these spells, he's being visited by his father, who wants to know what he has learned."

"Jesus, what a case!" Ted said gleefully.

"I think we should go at this thing tooth and nail, Ted. What do you think?"

"Agreed!" Ted snapped. "Hell yes, agreed!" He turned back to the book on his desk, then added more soberly, "But I'm going to run these tests. This could still be pituitary, Kyle."

With a sinking heart, Kyle read the reports handed him by Ted Drinkwater. He looked up at his associate.

"I didn't notice any appreciable change in the pubic area," Kyle protested.

"There is, though, Kyle."

"Well, goddamn it, Ted, I didn't see it."

"That's why doctors shouldn't minister to their families, Kyle," Ted said gently. "You're getting too close to that boy. Your eyes don't see. He's developing pubic hair, the scrotum is enlarged, not much but it has enlarged since we started examining the child. The testes are enlarged, too. At first, I thought there might be a low-grade infection there, but I pulled a prostate on the boy and Betty was right, it *is* semen. His development is that of a boy twice his age or more, despite his chronological age."

"For Christ's sake," Kyle hissed. "We don't need this complication now, damn it!"

"It strengthens my theory about the pituitary, Kyle."

"Anything else?"

"Nope." Ted retrieved his reports from Kyle's desk. "I'm doing a spinal tap tomorrow and a biopsy, just to be sure it isn't a tumor, but I'm relatively sure it isn't."

Kyle lit a cigarette and wheeled his chair around so his back was to Ted. "I didn't see any goddamned development," he said again.

"Forget it," Ted said. "Check him again."

"I will," Kyle said, smashing out his cigarette and rising.

Kyle found Damon sitting on the floor of his room, bored, looking at a magazine, the television playing. Mrs. Daniels was reading in a chair by a window.

"May I see Damon alone for a minute, Mrs. Daniels?"

"Certainly, Doctor."

Damon stood, uncertainly, and began untying his robe. Kyle said nothing, waiting for the boy to drop his pajamas. He sat down in a straight-back chair and felt the scrotum. It didn't feel swollen to him, by God. He tenderly felt the testicles. Looking closer, he saw the hair mentioned in Ted's report. He had to agree the development was there.

Then, as he examined the boy, Kyle saw the penis pounding erect, rising with each pulsation, the glans pushing through folds of skin.

"It's all right, Damon," Kyle said aloud, to reassure the boy that there was no reason to be ashamed or alarmed at this reaction. Abruptly, with a groan, Damon grabbed Kyle by the shoulders and semen gushed forth, striking Kyle in the face and chest. Stunned, Kyle held the boy's waist, thinking of the adverse psychological response that might come of this.

Damon's mouth dropped open, his eyes narrowed, eyebrows arching at the extremities as though going up into his hairline. The boy's tongue was livid, curved in his mouth; a sound rose from deep in his chest that was almost animal in origin.

"It's all right, Damon," Kyle said tenderly.

The boy's fingernails were cutting into Kyle's flesh despite the white smock and shirt he wore. Damon's eyes rolled back and he trembled in Kyle's hands as the final ejaculation pumped fluid from his body. Kyle looked down at the penis, which was purple with the pressure of its own blood. Why hadn't he noticed that before? Why had it escaped him before? Ted was right! He had eyes but had not seen.

"It's all right, Damon," Kyle said mechanically.

Damon's voice was deep. "I know," he said.

CHAPTER 5

"DAMON, LET'S talk about what we've been doing."

"All right." The boy sat, feet barely touching the floor, hands in his lap.

"Do you remember the things we talked about when you were sleepy on the couch?"

"I think so."

"Who is your father, Damon?"

The boy's demeanor was unchanged. "Edward Daniels."

"What does he do to make a living?"

"He's a lawyer."

Kyle pondered his notes a moment. "Has your father ever made you angry?"

"About what?"

"Anything."

"No."

"Would you say your father is strong, or weak?"

"Strong."

"Is he good, or bad?"

Damon laughed. "He's good."

"Do you love him, or like him?"

"I love him. I like him too."

"Do you know the difference between love and like?"

"I think so."

"What is the difference?"

"You like many people, but you love only a few."

"That's a good definition," Kyle said.

"What is your definition?" Damon asked.

"I would say that love is a deeper form of liking."

"But you can love somebody and not like them, can't you?" Damon questioned.

"That's right. Where did you learn that?"

"From you."

"What else have you learned from me?" Kyle asked.

"That people don't always know what they think they know."

"I'm not sure I understand what you mean," Kyle said.

Damon slipped forward on the edge of his seat, eyes sparkling. "People don't always tell lies because they mean to. They lie sometimes because they really think they're telling the truth."

"That's a very wise observation, Damon."

Damon smiled. "I know you better than you do."

"What do you know about me?"

"You are not who you think you are."

"Who am I, then?" Kyle asked.

"You are somebody different."

"You mean I'm not Dr. Burnette."

"Yes, but not who you think you are."

"Tell me who I am," Kyle urged. "Describe me, the real me."

Damon seemed to be taking stock of his words. Then his eyes dropped. "I don't want to," he said softly.

"Why not?" Kyle queried. "We're just playing a game, aren't we?"

"No."

"Do you dislike what you see in me?"

"Oh, no! It's all right. You can't help it, anyway."

"Please explain, Damon."

"No. I don't want to hurt your feelings."

Kyle laughed. "You'd make a bad psychiatrist, Damon."

Damon's eyes mirrored some inner wisdom and he replied soberly, "No, I'd make a good one. I could tell what is wrong with somebody right away."

"Very well," Kyle challenged, "tell me what is wrong with you."

Damon's eyes shifted and he stared at a far wall absently.

"Can you tell me what is wrong with you?" Kyle persisted.

"Yes. If I wanted to."

"All right, tell me, then."

"I'm afraid to."

"Afraid?"

"Yes."

"Afraid of me? Afraid of how I will react?"

"No. I know you wouldn't act ashamed or anything."

"Is there anything to be ashamed about?"

"I guess not. I can't help it, anyway."

"Can't help what, Damon?"

"What I am. What I'm going to be. I can't help it any more than you can help what you are."

"That's a very interesting thought," Kyle mused. "Let's discuss it. The only way we can help one another is by communicating, talking. I'll trade with you. I'll tell you something I think is secret with you and something you may not realize about yourself. You do the same with me."

"I already know what you think about me," Damon countered.

"No, you really don't," Kyle said sincerely. "I don't think about it when I'm with you."

His interest aroused, Damon sat back. "Okay," he agreed.

"You are spoiled," Kyle said bluntly. "You are an only child who has always had anything he wants and you are spoiled."

Damon's smile faded slightly, but he was still pleasant. "You are not sure of yourself," Damon said matter-of-factly. "You are slow to make a decision."

Kyle noted both responses, his own and the child's in two columns on a single piece of paper.

"You take advantage of people because you can read their minds," Kyle said.

Damon accepted this at face value. "You do too, because you know why they act like they do," he rejoined. The point impressed Kyle and Damon saw it and laughed. "I like this game," he said.

"Maybe you won't like it so much when I get tough on you," Kyle said, smiling.

"Maybe you won't either." ·

"All right, let's see," Kyle stated. "I think you put on a big act to scare people deliberately."

"What do you mean?" Damon asked.

"I think you know that your parents are frightened and worried and you deliberately cause this to happen," Kyle said firmly.

"That's not true," Damon said.

"Isn't it?" Kyle queried. "Don't you pretend to be in a spell when you really aren't?"

"A spell?" Damon questioned. Kyle could feel the boy probing his brain for a mental explanation.

"Like the sweven you talked about in your sleep," Kyle said sharply.

"I don't know any sweven!"

"I think you do, Damon."

60

"You don't know anything about me," Damon retorted. "You don't even know yourself!"

"All right," Kyle said, "It's your turn; tell me about myself."

"You don't like girls."

"That's ridiculous," Kyle replied easily. "What makes you say that?"

"Because you don't," Damon said, eyes glaring.

Seizing the meaning of the statement, Kyle did not pretend he didn't understand. "You mean I like boys sexually."

"That's right."

"Damon, that's absurd."

"You make love to a woman, but you don't really enjoy it," Damon said evenly. "Like Miss Snider."

"There are degrees of enjoyment, Damon."

"You would enjoy it more if it were a boy."

Kyle felt his face flushing. What could possibly have given this child such an idea?

"Because I know you," Damon said, catching the thought.

Kyle struggled to curb his brain. Why was he reacting to the statement so emotionally?

"People don't admit what hurts," Damon said, capturing information from Kyle's professional mind.

"It's my turn now," Kyle said. "You put on an act because you resent your parents. You resent them because they don't understand you."

"That's not true!" Damon shrilled.

"Then explain to me what happens to you when you sit without speaking, without moving, what is it?"

"I can't help it."

"But you do know about it."

"No."

"Then how do you know you can't help it, Damon?"

The boy's lips thinned and he glowered at Kyle. "Admit you are homosexual," Damon dared, "and I'll admit I know."

61

"I can't admit something that isn't true," Kyle said.

"Neither can I," Damon said softly.

For a moment they sat looking at one another. Kyle broke precedent and lit a cigarette.

"I made you worry," Damon said.

"I made you think," Kyle replied.

Damon responded soberly, "But I won."

Dr. Erich von Ulbricht sat with legs crossed, foot jiggling, smoking incessantly, the fingers of one hand tapping his knee. Before speaking, he had a mannerism of closing his mouth tightly sucking air through his prominent nostrils, and thus hyperventilating himself before expounding on his subject. His subject was endocrinology. Dr. von Ulbricht was author of a widely read text under the heading of neuroendocrinology. He was one of three men principally responsible for the recent development of radioimmunoassay, a highly technical and delicate process of testing and labeling hormone secretions in the blood-stream. He had been conducting tests on Damon at Ted Drinkwater's request. He was here now to give them the results of his findings.

"In the early sixties," Dr. von Ulbricht stated, "we had just begun to intelligently approach the glandular functions of the body. Only in nineteen sixty-nine were we capable of radioactively labeling hormones by the attachment of an antibody to the protein under investigation. You must understand that we are, in endocrinology, about where you are in psychiatry. We have a good concept of a particular hormone's primary purpose, a fair idea of its secondary effects, and practically no idea why."

"Yes, sir," Kyle said.

Teeth clenched, lips sucked against his teeth, Dr. von Ulbricht noisily inhaled through his hair nares and continued, "This case you have is intriguing. I've taken particular care with the tests, you know. When Ted told me some of the extenuating circumstances, the premature sexual development and so forth, I checked and double-checked everything."

62

"We appreciate that, Doctor," Kyle said.

"Bad situation, you know," von Ulbricht stated. He jabbed a finger at the reports he had placed on Kyle's desk. "The glandular activities are going crazy in that boy. Most amazing thing I've ever seen. It appears the negative feedback mechanisms are failing."

"Sir?"

The doctor's eyes disappeared under his eyelids; he sucked air into his lungs as he looked up into the dark of his skull. "You see," he explained, "the pituitary produces about ten commands, so to speak. Some commands go to the adrenal glands, some commands go to the ovaries or testes depending on the gender, some commands go to the thyroid, others to the pancreas, still others to the kidneys. These commands come in two forms, urgent and standard operating procedure. The SOP orders are constant, telling the body when to urinate, making a fellow horny, urging us to seek a mate, and such. The urgent commands give us our reaction to fear, preparing us for fight or flight. But, all these chemical orders are extremely delicate in balance. The amount of chemical and the urgency of the command itself is usually determined by the place the command is going. Let us use the ovaries for example.

"The pituitary issues chemical commands we call FSH and LH. Each one serves a separate function, but it takes both of them to get the job done. In the proper amount, these dual commands tell a woman's body to develop and release a single egg during her cycle which is then ready for fertilization. If she gets a super spurt of these chemical orders, she may produce two, three, four, five, or six eggs, resulting in multiple birth. That's what these fertility shots are all about, as you know, just our way of giving the ovaries extra commands, which is why multiple births so often result from such treatments.

"The ovaries then send back a negative message to the pituitary by way of the bloodstream and the message says, 'Got your orders.' This negative feedback mechanism halts the pituitary output of FSH and LH commands. If you remove those ovaries, the pituitary gets no stop order. It sends out greater and greater amounts of FSH and LH, assuming the message is not getting through for some reason, which it isn't—the ovaries aren't there anymore."

"I understand," Kyle said patiently.

"All right!" Dr. von Ulbricht said, lighting another cigarette from the remnants of a still burning butt in an ashtray. "In the boy's case, the pituitary is sending out urgent and increasing commands to various parts of the body. To his sexual organs come the commands to develop and perform and they are rapidly doing so, as you've seen. To his thyroid is coming a helter-skelter command which seems to be on again, off again, first spurting him forward and then retarding his development. The same thing is happening to his suprarenal glands. In combination with the activities of the other glands, his body gets a spurt of adrenaline, putting him into super high gear, and this results in phenomenal physical strength of short duration. His face contorts, his features twist, the voice alters, and his body is racked with missent orders from the chemical control center and blinko! Short circuit."

"Then," Ted Drinkwater asked, "you do think the problems with this patient are due to the haywire pituitary?"

"I do," von Ulbricht said. "As to what is causing the pituitary to go haywire, I couldn't tell you. I can't tell you medically. I can only give you my professional conjecture."

"Please do, Doctor," Kyle requested.

"The pituitary, as you know, is hanging on a stem from the hypothalamus at the base of the brain," von Ulbricht said. "In essence, it draws all commands from the subconscious brain. For years, it has been a theory well received in my field that the glandular functions are tied to the emotional activities of any given individual. In other words, the pituitary is causing the physical problems, gentlemen. But, psychological problems may well be causing the pituitary to do as it does. Now, having bounced the ball firmly back at you, I have a question."

"What is that?" Kyle asked.

"What subconscious force would so thwart nature's grand design this way? What mental processes would cause this boy's brain to make his mindless glandular functions go crazy?"

Kyle and Ted looked at one another and Ted said, "That's the big debate around here, Dr. von Ulbricht."

"Dr. von Ulbricht," Kyle said, "do you have any suggestions for treatment of this patient?"

With another chest-expanding inhalation, Dr. von Ulbricht looked first at Ted, then Kyle. "Your choices are limited. You can perform surgery, of course. Remove the pituitary altogether. You are aware of the consequences of such a move. The child will be enslaved to hormone injections for the balance of his life and that might not be very long. At this age, you doom him to the foibles of the laboratory and we would be literally developing and retarding him without much more accuracy than we expect with those fertility shots I mentioned. We may have a blithering idiot or a twisted dwarf; we would even have to control the coloration of his body with melanocyte-stimulating hormones. A terrible responsibility. Immediately after removal of the pituitary gland, the patient experiences diabetes insipidus as a result of losing the neutral lobe of the pituitary and its antidiuretic hormone. He will pass gallons of diluted urine with little or no sugar content and be consumed with an insatiable thirst. But this is usually controllable with ADH—antidiuretic hormone. It can be administered as snuff, actually."

"Do you recommend hypophysectomy?" Ted inquired.

"I do *not* recommend surgery except as an absolute life or death resort," von Ulbricht stated. "If the boy were a grown man, we might debate it, but not at this age. You have never performed this operation before?"

"No," Ted said.

"There's a Dr. Nelson in Baltimore who uses radioactive needles probed into the area which lead to disintegration of tissue causing the pituitary to atrophy. He's been successful at decreasing or removing only a portion, or all of a single lobe with little or no damage to the remaining lobes. You might consult with him."

"Yes, I already have," Ted said.

"Of course," von Ulbricht nodded.

"In your estimation, how much success may we expect using counterbalancing hormone shots?" Kyle questioned.

The endocrinologist shook his head. "I don't know. If, as I suspect, the negative feedback is the failure here, that may compound your problems. My suggestion would be to stick it out, let this run its course and try to find the underlying psychosomatic cause. I am not very encouraging. You aren't dealing with a single hormone problem, you have several. It will be a textbook case, as you must already know. Phenomenal, of course. Positively phenomenal."

Kyle sighed wearily. "Dr. von Ulbricht, would you venture a prognosis on this case?"

"Off the record?"

"If you wish."

Dr. von Ulbricht was motionless for the first time since his arrival. He sat staring at the floor, his hands clasped, elbows on his knees.

"I would say that the present indications of development will continue and possibly accelerate," von Ulbricht said softly. "I would say that the patient's penis and scrotum will attain monstrous proportions and you may see a satyric demand for sex. His body will get certain masculine secondary traits such as heavy, coarse hair. He will probably become hyperadrenaline and suffer Cushing's syndrome eventually. If I had to carry the prognosis to the extreme, you will very likely find enlargement of the extremities like Marie's disease would produce. Then, as calcium is consumed in his body, a reversal of the mental processes which will render him impotent, sluggish, dimwitted, and will culminate in death."

Dr. von Ulbricht looked up at the two psychiatrists and their silence moved him to add, "I'm sorry."

Kyle nodded. "To reiterate, you do not recommend surgery?"

"I do not," von Ulbricht responded, "as long as it can be avoided. You may only complicate the case with such a move and besides, it will eliminate any possibility of effecting a lasting cure of the psychopathic cause of the symptoms."

"Thank you, Dr. von Ulbricht," Ted said.

"You're welcome, gentlemen. If I can be any further help, do not hesitate to call me."

Kyle sank back in his chair as Ted followed von Ulbricht into the foyer. He swallowed hard and the lump in his throat rose again, bringing a sick queasiness to his belly. He pulled open the bottom drawer of his desk and tore the seal off a fresh bottle of Scotch. He poured a drink and downed it, still holding the bottle. He poured another and drank half, refilling the glass before placing the bottle back in the liquor cabinet.

"Time and research are our best tools," he told himself, repeating an axiom of his trade. Time and research. Only there wasn't much time.

CHAPTER 6

Seated at the conference table were Mr. and Mrs. Daniels, Ted Drinkwater, Betty Snider, and Kyle Burnette. A stenographer sat to one side prepared to take notes. Kyle assumed the position of director, standing at the head of the table, his medical records and tests carefully spread before him.

"This meeting is primarily for our benefit, Mr. and Mrs. Daniels," Kyle explained. "But I thought you would want to sit in on it. You may ask questions at any time to clarify a point."

"Thank you," Mr. Daniels said.

"First of all," Kyle began, "we have administered the Wechsler-Bellevue Intelligence Scale to Damon. He has been subjected to the Wechsler Memory Scale; Drawings of Human Figures was administered; he has been given the Rorschach in three separate sessions. The patient was cooperative, alert, and friendly. He displayed considerable interest in the mechanisms of the tests themselves and the ultimate deductions drawn from such data. In addition, we have employed a semantic differential form of psychotherapy utilizing a factor analytic scale of ten."

"We don't understand any of that, of course," Mr. Daniels interjected.

"This is for the benefit of a case report only," Kyle explained, nodding at the stenographer taking notes. "These are simply tests administered and various avenues we have taken in working with Damon. I mention them only for professional analysis of our work by other psychiatrists."

Ted Drinkwater sat slumped on his spine, one elbow thrown over the arm of the chair, his other hand occupied with a pencil he was stabbing at a piece of paper, peppering it with minute dots. When Kyle had finished, Ted adjusted his position and referred to his own notes. He summarized these into a few succinct paragraphs.

"The patient shows increased activity of the gonads. Prostate activation by the physician with a rectal probe resulted in discharge which, under analysis, proved to be semen with a high count of spermatozoa."

"For God's sake!" Mr. Daniels cried.

"The result of an increase of androgen in the system caused by an overactive pituitary gland," Ted explained. "The body is giving itself unwanted hormone shots. Once these are counteracted, the condition should reverse itself automatically."

The decision to have the boy's parents sitting in on this briefing had been bitterly contested by Ted. Kyle had insisted. Over the past few days Kyle had carefully informed them of Damon's "split" personality.

Ted glanced meaningfully at Kyle and continued, "It is the opinion of the attending physician that the patient is the victim of an overabundance of follicle-stimulating hormone and interstitial-cell-stimulating hormone as a result of the pituitary glandular activity."

For the next few minutes, Ted expertly summarized Dr. von Ulbricht's diagnosis in medical terminology. Then, turning to the parents, he explained in layman's language, "The pituitary is giving bad commands to the other glands."

Kyle interjected, "In Damon's case, the pituitary is the conductor of the body's glandular orchestra. It guides and directs all other hormonal production. The pituitary tells the thyroid how fast or slow it should develop the body, for example. If the command is too weak, a person remains frail for life, too much and his extremities spurt ahead giving him large hands, feet, jaw, and nose. The balance of the pituitary is a fragile and delicate thing. Imbalance can produce strange side effects. This is what is happening to Damon."

"What can be done about it?" Mr. Daniels asked.

Ted took a deep breath and exhaled slowly. "Unfortunately, very little. We might try radiation treatments as a last resort, to slow the pituitary processes. We are contemplating a rigid system of hormone injection to counteract part of the problem. But in reality, Mr. Daniels, every alternative is extremely serious. There are other factors involved here. We aren't sure that the psychological affectations which Damon exhibits are the results of the pituitary condition. There is some debate that the pituitary may be responding to the psychological condition."

"You don't know which is cause and which is effect, then," Mr. Daniels stated.

"That's right," Kyle said. "The multiple personality which is evident here may be the result of his physical glandular imbalance or, conversely, Damon's psychoneuroses may be the reason why the body is acting so adversely. Science has not reached a point where we feel that the mind and body are independent of one another.

There are many cases where neuroses are directly responsible for physical ailments. The most common example is the splitting headache brought on by mental fatigue or tension. There have been cases where the incurably ill have 'miraculously' cured themselves with a positive attitude. Also, there have been others who willed themselves to an early grave. Frankly, Dr. Drinkwater and I are at odds with one another on this subject. It is my opinion that Damon's primary problems are emotional and the body is responding. Dr. Drinkwater feels the problem is a physical one and the emotional reaction is the result."

"While you two debate the goddamned problem," Edward Daniels snapped, "what's being done about it?"

"We are pursuing both theories with equal fervor," Ted said calmly. "While Dr. Burnette concentrates on psychotherapy, I am working with Dr. von Ulbricht seeking any clue for the solution to the physical ailment."

"We work as a team here," Kyle added. "We have divergent theories, but that is good, not bad. Regardless of the theory of each physician, our common denominator is Damon; his symptoms and reactions are our clues. Now we are seeking the cause. We know the immediate cause is the pituitary, but we are now searching for the reason why the pituitary is doing what it does."

"Then send Damon to a specialist!" Edward Daniels said.

"Dr. Drinkwater and Dr. von Ulbricht are foremost in their fields, Mr. Daniels," Kyle replied. "Damon couldn't be in better hands."

Edward Daniels knew this. He had made inquiries weeks ago and was well aware of the professional standing of these men. He visibly composed himself and nodded. "I'm sorry. Forgive me."

"We will continue to do all we can," Kyle said, unruffled. "It will be necessary to continue keeping Damon here. This is why Miss Snider is sitting in on all this. She is Damon's companion at night. It's necessary for her to be kept abreast of the case developments."

Moments later, the meeting broke up and the Danielses

departed. When he and Kyle were alone, Ted wheeled on his associate angrily. "That's the most unprofessional god-damned thing I've ever been through, Kyle! I told you it was a bad idea to bring them in on a round-robin and by God, it was. What did you accomplish by admitting we have a difference of opinion on the boy?"

"I accomplished what I hoped to accomplish," Kyle replied.

"What was that?"

"We aren't mystics here, Ted. We're faced with a marked case of possible co-consciousness, possible schizophrenic catatonia, a runaway pituitary hormonal imbalance, and who in God's name knows what else with this case? Those people better know where we stand! My first consideration is for the boy, but I'm also thinking about Edward Daniels, attorney-at-law. I don't want my patient yanked out from under me at some short future date. I also don't want a malpractice suit. Daniels is an educated, thinking man. If he sees all the facets to the problem, the ramifications and potential disasters, he's going to be considerably more sympathetic if we fail to produce results. He is also going to be more appreciative of results attained."

"Shit!" Ted snapped. "He's going to go back to his office and worry himself sick, fretting over whether we are competent to handle the matter of his son, too."

"If he doubts that," Kyle insisted, "it's better to withdraw the boy now than later."

"Again, shit! Who could possibly do more for that boy than we can?"

"Nobody," Kyle admitted softly.

"Well, all right," Ted fumed, "now our guts are spread out for the public to see. I think we made a mistake not presenting a united front, regardless of our personal difference of opinion on the case."

"Frankly," Kyle stated, "I'm not sure either of us is totally correct."

"Since I'm not God," Ted snorted, heading for the door, "neither am I positive. But as far as is humanly possible,

73

I'm sure. Damon is the victim of an imbalanced pituitary, for Christ's sake! Who knows all the effects of such a thing?"

Kyle still stood at the conference table after Ted stormed out. He settled into a chair, lit a cigarette, and stared at the reports and tests on the table before him. Mumbo jumbo! When he first entered medicine and psychology, he thought the day would come when miraculously he would be handed a degree and some magic understanding of the human mind. Now, after all these years, it all came down to horse sense. A good psychiatrist learns that he knows very little about the human mind. He learns that psychotherapy is a blend of common sense, professional awareness of similar cases as his precedent, and he must be continually expectant of the unexpected.

There was something here, right before his eyes, in his mind, concerning this case—he could feel it, something he was overlooking. He was not sleeping nights, mentally examining each past session with Damon. He was spending the bulk of his working day and all his spare time on this case. He was consumed by it. He had trained his mind to be analytical, this was the essence of psychiatry; he was a detective of the mental processes. But there was something he was missing here; he was so sure of this, of this elusive factor, that he had an overwhelming sense of inadequacy for having missed it.

When he sat down with Damon now, Kyle had the eerie feeling it was himself they were examining, not Damon. Kyle felt the boy probing around in his professional brain. He found himself snatching incomplete thoughts away from the child, guarding himself. Perhaps, he admitted to himself, he should give the case to Ted or some other doctor. Even as he considered such a move, Kyle knew he would never do it. Damon was a once-in-a-lifetime case. Like a police investigator who secretly yearns for a monumental mystery, Kyle the psychiatrist was irresistibly drawn to the complex and beleaguered child down the hall. No, he would not give up the case. Not willingly.

He sighed wearily and snuffed out his cigarette. Pulling himself back to the present, he glanced up and Betty Snider was standing at the door looking at him.

"How about lunch?" Betty inquired.

He was ready to protest, then yielded. "Okay, where would you like to go?"

"Where the food is good and I don't want hamburger in any form."

"Mammy's Shanty suit you?"

"Kyle, do you know that's the only place you've ever taken me?"

"Very well," Kyle said, smiling, "make it the Camellia Room and we'll eat steak."

"Much better," Betty agreed. She helped him gather together the medical reports. Kyle's mind was off and gone again. There would be no great time at the Camellia Room but at least she'd have some company and, God, how she loathed eating alone.

The room was darkened, drapes drawn, lights turned down to a barely perceptible glow. Ted Drinkwater sat at Kyle's desk, observing. Betty Snider, at her own request, was assisting. Damon lay on the couch, eyes closed, succumbing to the flow of drug through his veins. His body was relaxed, face serene. The tape recorder had become an integral part of therapy and it hummed nearby as the reel revolved. Kyle sat beside the couch, holding Damon's arm, the loosened tourniquet still above the needle fixed in place in the vein.

"Damon, how do you feel?"

"Fine."

"Are you comfortable now?"

"Yes sir."

"I want to talk to your sweven, Damon."

"My father," the boy corrected.

"What does he look like?" Kyle asked.

"Like me."

"Then, he must be handsome; you are a handsome boy."

"He is to each man a different being," Damon stated. "Yes, he's handsome."

"What does he say, when he comes to visit you?"

"He says nothing. He listens."

"What do you say to him?"

Damon stirred slightly, eyes closed. "I tell him what I have learned."

"Give me an example of what you tell him," Kyle said.

Damon twisted irritably. "Whatever I have learned, this I tell him."

"Give me one example of what you have learned."

"My language."

Kyle consulted the list of questions he and Ted had compiled. "Damon, does your father teach you anything?"

"That is not his place."

"When you are awake, do you remember the meetings with your sweven?"

"How would I know the ones I do not remember?"

"Does he frighten you?" Kyle asked.

"Of course not!"

"By what name does he go, Damon?"

The boy tensed and Damon's eyebrows rose, a sign Kyle had learned to be the first indication that the boy's alter ego was intruding. "Enough of this." The voice came from that delicate head, but it was alien to the room, deep, sonorous, a tone that carried strength and command.

"Who are you?" Kyle asked.

"Damon Daniels," the reply.

"Who spoke to me a moment ago, Damon?"

"My father."

"Let me speak to your father again." Kyle could feel a clammy perspiration between his palm and Damon's arm, but he was not sure whether it came from Damon's flesh or his own.

"That isn't possible at this time," Damon said. His inflection had a singsong quality to it, like a carefully rehearsed response.

"Then you answer my questions," Kyle insisted.

76

"What is the question?" Damon's voice ranged some-where between a childlike tone and rasping baritone.

"Who is your sweven?"

"I answered that."

"Tell me again."

"My father."

"Not Mr. Daniels?"

"No. He is not my father."

"Then call your father by name. What is his name?"

Damon bolted upright, eyes wide, eyebrows arching, nostrils flared as he fixed his gaze on Kyle Burnette. Kyle still held the boy's arm to protect the inserted needle and he felt a flow through the youthful body which he could only describe as "electric."

"Who are you, Doctor?" The question rumbled. "Tell me and we will exchange answers!"

"I am Dr. Kyle Burnette."

"If that be so, I am Damon Daniels."

"This is not Damon Daniels speaking to me now," Kyle replied.

"Ah?" Damon's lips raised, exposing teeth and gums, the small white incisors catching the available light like porcelain. "If I am not Damon Daniels, then you are not Kyle Burnette!"

"Who do you think I am?" Kyle asked, deviating from the prepared questions.

"To whom?" the voice rasped. "You are to each entity a different personality, is this not so?"

"Yes," Kyle conceded. "But, to you, I am Dr. Burnette."

"So be it," the voice remanded, "and to you I am Damon Daniels."

"Heartbeat accelerating," Betty commented softly.

"May I ask you a few more questions, Damon?"

The child's voice again. "Yes."

"Was that your sweven?"

"My father, yes."

"Can you call him to speak anytime you please?"

"No."

77

"He comes when he wishes and you have no control over it?" Kyle questioned.

"Yes. I do as he wishes."

"What does he want of you, Damon?"

Damon turned his face to the doctor and his expression was completely guileless, and innocent. "I told you, Dr. Burnette. He wants to know what I have learned."

Kyle squeezed Damon's arm and removed the needle. "One more question, Damon, then you may go to sleep. Does your sweven, your father, does he ever tell you what to learn?"

Damon squirmed into a more comfortable position on the couch. His head turned aside and he sighed heavily. "Learn everything," Damon said sleepily. "He tells me . . . everybody teaches me, anyway."

"Who teaches you?" Kyle asked.

Damon mumbled incoherently.

"Damon," Kyle persisted, "who teaches you?"

Damon's smile was angelic. "You, for one," he said.

CHAPTER 7

TED DRINKWATER completed the paper Kyle had written for the *Journal of Abnormal and Social Psychology* and looked up, his face dark.

"It's all right, Kyle, as far as it goes."

"What do you mean?" Kyle asked.

"I mean, it's not a complete paper."

Kyle frowned and retrieved the article, scanning the pages. "Incomplete how, Ted?"

"I mean the goddamned paper is premature, erroneous in diagnosis, and lacking a professional conclusion."

Surprised at Ted's open antagonism, Kyle was deliberately slow to respond. "Do you have any suggestions?"

"Hell yes," Ted snapped. "You state in that article that Damon is a dual personality. You don't classify it as co-consciousness, you don't say whether Damon is the victim of his glandular responses. Multiple personality is exciting, yes! But you ignore my diagnosis altogether. How do you explain the catatonic seizures? Vigilambulism?"

"Of course not," Kyle replied quietly. "I'm willing to concede that the catatonic states are probably induced by the glandular imbalances."

"But, dammit," Ted said, "it goes further than that! I'm telling you that Damon's emotional responses are hysterical flights brought on by hormonal influences. You and I both know the reaction to adrenaline. Under stress, with adrenaline pumping into the system, perception becomes very acute. Just the surge of adrenaline that boy experiences might be a direct cause of his ability to exercise telepathy. It could certainly be the cause of his dual personality emerging. I'm not altogether sure his alter ego is a clearly defined personality, anyway."

"Ted, for Christ's sake, let's not argue. Be specific. Do you have any suggestions?"

"Would I be walking on hallowed ground if I prepare an article of my own advancing a theory of psychopathic response to a pituitary condition?" Ted asked.

"You know damn good and well that would weaken both our stands, to have conflicting articles on the subject," Kyle retorted.

"Precisely!" Ted agreed. "Yet you are about to send in an article stating your views with no recognition of my own, and damn it, I think I'm right!"

"Very well," Kyle said, "may I make an alternate suggestion to both of us writing separate articles?"

Ted nodded shortly.

"Any article for professional publication will be coauthored by the two of us and will be published under the clinic name."

Ted pondered this. It was brilliant. If he refused, he as much as admitted that there was an inkling of a possibility that their association might someday terminate and it was personal recognition he sought. Mentally, he said, "Touché!" and looked up, smiling.

"Excellent idea," Ted said. "Anything you write, I'll edit. Anything I write, you edit."

"For syntax, not content," Kyle insisted.

"Of course," Ted beamed. "Since our theories are so dissimilar."

"Now, with that out of the way," Kyle said, "there is the matter of when we should release the first article by either of us."

"When do you suggest?" Ted queried.

"This article I wrote doesn't truly cover the case, as you said," Kyle noted. "I think we should avoid drawing attention to Damon except to fellow psychiatrists. I was trying to avoid publicity in the lay press and I intentionally omitted some of the facts."

Begrudgingly, Ted nodded.

"Let's hold off on all reports," Kyle suggested, "until we know exactly what we have here."

"My God, Kyle, that could take years."

"Perhaps it will. But it'll give us time to get together on a ·diagnosis, prognosis, and etiology."

"I don't think we should do that," Ted countered. "We have a responsibility to our fellow journeymen."

"Come on, Ted," Kyle chided, "your motives haven't a damn thing to do with our fellow psychiatrists."

"No," Ted grinned, "but it sounds better. Okay, I tell you what, I'll yield to this extent. The one of us who is correct in his theory will go to the International Psychiatric Symposium in London to make a report on the case. Go at clinic expense and report in the clinic name."

"You mean next year?" Kyle asked warily.

"Right."

"Only on condition that we have reached some compromise between us as to the root of the problem here. And above all, I don't want this thing ballyhooed in the press, Ted."

"Oh, I agree!" Ted said, rising. "I'm assuming the case will have progressed to such a point that we can agree on a common theory."

Against his better judgment, Kyle consented and watched Ted leave the office with a bounce in his step. For the first time in their relationship, Kyle recognized a distinct rivalry between them over this case. Good practices had been ruined over less by men of equal maturity. Ted wanted to enhance his own personal reputation, but he was also every inch the professional. He would yield if Kyle were right. Obviously, Ted did not think that. Kyle drained the last of his drink and walked down the hall to the inpatient clinic.

"How's it going?" Kyle asked.

"We're fine," Betty said.

Kyle sat on the bed beside Damon and the two soberly studied one another. "You all right?" Kyle asked.

"I'm tired of staying here," Damon said peevishly.

"I know you are. I hope it won't be for too much longer."

"When do you want to see me tomorrow?" Damon questioned, head down.

"How about nine o'clock?"

"Are you going to put me to sleep again?"

"No. This time we'll talk wide awake."

Damon stared at his lap sullenly.

Kyle stood and addressed Betty. "I'll be home if you need me."

The television was tuned so low the dialogue was indistinguishable. Damon was on his back, arms thrown out to either side, mouth agape, sleeping. Betty put her book aside, bored with the sluggish plot, and sat staring at the child. He was a handsome boy, high cheekbones, dark hair tousled and slightly curly. She covered him with a sheet so he wouldn't get chilled as his body temperature dropped in the deeper stages of sleep.

Betty walked down the hall to the clinic kitchenette and

began preparing coffee. She should have taken a nap today. Already she was drowsy and it was just a little past eleven. Idly, she rummaged through a cabinet over the built-in electric stove until she found some cookies. Munching these, she waited for the coffee to brew. She was so sleepy! As a second thought, she returned to the percolator and added another heaping tablespoon of coffee. Perhaps after a cup or two of this, she would be more alert.

Finally, coffee in hand, she returned to the room and turned up the TV volume. Sound never seemed to disturb Damon's sleep. Like most children, he seemed to thrive on background noises. Betty sipped coffee, repelled by the taste of it with no cream and sugar. Her diet did not allow such luxuries and she refused to consider the cookies as anything but a necessary effort to rouse herself.

Damon was now turned on one side, facing her, an arm jutting over the edge of the mattress. His breathing was normal, with pauses at the end of each inhalation or expulsion of air. He would make a dashing man, someday. A lucky girl would be the recipient of his lovemaking—

He stirred slightly and Betty heard Damon's teeth gnashing together, a reaction common in children but unnerving to witness, nonetheless. He smacked his lips and swallowed, working fresh saliva over his tastebuds to dislodge the acrid flavor of stale spittle. His lips were now slightly parted. She tried to imagine those lips in the full bloom of maturity. That ever so tiny indentation in his chin would probably become a cleft, difficult to shave but sexy to the opposite gender.

He twisted at the waist, as though adjusting his body to the contours of the bedding. Betty put down her coffee and went over to smooth the sheet so he might rest more comfortably. She stood over him a moment, looking down on that carefree face. She brushed back a few stray hairs from his forehead. Then, impulsively, she bent down and kissed him lingeringly on the forehead. In his sleep he smiled and she again adjusted the sheet thrown over his body, going through the comforting motions of tucking him in. She had always enjoyed being tucked in as a child. She could still remember the pleasant sensation of that final adjustment her mother always gave the pillow and sheets before patting her on the rump and whispering, "Good night, my sweet baby."

Damon's smile still remained. She thought he must be having nice dreams; there was the faint sound of a chuckle. Betty gazed down at him and again bent over and kissed his forehead. He wiggled pleasurably. Love was the greatest healer in the world. She kissed him on the cheek, left then right, and her lips brushed his closed eyes. His chin lifted slightly and she kissed him fleetingly on the lips. If she ever got married she wanted a son; she wanted to caress him, hold him close, and rock him to sleep each night until he got so big he rebelled. Did that day ever have to arrive? Why couldn't she rock him forever? She wanted to rub away the growing pains in his legs and put a cool hand on his forehead, this future son of hers. She didn't want a mama's boy, God forbid! She wanted him virile, masculine, and headstrong. But for that precious period when he was all hers, she would treasure moments such as this now with Damon.

She brushed away the stubborn lock of hair which instantly flopped back across that small forehead. Love was a panacea, a balm, a tonic in any form. The sounds of love, the feel of love; to have a gentle and concerned hand adjusting your clothing while you slept. Surely, deep in his subconscious, Damon must know she was here, that she cared. Love has a way of seeping through the pores and nobody knew the ache of being without it more than Betty. She knew the loneliness of long evenings, sitting by a telephone which never rang. She knew the cancerous growth of solitude. In her years of nursing she had seen loneliness manifested in every elderly patient in her care. She knew the hunger in the eyes of the old, the eagerness of their recognition when she arrived to keep them company. It didn't matter that she was hired to be their companion, they would have paid with the last years of their lives for it!

A friendly gesture, an understanding touch, a moment of empathy between two beings, this was a hunger that could be satisfied only by one person to another. God, she had seen it hundreds of times.

It haunted her that someday she might be so alone. She thought about it often. She had nightmares of a time when she would be in a wheelchair, watching for a friendly face, listening for the crepe sole approach of a hired attendant. Jesus! She'd rather be dead.

She reminded herself she had just turned thirty-one. But then, she had once been *only* thirty, and before that only twenty-nine—

Damon touched her arm and his small hand squeezed. In his gentle, but unrelenting grip, she stood beside the bed. Perhaps, when all psychology was boiled down to its purest form, it was all a matter of love. Every problem stemmed from a scarcity of love, an inability to find it or adjust to the love available. If there were some magical serum extracted from human compassion, a liquid sympathy that could be injected in the libido of the mentally disturbed, it would surely solve every neurosis in the book. The goddamned world was fully of lonely people looking for lonely people. They passed one another at every turn and in their desperation for understanding they neither saw nor heard the whimpering of their fellow beings.

She kissed Damon's cheeks again, feeling the hand tighten on her fingers.

"I love you," Betty whispered. "I love you, Damon."

He smiled and in a childish mumble responded, "I love you."

She massaged his neck and shoulders with her free hand and when he ebbed back into total unconsciousness, she used both hands. She could feel those tender, taut muscles relaxing as she kneaded his legs and buttocks, his breathing so deep now that he was almost snoring. She turned Damon on his side, her fingers expertly but gently tracing his spine and working the shoulders. Could anything be more relaxed than that? Damon's body bent like surgical tubing, yielding

85

to the pressure of Betty's fingers and palms. His arms were as pliable as well-worked putty.

The smile on his face was gone and a trickle of saliva traced his cheek. Beneath his eyelids there was no movement, an indication he had entered the lowest level of slumber. Betty pulled the wrinkles from the sheet beneath him and once again spread the top covering over his inert form. One last kiss—then she returned to her chair. The coffee was cold. Betty walked down the hall to the kitchenette and washed away the viscous remnants of that first cup, refilling with fresh, steaming ebony coffee. To hell with it. She added two teaspoons of sugar and a touch of cream. She walked away a few steps, hesitated, then got another handful of cookies. She would cut down on lunch tomorrow to compensate, she decided.

The last TV program signed off shortly after one A.M. and she sat looking at the test pattern as though mesmerized. Finally, she turned up the background music and flicked off the TV. Returning to her chair she tried to make herself more interested in the novel she had selected for reading material, then abandoned it altogether. She kicked off her shoes and welcomed the pounding pulse in her insteps.

Damon stretched, turning onto his back. Betty glanced at her watch. It was about time for the catatonic reaction, if there were going to be one. It seldom deviated more than an hour. If Damon had not had a seizure by two-fifteen, she could stop thinking about it. Normally, if he were going to have one of the spells, it came around one-thirty or shortly before. Betty mechanically penciled the date at the top of a page in her notebook.

Damon stretched again, distinctly like a feline tensing muscles after a restful sleep. His fingers stiffened, his toes could be seen projecting through the sheet, pushing the percale into tents at the end of the bed. It looked like this was going to be one. Betty had come to accept these nightly experiences in much the same vein as she might the problem of bed-wetting. With Damon, it was a regular nocturnal event.

He opened his eyes, staring up at the perforated holes of the acoustical tile ceiling.

"Are you all right, Damon?" She pulled her chair nearer the bed so she could take his pulse later. "Do you need anything?" Betty asked, her tone that professional bland sound of the practiced nurse.

He sat up, eyes darting. Raising and lowering his legs in a bicycle pumping action, he kicked the covers onto the floor. Well, that was slightly different, anyway. Betty made a note of the hour and the throwing off of the sheet.

Damon's lips, normally compressed and thin, now appeared full and relaxed. His upper lip lifted, showing his teeth. The grimace was unnatural for the angelic face. Betty made a note accordingly. She reached for his pulse and his wrist was warm, a direct contrast to the usually cool tactile sensation she experienced in counting his heartbeat. She glanced up at his face and she was riveted to his eyes. His brows were lifting, the inner line of the eyebrows curved toward the bridge of his nose. He was looking at her, not beyond or through her, but directly into her eyes.

"How do you feel, Damon?" She felt a ripple of flesh as her arm erupted in goosebumps. She must remember to make a note—

Damon's facial contortions seemed fixed, a mask of fierceness, power, and maturity, eyes piercing. Perspiration collected on his forehead and trickled down his face. Betty's heart was pounding with such force she could hear blood drumming in her ears. She lifted the sheet and wiped away his perspiration. He did not blink as she passed the cloth across his face. His flesh! It was searing!

She felt for the calf of his leg to judge the temperature of his body by touch. Her arm bumped something hard. Startled, she jerked her eyes from Damon's face.

He had slipped through the opening of his pajamas and the organ was as large as that of a boy in his teens. The prepuce was stretched, the glans discolored with the pounding of his erection. Visibly it was still growing until Betty thought it must surely be about to burst.

A groan came from deep in his chest, a growling,

masculine sound, the same rasping baritone she had heard that day in Kyle's office during narcosynthesis. She couldn't make herself look back at his face, her eyes were drawn to that ever growing penis.

He seized her by the hair with a strength beyond reason for so frail a body. He was panting, nostrils flattened, widened; those eyes, those goddamned eyes piercing, she could feel them without looking! Was it a grunt? A groan? An animal sound—he was pulling her toward him. She resisted.

"Damon!"

She could feel the vibrancy of his muscles, sinews like cables, his body coming to meet her.

"Oh, God," she whispered.

The grunt again and he relentlessly pulled her nearer.

"Oh, God, no—"

But she didn't mean no. She didn't mean stop. She was not fighting, she was not struggling. This was not Damon. This was—she twisted under the pressure of his knuckles in her hair and she felt a hot probe against her cheek.

"Oh, God—please—"

CHAPTER 8

IN THE SEVEN months that Damon had been under Kyle's care, the boy's pubic hair had become a coarse, curly mat. True to Dr. von Ulbricht's prediction, the penis was greatly enlarged. Damon's testes had attained the proportions of walnuts and he now complained of a constant discharge. The thyroid cartilage commonly known as an "Adam's apple" was prominent. When Damon spoke, it was a voice with the timbre of a grown man, a rich, shocking baritone.

In desperation, the two doctors had turned to electrotherapy, hoping to dislodge the fantasy of Damon's sweven and free his mind to throw off the burden, whatever it was.

The effects of the mild electric currents had been negligible except to temporarily disrupt Damon's mental telepathy and memory. Kyle and Ted were expending dozens of hours each week researching, telephoning, debating, seeking a therapy which would produce results. Thus far, nothing.

Damon was going home today. The hormone shots could be administered when Mrs. Daniels brought the boy in three times each week. Dr. von Ulbricht had been carefully directing the injections, trying first one balance and then another. The doctor-patient sessions were becoming more and more frustrating. In these exchanges, under narcosynthesis, Damon reverted more and more to the second personality. Lately, even in the wide-awake periods of consultation, it appeared the ulterior personality was only a breath away, intruding obscenely here and there in Damon's mannerisms and speech. The somnabulisms were becoming more protracted, a further indication that the child was giving way to the overpowering and constantly growing "sweven" which seemed destined to dominate him.

"Dr. Burnette?"

Kyle depressed the answer switch on his intercommunications system. "Yes?"

"Mr. and Mrs. Daniels are here."

"Send them in, please."

Kyle nervously rearranged several objects on his desk and stood waiting for the parents to enter. The strain of the ordeal was telling on the Danielses. "Please sit down," Kyle directed. He offered Mr. Daniels a cigarette and lit one for himself. Jesus, how he hated to do this.

"Dr. Drinkwater and I have decided it is in the best interests of your son to send him home," Kyle stated. Mrs. Daniels's face lifted slightly, her eyes like an ember stirred to life in an open campfire by a capricious breeze.

"We will want to see Damon each Monday, Wednesday, and Friday," Kyle said. "I realize how inconvenient this will be for you, Mrs. Daniels."

"I don't mind," she said quickly.

"No," Kyle replied, "I knew you wouldn't."

"How is he responding to the shots, Doctor?" Edward Daniels asked.

"Thus far, there has been no positive reaction," Kyle admitted. "As I told you when we began the treatments, it's a hit-and-miss situation. Dr. von Ulbricht is working on the case many hours a week and we're faithfully applying his suggestions."

Kyle handed Mrs. Daniels a typed list of instructions covering Damon's diet. It had been some time since she'd seen one of Damon's spells and Kyle warned her of what she might expect.

"He's more active during these periods," Kyle explained. "He may glare at you, speak to you, even. Nurse Snider says he will sometimes grab her hand or arm and the pressure of his grip is painful. He may be quite oppugnant. When he does this, try to grasp him by the wrist, above the hand. If you must restrain him, try to keep something between you and him, such as clothing or bedding, to avoid bruising him."

"He's getting worse!" Mrs. Daniels said, her voice rising. Her husband turned to Kyle for a rebuttal and, significantly, Kyle said nothing.

"Is there anything else?" Edward Daniels asked weakly.

"Yes," Kyle said. "When was the last time either of you saw your son completely undressed?"

"Several weeks—four months ago, maybe," Mrs. Daniels said, her voice catching.

Kyle took a deep breath. "There are certain changes which have taken place," he said softly. "Damon is showing advanced development of the genitalia—"

"Oh, God!" Mrs. Daniels put trembling hands to her face.

"There's substantial growth of body hair and enlargement of the penis and scrotum," Kyle continued.

"Oh, God, Edward," Mrs. Daniels cried.

Mr. Daniels held her hand, his own eyes filled with tears, facial muscles taut. "Is there any goddamned thing good?" he demanded.

91

Kyle lifted his fingertips from the desk and dropped them again in resignation.

"I want to see my baby," Mrs. Daniels sobbed.

"Let's wait a few minutes, Mrs. Daniels," Kyle suggested. "It's important that Damon not see us upset this way. He will surely not benefit from it. We must try to give him the physical and mental impression that we are unalarmed and positive in our outlook."

"I want to know something," Mr. Daniels said, his voice contorted, "is there anything, anybody, anywhere, who can help our boy?"

"We're doing all we can do," Kyle reassured him. Kyle stood and offered Mrs. Daniels a box of facial tissues, then let himself out of the office, allowing them time to compose themselves. Ted Drinkwater was waiting for him.

"How's it going?" Ted questioned.

Kyle shook his head and walked past his associate to a water fountain. He drank the cold liquid, inhaled deeply, drank more, and stood up with a deep sigh. Ted placed one hand on Kyle's shoulder and squeezed, holding him steady for a moment. Then he walked back to his own office, leaving Kyle alone in the the corridor.

"You sent him home?" Betty Snider asked incredulously.

"Yes," Kyle said.

"You shouldn't have sent that child home!"

Kyle studied her blandly. "I'm sorry we couldn't notify you sooner. I'll be happy to pay for tonight since you came down here expecting to stay. However, I was going to take you out for supper, if you'll honor me with your presence."

Betty's eyes flashed angrily. "I'm not thinking about the money, damn it! I'm thinking about that boy and his parents. What if he has a catatonic seizure and—and hurts his mother?"

"I told her what she might expect," Kyle said. "I think it's best for everyone concerned that Damon be back in his normal home surroundings, Betty. The boy has been here for months, now. Outside of the expense to the parents, it is psychologically unsound to keep the child in an institutional surrounding."

"Oh, shit!" Betty fumed. "The first time he—"

Kyle held her coat. "The first time he what?"

"Nothing," Betty said sullenly. "Where do you want to eat?"

"Mammy's Shanty?" Kyle asked grinning.

"Is there any other restaurant in the world?" Betty asked.

After dinner, Kyle drove toward his apartment. "Would you consider participation in a scientific experiment?" he asked.

"Depends on the experiment, I suppose," Betty said.

"During abreaction," Kyle said hesitantly, "Damon informed me that he thought I was homosexual."

Betty lifted one eyebrow, looked at Kyle, then burst into laughter.

"That's funny," Kyle noted, "only if you aren't the subject under scrutiny. In all honesty, I have never had a ravenous desire to make love to the opposite gender. Fortunately, I have never had a conscious desire to make love to my own gender, either."

Betty slumped against the car tears streaming down her face. "Oh, that's good," she gasped. "That's really good! The psychiatrist is suffering post-patient suggestion. This is really rich!"

"Yes, well, I wish to disprove the statement with a practical demonstration of ardor. The fallacy of Damon's theory will become apparent when I stick my tongue in your ear."

"Umm," Betty murmured, "that's downright appealing."

"It will be necessary to have a heart-to-heart talk afterward," Kyle said. "I'll need an honest evaluation of my performance and your professional opinion of my androgen and estrogen balance."

"Naturally," Betty agreed snuggling up to him as best she could across the bucket seats.

"The ridiculous thing is," Kyle said, "it's really been

bothering me. I tell myself how stupid it is, how much like a freshman psychology student I'm acting, seeing every symptom of every neurosis in myself."

"I don't want to shake you up," Betty purred, "but it will take more than one time to get a perspective on the matter."

"More than one time when?" Kyle questioned. "More than one time in terms of nights, or more than one time tonight?"

"Right on both counts," she said.

"Oh, my lord."

"However," Betty reminded him, "I'll give you my most professional analysis afterward. I should make some topic headings for this. Let's see—technique, staying power, tenderness, tenacity, compatibility. Let's not forget dexterity, passion, attentiveness, and variety."

Kyle slipped one arm around her shoulder. "No," he said, "let's not forget variety."

"If you have any trouble, call me at the office," Edward Daniels said. His wife stood at the back door, nodding.

"I can be home in twenty minutes if necessary," Edward said.

"Stop worrying," Melba Daniels laughed. "Everything went all right last night, didn't it? Damon slept the entire night through with no sign of difficulty."

Edward smiled tightly and walked down a graveled path to his automobile. Melba was still standing in the door to give him a final wave as he made the turn downhill onto Decatur-Flat Shoals Road.

"Grandpa says you may go down to the milking barn and visit, if you like," Melba said, as Damon got down from the breakfast table. "He has a new pen of calves which were born while you were gone."

Damon grinned. "Has he named them yet?"

"Not yet. That's your job, naming the calves."

"Yeah!" Damon shrieked. "How many has he got?"

"I'm not sure—several." Melba dialed the office number of her father-in-law. It rang several times before he lifted the receiver.

"Damon is ready to come down now, Grandpa."

The boy was already at the door eagerly awaiting permission to race down the lane to the huge barn. His mother turned and nodded. Damon bolted out the door and ran pell-mell down the hill.

"He's on his way, Father Daniels," Melba said, and hung up. She stood at the back door watching the diminishing figure. He stumbled, recovered before falling, and halted only to shut and resecure the gate before going across the grassless holding pen toward the dairy section. He disappeared from her view and she busied herself with the dishes. Oh, God, she prayed, please God, don't take my baby.

Damon spent the morning sitting on a stool watching white-smocked assistants ushering cud-chewing Holsteins, washing swollen udders, and attaching pulsating milking machines. An odor of fresh milk and sorghum filled his nostrils, invigorating him. Grandpa insisted that Damon wear rubber shoes in the milking area so he wouldn't slip and fall on the wet tile floor. His feet were now so large he had to remove his shoes to put on the thin, flexible boots, but he didn't mind.

After milking was done, when the last cow ambled out the chute with a resounding slap to her hindquarters from one of Grandpa's hired help, Damon followed his grandfather up to the main house for a second breakfast of buttered biscuits, syrup, and sausage.

"How'd you like to ride the tractor today?" Grandpa asked. His white hair stuck up in the back where it had been pressed out of shape by a hat he wore constantly when outside.

"Sure!" Damon said.

"Buddy Latham is running a manure spreader on that

95

pasture over near the new project," Grandpa said to Grandma. "He'll be over there most of the day. He's careful. What do you think?"

Grandma took one look at Damon's eagerness and laughed. "It'll be all right, I'm sure. I'll call Melba and tell her not to wait lunch on him. He can eat with Buddy when they come in from the field."

"Hurry up then," Grandpa said gruffly. "You'll miss a dozen rides sitting there cramming your belly full of biscuits."

Sitting beside Buddy Latham, a musky odor of masculine perspiration in his nose, Damon rode high atop a big green tractor. The scene was one of the anomalies of the Atlanta area. To his left were pastures of fescue and clover. To the right, abutting a fence of the pasture and as far as Damon could see down a gently sloping hill, row upon row of houses in a new subdivision of low-cost homes. The land had all been Grandpa's. But as taxes overwhelmed him, he yielded to insistent developers and sold.

Damon ached from the hard contours of the tractor seat. He asked to be let down. Obediently, he took a position of safety beneath a spreading oak and watched Buddy Latham continue his labors. As the tractor receded in the distance, Damon heard the melodious laughter of children playing nearby. Drawn by the sound of merriment, he pushed his way through heavy undergrowth to a hogwire fence encircling the field. Grandpa deliberately allowed a border of native weeds around his land to "give the wildlife a place to breed and live." Damon followed the fence until he came to a point where he heard the creaking of a swing. Using squares of wire as steps, he pulled himself up higher. Now he could see.

The girl had long black hair and wore patent leather shoes. She was facing him as she swung, ankles together. She could not, or did not see him. She rose to the apex of the swing's course, paused an instant in flight, then disappeared from Damon's view to reappear at the opposite end of the arc. Her head was thrown back, hair flying, dress

96

blown up around her waist. She was so near when she came toward him that Damon could see freckles on her nose.

She was enjoying her solitude, smiling as she worked the swing, eyes half closed. He looked past the child. A woman was hanging garments on a rotating clothesline on a single post in the backyard.

"Janice, you be careful!"

Janice did not respond, continuing her body movements in such a way to maintain momentum, chains screeching. The act of spying on the girl exhilarated Damon. He broke off a shrub which partially blocked his view. She rose before him and he glimpsed her body beneath the dress and in that instant he saw blue panties with matching lace. Gone. Back again; he could see tiny transparent hairs on her thighs. Her legs were smooth, tanned. Gone. Damon let himself down on the far side of the fence, placing himself inches nearer. Her feet almost touched the overhanging growth along the embankment. Gone. Then back again. A shiver of anticipation now as she disappeared, reappeared afar, disappeared, reappeared near. Gone. Afar. Gone. Back again. Gone.

His hands were moist and from this clandestine position he gained a sense of superiority. He could see and not be seen. Her body was almost prone when she came toward him, her rear end level with his face just as she paused before falling into the return swing away from him. If he wanted, he could reach out and snatch her from her flight, or so it seemed. Gone. Afar. Gone. Here she came again.

He had not noticed the sound of the tractor now idling back in the field. The workman, Buddy Latham, was afoot, searching for the boy with mounting impatience. He had called and Damon did not answer. Latham trampled through the dense growth of the border to the fence, peered into the yards below and beyond. He heard the metallic protest of an unoiled swing, children yelling at some distant point.

"Damon!"

Buddy Latham swore softly. The boss had no right to

saddle him with this responsibility, him trying to put in an honest day's work. He returned to the tractor. When he came back with the next load of manure the boy would probably be standing here waiting. Wandered off to see the other children, no doubt. Like as not, he was as safe and sound there as here. Latham climbed back onto the tractor and adjusted the throttle, motor rumbling, smokestack belching fumes as he pumped the gas pedal. What would old man Daniels say if he saw the tractor and no child? Latham dismounted again and walked heavily toward the laughter of children he'd heard a moment ago.

He pulled aside the weeds and peered through. He heard only the creaking of a swing. Walking the fence line, Latham's irritation turned to anger. He glimpsed a girl's figure as she rose above the edge of the bluff, disappeared, then came back on a return swing.

"Hey!" Latham yelled. "You seen a kid around here? A boy?" The girl did not reply.

"Hey!" Latham shouted again. "You see a boy with dark hair come by here?"

"Mr. Latham?"

Buddy wheeled and Damon was standing behind him.

"Where you been, boy? I told you to stay under the tree."

"I had to go to the bathroom," Damon said.

"Well," Latham said, relieved, "come on, it's time for lunch."

CHAPTER 9

DAMON PLAYED in the yard, keenly aware of his mother's thoughts and attention. Through the morning she had busied herself with house cleaning, feeling better than she had in months. She had just talked to Dr. Burnette on the telephone.

"It's been nine days now," Melba Daniels reported.

"No seizure at all?" Kyle questioned.

"None!"

"Excellent," Kyle said. "Apparently the hormone treatments are having some effect. Very well, Mrs. Daniels, I'll see Damon at our regular time, tomorrow."

After a lunch of sandwiches and milk, Damon pleaded for more time to play. "I'm not tired at all, Mommy," he protested.

But she was exhausted. Her weariness had accumulated over the past months like grains of sand sifting through an hourglass. Since Damon came home from the clinic she had been sleeping in a chair at his bedside, constantly alert to every sound.

"Do you mind if I take a nap, then?" she asked.

"No. I'll stay in the yard," he said, anticipating her directive.

"I won't sleep long," she promised, kissing him on the forehead.

Damon waited outside the back door, his mind acutely perceptive to her movements. She fell across her bed fully clothed and set the alarm to allow herself one hour to nap. Ten minutes later, she was sleeping. Damon tiptoed down the hall and entered his mother's room. He quietly, ever so quietly, moved to the bedside table. Without lifting the clock, he depressed the alarm button. Then, with a single glance backward at his mother, he left the room, smiling.

For several days now, he had run down the hill to the milking barn, carefully latching the gate behind himself, ducking below the windows of the barn, and racing across the holding yard where he scaled a final barrier to freedom. Down a long twisted lane he ran, following a seldom used rutted road through a wooded area to emerge at the pasture where he and Buddy Latham had spread manure nine days ago. He avoided the open meadow, staying in a shaded border area as he made his way around the field.

The first day he had crouched at the edge of the yard and they had talked through the fence. "What's your name?" Janice had asked.

"Damon Daniels. My grandpa owns a dairy farm. He used to own this land where your house is."

"It's ours now," she replied.

"I know it. Grandpa got a lot of money for selling it."

100

Never completely out of touch with his mother, Damon had timed his return to coincide with her awakening. But today, having cut off the alarm, he would have much more time.

Damon approached the place where he and Janice met one another and halted, disturbed. There were three other children in the yard. A girl, perhaps two years older than Janice, and two younger boys were playing in a sandbox near the swing set. Janice was playing to one side, nearer Damon. When she came far enough away from the other children so they could not hear them, Damon said softly, "Come here, Janice."

She had been anticipating the arrival of this mysterious boy with the deep, commanding voice. She came to the fence and stood looking at him. She had never seen him clearly; he was always partially hidden by weeds that abounded on the far side of the barrier.

"Climb the fence and come with me," Damon said. She glanced at her playmates; Damon repeated, "Climb the fence and come with me."

"I can't," she whispered.

"Yes you can."

She was pressed against the fence now, trying to see him better. "Mama will be mad with me," Janice said.

"She won't know," Damon reasoned. "Come on."

Her fingers looped through the links. "I can't climb it," she complained.

"Take off your shoes. You can climb it. Come on."

One furtive look at the other children and Janice removed her shoes and hooked her toes in the wire, struggling over. On the other side, intuitively she crouched, glancing back to see if she had been detected. The other girl was giving commands for a sand city, her companions following instructions.

"This way," Damon urged. He took her hand and she resisted, looking at his face. His eyebrows were thick, the hair on her arms like that on her father's arms.

He smiled. "Come on," he said. He led her down the fence, helping her scramble up an incline, pushing through tangled honeysuckle vines to the pasture.

"Mama won't like this," Janice said, but her tone did not suggest she was about to rebel.

"It isn't far," Damon said.

"Where to?"

"To where we're going," Damon replied amiably. He took her around the perimeter of the meadow and they ran hand in hand down the lane. He detoured from the road into the woods, following a sound of water barely perceptible to him and totally unheard by the girl.

"The briars are scratching me!" Janice wailed.

"It isn't much farther," Damon stated. He veered around a blackberry thicket, sacrificing distance for ease of hiking.

"Oh, look, a river!" Janice exulted. They stood looking down at a flow of shallow water and a sandbar. Upstream, a kingfisher dived for minnows, the splash followed by a flutter of wings as the bird rose to regain a vantage point again.

"Let's go down," Damon said.

Janice hesitated, her eyes on his face. His eyebrows were lifted, upper lip raised, exposing his teeth.

"I better go home," Janice said.

"It won't take long." Damon's voice dropped.

"Mama will be awfully mad if she finds me gone."

"She won't know it," Damon declared. He was so positive, so definite, it assuaged her anxiety and she yielded to temptation. Growing from the steep bank were roots of trees which they used for handholds. As they descended, the air became noticeably cooler. Underfoot, sand shifted with each step. The shade was almost complete here, except for an occasional ray of sunlight through a break in the overhead foliage. In midstream, where the limbs did not reach, the rippling river shimmered with light, drawing her even nearer. Janice stood in the water and wiggled her toes into the fine sand bottom, watching eddies of silt drift away downstream. She glanced up and the boy was staring at her legs. She looked down to see what held his attention.

"What is it?" she asked.

"You have nice legs."

It was not a comment that disturbed her. "Look!" she said. "A shell!"

"You'll get your dress wet," Damon warned.

She lifted the hem, stooping to capture the prize.

"Why don't you take off your dress?" Damon suggested.

Before she could comment he was unzipping the garment and lifting it over her head. She wheeled and said, "Don't get it dirty! Put it some place dry." Damon placed it atop a partially buried log.

Janice waded out farther, intent on her search for more shells, clothed now in nothing but blue panties. Damon removed his shoes, socks, and shirt. He put them beside her dress. He pulled off his trousers, his underwear bulging from his excitement. He followed her into the water.

The hair covering his body, the jutting angle of his underclothes startled her. She stared at him, eyes wide, curious.

"You have as much hair as my daddy," Janice noted.

"Come here, Janice," he said. His command left no room for debate.

"What is it?"

He took her hand and led her out of the stream. He stood before her, his eyes hypnotically holding her as he took her panties in both hands, crouching as he pulled them to her ankles.

"What're you doing?" she asked.

"I want to look at you."

He pulled one foot out of the panties and she obediently stepped free of the garment. He removed his own underwear and she stared at his privates. She had never seen a boy completely nude, much less a mature man's body.

"Touch me," Damon said. She reached out and did so. He

gently maneuvered her to a place near their clothing, not pushing, but physically directing her to a sitting position. He traced her flesh with his fingertips, a movement she found pleasant. "Lie down," Damon said, his voice vibrant and deep. His eyes darted over her from feet to neck and he continued to touch her. His fingers sowed goosebumps up and down her naked body.

When he made an effort to become more personal, she did not object. Rather, she yielded to his manipulations, spreading herself willingly. Did she think of this as wrong? How does a child judge what has not been judged for her? Damon's attention, his touch, were pleasing. She visually examined his body. She attached no significance to the form and shape of him. His breathing became more labored, his excitement more overt, and for the first time she resisted slightly to his posturing of her legs.

"I better go home," she said.

"Not yet." The texture of the hair on his body was coarse and he now made a grunting sound. Her curiosity gave way to a tremor of distrust.

"Stop," she said quietly. "I want to go home."

His knee pushed between her legs and he wormed himself into position and suddenly, Janice felt vulnerable. She placed both hands against his chest. "I better go," she said.

He ignored her, forcing her into place. "Stop," she insisted. Her fingers were in the hair on his chest, her arms shaking from the slight exertion, holding him off. "Stop! Now!" He was probing at her with himself and she tensed, pulling away. "Stop it!" But he did not stop. He followed her as she squirmed upward away from him. His teeth were clenched, his breathing a hissing sound, almost a snorting of inhalation and exhalation. He grabbed one of her wrists and pushed it away from his chest and her other arm collapsed, letting his full weight descend upon her. She had an instant sensation of being closed in too tightly, of smothering.

104

"Stop it!" Her voice rose.

She felt him jab at her and the penetration made her suck air involuntarily. She was trembling now, trying to twist aside. "No!" Deeper he came, more forcefully.

"No!" Janice protested. She clawed at his shoulder and he pinned down her arms with a strength that totally overwhelmed her. She tried to close her legs but he was too well placed and with a savage thrust he buried himself inside and she split the woodland with a scream.

The cry had an instant effect. Damon froze, half lifted himself, holding her wrists. He was motionless a second, poised as though for withdrawal and flight. Seeing this and interpreting his action as defensive Janice screamed again, louder, as loud as she could!

His hand slammed across her mouth and he put his lips close to her ear. "Be quiet!"

Yes! Yes, this was the way to get free! The pain was mounting, his hair abrasively scouring her body, her groin burning viciously. She felt herself tearing. Her bones ached from the awkward posture and he drove into her with increasing force. Suddenly he stiffened, his probe so deeply imbedded it felt as though it were pushing at her throat. He pulsated, a groan rising from his chest. The movement was followed by a flood of liquid and momentary relief from the friction. Then it burned! She bucked and screamed.

Caught in the throes of orgasm, temporarily off guard, Damon was catapulted aside. For a moment he lay spent, caring not, until he realized Janice was scrambling up the embankment, shrieking and crying. He came up with a roar and grabbed for an ankle. She yanked loose, desperately dragging herself higher. Much as a cat responds to anything retreating, so did Damon now react. Filled with a nameless drive, a bestial urge, he fought his way up the bank, close behind her.

She somehow made the crest, legs weak from the ordeal below and the exertion of the climb. She wobbled an instant, stumbling, gasping for air. The sounds behind her summoned every ounce of reserve she possessed and sent her running as she had never run before. There was no screaming now, only flight.

Damon came over the top of the bluff and he too stumbled. This alone allowed her time to dash blindly through the woods oblivious to the snags of briars. Overtaking her, an oddly pleasant sensation throbbed in his belly. Instead of tackling, he gave her a sudden shove in the back. Already moving as fast as she could, impelled by momentum, she was thrown headlong to the forest floor. She tried to regain her feet but he was between her and home, having passed her as she fell. Janice slowly rose to her knees, sobbing, her chest scratched and bleeding.

He leapt at her with an animal growl and she fell back. He laughed, a heinous explosion of sound, and stood glaring down, his face twisted into a fierce mask. With horror, Janice watched his penis slowly pounding erect again and now this had meaning.

She scurried away on all fours and he grabbed her, jerking her to her feet. He deliberately allowed her to get away but kept himself between her and the pasture. Her escape carried her back toward the stream. She stumbled, exhausted, and he stood by until she recovered. Jumping at her again, he drove her deeper from the lane, farther toward the river. She collapsed on the bluff and he dragged her over the side, sliding down to the river bottom. Her lips were purple from exertion and she looked at him with aqueous eyes, whimpering.

He pulled her to a log and dropped her, rolling her onto her back again. She raised a trembling hand and he knocked it aside. She winced, mouth open, throwing her head to one side with renewed pain. He cruelly jabbed into her and she twisted with agony, grit getting into her mouth as she threw a hand over her face. Another, harder, deeper intrusion and she clamped her teeth together, the grinding of sand between her teeth audible even to her attacker. Deeper, stronger movement with such force that he drove her several inches with the thrust and her eyes rolled back, her arms falling aside limply. Again, with more force! As she ebbed to semiconsciousness, she felt the pulsating, a flow of hot fluid, excruciating, searing pain, his breath hissing in her ear as he clung to her.

She was unresisting. Wavering between twilight and pain, her sobs now muted, her body pliant except for an occasional fleeting muscular rebellion when spasms made her jerk and twist involuntarily. The horror continued until the shadows of her mind covered her consciousness completely and she felt nothing for several long minutes at a time.

She lay crumpled, face drawn, like a spool doll with a severed twine. Her flesh was cold, clammy, and livid bruises blotched her body. She made no move. There were no cries, no sobs, no more whimpers.

Damon bathed himself in the stream. The scraping of her flesh had left him raw and sore. He sat in the river, cool water making him cry aloud with the burning of his penis. Finally, he got up and walked back to the girl. She had not moved. Her breathing was barely visible. He lifted her under the arms and for an instant she was rigid, mumbling a weak protest. He dragged her to the water. The shock of the icy dip made her gasp, but it aroused her.

"Mama," she whispered. "I want my mama."

With genuine concern for the girl, Damon examined her body, still holding her under the arms. She was battered and torn. Mother would be awakening soon. Damon peered up at the sky and tried to judge the time. He tuned himself to his mother's mind. As of this moment she was still asleep, drugged by sheer fatigue. He needed to be there when she awoke. He needed to be there and pretend he had never been out of the yard. She would think the alarm sounded and in a stupor she had turned it off and and continued sleeping. But if she found him away, there would be no explanation.

The girl stirred in his arms, her shivering now joined by the chattering of her teeth. Damon realized he too was cold. He had to do something.

"Will you tell on me?" he asked, bending near her face and lifting her higher in the same motion. "Janice! Will you tell on me?"

Her eyes rolled slightly and returned to the half-closed position of a moment ago.

"Janice!" He jostled her in the water, dunking her deeper, and she gulped with the shock of the immersion. He pulled her up to his face again. Speaking directly into her ear, he questioned, "Are you going to tell on me, Janice?"

"Mama?"

"Are you going to tell on me?" Damon hissed.

Her lips twisted and she began to cry.

"Are you going to tell on me?" Damon demanded fiercely. Her body heaved with extended, heavy sobs, but she made little sound with her crying. She looked up at him now, eyes red, her face a façade of misery.

"Are you going to tell on me, Janice?" Damon asked, his voice ominous.

Sensing his fear, seeing his expression, aware of his strength, Janice responded instinctively. She shook her head negatively. Damon stood over her, his face upside down to her, holding her under the arms, her body stretched out in the water. He looked down at her for a long time, his odd expression impossible to interpret. Then, with a sigh, he said softly, "I don't believe you.'"

CHAPTER 10

"Lock the doors and stay inside," Grandpa commanded.

"We will," Melba said.

Mr. Daniels and Grandpa were dressed in old clothing,
each carried a flashlight, their faces grim. On a far hillside,
like a thousand fireflies, lanterns winked through the trees
and underbrush. Several blocks away, the sheriff's search
and rescue squad directed the hunt. A stark, white glare
pinpointed the location of filming crews from the Atlanta
television stations. Mrs. Daniels shut the door firmly,
bolted it and turned to smile tensely at Damon.

Damon returned to the television set, following developments and commentary. He seemed entranced by the story, and, truthfully, Melba Daniels did not relish the thought of being alone, so she let him remain up past bedtime.

Men in hip boots waded the creek, walking scarcely an arm's length apart from one another. Damon's eyes were on the television, but his mind followed the hunters as they closed on their quarry. Beams of light stabbed the night, shouts passed from one line to the next, eyes wide, peering into recesses and underbrush.

Damon stood abruptly. "I'm tired, Mommy. I'm going to bed."

"All right, Damon," his mother said heavily. "Go ahead. I'll be in after a while."

He took off his shoes, shaking sand from the soles into the toilet and flushed it down. He shook his socks over the bowl and picked off flecks of briars and leaf; these too he flushed away. He neatly dropped his clothing into a hamper and went to his bedroom.

Their feet made squishing sounds in the sand, boots sloshing as they walked the stream, muddying it with their sluggish movement. Ahead, an overhang blocked those who walked the bank and they were forced to take to the water or climb a steep incline to get past. There were curses from tired men and an occasional laugh as somebody stumbled, muttering, and pushed forward.

Damon crawled into bed, pulled the covers up around his neck, lying in the dark staring overhead. It was like a movie—a picture of what was happening hung there, he could see what they saw, feel what they felt, smell the odors in their nostrils. His eyes darted from one searcher to another, following the probing lights, peering as intently as they, searching for a child who might be asleep, crying, hungry, hurt, or worse.

Damon swallowed, his mouth acid, like it tasted after eating onions or garlic at Grandma's house. He watched the events unfolding before his eyes, heart pumping with increased vigor. A lone man decided not to climb the embankment. He had decided to crawl through the

110

overhanging bluff, to take to the water if necessary. He stopped, stooped low, shining a light ahead, more concerned with his passage and the possibility of snakes than his search. He stumbled, recovered, his foot slipped and turned as though he had trod upon a loose stone. He flashed his light down and a shiver traced his spine.

"Oh, Jesus," he whispered. He had to restrain his natural instinct to shout. He could be wrong. There would be derisive laughter if he were. "Spooked!" they'd say. He knelt down and dug away a bit of sand. His fingers touched something cold, leathery, and he jerked back, now trembling. "Oh, Mother of God," he moaned half-aloud. He brushed away more moist sand, throwing aside the hastily piled leaves and soil.

"Oh, my God," he said, his voice climbing. He scrambled backward from the concave overhang. "Hey!" he shouted. "Hey! Somebody? Hey!"

"What is it?"

"I—I think I found her ! Over here ! Hey! Over here! Jesus!"

Damon turned on his side, eyes still open in the dark, seeing the accumulation of lamps, flashlights, and lanterns, jabbing, stabbing, angling, reflecting then motionless as the holders of illumination peered down, unbelieving.

"Get the sheriff!" somebody shouted. "Yeah, hey, get the sheriff!"

New hands joined in now, raking away sand, shredded leaves, a stone here, a rotting branch there, uncovering the stiff form. "Oh, good God. No!" The men cautioned one another, "Don't move her, wait on the sheriff. Don't touch anything. All right, you men, get back over there! Don't touch anything."

Damon took a deep breath, his eyes seeing what the men saw: Janice, mouth agape, eyes not quite shut, nude, the soil partially covering her features. He sighed wearily and closed his eyes.

Mrs. Daniels telephoned Kyle promptly at eight when the clinic opened. "Dr. Burnette," she had said, breathless,

111

"Damon had one of those spells last night." She was close to tears.

"This is the first one in how many nights, Mrs. Daniels?"

"This was the tenth night."

"Is he all right now?" Kyle questioned.

"Yes. Apparently. I'm—I'm not really sure, Doctor. He talked strangely. He was crude. He cursed me." She sobbed audibly. "It didn't sound like my boy, Doctor! He swore, used filthy—"

"Bring Damon down as soon as you can, Mrs. Daniels," Kyle instructed. "Please try not to be too concerned. These manifestations often take such a turn. It shouldn't alarm you."

"There's something else," Melba Daniels said, her voice lowering as she held the receiver nearer her mouth.

"What is it, Mrs. Daniels?"

"It's probably my fault," she said. "I allowed Damon to stay up longer than normal last night. His father and grandfather joined the hunt for a little girl missing out here."

"I read about it in the morning *Constitution*," Kyle said.

"Yes, well," Mrs. Daniels continued, "there was a great deal of excitement, police cars and flashing lights. I didn't want to be alone with the men gone, so I, really selfishly, let Damon stay up."

"I doubt that staying up would directly cause a seizure," Kyle reassured her.

"No, that's not what I mean!" Mrs. Daniels hissed. "Damon was watching it all on television, the ten o'clock news. I guess that made him—I guess that influenced him."

Kyle waited. He heard Mrs. Daniels turn away from the telephone, speaking to someone. She came back to the line, whispering, "Damon just came in. I'm not sure whether he heard me."

"Don't worry about it, Mrs. Daniels, just bring Damon on in."

"I will," she said. "Doctor?"

"Yes?"

"Damon wouldn't be capable of—he wouldn't hurt anyone, would he?"

Kyle connected the significance of her disjointed statements. "Has he given you any indication that he would?"

"I really don't know whether I should even repeat this," Mrs. Daniels whispered. "Damon said, in his sleep, I mean in his spell, he said—" Kyle thought he heard her gasp, sob perhaps. "He mentioned the little girl, Doctor."

"That's a natural reaction to a traumatic occurrence, Mrs. Daniels."

"But he said the child was dead!"

"It was all on the news programs, Mrs. Daniels."

"No," Melba Daniels countered, "not when Damon went to bed, it wasn't. They had not found the girl when he went to bed."

"Damon has extraordinary powers of perception, Mrs. Daniels. He knows answers which elude the rest of us. You must not attach undue importance to such things."

"Oh, dear Lord," she said, hoarsely, "oh, God, Doctor! Maybe I'm becoming ill, too! I can't seem to control myself. I can't—my brain won't stop thinking—"

Kyle waited a moment for the woman to regain herself, then, calmly, "Bring Damon in now, Mrs. Daniels. We'll be looking for him. Let's try to be optimistic about the situation. This is the first seizure Damon has had in ten days."

"Yes. Ten days."

"That's an excellent indication the medication is having a positive effect, Mrs. Daniels. Don't allow the influence of a television program to affect your thinking about him. He's a combination of child and adolescent with a sprinkling of mature adult perceptions in a very intelligent mind. The most mature adult might be moved to dream about the death of a neighboring child."

"I'll be there as soon as we get dressed," Melba said.

"Fine!" Kyle said cheerily. "See you then."

He cradled the telephone and sat, hand on the receiver, debating a few minutes, then lifted the instrument and

113

called Betty Snider. "Can you be here at the clinic within the hour?" Kyle asked.

"I suppose so. What's wrong?"

"I want to put Damon Daniels under narcosynthesis," Kyle explained. "I'd prefer that you assist me, since it will involve some highly confidential questions."

"All right," Betty agreed. "I'll be right down."

Despite his assurances to Melba Daniels, Kyle was troubled. Could Damon be capable of hurting someone? The answer and its responsibilities fell to the attending psychiatrist. The difference between neurosis and psychosis is one of degree, like a common cold compared to pneumonia. However, the difference between psychosis and "insanity" is clearly defined by law. In most states, insanity assumed four forms: lunacy, idiocy, deprivation of understanding, and accidental loss of understanding. When the rhetoric of the courtroom attorney was distilled, it boiled down to: (1) Can the party in question distinguish between right and wrong? (2) Do his delusions or hallucinations prevent him from looking after his own affairs with ordinary prudence, or do such delusions constitute a menace to others? (3) Does the party suffer impulses of such intensity that they cannot be resisted?

So long as Damon's psychosis did not endanger himself or anyone else, releasing him to his parents was acceptable. However, if he should be otherwise—

Kyle related the conversation to Ted Drinkwater. Ted's reaction was predictable. "You'd better determine Damon's inclinations, Kyle," Ted said. "If the time comes, when it comes, it will be up to you to make a decision about having the boy committed."

"I know," Kyle replied. "I called Betty Snider to assist me. I'll put the boy under and question him directly about the little girl."

"You have no other choice," Ted said.

Kyle prepared for the consultation by drawing the blinds,

lowering the intensity of the indirect lighting, and pulling a chair near the couch where Damon was now lying. On the far side of the boy, Betty sat with a tray of paraphernalia, hypodermic, syringe, and cotton balls. The tray was covered with a white cloth. A smell of alcohol permeated the room from a single swab Betty used to cleanse his skin. She tied a rubber tube around Damon's upper arm to make the blood vessels rise.

"I don't want to do this," Damon stated.

"It won't take long today," Kyle reassured him.

"But I don't want to do it," Damon protested.

"A few more times, Damon," Kyle said, "then we'll be through with this form of talking." He had to place a hand on Damon's shoulder to encourage the boy to lie back again.

Damon's eyes darted from Kyle to Betty and his deep voice intensified. "I said I don't want to do this! Goddamn it! Let me up!" He vaulted upright, eyes glaring, fists clenched.

"Damon," Kyle said mildly, "why are you objecting so violently to this consultation? You've never done it before."

"I don't want to get stuck any more," Damon seethed.

"The needle?" Betty laughed. "You've never been afraid of the needle up until now."

"Well, I've had enough," Damon said gruffly.

"If I fix it so you won't feel the needle, would you agree then?" Kyle asked.

"I don't know."

"Come on, Damon," Kyle chided, "lie down again and let's talk."

Hesitantly, warily, Damon returned to the black couch and sat there, the rubber tubing still around his arm.

"I can't help you," Kyle reasoned, "unless you cooperate."

"I don't want to cooperate."

"Obviously," Kyle said. "The question now is, why?"

"I'm tired of all this."

"But evidently it's making you better," Kyle noted. "Your mother said you've slept soundly every night since leaving the clinic, except last night."

"I know."

"Why didn't you sleep as well last night?" Kyle asked.

"I did sleep well."

"I think something is bothering you, something more than we're talking about now," Kyle said calmly.

"I know what the hell you think!" Damon snapped. "I read your goddamned mind. I want to go home now."

"That won't be possible, Damon," Kyle said, rising and returning to his desk.

"What do you mean?" Damon asked.

"We'll have to commit you to a hospital until you're cured," Kyle said blandly, looking through several papers on his desk. He intentionally kept his thoughts neutral, avoided thinking ahead of his actions and spoken words.

"What are you trying to do?" Damon questioned, his voice dropping ominously.

"The day a patient ceases to cooperate," Kyle explained, "that is the day when he must go into an institution. It is a sign that his condition has worsened and he is unwilling to apply himself to treatment that will lead to improvement."

Abruptly, Damon snatched off the rubber tourniquet and threw it to the floor. He abused Kyle and Betty, first separately, then together, with foul, vitriolic language. Stunned, Betty listened as Kyle watched the boy stomp back and forth across the office.

"You add weight to my arguments for committal with that type of display," Kyle said softly.

"I know what you're after!" Damon said, his lip curling, eyebrows raising.

"Oh?" Kyle queried. "What am I after, Damon?"

"You want to know if I killed that little girl!"

Betty gasped. Damon wheeled on her, his back arched, shoulders forward. "You bitch!" he growled. Betty drew

116

back as though Damon were about to assault her physically.

"Did you have anything to do with the little girl?" Kyle asked.

The question tempered Damon's outburst. He turned, snorting, glaring at Kyle, eyes penetrating. "What do you think, Doctor?"

Kyle recognized the demeanor and voice of Damon's alternate and he met the fierce countenance squarely. "I think you did it!" Kyle accused.

The boy charged the desk, a short, blunt threat. His breath gurgled in his throat, almost a snarling sound as he stood facing Kyle.

"You queer," Damon's voice sneered revulsively.

"That won't work," Kyle commented, his hands wet.

"Homosexual sonofabitch!" the voice rasped.

Betty looked at Kyle, eyes pleading.

"You did attack the girl, didn't you?" Kyle persisted, his voice level.

"Goddamned queer," the voice rumbled contemptuously.

"You don't answer the question," Kyle said sharply. "Is it because you cannot, will not, or fear I'll see the truth?"

Damon's shoulders were now rounded, hunched over his chest, his features hideously taut, distorted. He grunted, "Afraid, Doctor? 'Tis you who should be afraid."

"Of what?" Kyle asked.

"Of me."

"I have no reason to fear you. You need me."

The grumbling voice chortled, "I need nobody."

"If I do not get a reply from you that convinces me otherwise," Kyle stated, "I am going to assume that you raped and killed her. I'll give you one more opportunity to respond convincingly, truthfully, and then I will prepare to have you committed to a security section of the state asylum, Damon."

"I am not Damon!"

"Yes," Kyle said, smiling, "so I have said."

"You are a fool!"

"Tell me," Kyle taunted, "which of you attacked the girl?"

The snorting, warlike form confronting Kyle sagged. The lip lowered, eyebrows settling, eyes becoming wider, more luminous and liquid, uncertain, petulant more than threatening. The shoulders·fell back, spine straightened, the hands on Kyle's desk slipping off to hang at the boy's sides. The voice smoothed, mellowed, warmed, became more childlike, despite the timbre.

"My head hurts," Damon whimpered. "I don't feel good."

"Sit on the couch, Damon," Kyle said, kindly.

"I wish I didn't have to do this."

"Go to sleep?" Kyle questioned. "Oh, we aren't going to do that now. We'll do that another day."

Gratefully, Damon smiled, lips thin, compressed. "You're going to make me stay in the clinic tonight?"

"I'd rather not think of it as 'making' you, Damon," Kyle replied. "I'd rather you agreed willingly."

"But I don't want to stay here," Damon said, tears in his eyes. "I want to go home. I want to be with my mommy."

"I hope it won't be necessary to keep you here long," Kyle professed.

"Please," Damon cried, "please, Dr. Burnette, don't make me stay here. I want to go home."

Betty hesitantly reached for Damon's arm and he threw himself against her chest, sobbing. She held him close, comforting a distraught child, but her heart still hammered from the scene a few moments ago.

"There, there," Betty said. "I'll be here to keep you company."

"No you won't," Kyle said. Betty looked at Kyle uncertainly.

Kyle said, "I want a man to stay with Damon."

"Now, wait a minute, Kyle," Betty protested.

"Not now!" Kyle snapped.

Sobbing, wiping his eyes with the backs of both hands,

Damon followed Kyle to the waiting room and down the hall to the inpatient clinic. Mrs. Daniels arose as they walked through, responding to Kyle's motion to follow them. Kyle ushered Damon into the familiar room, closed the door, and using a key from his belt chain, he locked it.

"Doctor, what is it?" Mrs. Daniels asked, her fears mounting.

"I want Damon to stay here for a few nights, Mrs. Daniels," Kyle said.

"Is it because of the little girl? Did he?"

Kyle gazed at her steadily. "No. However, apparently Damon is yielding more and more to the personality you witnessed last night when he was so crude to you. Come back to my office and let's talk a few minutes."

Kyle lit a cigarette and pondered the wisest approach to take with the visibly disturbed mother. "The nights are telling on you, Mrs. Daniels," Kyle observed. "You work at cleaning, cooking, other household chores by day and sleep fitfully by night as you try to look after Damon. I'm almost as concerned about your health this moment as I am about Damon's."

"I'll be all right," Melba Daniels insisted. "I'm just tired."

"Exhausted would be a better term," Kyle amended.

"Yes," she admitted, "exhausted."

"This is the primary reason I wish to keep Damon here," Kyle explained. "Plus, we need a more intensive consultation than we had today. Damon is rebelling, for which we cannot blame him. But for the necessity of the treatment, he must be properly reprimanded, restricted, so he will know the seriousness of continuing our work with him."

Melba Daniels nodded.

"You go home now," Kyle said. He reached in a cabinet drawer behind him and took out a package of samples sent to him by one of the pharmaceutical firms. "These will relax you," Kyle said. "Take one upon arriving home, another after supper. Get plenty of rest, Mrs. Daniels. All you need is rest."

She nodded again, lower lip tremulous. "I couldn't believe the way he spoke to me. Those terrible words. Where could he have learned such words?"

"From the minds of everyone around him," Kyle said. "But, again, let me remind you that the voice speaking those words is not your son, Damon. It was a totally alien personality, another person using his vocal cords and body, for all practical purposes. Try to think of it in that perspective."

She was breaking up now, the tenuous hold on her emotions cracking under the constant strain from the past several months. She sat, head ducked, tears splotching her conservatively cut suit, a crumpled tissue in one hand, both hands in her lap, palms up.

"It was frightening, Doctor. He looked at me with hate in his eyes. He threatened to—to attack me. Sexually. Attack me sexually. Oh, my God, how can this be happening? This is a nightmare."

Kyle saw Betty move from her unobtrusive position against the wall beyond the couch and make her way to the door. He motioned her back.

"He called me such filthy names," Mrs. Daniels wept. "I was afraid, Dr. Burnette. I was actually afraid. I wanted to call my husband, but I didn't want him to hear Damon calling me those things. Nobody ever said such things to me before."

"Try to put it out of your mind, Mrs. Daniels," Kyle said tenderly. "It was not your son speaking to you."

"Then who was it?" she asked, looking up. "If it wasn't Damon, who was it, Doctor?"

"He has no name as such, Mrs. Daniels. It's a twisted form of the subconscious. But we'll purge him from your son, believe me."

"Damon looked so strange, so angry!" Melba Daniels stared at her lap again. "Like he hated me, hated everybody, the world."

"Don't dwell on it, Mrs. Daniels," Kyle urged. "Think only of the positive things. Don't inflict mental pain on

120

yourself thinking about last night. It can serve no purpose. No good purpose."

Kyle circled his desk and gave Melba Daniels a box of tissues. "I'm using up all your Kleenex," she said.

"I have a good supply," Kyle said, smiling.

Mrs. Daniels took a deep breath and exhaled quickly. "Will this ever end, Doctor?"

"I hope so, Mrs. Daniels."

"If it doesn't?"

Kyle's eyes softened. "We'll cross that bridge when we reach it, Mrs. Daniels."

CHAPTER 11

MR. AND MRS. DANIELS sat close to Kyle's desk, sipping coffee; the atmosphere was relaxed and deliberately informal. Ted and Kyle faced the prospect of bringing these confused and terrified parents up to date on their son, to apprise them of the turmoil within Damon's mind.

"There have been only twenty-seven cases in medical history which approximate Damon's," Kyle said. "Of this number, all but half a dozen were many years ago, poorly reported and dubious at best. The most recent cases occurred in the late forties and early fifties. In London, in

May of 1955, a man named Kenneth Walker published an article entitled "The Strange Case of Miss Beauchamp" in the London *Courier*. In his article, Mr. Walker outlined a case concerning a woman with an alternate personality, a split personality you might call it."

"With Miss Beauchamp," Ted interjected, "the second personality was brought out under hypnosis."

"However," Kyle said, "more recently and closer to home, two doctors in Augusta, Georgia, had a patient they called 'Eve White,' which you may recall. Miss considered had a second personality who called herself 'Eve Black' and who obtained periodic dominance over the original Eve without the use of hypnosis, quite unexpectedly. The case received publicity worldwide when the facts were released. Dr. Corbett H. Thigpen and Dr. Hervey M. Cleckley wrote a book, *The Three Faces of Eve*, from which a film was made."

"I remember that," Mrs. Daniels remarked. "Eve White and Eve Black eventually yielded to a third personality," Ted said. "This third ego, named Jane, triumphed over the initial two and emerged the dominant character of the patient until she was considered cured."

"Then," Edward Daniels reasoned, "this can be cured."

"Actually," Kyle amended, "the word 'cured' doesn't apply. While Eve White suffered from the psychosis of hearing voices, it turned out she really heard Eve Black, her unknown and unsuspected second personality. Eve White had no idea that Eve Black existed, although Eve Black was aware of Eve White. The mind is a fantastic and little-known instrument, Mr. Daniels. We hesitate to say that Eve White, or Eve Black was ill. Each personality had problems but neither of them was mentally ill. In fact, had it not been for Eve Black, Eve White would probably have been all right. It was Eve Black who caused Eve White's headaches, made unexplainable purchases, and performed deeds which Eve White could not remember. So, who is to say that Eve White was suffering from a psychosis? Or Eve

Black? They were two separate and completely different people living in the same body, each attempting to survive independently."

The Danielses were struggling to comprehend the incomprehensible. "Then you are saying that Damon has such a split personality?" Edward Daniels questioned.

"Yes," Kyle acknowledged, "but with several remarkable differences. Damon is a child, whereas his alternate is apparently a mature man. We were positive at the beginning that Damon was unaware of his second personality. We are no longer so sure. It could be that the sweven is now using the child's personality to escape responsibility. Or, it may be that Damon knows the second personality exists and yields to it knowingly or unknowingly. At first, the second personality emerged under narcosynthesis. Now it comes and goes apparently at will."

"The most startling aspect of this case," Ted Drinkwater noted, "is the basic reason it has occurred at all."

"Yes," Kyle agreed. "The mind and body are one. In Damon's case, the mind may be creating the physical reactions. That is to say, Damon may be at the mercy of his glandular condition, or the glandular condition may be a direct result of Damon's sweven. Either way the two are intertwined. We face an alternate personality which is uncooperative and with a dual problem to overcome: one the psychological aspects and the other the physiological phase of the problem."

"Damon has no control over the second personality?" Melba Daniels asked.

"Apparently not," Ted said. "There seems to be evidence that the second personality has the power to control Damon, in fact."

"This is the person who spoke to you the other night, Mrs. Daniels," Kyle explained. "It was the sweven, not your son."

Mrs. Daniels shuddered. "He was vile."

"Again," Kyle said, "the sweven, as we are calling him,

may be a product of the glandular condition. Dr. von Ulbricht and Dr. Drinkwater believe that the body is totally at the mercy of an irresponsible glandular failure."

"It's difficult to believe such a thing is possible," Mr. Daniels said. "How can the glands create such a response?"

"Glandular malfunctions are considerably more common than personality dissociation," Ted commented. "Everybody has heard of the 'alligator boy' in the circus. The boy has clearly defined welts over his body which resemble an alligator's hide. The fat lady, giant, dwarf, all are glandular dysfunctions of one type or another. The results can be quite bizarre. The bearded lady, rubber man, all have a common problem of glands that did not do what they were intended to do. Every living animal is subject to similar failures at any time. What is happening to Damon could happen to anyone of any age. With Damon, the problem is more widespread, obviously affecting many parts of his body, including his mind. But the glandular condition is unique only in that it *is* so broad in scope and he is so young. That is why we think the pituitary is at fault. As we've said, the pituitary directs all other glandular activity."

"I think we understand about the glands," Mrs. Daniels said. "After you told us about them the first time, we did a great deal of research on the matter."

"Good." Kyle nodded.

"Do you think the glandular condition could be causing Damon to be so intelligent?" Melba Daniels questioned.

"Possibly," Kyle said.

"When he's cured then," Mrs. Daniels asked, hesitantly, "will his mind be dulled?"

"Hopefully not," Kyle stated.

"How about the mental telepathy?" Mrs. Daniels asked. "Will that disappear?"

"We don't have pat answers to such questions," Kyle noted. "It is theoretically possible for Damon's perception to be as acute as it is due to the glandular secretions, and therefore it is also possible that his keen perception would

126

diminish or vanish outright if the glandular condition is corrected."

"On the other hand," Ted added, "such perception could be inherent. Once these problems clear up, Damon might be more perceptive, brighter, responsive, and sensitive. We just don't know."

"I see," Mrs. Daniels said.

"Treating Damon's case is something like fighting a war," Kyle said. "There are several fronts to be considered. We fight all of them steadily. But the one that surges dangerously from an attack by the enemy, that is the front where we concentrate hardest to avoid a breakthrough. This is the case with the second personality. He seems to be trying to take over, winning his fight. We are still concerned with the glandular problem, no less intent on conquering it, but we are faced with a sudden onslaught by this second entity, aren't we? As your wife will tell you, Mr. Daniels, this second being within Damon is extremely unpleasant."

"Vulgar," Melba Daniels said softly. "Filthy."

"For this reason," Kyle explained, "I am asking you to leave your son here, this time for an indefinite period. Weeks, possibly months. You are aware of the cost involved. If you'd prefer, I will make arrangements to get him into a state institution."

"No," Edward Daniels declared, "we'd prefer that he stay here."

"I felt sure you would," Kyle said.

"What are the chances for Damon's partial or full recovery?" the father asked.

"I wish I could give a numerical percentage," Kyle said. "Unfortunately, we do not know. I realize how frustrating it is to get what appears to be a runaround. But it is fruitless to build hopes and expectations that might be disappointing."

"Then tell me this," Mrs. Daniels insisted, "how much chance do you yourself think you have?"

Kyle stirred uneasily. "We don't know. I don't know."

"You don't give a man much hope," Mr. Daniels said.

"In the hope department," Ted concluded, "we rank very high, second only to your hope. We do hope to see Damon living a full, useful, normal life. If we didn't have some iota of hope that this may happen, we would tell you. Our lack of positive response in no way reflects a lack of positive hope."

Mr. Daniels nodded, taking his wife's hand.

"Thank you for coming in, Mr. and Mrs. Daniels," Kyle said. "I know you want to spend some time with Damon, so feel free to go ahead."

"May we take him out for a soda?" Mrs. Daniels asked.

"Not just yet," Kyle suggested. "Let's wait a while on that. However, do utilize the kitchenette and lounge area. You'll have privacy there."

With the parents out of Kyle's office, Ted asked, "Did you locate someone to stay nights with Damon?"

"Nick Joiner," Kyle replied. Joiner had worked with them several times in the past. Big, powerful, the black man had a firm but gentle approach. Beneath a genial exterior was an iron will and Joiner had a genuine interest in his patients, too. He had worked in the psychiatric wards of several local hospitals. Most recently, he had been employed at Milledgeville State institution.

"Joiner will do fine," Ted said. "Have you given him the background on Damon?"

"Yes, I did."

"It doesn't worry him?"

Kyle chuckled. "No. He said it sounded like his first wife."

"Dr. von Ulbricht?" The voice on the telephone struggled with English. "This is Dr. Karl Christian in Copenhagen."

"Yes, Doctor?" von Ulbricht responded.

"You have been referred to me by my associate in London, Dr. Johann Dormann."

"Ah, yes!" von Ulbricht said. "How is Dr. Dormann?"

"He sends regards, Dr. von Ulbricht. May I come to the point immediately?"

"Of course, please do."

"I have an unusual case. I am a psychiatrist here in Copenhagen. Several months ago, a wealthy shipbuilder from Esbjerg brought his eight-year-old son to me for consultations. The child seems to have an erratic glandular condition unlike anything we have ever seen before. He is unusual in several ways, but the glandular condition is uppermost in our minds at the moment. The child is suffering enlarged extremities from advanced acromegaly and is rapidly deteriorating. We have sent him to London, Zurich, and to one or another of the various endocrinologists in the Scandinavian kingdoms. Dr. Dormann has recommended you. I am not in a position to appreciate adequately the work you have done, but Dr. Dormann says you have pioneered in radioimmunoassaying."

"That's correct," von Ulbricht replied.

"Dormann seems to feel, if anybody can help this child, it will be you."

"What are the symptoms?" von Ulbricht asked. "Anything other than acromegaly?"

"Yes, there are others, but I'd rather discuss them with you in person. The case must be held in great confidence, Doctor."

"You want me to fly over there?" Dr. von Ulbricht questioned.

"If possible, yes."

"It is not possible," Dr. von Ulbricht stated. "I could not get away that long, Doctor. I'm sorry. If you could send me samples, perhaps."

"No. This requires your presence," Dr. Christian said flatly. "If it is a matter of expense, my client is more than capable of payment. All expenses paid, of course."

"The expense is not altogether the problem," Dr. von Ulbricht said. "My own work has been considerably delayed here by a particular case and I am working overtime daily to keep abreast of it."

"Dr. von Ulbricht," Dr. Christian said, "this is a case that will no doubt be of worldwide interest. The child is, or was, an extremely bright boy. His intelligence tested well above genius when we first got him. He showed a remarkable ability to perceive the thoughts of people around him. Truly remarkable child. The death of this boy would be a distinct loss to more than the family. His case is unparalleled so far as we can determine. It is more than a child's life here, there are too many precedents involved. I urge you, please reconsider."

Erich von Ulbricht forced his voice to a calm he did not feel. "Tell me, Dr. Christian, have you tried hormonal injections?"

"We did, yes. The condition seemed to stabilize for a period of several months, then the acromegaly began."

"Have you considered operating?"

"It has been declined as an alternative by Dr. Dormann. He felt that to do so would endanger the life of the patient and preclude any hope of determining the cause of the condition, which we believe to be psychotic."

With perspiring hands, von Ulbricht held a pen. "Give me your telephone number, Doctor. Also the address. Tell your client that my fee is one thousand dollars, American, per diem, plus expenses of travel, lodging, and so forth."

"That will be acceptable, Dr. von Ulbricht. My client is sitting here at this moment and hears our conversation."

"I hope I can be of some benefit," von Ulbricht said.

"When do you think you can come?" the voice on the telephone asked rising above a crackle of line noise.

"I will try to fly out within a week," von Ulbricht promised. "I'll wire you when my connections are confirmed."

"Dr. von Ulbricht?" A strange voice.

"Yes?"

"God bless you. Thank you!"

"I'll wire you soon," von Ulbricht said.

He disconnected and sat staring at his desk, oblivious to his secretary, who had been taking dictation. Could there possibly be two cases of the same nature? Of course, with the little information he had, there might be no resemblance of the child in Copenhagen to Damon here in

130

Atlanta. But the parallel was too close to ignore. Dr. von Ulbricht looked up at the waiting girl, her pen poised.

"Make reservations for me on the earliest flight possible to Copenhagen," he said. "Find out what immunization I'll need for passport purposes, if any. Call my attorney and send someone over to pick up a standard contract for medical services rendered, billing in advance to—" He read the name of Dr. Christian and his clinic.

As the woman reached the door, von Ulbricht stopped her. "Call my wife and ask her if she'd like to accompany me. Then, clear my calendar for the next fifteen days. We might as well make a vacation of it while we're there."

"Yes, sir, Doctor."

"One other thing," von Ulbricht added. "Now would be a good time for you to go ahead and have your child's tonsils removed, while I'm away."

The secretary laughed. "Very well, sir."

"Get Dr. Burnette on the telephone for me, please."

"Yes sir."

He had already decided to wait until he saw the patient in Denmark before relating all this to Kyle. Nonetheless, to be absent fifteen days, he should advise Kyle and Ted that he would be unavailable to their patient in the interim. If indeed the Denmark case was like Damon Daniels's, the ramifications for Dr. von Ulbricht were enlightening! He had already considered an extensive paper on the case. But, two cases! There might be room for a series, possibly even a book.

"Your wife is not with you?" Dr. Christian questioned.

"No," Erich von Ulbricht said, "she's sightseeing. She took a tour up to Kronborg Castle for a day and night."

The two men walked a long tiled hallway, their footsteps echoing in a never-ending staccato. "Then, you'll be alone tonight," Dr. Christian surmised.

"So it seems."

"You must dine with my wife and me," Dr. Christian stated. He gestured for a left turn and they faced a shorter, narrower corridor. On either side were heavy doors with welded steel screens over small windows.

They halted before a door midway down the hall. Dr. Christian pulled a ring of keys from his pocket, peering through a latticed window before entering. They had to step down one foot to the floor of a sunken cubicle. The door closed into a recess that brought it flush with the wall and floor, concealing the step up to the outside hall. Above painted stressed steel construction wire, four naked bulbs illuminated the room. There was no bed. Except for the high window of the door, which was inaccessible at this level, no other portal broke the solid four walls. A heavy covering blunted all walls from floor to the steel grating overhead. The door was padded. It was the type of security cell assigned to hyperactive patients who might hurt themselves thrashing about.

An attendant wearing tennis shoes, dark trousers, and a white smock stood to one side. He had arisen from the only furniture here, a simple stool. In one corner, nude, crouched, with knees in front of him, genitals exposed, the patient glared at the newcomers.

The horror of the child was repulsing, yet infinitely touching. His head was preponderant, twice the size normal for a large adult. The hands and feet were huge. The child's legs were trunks, darkened, enlarged, and shapeless, bringing to von Ulbricht's mind the memories of photographs he'd seen in medical school of victims suffering from elephantiasis. The boy's legs were like the legs of the pachyderms which lent their name to that terrible tropical disease. His scrotum, in that crouched position, fell to the floor, fully large enough to contain two grapefruits.

Speaking Danish, Dr. Christian soothed the child, going through a perfunctory introduction of Dr. von Ulbricht. But it was obvious from the watery eyes and furtive glances that this was not a willing or cooperative patient. Appalled, Dr. von Ulbricht watched the child urinate under the influence of Dr. Christian's touch, quite like a nervous puppy might respond to a master's attention. Immediately, the attendant produced a towel and wiped up the area. Dr. von Ulbricht then saw that behind one of the cotton buffers was a chest of drawers and a disposal unit built into the wall.

An animal sound akin to a growl came from the pitiful gnome and he began to rock back and forth on his heels, eyes flitting from Dr. Christian to von Ulbricht.

"As you can see," Dr. Christian commented, "the condition is quite advanced."

"Too far for remedial therapy," von Ulbricht said tersely.

"I suspect so."

"Then," von Ulbricht said, testily, "why have you asked me to come here at great expense to the patient's father?"

"I want you to see the records."

They walked the return passage, this time with von Ulbricht setting the pace in long, angry strides. When they reached the seclusion of Dr. Christian's private office, von Ulbricht turned on the psychiatrist.

"You have asked me to fly here at phenomenal expenditures of time and money to myself and your patient," von Ulbricht snapped. "The case is terminal, as you must surely know! This is an irresponsible act on your part, Doctor. A needless cost in a hopeless situation. If my presence has given rise to one centimeter of hope to the parents, you are doubly damned for asking it of me!"

Dr. Christian stood behind his desk, eyes down.

"That boy is doomed," von Ulbricht seethed. "The best you can accomplish is a sad continuation, a prolonging of misery for all concerned."

"Please sit down," Dr. Christian said. "Would you like a drink? I have Scotch, brandy, tea."

"Hell no, I don't want a drink!" von Ulbricht exploded. "I want to return to my hotel and leave here as soon as possible."

"Please," Dr. Christian said calmly, "sit down."

"As a practicing psychiatrist," von Ulbricht said, "you

133

must surely have known the consequences of raising hope in the minds of the parents. What type miracle were you seeking, for God's sake?"

"For this boy, nothing," Dr. Christian replied. "He is, as you say, doomed. The parents knew that before we called you, Dr. von Ulbricht."

"Then, what in heaven's name possessed you to call for me?"

"Because," Dr. Christian said, handing von Ulbricht a glass of brandy, "we hoped you might solve the riddle of what could have been done."

"A postmortem of the still living," von Ulbricht sneered.

"Not quite," Dr. Christian retorted. "If you solve the riddle you may save future lives."

"Dr. Christian, you said yourself this case is unique. Solving the riddle in theory is pointless unless there are other similar cases."

Dr. Christian's eyes were steady on his American colleague. He sipped brandy and pursed his lips in appreciation of the flavor. Returning to the massive carved desk, Christian seated himself and withdrew a thick group of file folders from a drawer.

"I shall expect absolute confidence on this matter," Dr. Christian stated crisply. "There will be no release of papers, news stories, or even a general discussion among physicians." He extended the file folders at von Ulbricht and when the endocrinologist made no move to come forward, Christian dropped the material at the other side of his desk.

"Perhaps I did not make myself clear, Dr. Christian," von Ulbricht said curtly. "I am not interested in a postmortem. I do not wish to affiliate with the case."

"I think you will change your mind, however," Dr. Christian said. "Please take these reports with you. Study them."

"Why should I?" von Ulbricht challenged.

"You have seen an advanced case, the most advanced of three, Dr. von Ulbricht."

"Then," von Ulbricht said, "there are others!"

CHAPTER 12

"HE SAYS THERE are three cases documented," Kyle reported. "One extremely advanced, Caucasian male, age nine, in Denmark. Another, age unknown, Negroid aboriginal, confined in Sydney, Australia. The third is Indian, also male, age eight, presently in Hyderabad, India, but a native of some small village several hundred miles inland called Saugor."

"Four then, including Damon," Ted said angrily.

"Yes, four."

"Then, for Christ's sake, be sensible!" Ted demanded.

"Release the news of our case immediately. If we spent the next few weeks working on it, we could have papers ready for at least two of the major journals."

"It would not be in the best interest of the patients," Kyle replied.

"Goddamn it, Kyle," Ted said, "do you think for a minute you'll be able to keep this thing quiet? That doctor in Denmark, what's his name?"

"Christian."

"Do you think he's going to keep silent? He's going to print the case, his case. You know he will!"

"He said he wouldn't ."

"But he will!" Ted said, stalking the floor before Kyle's desk. "He'll scoop us while we stand by protecting our patient. Then it won't matter what we write, we'll just be one of four cases. If we go ahead now, get the papers out, it will be us, our clinic, that gets the recognition. By God, we've spent hundreds of hours on this thing. Our cumulative time far surpasses consultation fees. The prize goes to the swift and the victor."

"I promised Dr. Christian I would withhold all reports on Damon," Kyle said emphatically. "He agreed to issue our summations only in retrospect. It's in the best interest of everyone involved, Ted. Dr. Christian is concerned not only with his own case, which appears terminal, he's also thinking of ours. Seeking a cause, a cure, not just publicity."

"I'm not believing that," Ted snapped. "You mark my words, as soon as his patient dies he'll let his reports go. He's sucking us in, Kyle."

"It's a chance we'll have to take, Ted," Kyle said firmly.

Ted leaned forward, his weight on the knuckles of both hands atop the desk. "Kyle, at this juncture, you surely don't think this thing is going to be kept quiet. It's only a matter of time. The glory goes to the man who breaks it, not the poor bastard plodding along trying to protect his patient. I agreed to wait before, for the sake of the patient. But, when it is obvious that this whole thing is becoming general knowledge—"

"General knowledge?"

"Well, hell yes!" Ted countered. "You, me, von Ulbricht, Christian, some doctor or doctors in India, more in Australia! A secret is a secret, as someone once said, when two know it and one of them is dead. This story could break from any one of a dozen sources. A lab technician somewhere along the way could blab to a newspaper reporter, anybody!"

"Ted." Kyle put one arm on the other psychiatrist's shoulder and looked him in the eyes. "I don't want to oppose you on this. I don't want to argue over it. I don't want anything, no matter how trivial, to disrupt our services. Mostly, I don't want you unhappy with me personally. I'm not demanding that we withhold this case from report. I'm pleading with you on a single ground—Damon's welfare. The furor that will result from the press will be fantastic, I know it as well as you. But I think, I honestly think, we would hate ourselves for it someday. We would have done irreparable damage to Damon's future, we would have capitalized on his illness. To report on a case for academic, professional purposes is one thing. To use him for our own selfish motivations is something else. Believe me, I'm as frustrated as you over this. One side of me says, 'Go ahead, goddamn it, go ahead,' and the other side of me balks. How will we look one another in the eye someday? If I did anything else, I swear, Ted, I think it would be to our ultimate degeneration. I can't believe you would actually go through with releasing the reports prematurely. I think you'd write them up, all right. I think you'd even put them in an envelope. But, I know you too well; you wouldn't mail it, Ted. You have too much integrity, you care too much about that boy down the hall to do this to him."

Ted's face flamed. He dropped his gaze and shrugged away Kyle's hand, a smile coming to his lips sheepishly. "Oh, shit," he said softly.

"How about a drink?"

"Why not?" Ted agreed. He dropped into a chair, his long legs thrust out before him.

"I told Christian I'd see him at the International Psychiatric Symposium in London, month after next," Kyle said. "He invited me to Copenhagen to review his case."

"How'd he find out about the other two cases?" Ted asked sullenly.

"Searching for an endocrinologist to help him correct the hormonal imbalance in his patient there in Denmark. That's what brought him to von Ulbricht. One of Erich's old classmates from his Rhodes scholarship days recommended him. Evidently, the doctor in Sydney and the one in Hyderabad were also seeking somebody along the same lines."

"So," Ted sighed, "we become a company of dozens at the mercy of the weakest among us. It is the weakest who will let out the report and capitalize on it first."

"Let's hope not," Kyle said unconvincingly. He carried Ted's drink across the room and gave it to him. "Maybe, just maybe, everybody will wait until the final case is solved and we can all issue some sort of common report together. Better that than a premature grab for the glory and attention."

"Piss on it," Ted said heavily. "We're going to lose out, I can feel it in my bones."

"I really hope not," Kyle said. "For your sake, especially. It means so much to you, obviously. "

"Hell yes, it does," Ted admitted. "Every physician dreams of finding a one-time-only case, a supercase. Don't tell me you don't."

"It's exciting all right," Kyle said. "Maybe I'm wrong to ask that we hold back. I'm just thinking about Damon and—"

"Oh, Christ!" Ted flared. "That's enough. You want me to weep? I've agreed to wait, you hooker."

"Oh, Ted," Kyle purred, "you've been so sweet to me since the baby came."

"Bastard." Ted laughed. "If my wife didn't like you so much, and if you weren't my best friend and one whale of a psychiatrist anyway, I'd tell you to go to hell on this. I'm not falling for your childish psychology appealing to my

138

better half, I want you to know that. I'm yielding to a guy who's just too goddamned nice to buck, that's all."

Kyle nodded appreciatively.

"But you're still a bastard," Ted said morosely.

Erich von Ulbricht was his usual supercharged, energetic self. He jerked, twitched, jiggled one leg, and smoked constantly as he spoke. "The child's father is a wealthy shipbuilder," von Ulbricht explained. "This boy was his only child. He has agreed to finance us jointly, all of us, to find the cause of the trouble and correct it. He knows his own son's life is limited. But he wants to do it for the other three. He paid my fee in full and he's setting aside a generous sum for travel, intercommunications, laboratory analysis, and so forth."

"Tell us about the boy in Copenhagen," Kyle requested.

"I have the full case history with me," Dr. von Ulbricht said. "I also have a partial history on the other two. I felt sure you wouldn't mind my reporting your case to Christian. There was no other honorable thing to do, considering I was consulting on both sides of the fence."

"It's perfectly all right, I agree one hundred percent," Kyle stated.

"The causes are fundamentally the same," von Ulbricht noted. "If you placed the histories side by side, you'd be hard put to distinguish one from the others. Particularly Damon and this boy from Denmark. Well-to-do families, socially acceptable and all that. The youngsters have all suffered a similar imbalance and runaway glandular reaction. Each child has shown a fantastic ability to exercise mental perceptions above the norm, each has an extraordinary intelligence quotient. But as I predicted with Damon, the prognosis is inevitable. That child in Copenhagen was—terrible."

"You think what has happened to the Copenhagen case is the course Damon will experience then?" Ted asked.

"Unless we find some means of counteracting it, yes," von Ulbricht replied.

"How about the other two cases?" Kyle questioned.

"Of course," von Ulbricht said, "all I have is the medical history of each; I haven't seen the patients. But, except for the degree of the manifestation, they all have the same symptoms and affectations. Physically, I mean. I can only assume their prognoses are the same. As for the psychiatric end of it, there's no mention of any psychological testing with the cases in India and Australia."

"Well, shit!" Ted said hotly. "Has anybody got a suggestion?"

"Yes," von Ulbricht said, "I do. I suggest that one or the other of you go to see these other patients for yourselves. Not Copenhagen so much as Sydney and Hyderabad. I'm satisfied from the blood samples that were sent to me that these boys are all victims of a similar malady. That leaves the psychological aspects still in the fog, however. If they have identical neuroses, then we are back to the problematic question of which came first, the chicken or the egg. Is it gland over mind, mind over gland, or what? It isn't altogether a moot point, either. It seems to me, we can't afford to leave a single stone unturned in the investigation. If they are all identical and there is a single difference between them, that might help. Who knows?"

"I can't get away, that's certain," Ted said. "I have an operation a day for the next six months."

"Nor can I," Kyle added.

Dr. von Ulbricht drummed his fingers on Kyle's desk. "As you please, gentlemen," he said. "But be it known, the man who does the leg work between these cases is the master of them all. As it stands now, you and I are only one of four groups of physicians with similar cases. It appears to me that much has gone into this matter already. I'd hate to see us lose supremacy by inaction. In all modesty, at this point I am your only ace in the hole. After all, they did contact me for the hormonal work. I'm with you boys. But it won't be long before they know all I know and then everything will be par again."

"He's right," Ted said. "You should get on a stick and go see these other cases, Kyle."

140

"Me?" Kyle questioned.

"Well, who else?" Ted asked.

Erich von Ulbricht smiled expansively. "It is a wise decision!"

"You tell that sonofabitch in Copenhagen and the one in Sydney and the one in India that if they release this story without our permission," Ted said, "I'm personally going to hunt them down, if it's the last thing I do."

"That won't be necessary," von Ulbricht stated. "I already told them that you two have written a book which was just shy of going to the press and that you reluctantly agreed to withhold publication for their sakes."

"Beautiful!" Ted whooped.

"Of course," von Ulbricht said succinctly, "I wish to have an exclusive on the reports as they relate to the endocrinology of the cases."

"Of course," Ted agreed.

"Then," von Ulbricht said amiably, "we understand one another."

"Take me with you, Kyle," Betty pleaded.

"I can't justify that," Kyle said. "The father of the Copenhagen boy is paying the expenses, Betty."

"I can transcribe, take dictation, I'm acquainted with your case, I can be of great help to you. It won't be pleasure for pleasure's sake by any stretch of the imagination and you know it. My presence will save you many hours of work. It's a practical move. I don't have to have any salary. I'll live on my savings if you just pay my expenses."

"Betty," Kyle said tenderly, "I really can't do it. The gentleman is being generous now. Your going along would be taking advantage of him."

"I don't think he will believe that," Betty said adamantly.

"Nonetheless, when I spoke to him on the telephone, I didn't say anything about having a companion," Kyle argued.

"Come on now, Kyle, for crying out loud! You could do it with another phone call if you wanted to. Be sensible, damn it! We can stay in the same room. I'll prostrate myself for you. I'll eat crumbs from your dinner. I need to watch my diet anyway."

Kyle laughed and put his arm around her shoulder. "I'll speak to Ted and see what he says."

"Good!" Betty exulted. "I'll get my passport papers and be packing."

"You'd better wait to see what comes of it, first," Kyle warned. "Don't get your hopes up. If Ted agrees, which I doubt, I must then talk to the guy footing the bills for this junket."

"No sweat," Betty said. "I already talked to Ted."

"You did?"

"Yep."

"What did he say?"

"He said it would be worth it and if he were going he would certainly take me along."

"Not for dictation, I'll wager," Kyle said.

"It was dick something," Betty smiled. "I remember it distinctly."

"You're going away," Damon said simply.

"For a short while," Kyle acknowledged. "No longer than three weeks."

"I have to stay locked up until you get back?"

"You aren't really locked up, you know," Kyle said, a bit too sharply.

"The hell I'm not! I can't get out! What am I, if I'm not locked up?"

"Where would you go if you were out?" Kyle reasoned.

"Home."

"That wouldn't be wise right now, Damon."

The boy was becoming more and more recalcitrant. He sat on the edge of a chair, thick eyebrows lowered. Kyle had become more adept at concealing his thoughts. Or, was Damon's power weakening?

"You can't keep me locked up forever, can you?"

"I don't want to," Kyle said. "But it disturbs me that you

142

are showing less cooperation, Damon. Can you tell me why you're doing this?"

"Because I'm tired of this crap."

"People who have polio get tired of braces and iron lungs, too," Kyle responded calmly. "But those things are necessary for their welfare."

"That's a piss-poor simile."

"Why are you using such abusive language, Damon? It hardly becomes you. Swearing is a breakdown in the communications process, you know. A person swears, inserting the vulgarity when his mind fails to find an adequate word to replace it. With your intelligence, invectives should be completely unnecessary. They would also carry considerably more weight in an argument. Unless, of course, your sole purpose is to shock the listener. Even in that you fail with me, however. There isn't anything you can say that I haven't heard many times before."

"Fuck you," Damon said.

"Even that," Kyle retorted mildly.

"I'll tell you this," Damon said, lifting his head, his eyes intense. "You're going to make a trip that will cost that man in Denmark a lot of money and it won't do you one bit of good. The answer to everything you want is right here."

"Really?" Kyle mused. "Give me the source and I'll gladly remain here. Give me the answers, Damon, and you'll be home within a month, I can promise you that!"

"Ask the questions, then," Damon challenged.

"To begin, what is this sweven fixation that seems to obsess you?"

"Nothing obsesses me," Damon replied casually. "Part of your problem is that you are looking for the wrong answers."

"Did you have anything to do with that little girl's death?" Kyle asked.

Damon cut his eyes, half smiling. "What do you think, Doctor? Do you really think I did?"

"No," Kyle admitted.

143

"You see," Damon said, "we waste much time pondering stupid questions."

"All right, Damon," Kyle countered, "you ask the questions I should be asking, the ones you think are important."

"There is only one," Damon said, his eyes a peculiar hue.

"What is that?"

"Who are you?" Damon said. "That is the question."

CHAPTER 13

THE BURN of rubber on macadam occurred at 9:31 Hyderabad time. The jet settled onto a runway, engines whining, and taxied to a fixed position. Shimmering waves of heat snaked up from the concrete pad and lifted Betty's skirt as she and Kyle made their way toward the terminal. Having cleared customs in Calcutta, they passed directly into a crowded foyer of the depot. Kyle had just retrieved their luggage when a hand touched his arm.

"Dr. Kyle Burnette?"

Kyle turned to face a thin, slightly stooped Indian

wearing a loose-fitting suit, a smile crinkling weathered features. "I am Dr. Raul Jinnah."

They were escorted to a chauffeured Citroën and Dr. Jinnah wasted no time getting to the point of their visit. In the melodic English of an Indian who first learned Urdu, Dr. Jinnah briefed them on the child they were about to meet.

"If the boy were of a lower caste," Dr. Jinnah commented, "we might never have had an opportunity to see him. Being the son of a prominent man, having a father who is a wealthy textile miller, was good fortune. His father, Zakir Venkata, is a widely traveled man, he thinks with a western mind. If the boy—Khan is what he calls himself—if Khan had been born to a less fortunate lot, he might have been idolized or executed depending on the village where he displayed his extraordinary talents."

Dr. Jinnah proffered a dark cigarette and both Kyle and Betty declined. Jinnah lit his cigarette and twisted slightly to better face Kyle across Betty's profile.

"You have read the medical synopsis?"

"Yes," Kyle replied.

"There is no exaggeration," Dr. Jinnah stated. "Khan displays remarkable ability to exercise thought transference. He first exhibited this at age four when his parents were stunned to learn the child spoke fluently in the four major language groups of our nation. Further examination revealed that he communicates in dozens of dialects as well. This alone would bring him fame.

"The father, not wishing to make of his son a spectacle, hired the best tutors available and swore them to secrecy. Thus far, there was nothing which would not evoke pride from the parents. But they began to worry when Khan declared himself to be a prophet sent here to unite the Hindus with the Sikhs, Jains and Muslims."

"What made the father so certain the boy wasn't a prophet?" Kyle questioned.

Dr. Jinnah's eyes vitrified. "He caught Khan breaking a basic concept of all religions."

146

"What is that?"

"Khan murdered his brother."

Osmania Hospital and the university of the same name enjoyed a professional respect in India compared to Kyle's own alma mater in the United States. Passing through the general offices of the facility, Kyle noticed many employees dressed in the latest western fashion, while others seemed a mere step from their ancestral heritage. Brown-skinned girls in saris, with religious symbols on their foreheads, worked diligently and expertly over electric typewriters and posting machines. As he and Betty followed Dr. Jinnah, Kyle noted cartons from both Chinese and Russian ports being unloaded onto pushcarts for distribution throughout the building.

Dr. Jinnah had set aside a solarium for Kyle's use. One wall was dominated by full-length tinted glass. The other walls were covered with ivy of a climbing variety, growing up from carefully tended soil beds. Placed around the room on thick oriental rugs were couches, chairs, end tables, and low coffee tables creating a series of intimate gathering places for visitors. Khan was waiting.

As with Damon, it was difficult to realize this was a child chronologically. Khan had the wizened expression of an adult, his facial hair developed. He spoke before introductions were possible, a deep, rich tone of assurance and maturity.

"I have anticipated seeing you, Dr. Burnette," Khan said, his hand out to meet Kyle. He turned to Betty and, with an appreciation far beyond his years, looked her over.

"Ah, yes," Khan said softly, "Betty Snider."

His English was flawless. He stood silently appraising Betty with the overt expression of a man with an eye to feminine attributes. Betty's face suffused with a warming glow and her embarrassment made Khan extract himself from his reverie and comment, "Forgive me, Miss Snider. You are as beautiful and appealing as I knew you would be. I feel we have met before, don't you?"

"Yes," Betty stumbled, "I do get that feeling."

147

Turning to Kyle, Khan asked, "How long will you be here, Doctor?"

"Today. Possibly tomorrow."

"Excellent! Please be seated."

The interview began with questions of a general nature. Khan sat, short legs crossed, hands clasped and at ease in his lap. He looked Kyle directly in the eyes as they addressed one another. Suddenly, Khan's hands flicked the air impatiently.

"Doctor, you did not fly round the world to indulge in amenities. Please, feel free to go to work immediately."

"Of course," Kyle said, "thank you. That will save time."

Dr. Jinnah had taken a position to one side, smoking, watching.

"How quickly have you been able to absorb the information and emotions from my mind?" Kyle asked.

"Instantly."

"Do you, on meeting me for the first time, feel that you could seek out thoughts from my subconscious, as well as my conscious mind?" Kyle queried. Betty's hand moved in short, quick movements, transcribing questions and responses.

"With some people I absorb everything immediately, as I have just done with you," Khan said. "Others give me more difficulty getting past the conscious processes. Now and then, with very intelligent or very dull people, I have trouble getting through at all."

"In the periods of time when you lapse into a comatose, or catatonic state," Kyle asked, "do you know it is happening?"

The child's eyes averted for an instant, a hairline crack in his composure. Kyle pursued the questioning. "Do you know the meaning of the word 'sweven'?"

"Yes."

"Define it, please."

"It means dream, or illusion."

Kyle nodded. "Do you have such a sweven?"

Khan's fingers curled slowly, interlacing with one another. "If you mean in the same manner as Damon, no."

148

"You took his name from my brain?"

Khan smiled. "Of course."

"You know his case, then, from my brain."

"Yes."

"Very much like your case," Kyle observed.

"Very much."

"Can you tell me what is wrong with the two of you?"

"No."

"If you know what is wrong, tell us and let's get it cleared up. You are exceptional children, you and Damon."

At the term "children" Khan seemed amused.

"Despite your intellect and unusual abilities," Kyle explained, "you are emotionally a child. You're smart enough to know that."

"Dr. Burnette," Khan said imperiously, "you are chasing reflections. You should be home with Damon. That is where you are needed. I don't need you."

"You need somebody," Kyle said sympathetically.

"No," the lad said, "I don't. There is nothing you can do."

"Doesn't your condition worry you?" Kyle asked.

"No."

"I don't believe that's true," Kyle said tensely. "It scares you."

"Scares me?" Khan nodded. "Oh, yes, it scares me."

With the permission of the parents, Dr. Jinnah and Kyle supervised a session under the influence of narcosis. Dr. Jinnah administered the drug and Khan lay on a hospital bed, his body strapped down to prevent him pitching off involuntarily.

"Khan, you are sleepy?" Dr. Jinnah asked. Then, in a language Kyle did not understand, the Indian doctor said a few words to assure the patient of his well-being.

In English, Dr. Jinnah concluded, "I am going to ask you to speak with Dr. Burnette now, Khan. You will reply in English, please."

"Yes," Khan murmured.

"How do you feel, Khan?"

"Very well."

149

"Do you remember Damon Daniels?"

"Yes."

"Do you know that he is the victim of a glandular malfunction very similar to your own?"

"Yes."

"Then, you must understand this has to be corrected to achieve complete recovery for my patient."

"I understand."

"I need to know, Khan, are the catatonic seizures something you and Damon can control, if you wanted to do so?"

The upper lip curled, exposing Khan's teeth, and his eyebrows lifted, facial muscles taut. His body leaned into the restraining straps and then slowly settled back. As Kyle, Betty, and Dr. Jinnah watched, the body rose against the straps again, nostrils flaring. Slowly Khan's head turned until his eyes met Kyle's and a semblance of a smile stretched those tortured features.

"Go away, Physician." There was no mistaking that guttural voice.

"I wish to speak with Khan," Kyle said firmly.

"Go where you are needed, for you are not needed here," the voice commanded.

Dr. Jinnah sat, eyes wide, staring at his patient. It would be easy to see why a primitive society might reckon this to be possession, so complete was the transformation, so different this apparition from the boy who had been lying here a moment before. Snorting, sucking air into a heaving chest, teeth bared, the sounds from that body were animal. No less mesmerizing was the American doctor's reaction. Kyle sat with one arm thrown over the back of his chair, observing the phenomena with calm detachment.

"I shall wait for Khan to return," Kyle said mildly.

"What do you seek?" the voice rumbled.

"Who are you?" Kyle asked.

Khan's eyes bored into the American. The boy's entire scalp moved backward and the forehead seemed to grow larger.

150

"In due time, Doctor," the voice spoke sibilantly. Khan's head settled back, eyes fluttered, lips uncurling.

"Khan?"

A jumble of words Kyle did not understand, spoken rapidly, then Dr. Jinnah interrupted. "Speak English, Khan."

"My head hurts."

"A few more questions," Kyle requested. He glanced at Dr. Jinnah and the Indian hesitated, then nodded.

"Khan, who was that?" Kyle asked.

For an instant it appeared the transformation might take place again. The boy clenched his fists, holding handfuls of sheet in each, as though in pain. Abruptly, Khan wrenched to one side, his upper lip beaded with moisture, hair matted with perspiration. He coughed, tongue protruding, then swallowed, staring at nothing. The boy's eyes closed and his breathing slowed to a more normal rhythm. His fingers uncurled slowly, leaving bunched, wrinkled knots of bedding soaked from moist palms. Exhausted, the boy succumbed to sleep.

"I'm afraid that is all, Doctor," Dr. Jinnah said softly.

"Yes."

"Would you care for coffee?" Dr. Jinnah asked.

Kyle was still seated, his hands hanging from wrists like unstarched cloth. "Yes. That would be fine."

"Are you all right, Kyle?" Betty asked.

Kyle looked at her with vacant eyes, his thoughts writhing on some distant horizon of the mind.

A nurse was ministering to Khan's inert form, wiping the child's face with a damp washcloth, unbuckling the straps. Dr. Jinnah was waiting, standing, at the exit.

"My Lord," Kyle whispered.

"Come," Dr. Jinnah urged gently, taking Kyle's arm. "Let's go have coffee."

CHAPTER 14

KYLE HAD SAID very little since Sydney, Australia. They arrived there in late evening and saw the aborigine boy the following morning. The aborigine child was homuncular, his dwarfed body warped as though with age. He was indeed intelligent, above average, but nothing to compare with Damon or the Indian boy. His fugues were more the confused state of a narcoleptic with an insatiable desire to sleep. Kyle had uncovered no evidence of a sweven in this patient. There were no appreciable changes of voice timbre, no sudden displays of personality alteration. Yet, according to the medical records, such changes had occurred in the past. The aborigine had once shown a distinct ability to perceive the thoughts of those around him. Abruptly, several months ago, there was a cessation of those extrasensory powers. Had the aborigine shown evidence of an alternate ego? Indeed! His tribesmen thought him possessed. There were stories that the boy had killed two fellow members of the tribe simply by pointing at them! But, the doctor in Sydney explained, the uncultured and isolated tribe was prone to indulge in fantasies of this sort. Their cult-totemism endorsed the concept that a man's nocturnal dreams were conclusive evidence signifying a continuity of life unlimited by space and time. Their medicine was administered by a witch doctor known as the "clever fellow." All disease terminating in death was attributed to sorcery unless the victim was very young or very old, or killed in an obviously accidental manner. The "clever fellow" extracted his tribesmen's "badness" with countersorcery. Failure was explained in one of several convenient ways. Being a psychic and psychologist, the "clever fellow" merely told the bereaved that he had been called too late, or the sorcery he combated was too powerful, or the hapless victim deserved his fate, anyway.

However, the young aborigine Kyle and Betty had seen supposedly rocked the career of the tribal clever fellow assigned to purge the spirits from the boy. For fear that the death-by-touching might recur, the tribe carried the boy to the witch doctor, who agreed to an exorcism in return for a stipend from each of the tribal members, since the threat was universal. The bargaining completed, the confident witch doctor proceeded to cleanse the child's soul with exotic potions, incantations, and histrionics.

As the clever fellow indulged in his theatrics (so the story was related to Kyle and Betty) the possessed child rose from his mat, glaring ferociously, snorting like a wild beast. His face a mask of "badness," he roared with the voice of ten men. Then, before the terrified audience, the child conjured up images of fearsome animals, created fire that danced and

154

other visual impressions which the Sydney doctor attributed to mental transference and a form of mass hysteria.

Truly frightened now, the witch doctor urged the banishment of the child, and forthright this was accomplished. Shortly thereafter the boy was found wandering on a highway miles from the nearest settlement, emaciated and delirious. During his stay in the general ward, his amazing intellect and abilities were discovered. The chart listed him as "approximate age thirty" but the boy professed to be only a child. Further investigations by authorities revealed the story and the boy became a dependent of the state since it was obvious he no longer had a home.

He still had a glandular condition, as marked and advanced as Damon's and Khan's. But his perceptive powers had diminished "abruptly," as the doctor in Sydney stated. What happened? Why had the boy lost the powers? Was it a sign of improvement? Or degeneration?

On the return flight to New York, Kyle brooded in silence. Betty found herself guiding him through the motions of eating, clearing customs, checking in and out of lodgings. For hours he sat motionless, staring into space.

"Is anything wrong?" Betty inquired.

"No." No further explanation. Simply, "No."

"Are you planning to call Ted Drinkwater?" Betty asked.

"Not yet."

"Would you like me to call him?"

"No. Thanks."

Then back to his thoughts. Once, in a sudden flurry of activity, Kyle vaulted from his chair, opened a briefcase, ransacked the contents, and paused to study some notations for several minutes. Then, shaking his head, he returned to his seat and, oblivious of Betty, his expression clearly indicated his mind was elsewhere.

Briefly, she had tried to draw him out during a layover in London.

"Have you reached any conclusions, Kyle?"

"No."

"Do you think the Sydney case is similar to the Indian boy and Damon?"

"Somewhat. Please, Betty."

She had occupied her time transcribing notes, using a portable typewriter they had brought along for the task. Thus it had been up to and through today. Now, on the last leg of their journey, here in the most exciting city in the world, they sat looking at that part of New York City visible through a window of the multistoried motel. Having finished supper, Kyle sat in bed, nude beneath the sheets, his tray set aside, smoking a cigarette. Betty sighed heavily and left the room to begin a bath.

"You didn't go to Copenhagen to see the Danish boy?" Ted Drinkwater queried.

"No," Kyle said. "I'm going to the symposium next week. I'll run over and see him while I'm there."

"Have you talked to Dr. Christian?" Ted questioned.

"A couple of times," Kyle said, sorting mail on his desk. "I told him I'd see him at the meeting in London."

"Did you ask the other psychiatrists to withhold reports on their cases?" Ted persisted.

"No. Frankly, it slipped my mind."

"Slipped your mind?" Ted's irritation was evident. Kyle continued opening mail, perfunctorily glancing at it and discarding it in a wastebasket.

"Don't get angry, Ted," Kyle said.

"Okay," Ted said, without rancor, "just try not to blow it, Kyle."

"I'll try."

When Kyle entered Damon's room, the boy jumped off his bed and ran barefoot toward the psychiatrist. He halted shy of touching the older man and stood uncertain, hestitating. Kyle knelt, holding Damon's shoulders, smiling.

"Hey, I missed you," Kyle confessed.

"I missed you," Damon responded.

156

"Come to my office and visit with me?"

"Sure!" Damon scrambled under the bed for his shoes. A Negro attendant stood by.

Seated in the office, Damon's obvious pleasure warmed the physician. Kyle asked the receptionist to bring a soft drink and coffee. When these had arrived, Kyle relaxed, lifted his cup as a toast, and said, "Here's to you, Damon. You're a fantastic person."

Damon laughed and sat cradling the cold drink, looking at Kyle.

"I went around the world to meet a boy in India," Kyle reflected. He deliberately formed a mental image of Khan's face, and Damon's eyes took on an expression of concentration, then he smiled and nodded.

"His name's Khan," Kyle explained. "He seems to be very much like you, except he's older."

Damon nodded, rapt.

In an unhurried manner, Kyle spoke of and thought of his trip, his mind revealing what his words did not. Thirty minutes later, Damon was informed and contemplative.

"Let's see," Kyle said, thumbing the material. "Here are four similar cases. Three similar cases, actually. All from better-than-average-income families, high intelligence, telepathic ability, glandular conditions causing rapid maturation but eluding etiological explanation. Then there is the Australian boy who is not like the other three. Born to impoverished and uncultured parents. He is reputed to have caused the deaths of two villagers by pointing at them. He defied a witch doctor and was banished. He eventually suffered a loss of intelligence and his telepathic powers waned. The pituitary condition began to stabilize despite the fact that he had not received the first hormone treatment."

"You're worried about me?" Damon questioned, really making more of a statement than a query.

"Yes," Kyle admitted.

"What are your deductions from all this?" Damon asked placidly.

157

"I'm going to present the matter to my fellow psychiatrists in a few short weeks. It will be a case of hyperactive pituitary. Dr. Drinkwater and Dr. von Ulbricht will concur in that. We are going to show some—not all—some of the psychological manifestations that emanated from these malfunctions."

"Since there are four of us," Damon said, "how do you explain the dissimilarity of the aborigine boy?"

"There is no such thing as a unique and totally isolated case of anything," Kyle said. "Millions of people suffer glandular problems to one degree or another. There are extremes, of course. I am convinced that the aborigine boy falls somewhere between the other cases."

Damon's chest rose and fell heavily, adrenaline flowing into his veins, his face contorting. The boy's shoulders drew forward; his chest concave, he rose from his chair and approached Kyle's desk with a catlike stalk.

"What of me, Doctor?" The voice was deep.

"What of you indeed?" Kyle said evenly.

"How do you explain my presence in India?"

"I had hoped you would tell me the answer to that," Kyle said, watching the boy's face twisting to the mask of the sweven. "Like Damon, Khan was sensitive to my thoughts. I think he conjured you from my mind. I think you are a vision, a passing thought. Without a carrier, you do not exist."

"Would you ignore me? Hide me from your fellow psychiatrists?"

"I see," Kyle said softly. "You want attention."

Damon gripped the edge of the desk as though to push it toward Kyle. His eyes flickered with flintlike sparks of anger, pupils constricting to pinpoints. From his chest came the gurgling rale of air passing through liquid and his breath smelled of blood, like a dental patient who has just undergone oral surgery. With the fetid air surrounding him, Kyle sat with equanimity, his eyes betraying no emotion at the ferocity of the chimera confronting him.

"You dare to refute me!"

158

"You are nothing," Kyle said, his voice hard.

"Know ye now, I am not your benefactor."

"I did not think for an instant that you were," Kyle retorted mildly.

The door flew open and Ted Drinkwater stood in the portal, the receptionist and several patients behind him in the lobby.

"Everything all right?" Ted asked.

"Most assuredly," Kyle said.

Ted closed the door and stood inside against the wall, observing.

"It would not be wise to ignore me, queer one," the voice rumbled. "You are unaware of your weaknesses, therefore you cannot know your strength."

"Perhaps," Kyle acknowledged. "Nonetheless, I know your weaknesses better and better."

"Amen," Ted said.

Damon wheeled and advanced on Ted, his obscenities flooding into the front office.

"Get out!" Damon roared.

Kyle nodded and Ted hesitated a moment, then let himself out with the comment, "If you need me, call."

Damon turned on his heel, body bent, fingers curled, snorting through flattened nostrils, bushy eyebrows lifted, teeth exposed. He thrust his chin forward, head tilted slightly, the muscles in his neck taut, corded, the veins protruding.

"Hear me well," the rasping tone warned, "you are no match for me, Physician. Do not offend me."

"Let's get one thing straight," Kyle said firmly. "I am your master, you are not mine. You are a freak of hormonal structure and when we balance that structure, you will disappear. I am not an aborigine witch doctor to be bullied by superstitious emotions. You will do as I tell you, when I tell you. In due time, I will evaporate you with pills!"

Damon lunged at the desk, his breathing coming in chortled hissing sounds, his words trembling with sibilant malevolence. "I warn thee, Physician! Provoke me not!"

159

"Now you hear me, you pompous sonofabitch," Kyle snapped, rising from his seat. "You don't intimidate me. Would you have me believe your powers are omnipotent?"

"Surely you are damned, Kyle Burnette."

"Not me," Kyle retorted. "You are the damned one. I will see you gone, whatever you are. I will see you vanquished and forgotten. These are not the days of the aborigine, by God!"

"By God?" The garish configuration withdrew an inch. "By *God?*" he repeated. "What do you know of God, Doctor?"

"Come along, Damon," Kyle said, his tone one of complete calm. "It's time to return to your room."

"Tell me about God, Physician! Tell me of your faith. Tell me, what do you say to God?"

Kyle reached for Damon's hand and for an instant he thought he would be attacked as Damon threw himself between the doctor and the door, a constant stream of curses assailing Kyle.

"Come along," Kyle repeated, circling Damon.

"I'm not going," the boy growled, his posture defensive. He still blocked the door.

"'You mean you will physically resist me?" Kyle asked.

"I'm not going, goddamn it."

"You'll go, Damon. You'll go because you have to."

"I don't have to do anything!"

"You have to," Kyle said emphatically.

"You dare to make me?"

"I don't have to make you," Kyle said flatly.

"Then, I will not go."

"Listen to me closely and hear what I say," Kyle said, advancing on the angry being confronting him. "You need me. I don't know why, yet, but you need me more than you need this child's body. You cannot survive without me. Without me, you perish."

"Why think you this, Physician?" Sneering.

"You had never revealed yourself to Dr. Jinnah, yet you spoke to me through Khan. Would you have me think you

160

have something to do with the other boys? Oh, no, not true. Until I saw Khan, you'd never been there. Oh, yes, you need me. You are here because you must have *me*. You will obey me, or be gone. Now get back to that room!"

Damon backed away with each advancing step of the psychiatrist. He stood against the wall, his movement blocked by a bookcase and the desk. Kyle towered over him, glaring down at the dwindling emotions ensconced in this boy. Trembling, the boy's external posturing altered, the eyebrows descending. The irises blossomed from pinpoints, enlarging, passing from aggression to submissive uncertainty.

"Dr. Burnette?" Damon's childlike tone now.

"Yes?"

"I'm afraid, Dr. Burnette. Why are you looking at me like that? I'm afraid."

Kyle extended a hand. "Don't be," he said. "Come with me, it's time to go back to your room."

Damon's hand was cold, the delicate fingers quivering in Kyle's hand.

"Please, Dr. Burnette—" Damon held back, eyes wide, still looking at Kyle's face.

"Come on, Damon."

"Oh, please!"

"What's the matter, Damon?"

"I'm afraid!"

Kyle knelt before the boy, looking at him. What must his expression have been when this child looked up a moment ago?

"Come here, son," Kyle said gently. He took Damon in his arms, holding him close, the child crying against Kyle's shoulder.

"I'm afraid," Damon sobbed. "Please, Dr. Burnette, I want to go home. I'm afraid here."

"Don't be," Kyle whispered.

"But I am!"

Kyle held him tightly, rocking their bodies to and fro, caressing the boy's back, holding Damon's head. He

161

enveloped the shivering form in his arms, muffling Damon's cries with his own body. Desperate, clutching hands held on for dear life and Kyle's eyes burned with the saline of his own tears.

Suddenly, Damon pushed away and looked up at the physician's face. Gently, with tenderness and compassion, Damon brushed Kyle's tears with one, small finger.

"It'll be all right now," Damon said, very softly. "Come on, it's time for me to go back to my room." He extended a diminutive hand and took Kyle's hand, smiling.

"Come on," Damon said. "It'll be all right now."

CHAPTER 15

DR. KARL CHRISTIAN settled himself in the better of three chairs in his hotel room. He had never cared much for the Ritz, which had seen better days. He personally preferred Claridge's. But the British Medical Association had arranged lodging and coordinated the convention and this was the site selected, so here he was. He scanned a program bearing the title "International Symposium of Psychologists and Psychiatrists—London." He traced the fine type with a finger, adjusting his position for light and his bifocals to the reading matter. He swore softly in Danish and sat back a moment. They had spelled his name "Carl" Christian. He was scheduled to speak Thursday afternoon. The time allotted to him carried the innocuous heading "Etiology of Schizoid Catatonia: a case history."

He had asked for an hour and a half, but was refused. He had also requested the prime evening hours in which to speak and was forced to settle for the thirty minutes following three o'clock tea. Dr. Christian opened his valise and withdrew a thick, bound sheaf of papers. In the same compartment were film, recording tapes, photographs, and one thousand brochures summarizing the case he intended to present. The leaflets were strictly for the benefit of the press, written in layman's language and bereft of terminology which might cause some bored reporter to abandon the matter for lack of comprehension.

He had made up his mind to release the story after his patient died. The boy strangled to death on his own vomit during a particularly severe period of catatonic seizure. The attendant had not recognized the problem immediately and had reacted too slowly to save the child. In the interim, Dr. Christian had observed how the American, Kyle Burnette, traveled to Hyderabad and Sydney, the implications all too clear to him. With Burnette gathering extensive data on all the patients, his own patient still alive and in therapy, Burnette would soon assume control of the cases. So, Christian had covered the death of his patient with lies to Burnette and von Ulbricht. He told the endocrinologist that the parents had taken the boy to a retreat for a while. In the meantime, Christian carefully maintained a façade of interest and exploration. He continued to ply von Ulbricht with queries and answered each suggestion with detailed, albeit false reports of hormonal treatments undertaken.

Karl Christian had learned his lesson about men of German extraction and Americans, during World War Two. He had watched hordes of Nazi Panzers flood his nation, usurp local authority, and virtually enslave the populace for the German war machine. He had his fill of Americans too, during the same period. Having been very active in the underground movement, Christian was placed on an

164

execution list and had to flee to Yugoslavia. There, under the protection of Draja Mikhailovitch, Christian had fought the Germans for the duration. But his friend Mikhailovitch was betrayed by the Americans in one of history's most dastardly political sellouts. In an agreement with Stalin, support was thrown to Josip Broz, who would later be known to the world as Marshal Tito, dictator of Yugoslavia. The duplicity of the Americans ultimately led to the annihilation of Mikhailovitch and his followers, hunted down in forests and executed one by one. Oh, yes, the Americans and Germans were a fine pair, as witness the resurrection of the German nation since World War Two.

Christian wasn't about to be caught napping this time. He did not tip his hand with a detailed synopsis to the placement and selection committee. During his half hour, he would give them the hard facts, using films to demonstrate the phenomena of his patient. Then, with any luck at all, he would be allotted time on the final day of the meeting to continue his session. Either way, more time or not, he had already arranged to have reporters present, including one American whose syndicated column appeared in several hundred newspapers. No, this time he would not be caught snoozing.

"Yes, Ted, goddamn it," Kyle snapped into the telephone, "I've seen Christian! I'm going to Copenhagen the day the convention ends and I'll see the boy then."

Ted's voice crackled on the line. "Try to get some photographs of him if you can. Erich says he's positive the boy is going to die soon and we'll need that type of material for a book."

"All right, Ted."

"And, say," Ted asked, "do you suppose you could interview the parents?"

"Ted, for Christ's sake!" Kyle said. "I can't give the appearance of trying to take over. I'm going to see the boy and review his case with Christian soon enough. My purpose is investigation, not subterfuge."

"Okay, okay," Ted soothed. "Keep your cool, Kyle. I

165

know you'll do the best you can. But listen, I've got the first draft of a manuscript ready to read when you get back."

"Now, Ted, we agreed—"

"Look, Kyle"—Ted's voice took a sharper note—"I haven't shown it to anyone yet, I have it prepared in first draft form, that's all. We must begin assimilating it sooner or later. We can always revise and delete, you know."

"All right, Ted."

"Try to get the photos, anyway," Ted added cheerily. "I'll talk to you when you get home."

Kyle cradled the antiquelike French-style receiver and shook his head. The strain of keeping Ted down was affecting his manner toward his associate. He was losing patience. Goddamn it! He had forgotten to ask about Damon.

As with most symposiums of learned men, particularly if their interests are scientific, the days are filled with hour upon hour of meetings, demonstrations, and lectures. The times between are designed as social relief. The day began promptly at six-thirty with breakfast and a speaker from the local medical society. Every hour thereafter until ten at night was scheduled with one or more activity, including a respite set aside for sightseeing and a bus tour of London for those who wished to go. Rare indeed was the dedicated soul who persevered throughout and attended all the lectures. One's strength would ebb, his mind boggled, and he soon resigned himself to selecting those talks which mirrored his own particular interest.

By the third day, at three-thirty in the afternoon, the banquet room of the Ritz was sparsely attended as Dr. Karl Christian supervised the setting up of a 16mm projector and a second machine designed to show 35mm slides. He had spent hours putting the slides in proper order, working from the the first day he had met his patient to the dramatic final weeks when the boy was transformed by his affliction from a charming, smiling, personable lad into a hulking, dwarfed, and ghastly semblance of a human child. His

166

lecture was timed to the second, his talk interspersed with highly emotional scenes of the patient during somnambulisms when a second personality emerged before the eyes of the viewer. The sound recordings were of a snarling entity, destined to chill the blood of a listener. To cap the performance, Karl Christian would show the slides, in silence, as the audience observed the boyish face change to what it had become just prior to death. The lecture was a fine blend of scientific explanation and blatant drama with more than a touch of pathos. If it did not leave the audience emotionally spent, nothing would.

Fewer than thirty people sat in the four hundred chairs set up for the symposium members. Scattered here and there were a dozen or so doctors who specialized in various forms of schizophrenia. In addition, there were two porters from the hotel staff, a straggler from off the street, a couple of ladies caught between limousines to the airport, and four reporters. The American, Larry Reirden, a syndicated columnist, did not arrive until Christian had been speaking for a full ten minutes. He settled himself in a back row, threw an arm over an adjoining chair, and took another five minutes to realize the importance of what he was observing.

For a man with a scant thirty minutes, and a subject as complex as this, Christian had done a superb job of organizing his material. When the last horrible color slide filled the screen, and he left it there for a full fifteen seconds, there was not a person in the room who was not welded to that pitiful, grotesque image.

"That concludes my lecture, ladies and gentlemen," Dr. Christian stated. "I'm sorry, my time restriction does not allow a question period. However, I will be available for inquiries in my own room immediately following the disassembling of equipment here."

With an ascending heartbeat, Karl Christian gathered his material, packaged the projector, canned the films, and made his way through an empty hall toward the foyer. He could feel the electricity of excitement racing through the delegates lounging in the lobby as the facts were relayed by those who had been present for the speech. The hum of the news lines was something he could sense and he was trembling as he stood at the lift, waiting for the doors to open.

"Karl!" The American reporter pushed through to Christian's side. "May I assist you with your luggage?"

"Yes," Christian said, smiling, "please take the projector, if you will. It unbalances me."

"Certainly," the reporter agreed. "Good to see you again, Karl. May I have a few minutes alone with you?"

"Surely," Christian smiled. "Come on up."

"Have you seen the goddamned newspapers?" Ted screamed.

"Yes, Ted, I saw them."

"It's on the front page of the Atlanta *Journal*!"!"

"Yes," Kyle replied huskily. It was also on the front page of every London and most of the continental ones, as well.

"That lying sonofabitch had von Ulbricht spelling out treatments after the boy was dead!" Ted seethed. "He fucked us, Kyle. I guess you know he fucked us."

"Yes, I know," Kyle said.

"Goddamn it," Ted said, his voice wavering, "I knew we should've broken this story. I knew it! But, no, goddamn, oh hell no, we had to think of the patients!"

"I'm sorry, Ted. I really am."

"That's a crock of shit," Ted said crisply. "That Danish bastard has stolen the show now, old buddy. What we have left is piss poor and slim pickings. Some American writer has already announced a forthcoming book on the subject and the Danish boy is his focal point. We lost out. It's that simple."

"I'll be home this weekend, Ted," Kyle said. "We'll go to work on your material right away."

"Aw, shit, Kyle," Ted said, and hung up.

Kyle had masked his anger, talking to Ted. He had assumed a placating composure which in fact he did not feel. He was furious over the Danish doctor's deception. He had learned of the lecture that evening when it was the talk of the delegates. The selection and placement committee had set aside two hours tomorrow for Dr. Christian to repeat his sparsely attended lecture and to expound on the subject. When Kyle fully realized what had transpired, he was red with rage. He had raced upstairs to Christian's room only to be barred at the door.

"We have nothing to talk about, Doctor," Christian had said.

"You sonofabitch," Kyle retorted. "You deliberately and unethically connived to break our agreement to keep silent. You lied about the boy being alive."

Kyle was brought up short by the physician's response. "Unethical?" Christian snorted. "Connived? Tell me something, Dr. Burnette, you were running all over the world for the sake of your own patient? If that is so, why was everybody consulting you and von Ulbricht? You were not consulting anyone. You were investigating, compiling, preparing to do just what I did. Please do not insult my intelligence by suggesting otherwise. You withheld publication of a book merely because you wished to assimilate further information on other cases."

How far was that from the truth? Kyle fumed in frustration, afraid of Ted Drinkwater's reaction and resenting his own position. What Christian had done was precisely what Ted wanted to do, was it not? The only honest regret Kyle would allow himself was that he had not given Ted his blessing and released the material first.

Christian had told the reporters there were three similar cases: one in India, another in Australia, and the last in America. He had dared to draw the other cases into his speech when he compared the glandular malfunctions, cause and effects thereof. However, he did not mention the other patients or doctors by name. If this was a concession to protect the patients themselves, Kyle blew it. When he angrily accosted the Danish psychiatrist, sitting in the room with pad in hand was the American columnist who

169

soon enough had Kyle's name and home city from the hotel register. Even before Kyle departed from the convention, Larry Reirden was winging his way to Atlanta.

Reirden had come through the ranks with Associated Press. He began as a copy boy with the Baltimore *Sun*, worked his way through college as a cub reporter with the Chicago *Daily News*, and joined AP in 1937. He had spent most of his bachelor existence covering wars, famine, pestilence, and politics, his dispatches repeatedly giving him national attention. If there was one thing Larry Reirden knew about newspaper journalism, it was the value of investigative reporting. He had the temperament for it, too. Thousands of hours of his life had been spent in one archive or another, tediously examining records, keenly alert for a hidden clue.

He had attended the symposium of psychologists and psychiatrists for the simple reason that he had been asked to do so. During the war, when he was freezing in Trieste and following the political evolutions there, he had once been befriended by Karl Christian. Karl had led Larry Reirden into the mountains to the secret headquarters of Mikhailovitch for an exclusive interview with the doomed leader. The columns Reirden wrote on Mikhailovitch were the ones which began his now sizable syndication. Reirden had always leaned toward the human element in any story. He went to the convention anticipating a boring, technical, nonnewsworthy event. He couldn't have been more wrong.

Here was a story bordering on the occult at a time when the arcane was much the vogue in America. Meticulously documented and professionally prepared, the story of the Danish boy was both frightening and enthralling. Karl Christian had agreed to give Reirden the exclusive rights to a book on his case, and with a single call, Reirden had arranged for his publisher to send fifteen thousand dollars as a binder for the Danish psychiatrist, thereby making the offer firm.

Now crossing the Atlantic in a huge 747 jet, Larry

Reirden felt the exciting tingle of a hot story in his blood. This was the electricity that made a reporter run, the promise of a scoop, the satisfaction of getting something into print that would send millions of people to purchase books. Reirden let his seat back and closed his eyes.

Despite all his persuasive efforts, Karl had refused to give Reirden the names of the patients or doctors in Australia, India, and America. Reirden had yielded to the professional ethic, but by no means intended to let the matter drop. This story was bigger than a single country. It had world appeal and with an American kid in the book, it would sell all the better to the lucrative U.S. market. Then, out of the blue, up comes angry American doctor, Kyle Burnette, blocked at the door by Karl Christian as Reirden waited inside to continue his interview.

So, okay, Burnette had the other patient. You could be sure he would not cooperate. In fact, judging by his reaction to Christian, Burnette would be antagonistic. Reirden had been working with the peoples of the world long enough to know human nature. A man in a court case hates the opposing attorney, despite the fact the attorney is merely performing his legal profession. Just as true, the doctor from America would resent Larry Reirden because he was the journalist who publicized the other doctor's case. Was it not feasible that the angry American might approach another reporter to pour out his own story? Then, as Reirden well knew, the race would be on between two professional writers, each working toward a publication deadline.

Reirden squirmed in his seat and adjusted a small pillow beneath his head. The vibration of the craft was not lulling him tonight. He saw images of the Danish boy slowly altered by a remarkable mental or physical disorder. Reirden recalled the heavy masculine voice that predominated during the personality transformations. The movie films had shown the metamorphosis as more than a tone of voice and vocabulary, the boy's features actually twisted in a Jekyll-Hyde manner. Fantastic story!

171

There was only one thing to do so far as Reirden was concerned. He had to get to the American boy and sap as much of that story as possible to make it less appealing to a competitive writer. Otherwise, as surely as this plane now flew to Atlanta, the market would be flooded with half-assed accounts that would jade the prospect for Reirden's own book.

He tried to sleep, but the contorted face of that poor Danish boy kept popping into Reirden's memory. Dear God! One does not appreciate his health until he sees something like that.

Ted Drinkwater was more than willing to cooperate. He spent two hours talking to Larry Reirden and with a voice laced with anger recounted the case history of Damon Daniels without ever mentioning the boy by name.

"Would it be possible to see this child?" Reirden requested.

"We would have to have the permission of his parents," Ted balked, "and frankly, I doubt they would allow it. We must protect the boy from sensationalism. You must understand, the press would have a field day. It could not possibly be beneficial to the patient, especially at his age. He is a curious blend of immature child and young adult."

"I can respect that," Reirden said. "Nonetheless, for my own personal background material, I would like to speak to the parents and, if possible, to the boy. I would agree to withhold his name if you wish."

Ted stood firm. "I'm sorry, Mr. Reirden. It can't be done. We aren't being bullheaded about it. The patient is our first concern. Out of deference to his welfare, we have withheld the case even from scientific scrutiny. Only because our Danish colleague chose to release the story am I talking to you about it at all. He shouldn't have given you our names. It was a breach of ethics to do so."

Reirden could not miss the bitterness in Ted's tone. Taking advantage of this, he allowed Ted to continue thinking Dr. Christian had supplied the names of the American psychiatrists.

"According to Dr. Christian," Reirden lied, "he has been leading the efforts to determine a cause of these four cases, and to effect a cure."

"Oh, for God's sake!" Ted exploded. "That's utterly ridiculous. Dr. Erich von Ulbricht has been working hand in hand with us as we mapped out a hormonal therapy for these children and our own case was the first to receive such treatments. All the others are following our example. I'm surprised that Dr. Christian would make such a patently false statement."

"This Dr. von Ulbricht," Reirden said, "he's American?"

"Why, hell yes," Ted said, his face flushed. "We brought him into our own case seeking a counterbalance for hormonal changes transpiring in our patient. In fact, when the other doctors, including Christian, began seeking the best endocrinologist available, they came to our attention by way of von Ulbricht."

"Would you say von Ulbricht is the keystone to the cases, then?" Reirden asked.

Ted saw the emphasis of the story slipping away. "No," he said, "I wouldn't. My associate, Dr. Kyle Burnette, is the one of us who has actually seen all of the cases, except the Danish boy since that child died sometime back. Dr. Burnette is probably as near to being an authority on the cases as a group, as a whole, as anybody can be at this point."

"You say there's no chance of my seeing your American patient?" Reirden persisted.

"Not without Dr. Burnette's permission, no," Ted said. "He will not agree without the permission of the parents, of course. I can tell you now, they won't do it, any of them. They are concerned with the effects publicity might have on the boy and his future, as I've said. You can understand that."

Reirden nodded. He had all he needed. It was a matter of

plodding investigation now. He might not ever release the name of the child, but he would certainly interview the parents and hopefully the boy himself. Good reporting, like good salesmanship, is a matter of never taking "no" for an answer.

CHAPTER 16

LARRY REIRDEN checked into a room at the Heart of Atlanta Motel. He then spent time finding a detective. He had noted with satisfaction that there were facilities for inpatient treatment in a wing of the psychiatric clinic. Circling the building by day and again by night, he had no difficulty spotting the lighted windows of Damon's room.

The detective had soon installed a microphone against the glass of the marked windows and windows thought to be offices of the two psychiatrists. A day later, Reirden had the name of the child and his parents.

Utilizing the bulk of material given to him by Dr.

Christian, Reirden employed a secretary-typist and was well under way with a manuscript by the end of a week at the motel. He mailed the first few chapters to his publisher, received a go-ahead, and renewed his lease on the suite for two more weeks. In the meantime, he churned out his daily column with datelines placing him in a dozen cities.

Reirden soon had a history of the Daniels family, a complete dossier on Kyle Burnette and Ted Drinkwater. In addition, he had surreptitiously acquired dozens of hours of recorded conversations which he could never use, but which armed him with an understanding of the boy, Damon, and the personalities of the psychiatrists and the parents.

He wangled an appointment with Dr. von Ulbricht, tricked the physician into releasing information based on what he thought Reirden had already learned from Dr. Christian and Dr. Drinkwater.

When he next visited the clinic, Reirden was well aware of the reception awaiting him, but he was also prepared to go on the offensive. Ted and Kyle ushered the columnist into Kyle's office and without further ado proceeded to lambaste him for approaching von Ulbricht.

"Let's have an understanding," Reirden said icily. "I am a reporter. I have a story. Fully half of a book is in the hands of a publisher at this hour. I can take one of two courses in this matter. One, I can publish everything as it is, without your cooperation. Including more or less factual reports of what this boy is probably like, since the cases are so similar. If I do this, there isn't a leg for suit against me, no recourse for anybody, and you gentlemen go unsung and unknown by name. But, then, reporters will descend on you, this clinic, the parents, and the child like vultures. The lack of names alone will guarantee it. On the other hand, with your cooperation, I will write a book more sympathetic, more scientific, thereby alleviating any future pressures by having the entire story documented with your help."

"We must consider our patient," Kyle declared flatly.

"Consider your patient?" Reirden scoffed. "If the patient is truly your prime concern, then it appears to me you have but one choice: cooperate with me."

"Goddamn it, man," Kyle said angrily, "you're asking us to condemn this child to the glare of publicity, to make a freak of him!"

"Again, let me make myself clear," Reirden stated. "I intend to release this story in book form within four weeks. The publicity is a foregone conclusion."

"Don't you people give a damn about anybody but yourselves?" Kyle asked.

"I look at it this way," Reirden said, "this boy is like a prince, a king, an accident victim, an unfortunate or fortunate pawn of fate, if you will call it that. He is destined to be written about, discussed, and examined. In my years as a reporter, I have felt sympathy for the wives of embezzlers, the children of assassins, the lovers of presidents, and I reported on them anyway. When all is said and done, these same pawns of fate are reading the newspapers every day themselves and what do they read? They read about other poor bastards caught in the imagination of the public. Do I make myself clear? This story will break. I will do it. You have only the choice of a slant to be taken. I would strongly recommend a sympathetic and cooperative response. It will save you many hours of dodging reporters, cameramen, and television people. They will still come at you, but with less tenacity if you are cooperative. I have always suspected Greta Garbo would have sunk to obscurity if she hadn't been so dogmatically seeking it. Open up with the story and it will go away faster. Try to play it close to your chest and they'll dig it out of you anyway. Believe me. I have my story now. It isn't hard to get."

Ted Drinkwater sat to one side, fingertips touching, his nose on the forefingers of the hands, watching Kyle. When Kyle turned to face him, Ted shrugged his shoulders, indicating he had no advice to offer.

"I'll have to speak to the parents," Kyle said. "I will not

encourage them to do this, but I'll tell them the alternatives."

Reirden stood and turned at the exit, one hand on the doorknob. "I'll speak to them, too. I feel sure they'll see the light."

With the reporter gone, Kyle sank into a chair and lit a cigarette. "Jesus, what a mess," he said.

"Yep," Ted agreed.

"I wish I'd let you release the story before," Kyle confessed.

"Me too," Ted said. "It would've made a different splash being issued as a properly prepared scientific report. Now we only have a choice of infamies, don't we?"

"Apparently so," Kyle sighed. "Well, I'm sorry. I don't know what else to say except that."

"Better call the Danielses," Ted suggested. "I suspect Mr. Reirden is the type of man who expects immediate results and will move without us if he thinks he isn't getting a response."

"The sonofabitch," Kyle steamed. He lifted the telephone and put it down again. "What would you think about sending Damon away somewhere?"

"That won't stop the story from breaking. Although, eventually, we may have to do something like that."

Kyle nodded and lifted the receiver again. He dialed Mr. Daniels's number.

"What do you expect out of us, Mr. Reirden?" Edward Daniels questioned.

"Your sympathetic cooperation, Mr. Daniels. I want to portray this case as accurately and truthfully as I can. I would want to spend some time talking to you and your wife, to the doctors here, and to your son. This will not be a sensationalized account, although the case itself is sensational by its very nature."

"Will we have a right to delete?" Mr. Daniels asked.

"I'm sorry," Reirden said, "I can't agree to that. I have written about some of the most famous men in the world,

178

Mr. Daniels, and I did not allow them such prerogatives. I will give you my word that this will be handled tastefully, however. As I said, it won't be sensationalized. It will be factual."

Mr. Daniels looked to Kyle and Ted; both physicians were acutely discomfited, but they gave no external indication of their feelings.

"You're going to write the story anyway?" Mrs. Melba Daniels asked.

"Yes."

"Then"—she turned to her husband—"wouldn't it be better to help him get a true perspective, rather than have him make wild guesses at the facts?"

Edward Daniels sighed wearily. "All right, Mr. Reirden, I'll sign a release allowing these doctors to assist you to the limits they feel advisable." He looked at Kyle. "This is not a carte blanche release, nor an order to release anything you deem advisable to withhold. I simply leave it to your discretion."

Kyle forced himself to remain silent, glancing at Ted for assistance, which was not forthcoming.

"What's the first thing we do?" Melba Daniels asked.

"Nothing," Reirden stated. "I'll be in touch with you off and on to clarify one point or another. I'll want to talk to you about many things, not just Damon. In-depth stuff, if you know what I mean."

Edward Daniels looked pale as he stood and took his wife's arm. "I guess it's all beyond our control now," he said hoarsely.

Kyle tried to smile, but his lips twisted and he settled for a quick nod. Reirden followed the parents from Kyle's office.

"Oh, God Almighty," Kyle declared, "this is terrible."

Ted sat, pose unchanged, eyes on Kyle.

"Damon will be at the mercy of the ogling world now," Kyle said. He pulled out the Scotch to pour drinks.

"Maybe it was destined to be from the beginning," Ted observed, "just like Reirden said."

179

"It didn't have to be," Kyle noted. "If that bastard Christian had kept his mouth shut."

"Christian is the only winner among us all," Ted said tersely.

Kyle carried a drink to Ted and sat on the couch. "I'm afraid you're right."

"Personally," Ted said bitterly, "I'm going to drink this drink, go home and screw my wife, take a hot bath, and have a steak in bed, not necessarily in that order. To hell with it all."

Betty Snider was in the shower when the doorbell began to ring, unrelenting, as somebody leaned heavily on the button. Her initial irritation had turned to anger by the time she reached the door, dripping wet, her robe clutched with one hand to keep it closed.

"Who is it?" she demanded through the door.

"Just little old queer me."

"Kyle?" Betty threw back the bolt and opened the door to the end of the safety chain.

"See!" Kyle exclaimed. "You recognized the description."

"I recognized the voice," Betty said, shutting the door long enough to remove the short chain.

Kyle lifted her robe with one finger. "Getting all the smellies off?"

"You're drunk," Betty observed.

"Now, that's astute." Kyle grinned.

"Sit down and I'll make coffee."

"Hell no! The last thing I want is coffee. I brought along my bottle in hopes you might join me in my mellowed condition."

"Is something wrong?" Betty questioned.

"Yep."

"It's a bad sign to drink when something is wrong," Betty said.

"Yep."

"What's wrong?"

180

"I can't get the cap unscrewed from the bottle."

"What is it, Kyle?"

"Oh, it's a long story," Kyle said. "I'll tell you over breakfast tomorrow. Tonight, I'd like to be held close and kissed some, mothered in fact. I promise to return the favor sometime."

She began undressing him as he lay back on the couch, eyes closed, mumbling, holding the liquor with one unrelenting hand.

"Don't pass out, damn you," Betty said softly. She wrested him to his feet and maneuvered him into the bedroom. Kyle succumbed to a stupor within a minute of hitting the mattress.

Standing over him, Betty pondered the snoring man. This was as out of character for Kyle Burnette as it would have been for him to show up at her door dressed in a bikini and a party hat. Supercomposure, that was his bag. Although you'd never guess it looking at his mouth agape, slobber on his cheek, the bottle neck now resting in the relaxed palm of one hand.

She completed the undressing, pulled a sheet over him, wiped his face with a warm, damp washcloth, and doused the lights. Retiring to the kitchen, she cursed her habit of staying awake all night. Years of pulling a graveyard shift had ruined her for nocturnal slumber. How nice it would be to curl up around him, her body against his, despite his drunkenness. He came to her. It struck her for the first time, he came to her. He didn't go home, or pass out at the office, he came to her apartment. In every man was a little boy who needed somebody to look after him. He wanted to be strong, brave, and cavalier, but deep inside was a child with a runny nose who wanted only his mommy. It was, after all, a basic male trait. It was also an indication of love.

Not for the first time, Betty Snider wondered if Kyle would ever marry her.

Damon had accepted the new clothing, the tags still sewn to the trousers. The smell of newness came pungent to his nostrils as he dressed. A complete ensemble, underwear, shoes, socks, shirt, and pants. He did not have to ask why—he'd already walked through his mother's mind and with less success plumbed the thoughts of Kyle Burnette. There was to be a visitor, a man named Reirden, a reporter writing a book. The reporter had already talked to both parents extensively. He had seen Damon's medical reports, listened to hours of recorded sessions between Damon and the doctor, watched films, and read thousands of words of transcript.

"Be careful not to scuff your shoes," Melba said.

"I will," Damon agreed. "What time will I see Dr. Burnette?" He knew his mother did not have the answer when he asked the question.

"I don't know, darling."

"I love you, Mommy."

That deep voice, so mature, so adult, still held the childish inflections of a boy approaching his sixth birthday. Mrs. Daniels took him in her arms and held him close, his head against her bosom. He could smell her powder, deodorant, and perspiration mingling into one, the aroma of an adult woman, the scent of a mother.

"I love you, Damon. You are my life."

"Do you believe in God, Mommy?" Damon's voice was muffled by her body.

She pushed him back to arm's length. "Of course I do."

"Today is an important day for me," Damon stated. "Pray for me, please."

Her hands were shaking. "I always pray for you, Damon," she said tenderly. There was a sheen of moisture in her eyes.

"Pray very hard for me today," Damon said. His eyes were huge.

"I will," his mother promised.

"Don't worry, Mommy. Everything is going to be all right."

"Oh, Damon." She pulled him to her and squeezed him hard. "Oh, Damon, I love you so much!"

He submitted to her emotional response, his eyes open wide, staring at nothing, his breath trapped by her fierce embrace.

"My name is Larry," Reirden said, extending one hand to Damon. The boy accepted the gentle shake and took a seat across a table from the reporter.

"I want to be friends with you," Reirden began. "I'm planning to write a story about you."

"I know," Damon said. "I've been expecting you."

"Fine," Reirden smiled. The boy seemed normal enough. Not a bad-looking kid, despite thick eyebrows and a few hairs showing over the open neck of his shirt. Still, he had a childlike demeanor.

"I think you should know," Damon said evenly, "I will not cooperate in the presence of the doctor."

Kyle realized he had gasped involuntarily.

"Oh?" Reirden said. "Why not?"

"I will not discuss my reasons in the presence of Dr. Burnette."

"Damon, what are you up to?"" Kyle questioned.

Damon's eyes were straightforward on the reporter's face. He sensed the journalist's rising interest. Reirden looked to Kyle for a response and Kyle hesitated, debating Damon's motivation, the advisability of leaving or staying.

"Damon, what is this nonsense?" Kyle asked, his voice unchanged.

"It is between Mr. Reirden and me," Damon said.

Reirden waited expectantly.

"How long will it take, Damon?" Kyle asked.

"That depends on Mr. Reirden."

"Very well," Kyle acquiesced, "but let me tell you, Damon, any nonsense and this will be the last meeting of this kind. Act in a responsible manner." Reirden was studying Damon's face, his writer's mind taking in the expression, set of the jaw, the expressive lips. The boy waited until Burnette was completely gone, the door firmly closed.

"All right now, Damon," Reirden said, "what's the deal?"

"I'm being held a prisoner here," Damon stated. "I have been threatened with incarceration for the balance of my life."

Reirden had been warned to regulate his thoughts, but the mind is often the least manageable of the bodily functions. Reirden did not realize the flickering thoughts and subthoughts being passed to the boy.

"I'm not sure I'm following this," Reirden confessed. The boy was intelligent, that was obvious. Equally as obvious, he was mentally disturbed.

"I mean I am trapped," Damon said. His voice was scarcely above a whisper. "With the right kind of publicity, they would be forced to release me."

Reirden leaned across the table, his own tone dropping. "Tell me, Damon," Reirden said, "tell me about the sweven."

CHAPTER 17

NOBODY COULD top Larry Reirden at making a topic hot. Like a mason laying bricks, Reirden concentrated on the foundation, constantly building the intended story in the minds of the readers. Therefore, in his initial column on the subject, he wrote of Damon and the other children from a medical viewpoint only. When Kyle read the article, he heaved a sigh of relief and prematurely dismissed his fears.

Releasing columns on the subject once a week, Reirden shifted his emphasis with deliberation. He documented the Copenhagen and Atlanta cases without divulging names or places. He tantalized his readers with the horror, intrigue, and mystification of the body gone berserk. He detailed the medical phenomena and the psychological implications. His story wrung the hearts of the readers with sympathy for the tortured parents. There was little need to do more than report the facts, which were sensational in themselves.

Reirden timed his bombshell with a variety of factors. There was his book, just now going to press, and his carefully placed "drops" to friends with the wire services. He had written and placed a side article with a Sunday news supplement, including photographs of Damon and the child in Copenhagen which would run as the cover. He tipped a friend with network news, filled him in on the story that was about to break, and secured footage of the Denmark boy for use on television. He booked himself onto every major television talk show as a trade-out to push the book. Like meshing gears, the masterful plan clicked into place. The story broke, as fresh as though it had never had a word written about it, worldwide. In the course of a single Sunday, it seemed a reader could not turn without seeing something on the subject. In his Chicago apartment, Reirden stood alone with his first drink of the day and lifted a toast to himself.

"Did it again, old dude," he said aloud, and downed the bourbon and water. From here on in, it was a familiar story. There would be screams from the "victims," threats of lawsuits, more publicity therefrom. He could expect anger from all parties. The film clips he had secured from Dr. Christian were scheduled to run on the evening and morning news. By the end of the week, Damon Daniels would be a *cause célèbre* and Reirden's book would be a sellout. His column would be picked up by a dozen or more new publications.

He prepared another drink even as the telephone began to ring. With a smile, he strolled to the phone. With every load of fertilizer, a man must take a little shit.

"Reirden here," he said abruptly. "Yes, operator, this is Larry Reirden. Who? Dr. Christian? Well, hello, Doctor—how are things in Copenhagen?"

"Did you see this goddamned newspaper?" Ted seethed.

"I saw it," Kyle said.

"That sonofabitch!" Ted screamed. "That muckraking sonofabitch!"

Kyle nodded, motioning Ted to the far side of the breakfast table. Ted's rumpled hair and puffy eyes attested to the fact he'd bounded straight from his Sunday morning sleep to Kyle's apartment.

"Coffee?" Kyle asked.

"Yeah. Jesus. I hope Daniels sues Reirden for ten million."

Kyle poured coffee, sat opposite his associate, and silently studied Ted's troubled face. Ted was reading anew the Sunday supplement with Reirden's story. He grunted here and there and read aloud from time to time.

" 'From the dark recesses of our caveman days comes a horror that defies explanation by modern medical authorities,' " Ted read. " 'Have demons possessed the minds and twisted the tormented bodies of these innocent children? As we stood looking down on the grotesquely deformed shape of that Copenhagen boy, I felt a fear that primitive man must have experienced when first he saw the misshapen hulk of a purple wen covering the face of a stranger. Squatted on the floor like an animal, this human vegetable was, a few short months ago, an extremely intelligent and gifted child. Seized by some demonic force, this pitiful child looked up at me with agonized eyes and puddled involuntarily.' Jesus, you wouldn't think they'd publish shit like this in a family magazine," Ted said.

"Plus the fact that Reirden never saw the Copenhagen boy," Kyle noted. "The boy was dead when Reirden learned about it from Christian."

Ted continued, " 'Are we so removed from the primal taboos after all? How else can we explain the transformation from the highly telepathic and remarkable beginning this child knew, to this monstrous being that now exists?' "

Ted looked up. "Did you see the photos with this? He must've gotten them from Dr. Christian."

"I would assume so," Kyle said. As Ted lifted the

187

magazine to continue, Damon's face shared the front page with the contorted image of the Copenhagen child.

" 'It is easy to accept the fact that this is possession—' Goddamn Reirden! Possessed!"

"Which in fact they are," Kyle commented.

"Bullshit!"

"By hormonal imbalance, psychosis, that's possession. It's a medical possession and can be scientifically eliminated."

"All right, I'll buy that," Ted agreed. He slammed the newspaper to the table. "They ought to shoot Reirden."

The two men looked at one another a long moment, then Ted sipped his coffee and sighed. "To hell with it," he said softly. "I guess we'd better think about the future."

Kyle listened, not really catching more than the substance of the statements as Ted spoke rapidly of the impending problems that would arise from Reirden's article.

"The effects of this on the family . . . publicity seekers, the curious . . . queries from reporters . . . must manage all this . . . Damon's welfare . . ."

Kyle nodded absently. Personal frustrations and personal motivations had clouded the real issue here. Damon's welfare was paramount as it should have been all along. They had been sidetracked by Ted's desire to write a book to put the clinic on the map and by Dr. Christian's quest for similar goals. Reirden had forced them all to return to concentration on Damon's illness, Damon's ultimate cure.

"I want to go home," Damon stated.

"In due time, Damon," Kyle countered.

Damon's lips were tight. "I'm tired of being here. I don't like Mr. Joiner."

A man of little formal education, the attendant, Joiner had a quiet manner and great physical strength.

"What's the matter with Mr. Joiner?" Kyle asked.

"He's stupid."

"The world is full of stupid people, Damon."

"Their companionship is not forced on me," Damon snapped. "I spend eight hours each day with Mr. Joiner."

Kyle nodded. "We'll try to find somebody more compatible for you."

"If I must remain here, I want Miss Snider back."

"We'll see."

"Until I have Miss Snider back, I don't want to talk with you any more," Damon said.

"I see."

After a long silence, Damon asked, "May I return to my room?"

"As you wish, Damon."

Damon slipped from the chair and was met at the door by Joiner.

"Ready to go back to the room?" the attendant asked.

"Avidly anticipating it," Damon replied. The orderly laughed and took Damon's arm.

"You sure go on with them two-dollar words, Damon."

Kyle winced at the pained expression on the child's face. He made a mental note to speak to Betty about returning to work. Television and Joiner were hardly conducive to mind expansion.

Damon requested a *Book of Knowledge* set, which Mr. Daniels had promptly purchased. Despite Kyle's own high appraisal of Damon's intellect, he had been surprised to discover the boy teaching himself to read. A tutor was hired to assist the child.

"It isn't a matter of teaching him," the tutor said. "Damon leads the way, directs himself, and I merely answer questions and expedite the procedure. In fact, he resents any effort to channel his process of learning. He has asked for an unabridged dictionary, which I think he should have. He is methodical in his learning, which is rare. He's reading that set of encyclopedias by number, in sequence, and from page to page. I haven't attempted to test him for comprehension because he rebels so violently. He informed me that he wanted me to answer questions, not ask them."

The teacher adjusted rimless glasses and his prissy

pinched lips pursed a moment. "He's precocious, a genius as you said, Dr. Burnette. Positively astounding. Did you know he can read, watch television, and follow a side conversation at the same time? How much he gets from any of them I don't know. But, he does it."

The male nurse in nightly attendance grumbled, "The damn kid doesn't sleep! He sits up until three A.M. reading books. He goes to sleep, wakes up at six, and goes back to reading again."

Kyle administered a vocabulary comprehension test and Damon scored on a level comparable to a third-year college student. In contrast to his earlier protests against being confined, Damon had come to resent intrusions. He relished the hours of solitude, even to the exclusion of his mother. In her effort to please the boy, Melba Daniels soon learned to sit quietly, now and then giving a rudimentary definition of a word, or helping Damon by looking it up as he continued to read, one finger poised on the term in question.

The hormonal imbalance was holding steady. Damon's treatments were having beneficial results. His physical development had slowed, his condition stabilized. Unfortunately, the same could not be said for the other known cases. Khan, the Indian boy, died of cerebral occlusion, his heart already damaged by repeated hammering caused by adrenaline surges in his system. The aborigine child in Sydney died a few weeks later with bronchial pneumonia. Knowing this, Kyle remained constantly alert for a sudden turn in Damon's condition. The psychiatrist was not comforted by the medical synopses he received on Khan and the aborigine. Both children had apparently been doing well under similar hormone treatments, following Damon's example. Adverse developments came quickly, unexpectedly, and death was not long after. As for Damon, the therapy routine required injections thrice weekly. The boy was subjected to a continuing battery of tests, merely to compare them to tests administered months before. On the charts, physically, mentally, Damon appeared to be faring well.

190

There had been a brief experiment of withdrawing the hormone treatments, at Dr. von Ulbricht's suggestion. Was this boy to be a slave to hormones indefinitely? Or, hopefully, would the body correct itself? Until they reduced the hormone treatments, they had no way of judging.

They did not have long to wait. Ted's report summed it up: "Facial hair, hair on lower arms and chest, as well as pubic area, rapidly accelerated growth evident. Return of prostate gland condition noted and patient complains of discharge and resulting discomfort. Growth of fingernails and toenails accelerated. Body weight increase in seven days, five pounds. Extremely irritable. Expresses a desire to sleep."

During the same period, the "sweven" returned on the fifth and seventh nights as Damon experienced catatonic seizure for the first time in weeks. Betty Snider, now working days with Damon while the tutor was present, and during clinical testing time, reported Damon to be more aggressive, short-tempered, and argumentative. Dr. von Ulbricht reluctantly ordered the hormones back to the former successful schedule. Damon's condition immediately improved. His temperament leveled and he returned to his books with renewed interest.

Intrigued, Kyle observed a metamorphosis in the parents themselves. Their initial fears soon subsided to regulated concern. Then, with Damon progressing with studies, consuming reading material Mr. Daniels brought in, they began to act like the parents of any prodigy. Proudly, they told their friends of Damon's intellectual accomplishments.

A reporter from the Atlanta *Journal* requested an interview concerning Damon, only to be turned away. Later in the same day, the reporter returned with written permission from the parents to see Damon. It took a telephone call and much persuasion to discourage the idea. The reporter professed a desire to "cover only the boy's intellectual achievements," thereby convincing the parents that no harm could come from such an interview. Kyle pointed out the probability that this would signal an onrush of other reporters who might not be quite as honorable in their intentions. Larry Reirden's book on Damon was selling too well to take the gamble of a further avalanche of unwanted publicity. The parents yielded, the reporter was denied.

Kyle had the helpless feeling that the situation was getting out of hand. During the three months following Reirden's book publication, Kyle had a wriggling uneasiness in his belly. Furthermore, his attempt to pursue a constructive course of psychotherapy was bogged down by Damon's lack of interest.

"I'm at the end of my wits on this case," Kyle confessed to Ted.

"What do you suggest?" Ted asked.

"I don't know, really," Kyle admitted. "We don't seem to be getting anywhere, Damon and I. It's like we've talked until we're talked out. He is most uncooperative. He limits his conversation to topics about which he is currently reading. Frankly, I don't know where to go from here."

"Perhaps it's time to send him home, Kyle."

"I'm afraid to do that just yet."

"Afraid of what?"

"I'm not sure what. Afraid of what Damon might do, I guess. Hell, I don't know."

"Kyle," Ted said, "you can't keep that boy the rest of his life. Your task isn't to raise him."

"I'm aware of that."

"Better think about returning him to some semblance of normal living," Ted counseled.

"Guess I'd better," Kyle sighed. "I suppose what's worrying me is that little girl who was raped and killed. Damon has flatly refused to submit to narcosynthesis since then and—"

"Kyle, Jesus! Assuming he did and assuming you determined he did under narcosynthesis, then what? Would you report it to the police? And if you did, what would they do? They still need evidence for conviction and a confession under narcosynthesis doesn't qualify as evi-

192

lence, especially from a six-year-old! Declare him mentally incompetent at the time of the act? If Damon did assault that girl, it wasn't Damon. We'd both go to court and testify that it was a schizophrenic act and Damon was not responsible. The court would remand him to psychiatric care and that's where he is now. There'd be no trial, no jury, nothing but a stink. The only question is, will he do such a thing again, if he ever did it at all? In other words, should Damon be institutionalized and for how long? Personally, I think the idea is absurd."

"You're right, of course," Kyle said wearily. "What do you think I should do?"

"Send the boy home," Ted said strongly. "Get him back to a somewhat normal life!"

"You're probably right," Kyle said. "Okay, thanks for helping me think it out."

Kyle poured himself a drink and sat alone in his office, nursing the beverage slowly. What the hell, Ted was right. A psychiatrist's purpose is to achieve normalcy as much as possible and release the patient to a happier existence. He was getting too close to this goddamned thing. He lifted the telephone and dialed Betty's number.

"What's happening for supper?" Kyle asked.

"Eating with my favorite shrink, if I'm lucky," Betty replied.

"Mammy's Shanty?"

There was an audible sigh from the other end of the line and Kyle heard Betty say, "Listen, how about you stopping to buy some beer and steak and bring it over? I'll cook. I'm sick of eating out, if you want the truth."

"That sounds good."

He paused outside his office, looking down the hall toward Damon's door. Piss on it! There was no need to check on that boy every night before leaving. He walked directly to the exit, secured the latch, and climbed into his automobile. He spent a few minutes dusting the dustless interior, cranked the motor, and pulled out to the edge of the parking lot, watching traffic. He sat, thought a moment, then threw the vehicle into reverse and backed to the door of the building again. He reentered, walking with long strides the length of the clinic to Damon's quarters. He stuck his head in the door. The boy was looking at him as Kyle appeared. Damon smiled, looking almost embarrassed.

"Good night, Damon."

"Thank you," Damon said.

"For what?" He knew what.

"For coming back."

Kyle leaned against the doorjamb, his eyes on Damon, ignoring the attendant they had just hired, a college student working his way through premed.

"What am I going to do with you, boy?" Kyle asked gently.

Damon lifted one shoulder. "I don't know," he said.

"Well," Kyle nodded to the college kid, "good night."

Damon's eyes were aqueous. "Thank you," he said again.

Kyle let the door close and hurried down the hall. Damn it. Damn it. Goddamn it! He yanked the office door shut to trip the internal lock and got into his car. Really now, damn it all! He gunned the motor to life and flicked on the headlights. Smoothly, he slipped into the Peachtree traffic and turned south toward Betty's apartment. What was it she said to get? Steak and beer? As he unconsciously sought a supermarket, Kyle's mind churned over the boy back at the clinic. With a sick, sinking feeling in his stomach, Kyle dreaded the moment of their parting. Even as his insides tightened, Kyle made his decision.

CHAPTER 18

MELBA DANIELS sat on her back steps, the kitchen door open behind her. Between her fingers, in the gingerly fashion that marks a beginner, she held the first cigarette she'd ever smoked in her thirty-six years. Thirty-six. Her first cigarette.

"We've decided it will be all right to allow Damon to return home, Mrs. Daniels," Dr. Burnette had said. "It will be necessary to bring him in three times weekly for treatment, of course. But we feel he has progressed sufficiently to warrant a return to the normalcy of home.

Can you pick him up sometime today?"

Now, why was she reacting like this? Why was she sitting here smoking this foul-tasting tobacco? What if Edward saw her smoking, what would he say? Her lips twisted into a half-smile at the thought. Even her wry humor at his imagined chagrin was out of character.

Don't I love my son? Why should I not want him home if I love my son? What kind of mother would want her child to stay in an institutional surrounding when she could have him home?

She sat with her knees apart, her dress forming a valley between her legs. She drew on the cigarette, held the smoke in her mouth a moment, and puffed it out.

"His treatment has reached a point where his physical condition is stable, we think," Burnette had said. "A respite from psychotherapy is sometimes therapy in itself."

What is the life expectancy of a caucasian, American female? Statistically, half her life was spent as of this moment. Today was her birthday. Edward was in Toledo, attending a convention. Or was it St. Paul? He'd said something about St. Paul. Anyway, she had it all written down by the telephone in case she needed him. She dismissed it from her mind. Why worry about where Edward was? If she really cared, she could go look at the pad by the telephone.

That summed up her life very nicely, didn't it? She was not a worrier. Or, perhaps more precisely, she didn't care? She didn't worry because she didn't care? Was that it? Of course she cared. Everybody cares about their loved ones. Then, why did she not care enough about Damon to want him home?

Shit!

Did she say that? Shit?

Melba dug a thumb and forefinger into her eyes, partially to dispel these alien thoughts, partially to clear the smoke that had burned them. What was wrong with her?

"She never gave us a minute of trouble, our girl," Mother once told Edward. "The perfect child."

196

"Ah, my Melba," Edward once smiled, "the perfect wife."

Ah, shit! She did say that.

It was her birthday that was upsetting her, that's all. Half a spent lifetime. For the first time ever, she was thinking thoughts that marked—what?

She was at the far turn and approaching the home stretch, that was it. She stood at the milestone and from here she had the vantage of the past and the future. Who knows what the future holds? As for the past . . .

Exactly what did she feel? Not just now, just about Damon. What did she feel about anything, everything?

Melba systematically clicked them off, mentally. Her childhood, her parents, her school days, her marriage at age thirty when almost everybody had given up hope that she might ever marry. Then, she married Edward after five years of courtship. Had her mother sighed with relief? If Mother was worried, why hadn't Melba worried? She hadn't worried. She faced the prospects of being an old maid with the same stoic attitude with which she had approached every other turn in her life. It was as if she were anesthetized. Her whole life a benumbed existence. She was born, lived, attended school, grew up, attended college, got a job, married, had a baby, and it all just *happened*. She was neither apprehensive nor elated. She couldn't remember being elated, not ever. Not about anything. On the other hand, she couldn't remember being depressed either. Upset about Damon, disturbed, perhaps, but not depressed. She accepted life. She accepted the risks and fortunes, the happenings around her. She didn't worry needlessly, she didn't borrow sorrows about events that had not as yet unfolded. The few adversities in her life had been well met and none too serious.

Shit.

That just about covered it.

Her entire life was neither good, nor bad, up nor down. Neither retrospective nor introspective. Until today. Until this moment. Her first cigarette in thirty-six years.

Her dread at bringing Damon home had totally surprised her. Surely she had thought about the moment when he would come home, that would be natural, wouldn't it? Why was she so stunned when Dr. Burnette called and asked her to come get her child?

She did love him. Of course she did. A mother loves her child. She loved him as much as she loved Edward or her father or—

She did love them, didn't she?

This was ridiculous! Melba threw the cigarette to the ground and tapped it with the toe of one foot until it was out. She picked up the stub and carried it into the bathroom, where she flushed it down the toilet. She paused before the medicine cabinet, perfunctorily examined her appearance, and then hurried herself along.

"Get dressed, get dressed," she said aloud, in the same tone she might employ with a tardy child.

Her hosiery was neatly folded in the top drawer, her better and newer pairs at the bottom of the pile so she would use the older pairs first. All her hose were the same color, so that a run in one would not necessitate the disposal of both. That was in character.

Neat, tidy, efficient, sufficient: Melba Daniels. Quiet, steady, dependable Melba. Dull? Drab? Boring? How did a man like Dr. Burnette view her? Did he see her as the worried mother of an exceptional child? Did he see her as handsome? She could not think of herself as "attractive" or "pretty" and she was too practical to think of herself as "beautiful." Did Burnette think of her as practical? Did he see her as—anything? Perhaps he didn't see her at all.

She closed her eyes and immediately a sharply focused image of her son came to mind. His puerile face dark with a growth of hair that nature had cruelly placed there prematurely. She let her mind kaleidoscope, her picture of Damon shattering into fragments: coarse hair protruding above his undershirt, enlarged knuckles, the veins on the backs of his hands giving them the appearance of a mature dwarf's appendages. His voice resonant, mature; mature.

198

That was it. Damon wasn't actually a child. He was a little man in a little body. His chronological lifetime was a lie.

"Isn't it amazing how quickly that child learns?" Mother had exulted with grandparental pride.

Yes, it was amazing. Why wasn't Melba amazed? She had sat with Damon as he pored over those encyclopedias and she wasn't amazed. Was there something wrong with her? Didn't she feel anything about anything?

Yes! She felt something. Right this moment. She felt—dread. Not fear, not anger, not love, not anticipation of her son's return. She felt dread.

Melba halted her movements, holding one stocking halfway up her leg, her eyes on her reflection in the bureau mirror. She looked haunted, haggard. She was, she suddenly realized, very tired. She could, right this second, fall back on the bed and sleep for hours.

Oh, God. What is wrong?

"Get dressed, damn you!"

Her own voice urged her to action again and she completed the act of hooking her hosiery. Why was she still wearing garters? Every woman in the world was wearing pantyhose now. It had become difficult to find these hose and yet she persisted in seeking them out, specially ordering them to be sure they were all the same color.

She went to the dresser and pulled it open, seized with a desire to take all of the hose, throw them in the garbage. But she did not. She gazed down at the neatly laundered, tidily stored garments. Her arms felt heavy. Her whole body was heavy. There was a weight suspended in her chest that pulled her down with a sickening effect on her stomach.

The drive home was completed in silence. Damon peering out the window on the far side of the automobile, Melba driving. In the back seat were his clothing, books, and personal items from the clinic. It was astounding the bulk of belongings which accumulate around a person when he resides at a given place for any period of time.

"I'll be available any time you need me for night work,"

Miss Snider had said, as they closed the trunk of the vehicle and Damon slipped into the front seat.

"I know you're glad to be going home, Damon," Miss Snider had laughed. It was obvious, she and the boy had become very close. Damon had a certain look in his eyes when he talked to the nurse.

"You will call me, if you need me," Miss Snider had urged.

Melba turned out of Decatur toward their rural home.

"When is Daddy coming home?"

"In about a week."

Damon's eyes turned to the passing scenery again.

"He's attending a convention," Melba stated.

"I know. You told me."

"Did I?"

Whether consciously or otherwise, Melba was guarding her thoughts, carefully concealing her doubts, holding her emotions in check. This had become an automatic reflex, to shield her mind from this boy. It left her no recess into which she could dart, mentally. It left her exposed, feeling naked and vulnerable.

"I'm hungry, Mommy."

"We'll eat when we get home."

Automatic responses. So it had been all her life: automatic responses.

"What is it, Damon?"

He stood at his bedroom door as though lost.

"It's time for bed," Melba persisted.

The room was still cluttered with various belongings she had not found time or space to store.

"Damon?"

"I'm going."

She brought the covers up around his shoulders and he lay unresisting as she tucked him in. She stared down at him and, with a start, realized she was hesitating at kissing him good night.

"Good night." She kissed him.

200

"Good night." His eyes had a distant expression.

She turned out the bedroom light and pulled the door closed to within a half inch. She flicked off the hall lights on her way to the kitchen. Checking everything, stove off, door locked, she returned to the bathroom and undressed. She did not close the bathroom door completely. If Damon called, she wanted to be able to hear him. She dropped her clothes in a hamper, empty except for Damon's clothing just discarded. Then, she adjusted the shower and stepped inside.

She was standing, head forward, chin on chest, letting hot water beat at the base of her skull. Her eyes were closed. How long she had stood this way, she had no idea. Certainly no longer than a few minutes. Suddenly, she jumped, as though to a loud noise. She found herself pressing against the tiled wall, away from the opaque glass shield between shower and bathroom.

Had she heard something? Seen something? She couldn't possibly have seen anything, her eyes were closed. She must have heard something! Melba wrenched the taps closed and stood listening. She pulled a towel across her breasts as though expecting someone to be there when she opened the shower doors. Nobody. The mirror was clouded with steam. The door was still ajar. Had she left it that far open?

Letting her imagination get to her. Being stupid. For heaven's sake, take a shower and go to bed!

She was about to close the shower doors when her eyes touched on the medicine cabinet mirror again. She stepped out of the tub with one foot and leaned nearer. At the base of the mirror, at the edge, droplets of condensed moisture had been disturbed. Four small, almost unnoticeable smudges had appeared there. Four short fingers had touched the steamed glass! Melba stared at the crack in the bathroom door, her eyes wide, trying to see into the dark beyond. She stepped completely free of the tub and pushed the door closed. She turned the latch gently, slowly, so it wouldn't click. Why in God's name was she trembling?

201

She reexamined the mirror. She could be mistaken. The mirror had not steamed evenly, perhaps, and it only appeared to be fingermarks. Melba returned to the shower and quickly completed her bath.

In bed, she read at length, trying to relax. In desperation, she arose and took a bottle of sleeping pills from one of Edward's dresser drawers. He kept them for those times when a case was causing him so much concern he could not put it out of his mind.

Melba took one of the pills; she debated two, but did not know the strength of them. For another hour she tossed and turned, lights out, eyes closed. Finally, she changed from the pajamas she was wearing to a short gown that was less binding. She took another of Edward's pills. It had been several hours, hadn't it? She took two.

She paused to look in on Damon. He was asleep on his back, arms extended. Melba returned to bed and took up her book for yet another hour. It was not long before dawn. Really! This was ridiculous.

Frustrated, she took another sleeping pill, this time bracing herself with a stiff drink as well. She wished Edward were here to make love to her. That always relaxed her, helped her sleep. She briefly debated masturbation, then decided it wasn't worth the trouble. Besides, there was Damon—

She did not remember falling asleep. She only knew it was almost daylight. When sleep did come, it came with a heavy veil. When she awoke, it was noon.

Melba grabbed her robe and threw it on as she moved toward the bedroom door. Damon's bed was empty. She rushed down the hall and when she did not find him in the house, she became alarmed.

"Damon!"

She opened the back door and looked across the yard.

"Damon!"

She was outside, barefoot, yelling, "Damon!"

"Here I am, Mommy." Damon emerged from their pump house, always a favorite playing area.

"I overslept," Melba confessed. "Are you hungry?"

"No, I made a sandwich."

"I'm sorry, Baby."

"It's all right." Damon smiled.

"I'll be happy to prepare breakfast," Melba insisted.

"No. I ate the sandwich. I'm not hungry."

She returned to the kitchen, perked coffee, then went to the toilet. The sleeping pills must have been caustic. Her rectum hurt as though she had eaten hot peppers. She fingered the area and the touch of her hand made her skin burn. Even her vagina was sore. She vowed to wear herself out with manual labor to avoid the misery of another restless night. Having slept so late, she would surely be sleepless again if she did not expend her energy somehow.

It occurred to her shortly after four in the afternoon, she had not so much as offered the boy lunch!

"Are you getting hungry, Damon?" Melba called.

"Not really."

He was still in the pump house. There was nothing out there that could hurt him. Grandpa had built it as more than a housing for the deep well pump. There were Knox canning jars on shelves and wicker baskets for storing potatoes, but nothing dangerous. Damon had often spent many hours there, before he went to the clinic.

Melba's day consisted of cleaning house at a feverish pace. She washed the few items in the dirty clothes hamper and otherwise busied herself with the sole purpose of achieving exhaustion by bedtime.

Long after Damon was asleep that night, she was still scurrying, pushing herself. She felt considerably better than she had upon awakening, so she dared to take two more of Edward's sleeping pills. To be doubly sure she slept, she had a drink. These past few days had seen her do things she'd never done before. Her first cigarette, a drink before retiring, and sleeping pills.

However, it worked. She fell into bed like a sack of rocks and five minutes later she was dead to the world.

Melba sat in the bathroom, holding a mirror to see hidden parts of her body. The tenderness of the previous day was even more pronounced this morning. When she awoke, she was extremely sore and there were blood flecks on the sheet. Perhaps her IUD was causing trouble. Once before she had to have it removed for several months. Still, that would not explain the ache in the rectal area. She maneuvered the mirror so she could examine herself. Inflamed, but not enough for undue concern. She'd never had hemorrhoids, but she could well imagine this was how they felt.

"Mommy!" Damon's voice came through the locked bathroom door.

"Yes, Damon?"

"May I go to Grandpa's barn? He's waving his arm at me to come."

"I suppose so. Don't get in their way down there."

"I won't."

Melba sat on the commode, mirror in hand, until she heard the back door slam. She waited another full minute before allowing herself to resent Damon's presence outside the door a moment ago. Surely, he knew what she was doing. Just as he knew every other unguarded thought in her brain. She was imprisoned in her own skull, restricted to what she could and could not think, for God's sake!

She put the mirror aside and undressed completely. She turned back to the commode, straddling it so she faced the wall. She switched on the electric toothbrush.

She did not think of Edward. She refused any longer to allow her realization that Damon knew her thoughts and what she was doing to inhibit her. She did not want them to cross her mind. She wanted her thoughts free, to go where they wished, without slinking. She wanted her mind to roam where it would, go as it pleased, not like a frightened animal quivering at the edge of a glen, but free!

She turned loose, releasing the last tenacious barrier which hemmed her thoughts and channeled her thinking, stifling her imagination. She sighed with contentment, submerging into fantasy as the soft bristles of the vibrating brush touched her clitoris.

204

CHAPTER 19

"Is EVERYTHING all right?" Edward's voice always sounded so far away when it was long distance.

"Yes, fine."

"Damon is doing okay?"

"Yes, darling. Fine."

"Good. I'll be home Sunday afternoon, Melba. It'll be the five o'clock flight. Can you meet me?"

"Of course."

"I'll see you then."

"Good."

"Melba?"

"Yes, Edward?"

"Everything *is* all right?"

"Yes, fine, Edward."

"You sound worried."

"No, I'm fine. I'm just tired, I suppose."

"Get some rest, Melba. You need your rest."

"I will."

"See you Sunday, then."

"How is the convention going?"

Edward grunted. "You know how conventions are."

"Try to have fun, Edward. Don't make it all work."

"That's the trouble with the convention now, everybody is having fun and the constructive work is a byproduct."

"Oh."

"I love you, Melba." As though by rote.

"I love you, Edward." Automatic response.

She cradled the telephone without rising from the kitchen table. Her coffee had gone cold. She sipped it anyway. Through the window she could see Damon down by the rose-bordered lane to the barn. The roses were coming into blossom again. Had it been a year since he touched the roses? Two? She had lost all concept of time.

Grandpa said Damon didn't kill the roses. "When the temperature drops below a certain point," Grandpa had explained, "it causes the petals to separate from the stem. They hang there and look fresh for a day or so, but they're really dead. All it takes is a touch and they fall away. You've seen magnolia and gardenia blossoms turn brown immediately after you touch them, Melba. There's nothing supernatural about that, is there?"

It occurred to her, Damon was standing very still in the same place, the same way he used to. Only now, with his broadened shoulders and thicker torso, he was not as defenseless in appearance. What thoughts coursed that brain? With his superior intellect, what must he be thinking? He played children's games, but he spoke adult thoughts. Melba had found herself irritated when he acted like a baby.

She had talked to the mother of a genius attending a special school for exceptionally bright children. Melba had gone there at Edward's urging some weeks back, to see about enrolling Damon into classes. "It's an onus, having a bright child," the lady had related. "He responds with maturity to some things and complete immaturity to others. He has the scholastic capabilities of a senior in high school when it comes to mathematics, but he can't master brushing his teeth properly. He forgets where he left his shoes. It isn't easy being his mother."

Melba finished the cold coffee and poured fresh hot liquid into her cup. It wasn't going to get any easier, either.

"My boy still wets the bed," another mother at the same school had volunteered. "The psychologist says he's insecure. Then the boy sits down at a piano and plays a complicated sonata. Jesus Christ! *I'm* insecure!"

Melba gazed at Damon, still transfixed, unmoving. It was with detachment that she observed this now. She wished she could afford the luxury of psychiatric care. Maybe a psychiatrist could explain her change in emotions. How nice it would be to have someone explain illogic in logical terms.

"You do not suffer highs or lows, Melba," they would probably say, "because you are normal. Perfectly normal."

What else? The perfect child, the perfect wife, the perfect mother—perfectly normal.

She was exhausted and her day had not yet begun. She wanted to sleep. Sleep for days! If she could go somewhere, find a motel, and hole up there; no telephone, no television, just a comfortable bed and a "do not disturb" sign on the door.

He moved. His fingers stretching, arms extending, head coming back to a normal parallel with his spine. Melba felt her lips twisting bitterly.

Why did God complicate things? Was there any person

207

anywhere who did not suffer complexities? Melba could understand why people combed desolate beaches and ignored the world. Having anything, home, automobile, husband, child, complicated things. The more one possessed, the more complex—

She was trembling again. It was unlike her to react this way. It was unlike her to react. Period. Automatic response: Melba Daniels.

Damon had wheeled and was now facing the house, staring at the kitchen window. He was reading her mind again! Her thoughts darted into nooks and crannies of her brain to hide themselves. This couldn't go on. Not for a lifetime. She wouldn't be able to stand a lifetime of this. Shield that thought!

"Are you hungry, Damon?" She fed the child too much. Action covers thoughts, scatters them.

"No."

"I'll be happy to make you a sandwich."

"I just had breakfast, Mommy."

The dishes were still in the sink.

"If you get hungry, call me."

She must seem inane to him. Shallow and inane.

"May I go see Grandpa at the barn?"

"I think not, Damon. He may be busy."

No argument. The boy moved toward the pump house. He was a solitary child. But then, she realized, so was she as a child. And, Edward. Edward was an only child, too. Could this have contributed to her failure as a mother? Failure? Where did that idea come from? She was a *perfect* mother, remember?

Wash the goddamned dishes.

Shit. And goddamn. In three days. Trench mouth her father called it, when someone swore unnecessarily.

"Think of Damon as a reflection," Dr. Burnette had once advised. "He expresses what his mind gathers from everybody around him. His vile language is a reflection only."

208

She attacked the house not because it needed cleaning, but because she needed the exertion. She wanted to be tired tonight. For two nights she had turned to Edward's sleeping pills and she absolutely refused to do so again. Work was good for her. It dispelled her weariness and occupied her mind. Perhaps she needed vitamins.

Why be a fool? She didn't need vitamins. She didn't need sleep. Her exhaustion, her lassitude, her aching posterior were symptoms! Attack the cause, or ignore the symptoms.

She refused to consider the cause.

"It's Friday, Mommy, may I stay up late?"

"No."

"Mommy, I stayed up late at the clinic."

"This isn't the clinic. You can't stay up late here."

His voice rose sharply. "I can look after myself!"

"Be that as it may, young man, you are going to bed at your regular time."

"Goddamn it, I'm tired of being treated like a baby!"

She slapped him so fast it had happened before she realized it. Her hand left her side and squarely connected with his face as though by reflex. The blow sent Damon back a step and the two of them stood looking at one another, both equally shocked by the unexpected and unnecessary physical response.

"Damon. I'm sorry."

She tried to read the expression in his eyes. "I don't know what came over me, Son."

"It's all right." His voice was extremely deep.

She crouched and held out her arms. After an instant of hesitation, he came forward and allowed her to embrace him. She kissed his forehead.

"To bed now?" she asked softly.

"Yes."

She stood at the hallway door and as he reached the bathroom, Damon turned.

"Mommy, it *is* all right."

"Good. Thank you."

She could not allow herself the debate that any other parents might experience, rationalizing, recriminating against herself, coming to grips with her own involuntary action. She stood there numbed, frustrated, angry with herself, furious with her weakness, angry with—Damon. She could hear water running in the tub.

Shivering, Melba sat in a dinette chair and rested her elbows on the table. She covered her face with her hands and stared at the dark caused by her cupped fingers. She was not equipped for this. Not mentally or physically. She was lacking in the strength of character and the will of resolution. She just couldn't handle it. Not all by herself, she couldn't. Something had to be done. Things couldn't go on this way.

Despite her resolve, Melba took a glass of wine and a sleeping pill. She steeped in a hot tub of water, letting her mind idle, absorbing the creature comfort of the relaxing bath. She was careful to daub herself dry, as opposed to an invigorating rub with the towel.

Naked, she walked down the hall. She adjusted the sound system and opened the files of taped music which Edward collected. She selected titles to lull her. She had never used the system before and it took several minutes to remember Edward's initial instructions given when they first moved into their new home. There were a dozen dials to control balance, tone, volume, with switches to throw the system to a record player or convert it for use as a communications network, something they had never used.

With the refrains of Strauss waltzes flooding the building, she poured herself another glass of Mateus slightly larger than before. Rather than reading, which took a semblance of concentration, she lowered the rheostat until her bedroom was barely lighted, and lay abed nude, sipping wine, pleasantly inebriated.

She really should put on her gown and get under the covers. She really should. Or turn out the light. She roused herself enough to set aside the empty wine glass and to push the button that doused the last vestige of light. Then, content, she fell back across the bed and slept.

She was enjoying it, that was what haunted her later. Even when she rationally explained to herself that she had been asleep, it bothered her that she awoke enjoying it. She told herself that, after all these years of marriage, she often yielded to Edward in her sleep and he had admitted that he sometimes awoke to find himself making love to her. So, she knew her physical response was as natural as marital love. Still, it disturbed her that she was enjoying it, despite the logic as to why. Her movements, might they have encouraged him?

In that twilight moment between complete awareness and sleep, she dimly realized he was too short to be Edward. His hands clutched her waist and he moved with the rhythm and expertise of a practiced adult. Therefore, she did not quickly come awake.

She struggled to clear her sleep-fogged mind, to calmly make a decision as to how she must react. He knew she was awake. His hands slid from her waist to her wrists and he gripped her arms as he continued. Long, pulsating drives as deeply as he could. She heard his toenails scratching the sheet as he pushed inward. She brought her knees together, resisting, and he snorted, twisted, shoving her thighs apart.

"Damon!" Had she shouted? Whispered? She wasn't sure.

"Damon, stop."

She had never realized his strength. When she tried to pull her wrists free, he clamped them with such force the pressure caused pain.

"Damon, stop this."

She felt him probing. He was still erect. Melba jolted as he tried to reposition himself. She flipped suddenly, trying to dislodge him.

"Be still, bitch!"

His guttural, alien voice galvanized her. Melba lunged to

211

one side and cast him off. She heard his knees strike the floor. Instantly, he was back at her, snarling, clawing at her body. She brought up one knee to block him and he hit it so hard she cried out in pain. His reaction brought her to the brink of panic and for an instant she relaxed, seeking composure. It gave him a split-second advantage and he regained his leverage. His teeth settled over her breast. It was, she later told Dr. Burnette, like a dog clamping his mouth over your arm—a threat, a warning, but harmless if not resisted. In the same second, his hand dug into her vagina and thus held, she lay breathing hard, trembling, uncertain as to what action, how forceful she should be.

The pause in her defense must have been interpreted as submission. Damon's lower hand eased and he began massaging her. With horror, Melba realized it was exactly as she liked it, exactly as she would have done to herself.

"Damon, you must stop."

His tongue circled the nipple, suckling. Dear God!

"Damon, stop it!"

She arched her back and catapulted him so violently that he was thrown clear. She heard his teeth click and she knew she had scarcely avoided being severely hurt. Immediately, he came back at her, shoving her down, reviling her with abusive and filthy language. She groped wildly for the lamp and the fixture crashed to the floor. He was on her back now, his fingers holding her hipbones, dragging her buttocks toward him. She felt his still erect organ stabbing at her. She bucked and his fingernails raked her sides as he was knocked away. She reached the far edge of the bed and attempted to drag herself free, but he was atop her back, straddling her, his teeth sinking into her shoulder at the base of her neck.

He was intentionally hurting her. Causing her pain and threatening more pain if she resisted. As his teeth crunched and searing pain made her scream, Melba abandoned any thought of trying to exercise care not to hurt him. She rammed her elbow backward and caught him in the chest. She heard the air go from his lungs and he released his hold on her with his teeth. He fell back, gurgling, but as Melba

212

stumbled over the fallen lamp, he was at her again and once more she heard his teeth click as she knocked him away from her legs with a suddenly raised knee.

Her fist caught him beside the head and her full weight was behind the blow, driving him into the dresser. Melba heard the breaking of glass and a smell of perfume filled the room. She fought him off again, getting across the room to the light switch. She had forgotten the rheostat was turned so low and when the light came on, it bled the scene into shades of amber and brown.

He was crouched, like a wild animal, facing away from her when the illumination came up. He wheeled and she stood aghast, his enormous penis projecting upward, the hair of his chest and abdomen matted with perspiraton.

"Oh, God," she whimpered. "This can't be happening."

He advanced toward her and Melba backed into the hall. She felt along the wall to the light and flicked it on.

"Damon, go to bed," she commanded.

He was bent, shoulders hunched, stalking.

"Damon, I said for you to go to bed!"

She eased toward the safety of the bathroom and he correctly read her thoughts. He lunged forward and she jumped away. He passed her and stood now between her and every exit in the house.

"Damn you," Melba seethed.

A sickening smile parted those curled lips and his tortured features wrinkled into a mask of utter ugliness. Saliva coagulated at the corners of his mouth and her blood was smeared across his cheek.

"Get into your room, Damon."

He was inching forward again. She intended to stand her ground, pointing at his bedroom door, but she fell back as he enough!" She threw her heavy powder jar at him and it barely missed his head. He ran at her and with another jar as her weapon, Melba crashed it against his forehead, knocking him to his knees. She brought the jar down with all her might and only his quick dodge kept her from smashing him squarely atop his head.

He grabbed at her, his aim being her pubic area. Melba

brought up her knee with every ounce of strength she could muster. She heard his nose crunch and she held the back of his head and brought her knee up again, a sick thud and a gush of blood spewed from his nostrils. Again! Damon sank to his knees and with a final, furious blow, Melba knocked him flat. The penis began to ebb as she stood over him. Melba looked around the room, eyes darting, and she ran to the closet. Edward's golf bag was there. She grabbed one of the irons and moved toward Damon, club raised. He was gasping, reeling, struggling to his knees. Melba lifted the club for the decisive, killing blow and he met her eyes.

"Mommy!" Damon screamed.

Why did she halt? Why didn't she drive that steel shaft down on his skull? One well-placed blow and he would fall dead at her feet. Kill him. Hit the beast and kill him!

"Mommy!" he was shrieking. "Mommy, stop! What is it, Mommy? Please, stop!"

Her eyes mad, club raised, Melba stood nude over the cowering child. Kill him, Melba. Be done with it. Kill him!

"No, Mommy. No! Please!"

Which one is real, Melba? This crying child, or the animal that was here a moment ago? Kill him! She moved a step nearer.

"Mommy, don't hurt me, Mommy. Please don't hurt me any more!"

Her voice was rasping. "Get in bed, Damon. Get in bed and don't get up until I call you."

"I will, Mommy. I will. I'm going to bed."

After he left the room, she still held the club in both hands, poised for a strike. How long she remained there, she would never know. Then, finally, she let the club down, but did not release it. She sank to the side of her bed, trembling violently, and there she sat, club in hand, when daylight finally came.

214

CHAPTER 20

THE CALL from Melba Daniels awoke Kyle shortly before seven. He agreed to meet her at the office. Damon's presence caught him by surprise. The boy's face was puffed.

"Wait in your room," Mrs. Daniels instructed.

Obediently, Damon disappeared down the hall and into the room that had been his.

"I brought Damon back to stay," Mrs. Daniels said, her voice evenly modulated.

"There's no one here to stay with him today, Mrs. Daniels."

"Then, we must get someone. He cannot come home." Despite the adamancy of her tone, she did not seem unduly upset. Tense, yes, but not distraught.

"What's the trouble?" Kyle questioned.

She sat, seemingly composed, her voice low as she related the events of the night just past. Her story was devoid of histrionics and betrayed no rancor. When she described the sexual onslaught, she was neither sparse with details nor verbose. She might have been reading a text, so level and unchanging was her voice. With a pounding heart, Kyle sat with practiced professional calm and listened. He had grossly misjudged his patient and thereby inflicted a deep hurt on this woman.

"May I see your shoulder?" Kyle asked. "A human bite is rather serious. You may need treatment."

She unbuttoned her blouse, head hung, and exposed the wound. Damon had bitten a plug from her flesh.

"I'd better dress that," Kyle said. "Please remove your blouse. I'll be back in a moment."

He was shaking as he let the office door close behind him. He walked to the receptionist's desk and dialed Betty Snider.

"Betty, please come to the clinic immediately."

She agreed without question and hung up.

Kyle walked down the hall, breathing heavily, his emotions less than stable. He gazed through the one-way glass of the ward door. Damon knew he was there. Kyle pushed the door ajar and with a tone he hoped was casual, asked, "You all right, little buddy?"

"Yes."

"I'll be with you in a little while."

"All right."

Damon's eyes were huge, moist, and slightly swollen. He appeared to be approaching tears.

When he returned to his office, Kyle found Melba Daniels sitting with her blouse off, but her arms still in the sleeves, elbows at her sides, head down.

He prepared a shot of penicillin, asking, "Any allergies?"

"No."

As he approached her with the injection, she added, "No allergies. I'm perfectly normal."

"With the ratio of allergies to the population," Kyle said lightly, "I'm not sure that being without an allergy is normal."

"In that case," Melba replied, "I probably have one."

He dressed the shoulder, swallowing hard now and then to cover his own distress. As he finished, he told her, "You may put on your blouse now. Anywhere else you're hurt?"

"No." Very softly.

"Would you like coffee? It'll only take a minute."

"No, I've been drinking coffee all night. All morning."

"Can you spare a few minutes to answer some questions?"

"Yes. Of course."

"Second thoughts about the coffee?"

"No."

Nonetheless, he made a pot, again checking on Damon. He was stalling. Waiting on Betty. Trying to recompose himself. Giving himself time to think this thing out before speaking. He couldn't just let her walk out without saying something. Despite her apparent control, she was extremely upset.

"Has this upset you, Mrs. Daniels? I know it has, but what I mean is, are you very upset?"

"I suppose so."

"Do you have a grip on yourself?"

"If you mean, do I feel dirty, or raped, I don't."

"What do you feel?"

She looked up slowly, her eyes clouded. "I feel tired. I want to take a hot bath and sleep for a long time."

"That's probably a good idea. Is Mr. Daniels home?"

"No. He's at a convention in St. Paul or someplace."

"Would you like me to call him?"

Her voice was sharp. "No!"

Kyle pondered a moment, putting sugar and cream in two cups of coffee. "Perhaps you would rather not tell your husband anything about this," Kyle said.

"Yes."

"He'll ask about the bruises," Kyle stated. "He'll see your shoulder."

"Oh." Her face twisted and discolored and she began to shake her head slowly from side to side. "I just can't tell him, Doctor. I don't want Edward to ever know."

"Do you think he would be upset with you? Blame you?"

"I don't think so." Her voice was squeaking now.

"I don't think he will," Kyle said. "He'll know it isn't your fault in any way, Mrs. Daniels."

"I do not want him to know," she said fiercely.

Come back to this later, when she was better prepared to handle it. Kyle changed his approach. "What happened to you last night was not the doings of your son, Mrs. Daniels. It was somebody, something else."

He watched for a reaction. There was none. He held out a cup of the coffee and she shook her head, her hair falling down the sides of her face, hiding her expression.

"You must try to put this in proper perspective, Mrs. Daniels. The thing you saw last night was not your son. You must not think of it as Damon."

Still no response.

"I called Nurse Snider," Kyle said finally. "She's coming down. We'll make arrangements to care for Damon over the weekend. I'll drive you home."

"No. Thanks. I'll drive home. I'm all right."

With this, Melba Daniels rose and without a backward glance left the building. Kyle worked his temples with the thumb and forefingers of one hand. He lit a cigarette and sat back, staring ahead at space. He had really messed this one up. One miscalculation atop another. How deeply was Mrs. Daniels hurt? How long would it take her to recover? What would be the effect on Damon? Goddamn that sweven. A loathing arose in Kyle that was far from professional. He conjured mental images of the mother towering over her

218

son as the sweven evaporated and the boy emerged. He could well imagine what Melba Daniels meant when she said, "I was ready to kill him. I don't know why I didn't. Even when I saw it was Damon, my son, a little boy. I still wanted to kill him. I nearly did it. I nearly did. I—I don't know why I didn't."

"Murder is foreign to most of us, Mrs. Daniels."

"Not when it comes to animals," she had replied.

Kyle opened a desk drawer and removed several tissues which he used to dry his palms. Damn himself! Damn his mistakes!

Betty's expression revealed her concern. "What is it, Kyle?"

"Come in."

"It's Damon, isn't it?"

"Yes, come in."

"I was afraid of this."

His frustration erupted in an angry retort. "Afraid of what, goddamn it? If you were afraid of something, why didn't you tell me before I sent that child home?"

Betty stared at him, eyes wide, and wisely held her tongue. She followed him into his office. Her trained eye immediately took in the used syringe, opened cotton, and discarded swabs. Two cups of coffee, one untouched.

"Let me make some good coffee," Betty said mildly. "Yours always stinks."

Kyle had dropped into his desk chair and sat morosely glaring at the floor, hands clasped, elbows on knees.

Betty paused at the door to Damon's room and stuck her head inside. "Hi, Sweetie!"

"Hello."

"Why's everybody so glum this morning?"

"Because I fucked my mommy."

Betty's smile froze. She found her eyes blinking rapidly. Then, like a remotely controlled sound, she heard her own voice speaking with nurselike cheerfulness. "Have you had breakfast?"

219

"I'm not hungry."

"That wasn't the question," she said, a bit more sharply than she intended. "I asked if you had eaten."

"No!" Damon screamed. "No, I did not have breakfast! I don't want anything to eat. Get out! Get out of here!" Numbed, Betty let the door close. She turned the external security latch that held Damon inside. Kyle was at his office door, looking at her. For a moment, they stared at one another, then Betty moved toward him with quick strides.

"Sit down, darling," she said tenderly. "Come on." She took him by the arm and returned him to his chair. He looked exhausted, eyes red, head wobbling like an old man's.

"The coffee will be ready in a few minutes," she soothed.

He opened his mouth to speak and she placed a finger across his lips. "Wait for the coffee, my baby."

Kyle nodded. Then, as Betty held him, he began to sob.

Melba Daniels carefully set the emergency brake, locked the car doors, and went directly into the house. The telephone was ringing, but she walked past without answering. She went down into the basement and found a hammer on Edward's workbench. She moved things about until she chanced upon a large nail which, with the hammer, she took upstairs. The telephone stopped ringing.

Melba opened several of her dresser drawers, carefully stepping around the litter of broken glass and overturned items. She examined several cloth belts which she used as accessories to various spring outfits, then rejected them all. She opened the drawer with the stockings. She pulled out an old pair, dropped them on the floor. At the base of the pile were two new pairs, still wrapped in cellophane. She chose one of these and opened it, dropping the torn wrapper where she stood. She tied two of the stockings together at the toes and then nailed both of them to the doorjamb. The other end of the stockings were knotted together to make a hanging loop from the nail. Giving the stockings a half twist, she formed a smaller loop at one end and put this over her head. She tossed the hammer onto the bed.

Slowly, deliberately, she let her weight down, adjusting the noose so that it first brought pressure on her jugular veins. There was no pain. As the circulation of blood to her brain was impeded, she became dizzy. Then, without really realizing it was happening, she passed out and her full weight yanked the stocking taut as she slipped down the wall, arms at her sides. Her legs twitched, her face discolored as death overtook her. If she had opened her eyes, if she could have seen herself, she would have been stunned at the distorted expression on her face, the protruding tongue and purple lips, saliva corded between the roof of her mouth and her lips, eyes bulging. It looked very much like Damon this morning, just as the lights came on in the bedroom when he had wheeled to face her.

Edward Daniels missed the call to him at the hotel. He'd already left to catch his plane by the time they traced him. He was airborne and only a few hours away from home when his name went out over the speakers at the terminal. So, he arrived in Atlanta unsuspecting and unexpected. He waited, becoming more and more irritated as he shifted from foot to foot, watching for Melba. She was generally punctual, but there had been a few times she had allowed herself to become delayed when she was scheduled to meet him. Therefore, by the time three-quarters of an hour had elapsed, Edward Daniels was angry. Rather than call her and risk waiting an additional hour and a half for her to get here, he decided to pay the fifteen dollars cab fare required and use that as further ammunition to berate her for this.

He did not hear them paging him. He was in a telephone booth trying to reach Decatur for a taxi. Now very irate, he stalked outside and grabbed the first cab he saw. He had been told the Decatur cabs could meet him in Decatur, but wouldn't come this far for a telephone call.

He arrived home and instantly knew something was

221

wrong. There were strange automobiles parked on the lawn. Edward threw his baggage from the cab and with the driver's shout in his ears, raced toward the back door.

"What is it?" Edward demanded of the first person he saw.

"Oh, God, Edward!" His mother came toward him from the living room. The house was full of people.

"What is it, goddamn it, somebody tell me what it is?"

"It's Melba, Son," his father said.

"Oh, no, Dad, no—what is it?"

"She's dead, Edward."

"Oh, Dad, no, not Melba!"

"Come sit down, Son."

"Not my Melba."

"Come sit down."

"What happened?"

"We're not sure, Edward."

"Are you sure she's—"

"Yes, Son, we're sure."

"Please, I don't believe this. She was supposed to have met me at the airport."

"We tried to reach you, Son. We called the hotel and you had left. We paged you there and here at the airline but we weren't sure what flight you'd take, or what airline. They refuse to give out that kind of information, you know."

"How did it happen?" Edward demanded.

"Edward, they think it was self-inflicted."

"Suicide?"

"Mr. Daniels?"

"Yes?"

"I'm Elliot Jones, detective with the De Kalb County Sheriff's office. I hate to disturb you at a time like this, sir. But could you answer a few questions?"

"Must you now?" Edward's mother snapped.

"I'm sorry," the officer said gently. "Does anyone know the whereabouts of the boy?"

"The boy?" Edward's legs wobbled as he stood.

"Your son Damon, Mr. Daniels. We can't seem to locate him."

"For God's sake!" Edward screamed. "What has happened here?"

"She was the perfect mother," Edward Daniels said. "The perfect wife. Always so steady and easygoing. Never lost her temper, never even raised her voice in anger."

Melba's grieving parents acknowledged, "She was always such a good child, a joy. We had no idea she was so upset. She didn't call. That's just like Melba, not to burden others with her troubles. Our baby—she didn't even say good-bye."

To the clamoring reporters, the investigating officer said, "There was no note. Mrs. Daniels was apparently very depressed over a son under psychiatric care. Evidently the boy had a temper tantrum the previous night. It was the child who broke up things in the bedroom and upset the furniture. You can see why we suspected foul play at first. The autopsy says the blood came from cuts on Mrs. Daniels's feet. There was a lot of glass on the floor. I don't think this is a story you'll want to dwell on."

"How old is Damon now?"

"Still under six."

"Jesus, this family has really had problems," a reporter said. "OK, that covers it. Thanks."

"Dead?" Kyle repeated.

"Suicide," Ted Drinkwater said.

"When?"

"Saturday morning. Betty's been trying to reach you for hours. She finally decided you had your telephone cut off."

"Yes," Kyle stuttered. "I do."

"The police called the clinic and Betty verified that Damon was there and when he had arrived. Evidently, Mrs. Daniels went straight home and did it."

"How?" Why ask that? He didn't want to know.

"She hung herself with some nylon hose."

"Hung. Jesus."

"I just came by to tell you," Ted said. "I'm on my way to Lake Martin, over in Alabama. Want to come along? I hear the fishing is great."

Mechanically, Kyle rejoined, "No. You don't have any appointments next week?"

"No. I told you three weeks ago I was holding this week for my vacation. Don't you remember?"

"Oh, yes, I do now." He didn't though. He couldn't remember the subject ever arising.

"You aren't going to be in much shape for work this week, Kyle. Come with me."

"No." With more resolution in his voice, he repeated, "No! I have some research to do."

"Okeedoakee." Ted shrugged. "I'll bring you back some fish, if I catch any."

"Thanks, Ted."

"See you next weekend."

Kyle dressed as quickly as he could. He drove through the sparse Sunday traffic to the clinic and pulled in beside Betty's battered Chevrolet.

Betty was sitting in the anteroom.

"Where's Damon?"

"Asleep," Betty said.

"Everything all right?" Kyle questioned.

"Yes. How about you?"

"I messed up, Betty."

"You're not God, Kyle. You can't possibly know everything."

"I should have seen the extent of her trauma. I should have known my patient's capabilities and weaknesses. I really messed up on this one."

"Kyle, you see what you're doing to yourself, surely. It doesn't take a psychiatrist to see that. You must know it's ridiculous to suffer even an iota of recrimination over this.

224

It just—happened. That's all."

She saw she had not assuaged him. She also saw it was fruitless to try.

"I'm going to kill that sweven," Kyle said. "If there's such a thing as murdering a nonentity, I'm going to do it."

"Good," Betty said.

"I've been lenient with him up to now."

"The sweven?"

"Yes. I've been lenient, but now I won't give that sonofabitch a chance."

It startled Betty to hear Kyle speak this way. Or, perhaps it was the utterly cold, almost expressionless look in his eyes.

"Would you like a drink?" Kyle asked. His change of tone caught Betty off guard.

"I'm on duty, Kyle."

"You've been here since yesterday morning?"

"Yes. I couldn't reach that college kid, whatsisname? Probably out doing what college kids do on weekends. Anyway I'm charging you time and a half for it and I need the money."

Kyle grinned. "In which case, suffer as I drink alone, Nurse Snider."

She took his arm and they stood in Kyle's office, his finger on the light switch, waiting for the fluorescents to catch up and flicker bright.

"I like you, Kyle," Betty said softly.

Kyle laughed. "I like you, Betty. Very much."

"That's important," Betty said, seriously. "I think it's more important than loving, actually."

"A good point," Kyle replied, opening the liquor drawer. "A good point psychologically, I mean. If there were more like and less love in this world, there'd probably be less violence, did you ever think about that? People who love one another are the ones who commit crimes of passion, generally. But, people who like one another suffer less emotional turmoil in their relationship. Two likers would hardly be likely to murder one another. 'Like' is a much less volatile emotion and—"

Kyle stood with his bottle in hand. He was alone. Betty had left the room.

CHAPTER 21

KYLE AND TED had decided not to tell Edward Daniels the story behind his wife's suicide. They explained only that Mrs. Daniels brought her son to the clinic because she found it impossible to control him. This covered the cause of the vicious bite on her shoulder, the melee that had obviously transpired in the bedroom, and Kyle's refusal to allow the child to attend his mother's funeral.

To tell Mr. Daniels the full truth would invite new problems for Damon. There was the very real possibility that the father would, or could, never forgive his son.

Realism and rationale often take a backseat in such traumatic events. Hence, Edward Daniels would never learn the story. Not from the psychiatrists, anyway.

The human mind is a complex study. Damon with his extrasensory powers seemed completely unaware of his mother's death. This is a protective shield the mind erects to avoid coping with the unbearable pain such realization would cause. Quite often, extremely sensitive people are keenly perceptive to the problems of strangers while blind to the mental anguish of those nearest them. It is easy to be objective where strangers are concerned. Not so easy if it is a loved one. Hippocrates had wisely ruled, a physician should not minister to his own family.

Kyle's psychoanalysis of Damon, or to be more precise, his psychotherapy, had faltered. Step one in effecting a cure is, the patient must wish to be well. An alcoholic is an alcoholic forevermore. Before he can put aside the slave of liquor, he must want to do so badly enough to gather his strength to that end. Unfortunately, the drunk often hits absolute bottom before he begins the bounce back. He allows his health to dissipate, loses his family, forfeits his career, and awakes friendless and cold in a bowery gutter one morning. If he is lucky, if he is strong enough, when there are no greater depths to which he can descend, he summons courage from some hidden reservoir and initiates the moves essential to claw his way back upward again.

Thus it had been with Damon. He was not unhappy with the status quo. He accepted his sweven, tolerated the aberrant behavior in himself, and actually began to resist Kyle's efforts to purge the problem. Damon had been, up to now, unmotivated to assist in uncovering the cause and actuating a cure. So long as Damon did not care, progress was virtually hopeless. Now, however, Kyle had the ammunition to motivate the boy. When Damon realized his mother had died, almost directly because of his actions, what would the result be? Would Damon fall into a shattered heap, beyond psychiatric help? Or, hopefully, would he rise in self-anger and demand to be well?

228

Directing, controlling this bitter resentment was what Kyle now faced. Damon had admitted to Betty that he had sexual relations with his mother. So he *knew* what had happened. Furthermore, he said "I" when referring to the event. He had not blamed it on the unknown, the sweven. It was this factor that stayed Kyle's next move. The last thing he wanted from Damon was self-guilt. He needed Damon's alliance against the sweven. Without Damon's support, the sweven would win and the child would be conquered.

"How do you intend to handle it?" Betty asked.

"I haven't decided," Kyle admitted.

They were in Betty's bed, smoking. Kyle had been plying the nurse with questions, seeking some elusive clue that might help determine a wise course of action.

"We must show Damon that sex is normal. Even sexual attraction for one's parent is normal," Kyle said. "Every boy is drawn to his mother, every girl to her father. Long before they translate this as 'sexual attraction,' they feel it. Healthy sex is an extension of love, of course. Not necessarily an expression of it, but necessarily if we love someone, we have a desire to make love to them."

"I don't remember being sexually attracted to my father," Betty said.

"Did you love him?"

"Of course!"

"Then, you were," Kyle said. "However, in most societies, copulation between family members is denied. As we mature and our drives take on the tag sex, we subdue our natural desire to make love to the parent or vice versa. It is one of the basic conflicts in every mind. This emerges in a dozen ways that a psychotic cannot explain. He may be riddled with guilt about his desires and covers it so deeply that it erupts in an unexplainable and apparently senseless murder of a stranger. The same latent guilt may produce sadism, masochism, or result in punishment of one's marital partner with the psychotic completely unaware of what is motivating him.

229

"Were you drawn to your mother?" Betty asked.

Kyle stubbed his cigarette into an ashtray on his stomach. "I just told you, it's natural."

"Not many of us think of it as natural," Betty laughed. "You actually wanted to have sex with your mother?"

Kyle put the ashtray aside, his tone peevish. "It is a fact of life, like masturbation, Betty."

"When did you recognize your desires?" Betty questioned.

"I was a perceptive child, consumed with dubiety about my thoughts and motivation from the first time I can remember. I knew it and recognized it prior to puberty."

"I'll be damned."

"You make me ill at ease discussing it," Kyle admitted. "You seem to convert the subject from clinical to personal."

"I don't mean to," Betty said seriously. "It's interesting. I learn something about myself when you talk to me like this."

After a moment of silence, Betty asked, "Did it shake you up when you realized your mother turned you on?"

"Oh, shut up," Kyle said mildly.

"I'm being serious! Did it bother you?"

"Yes."

"What did you do about it?"

"I didn't do anything about it."

"Nobody does nothing about something. Doing nothing *is* something, Kyle Burnette. Did you fantasize when you masturbated, thinking about it?"

Kyle was dressing. "I think this is enough of this," he said calmly.

"I'm sorry. Please don't leave."

"I must go to the office."

"You told me you didn't have to go to the office today, Kyle."

"I remembered some reports I was to have ready by Monday. I'd better go on, while the mood to work is on me."

She'd lost and she knew it. Betty offered to cook breakfast, but Kyle declined. He completed his toilet in silence and with a terse good-bye departed.

"Let's see," Kyle said, scanning Damon's chart, "the sum and substance of our last few weeks has been this: I talk, you pout. I try to find a way to help you and you refuse to cooperate. We seem to be at an impasse, don't we?"

"I'm sick of being in jail," Damon snapped.

"This is not a jail, Damon. Walls do not a prison make. Or, haven't you reached that quotation in your literature, yet?"

"Piss on you."

"Well, let me tell you, young man, you're going to be here or someplace like this, for a very long time. Is that clear? Until the day you get smart, you can wallow in your stupidity if you wish. But make no mistake, it's stupidity!"

"You aren't helping me!" Damon shouted.

"You aren't helping yourself, Damon."

"You're a stinking doctor!"

"I don't think you're in a position to judge," Kyle retorted. "I might add, you're a lousy patient."

"I want out of this goddamned prison, goddamn you."

"To do what? To go where? Run and play? Travel? Or to watch TV and read? That's what you do here, watch TV and read. This is a 'prison' only because you insist it is."

"I want to see my mommy." Sullen. "Why doesn't she come to see me anymore?"

Damon looked up at Kyle through thick brows. "It's because she hates me now, isn't it?"

"Nobody hates you."

"I do."

"You do what?"

"I hate me."

At last. Kyle's voice softened in tone. "Why do you hate yourself?"

"You know why."

"I want to hear you say it."

231

"I hate myself because—" Damon's voice choked and his head dropped. Perspiration glistened on his forehead.

"I'm waiting."

"I hate you!" Damon shrieked.

"I don't hate you," Kyle said evenly.

"I hate you! I hate you!"

"Sit down, Damon."

"Shut up, you goddamned queer!"

"Is that you, Damon? Or is that the sweven talking?"

"It's me all right."

"Really? It sounded like something the sweven once said to me. Or is the sweven just you, with another name?"

Damon lunged at the desk, teeth exposed. "I hate your goddamned guts! I want out of here!"

Kyle found himself standing, leaning across the desk, as he responded in kind, "Then get smart. Get smart! Stop blaming everybody else for your problems and let's see if we can start straightening some of them out!" ·

"I don't blame everybody else."

"Who do you blame for the thing with your mother?"

Damon stepped back as though Kyle had slapped him.

"You do hate me," Damon seethed.

"I do not hate you."

"You hate me, goddamn you! You're trying to make me feel bad for something that wasn't my fault!"

"Ah, who are we blaming, then?"

"Goddamn you, you goddamned queer doctor!"

"Was it you?" Kyle shouted.

"Yes!" Damon screamed. "Yes! It was me!"

"Not somebody else? Not the sweven?"

"No!" Damon's face was starkly pale despite the tears pouring down his cheeks.

"I don't believe that!" Kyle railed.

"You're a stupid doctor!"

"I don't believe that you think it was you, either, Damon."

"It was! It was—oh—" Damon wrapped both arms across his stomach and bent forward as though cramping.

232

"It was *not* you, Damon," Kyle said with finality.

"It was. I couldn't help it."

"Precisely. It was not you."

"It was—it was me."

"I can prove it was not you," Kyle said gently.

Damon's sobs racked his body with wretching force.

"It was something else, Damon. It was this thing we call your sweven. Whatever your sweven may be, he is not you. He is something separate and apart. It's like another person altogether. He used your body. Have you noticed, it is always him that uses you? I don't believe I have ever seen you use him. If you used him, then I could believe it was you that did what happened to your mother."

"I couldn't help it."

"I realize that. So does your mother. You should realize that, also. It could not be helped because it was somebody, something beyond your control. Whatever it was, it was not you."

"I want him dead."

"Who?" Kyle covered his mounting excitement.

"I want the sweven dead."

"So do I," Kyle agreed emphatically.

"How?" Damon's puffed eyes lifted.

"I'm not sure, yet. But together we can kill him. We will kill him."

Damon sank to the floor, hands covering his face, crying. It was a different sound he now made. It was a weeping of frustration mingled with relief. Kyle circled his desk and lifted Damon by the shoulders, helping the boy to rise. He placed Damon in a chair and knelt at the boy's side.

"Listen to me, Damon. Nothing is more important to me than finding out about this sweven and eliminating it. I lie awake nights thinking about it. I have studied every book I could find, delved into every possibility. I have learned a great deal about it, I can tell you that."

"What is he?"

"If I knew that," Kyle replied, "I would be armed to defeat him this minute."

"How can we find out?"

We. Kyle put a hand on Damon's arm.

"By hunting him down," Kyle whispered. "By working together we'll hunt him down and we will eliminate him."

"But how?"

"Together, Damon. Together. As for the system, the method, that we must discover together, too. I'm willing if you are."

"Please," Damon implored, "I want to see my mommy. I want to tell her I'm sorry."

"She knows that."

"Please?"

There was no way to turn. Damon forced Kyle's mind to the thought when Kyle would have preferred a more stable moment. Before Kyle could formulate an approach, form the words, Damon's eyes widened and he jolted, stiffened, withdrawing his arm from Kyle's hand. The boy stared straight ahead, his face stricken with horror, his tongue moving in an open mouth, but the lips ovate.

A thin, high-pitched wail rose from Damon's throat. When Kyle reached for him, Damon slapped away the doctor's hand and then sat, the outflung hand suspended in midair, fingers crooked and frozen. Again the piercing sound came.

"I want to hold you, Damon."

Louder, the same cry.

"Please let me hold you, Damon."

Seeing that this was not possible, Kyle went to his desk communicator to call for a sedative.

"Ask Dr. Drinkwater to come in, please."

His eye had left Damon only an instant. When he looked at the boy again, Kyle felt an electric shiver of shock trace his back and arms. Damon had seized his cheeks in both hands and had torn at his eyes. Blood flooded the ocular openings and Damon was smashing himself with both fists, tearing at his ears. As Kyle raced around the desk, Damon sank his teeth into his own forearm and Kyle heard a nauseating crunch of molar against bone and flesh.

234

"Nurse!"

Damon threw Kyle aside with a strength borne of madness. "Nurse! Quickly!"

When she entered the door, the woman gasped and tears jumped into her eyes. "Oh, my God, Doctor—"

Kyle knocked away Damon's free arm, trying to pin it as blood rose around the boy's mouth, his own teeth embedded in his other arm.

"Get help," Kyle said, "hurry!"

Damon shook his head, like a mongrel with a rag between its fangs, tearing the meat from his arm. "Damon! Damon! Let go, Damon!"

Ted Drinkwater was on the boy from the other side now. He reached up under Damon's chin and tried to staunch the flow of blood to the brain, causing the boy to faint.

"Get something to knock him out, Nurse," Ted commanded, "three hundred cc's of Pentothal. Hurry!" Then, to Kyle, "Get him on the floor. My hand is slipping on the blood."

They had to pin him with body weight.

"Hold his head so he can't tear himself that way," Ted ordered.

"Here, Doctor." The nurse held out a syringe. "Shall I cleanse his arm?"

"Fuck the cleansing. Shoot him!" Ted groped for the jugular vein, his fingers slippery. "If I could just get hold of—Kyle, hold his head back. Get me a towel, somebody!"

"Oh, God!" The nurse was sobbing, but still her actions were the deliberate ones of a professional nurse.

"I missed the vein," she said.

"Goddamn! He's strong!" Ted was shivering from the strain, still groping for those lifelines to the brain.

"There!" the nurse rasped. "Got it. Easy, easy."

An unbelievable sucking sound preceded the separation of flesh from arm and Damon's head was shoved free by Ted's weight as the torn arm was forced to the floor.

A scream of sheer agony split the air and Damon's open mouth and bloodied face gave him an appearance none of them would ever forget. Ted held the boy's head down by the hair. The nurse was already working on the chewed arm. Two associate doctors from down the hall had arrived and between the four of them they had Damon where he could not move.

"How much do you think I should give him of this?" the nurse asked.

"Whatever it takes," Ted replied.

The boy began to relax. Steel taut sinews and muscles gave way as the drug took effect. Still, they held him, lifted him still holding, and got him down the hall to his room.

"That's a nasty wound," Ted said, dressing it. Kyle sat on a chair across the room, spent, smoking a cigarette someone had given him.

"What happened?" Ted asked finally.

"He found out about his mother. Read my mind."

Ted nodded, features grim.

"Maybe I ought to come off this case, Ted."

"This is not the time to make that decision," Ted said sharply.

With the rebuke, Kyle left the room. He closed his office door behind himself and stood watching an orderly cleaning the chair and floor. Someone bumped him from behind, trying to enter, and Kyle numbly stepped aside. Betty Snider came in, took his arm, and led him out. Without a word, they walked the length of the hall, past hushed patients awaiting appointments and out into the sunshine.

"Get in," Betty said, directing him to her automobile.

They drove in silence to Kyle's apartment. Betty held his arm as they made their way into the elevator and then down the passage to his door.

"Give me your key."

He did so.

Inside, Betty ran a tub of hot water, forced four Bufferin on him, and then undressed him. He sank into the tepid water with a soblike expulsion of air, much as a child makes after a long, hard cry.

"Oh, Jesus," Kyle said, closing his eyes.

236

Betty was in the bedroom turning back the covers. He heard her practiced slap at the sheets to smooth them.

She bathed him as he lay unresisting. She lifted first an arm, then a leg. She leaned him forward and washed his back with firm, relaxing strokes. Cupping water between her hands, she rinsed him, drained the tub and toweled him dry. Once in bed, she gave him a rubdown from insteps to scalp, using oil followed by diluted alcohol. He succumbed to sleep and there she remained until the following morning.

CHAPTER 22

TED DRINKWATER settled into a chair facing Kyle's desk and lit a cigarette. Betty Snider had just left the room with transcriptions which must now be typed and placed in Damon's file.

"How's it coming, Kyle?"

"Better."

"Damon cooperating?"

"He wants to, anyway."

"That's the first step."

Kyle poured two drinks. "He now feels we have a common adversary in the sweven."

239

"Excellent!"

"Yes," Kyle agreed, "it is."

"Going back to narcosynthesis?" Ted asked, sipping Scotch.

"Not yet. I'm afraid Damon isn't stable enough to handle it afterward. I want to be absolutely sure he blames the sweven and not himself for what happened to his mother. However, today we did talk about the sweven and it was all in the third person. 'He' and not 'I.'"

"Good, good," Ted said. He extended long legs, crossing them at the ankles, slumped low on his coccyx.

"Ted, what do you think of Betty Snider staying with Damon at night?"

"I think it'll be all right."

"She wants to do it."

"Then let her."

"She's very good."

"She's superb," Ted amended.

"Yes, really she is. But I don't want to subject her to the same thing Mrs. Daniels experienced."

"I think Betty can handle herself," Ted said.

"I suppose you're right."

"Well," Ted said, downing the last of his drink, "I'm speaking to a group of student nurses at Georgia Baptist Hospital this evening. Goddamn, I don't know how I get sucked into things like this."

"Why do you do it?"

"Oh, I don't know," Ted said, grinning. "Keeps one in touch with fresh stuff, I guess. Student nurses always feel so clinical about sex. They've been carrying those bedpans and bathing masculine privates and to them it's just so much meat. They're prime targets for subtle psychology."

"Ted, I swear."

"Banish those thoughts of condemnation, lad," Ted responded airily. "You might do well to try following my example. The worst it can get you is claps and I can cure that. Besides, after classes on the gamut of venereal diseases, student nurses are the best-douched dolls around.

Disgustingly healthy girls. Balanced diets and all that."

"Get out of here!"

"My advice to a virile young medical man would be, seek out a student nurse and teach her anatomy," Ted expounded.

"Go give your lecture," Kyle said soberly.

"More than a lecture," Ted exulted, "it's a Drinkwater demonstration!"

Betty tucked a quilt around Damon's shoulders and sat on the side of his bed. With firm, comforting strokes, she pushed hair back from his forehead.

"Do you like me?"

"Yes I do, Damon. Very much."

"Why?"

"Oh, I don't know. Because you like me, I guess."

He smiled, but the expression was short-lived. He closed his eyes and submitted to a shuddering sigh.

Moments later, he mumbled, "I'm glad you like me."

"Well I do," Betty acknowledged, still massaging his head.

She moved away only after he was fully asleep, having watched for the revealing flicker from side to side which the eyes undergo as a person slips into the final stages of slumber.

To avoid a hospital atmosphere, Kyle had placed two beds in the room, neither of which would be out of place in a home. Betty normally eschewed the bed that was meant to be hers, preferring to sit up most of the night, reading. But these past few weeks she had spent much of each day here at the clinic helping Kyle during sessions with Damon. Tonight, she welcomed the prospects of sleeping.

She was taking a shower when Damon entered and stood staring at her. Betty knew at once what was about to happen.

"Let me finish bathing first," she said calmly.

He stood without speaking, the front of his pajamas extended. Betty rinsed away the suds, toweled dry, and

241

stepped out. As she wrapped her hair in a second towel, she felt his hand, hot and firm against her thigh.

"Let's go to the bed," Betty said.

She paused only to cut off a lamp, reducing the room to a half-light from the bathroom. She went to her own bed, not Damon's, and instantly he was on her.

She yielded, accepted his thrust, and met the quick climax with reassuring sounds and movements. He withdrew and she felt his tongue tracing her abdomen, going lower, lower. When he moved to cunnilingus, she was astounded at his ability. Several minutes later, she reached an orgasm. There were no words between them at any time. Totally possessed by the sweven, he turned her over and made a new approach. Betty reached between her own legs to hold him.

In all that he did, Betty participated. She was not the unwilling victim. This was a virile, aggressive, and masculine person and he knew how to do everything well. She gasped as his tongue moved from one sensitive area to another and when he had aroused her sufficiently to accept anything he desired, he changed his direction. As he pushed into this unaccustomed region, he employed a gentleness that made even this exhilarating.

When, finally, it was over, Betty lay beside the boy, kissing his forehead, holding him to her breasts, one hand cupped over his buttock.

From the depths of contentment came a whispered question. "Do you like me?"

"I like you very much."

"I couldn't help it," he said.

"It doesn't matter. It was nice."

He began to cry, muffled sobs. "It's all right," Betty soothed. "It was nice, Damon."

"I'm sorry."

"There's no reason to be sorry."

"I couldn't help it."

Her voice carried more emphasis. "It does not matter."

Small arms wrapped around her and he held her tightly.

242

"I'm glad you still like me."

"Well, I do." She rubbed the small of his back, kneading away knots of anxiety.

Later she carried him to his own bed and positioned the sheets and quilts over him. She bent low and kissed his forehead.

If she had not resisted, Betty thought, it would have ended this way.

She lit a cigarette and sat on a towel in a reclining rocker. The glow of the burning tobacco gave her warmth. Damon needed that. He needed to know that sex was not violent, or dirty, and did not necessarily alienate the partner. He was two people, she told herself; was she rationalizing? He was the child. He was the man. They both demanded, craved, required. It was not her job to separate the entities. If she was supposed to feel shame or degradation, it was not there. To the contrary, she had been satisfied. He knew precisely what she liked, how she liked it, and he had shown an ability to please her.

The unnatural acts? A stupid term to cover something so natural! She crushed her cigarette and debated going to bed. There was something nagging at the back of her mind and she could not bring it to full thought. Her desire for sleep had vanished. She lit another cigarette. Good psychology was nothing but good horse sense. Psychiatry was an educated approach to the horse. She did not profess to be a psychiatrist, but a psychologist she was! One thing she had learned in all these years around this business, everything had significance to one degree or another. It might take analysis, but the significance of everything was not to be denied. How much significance was another question.

Betty laughed softly. How significant would Kyle find it if he knew that the sweven employed Kyle's bedroom manner? That was not altogether true, of course. Kyle was by nature an inhibited man. He was no more adventurous in sex than he was in food. It had always been Betty who led the way to Chinese restaurants and wheedled Kyle into tasting new delicacies she ordered. If left to his own

243

devices, Kyle would still be eating the same fare his mother prepared for him as a child. It was Betty who maneuvered Kyle in bed. God, if you asked him to stick his weewee up your anus, he'd probably flee to the nearest closet and barricade himself! Yet, once he tried new things, Kyle usually loved it. Betty had once teased him, "Think of me as a broadening broad. If it hadn't been for me, you'd never have tasted green pepper steak, guacamole salad, or me." Kyle twisted uncomfortably at this barb, but acknowledged it, nonetheless.

Long ago Betty had decided that a person's sex life was a direct and equal barometer of his life as a whole. A person who was free and easy with sex was also free and easy in the rest of his life. If he was inhibited and unhappy in sex, so was he in other aspects of living. If he was selfish and refused to give of himself in sex, he was also possessive with material things. Betty had concluded that a wise woman best attacked such personality faults in bed. If she could alter a reclusive, introverted mate and convert him to a freer, less stagnated and more adventurous lover, she would see his entire personality transposed accordingly.

"The root to most of mankind's obsessions," Betty once told Kyle, "lies ventrally located an equidistance between the septum and the tarsus."

"That is the most painful play on words I've ever heard," Kyle protested, laughing. Then, soberly, "And true."

Was she rationalizing? If so, it was working. Betty viewed her experience with Damon as an extension of her philosophy. Her psychiatric horse sense, if you will. In her mind, she had just performed an essential service with therapeutic value. Needless to say, this would remain a confidence between patient and nurse. Kyle Burnette would vehemently protest this breach in professional ethics. He would remove her from the case if he ever found out. She would never find another job in this line of work, either. But Damon, what of Damon? That fantastic and unbelievable person, he needed her. Kyle would never know. Nobody would know but Betty and her patient.

Kyle snuggled nearer and his hand traced Betty's leg. After a few minutes of this, he asked, "What's wrong?"

"Nothing."

"You're sure?"

"Sure I'm sure," Betty said. "Why do you ask?"

"You seem preoccupied."

Betty realized her muscles had tensed at his touch. "I was thinking about Damon."

"What about him?"

"I guess I was worrying, without realizing it. I was thinking about the new man you hired, wondering if Damon would like him."

Kyle rose up on one elbow and looked at her. "Betty, you can't work seven days a week."

"I don't see why not. I'm not charging overtime."

"That wasn't my consideration," Kyle said hotly.

"Then what difference does it make? I told you I wanted to stay with Damon every night."

Kyle turned and sat up, his back to her. "We've been over this half a dozen times, Betty."

Betty rolled away from him, lying on her side staring at the bedroom wall. The cold silence passed and Kyle finally sighed and rounded the bed to sit beside her, his hand on her shoulder. "Betty?"

"What?"

"Let's not fight over Damon. I would like to turn my brain to other things. We both need to do that."

"To keep our perspective," Betty said.

"Yes, that. But too, I want to think about you. I want you to think about me."

"For the moment."

His hand pulled away. "Now what does that mean?"

"Just what I said," Betty declared. "If you want to make love, if it suits you to spare a microsecond of thought toward that end, you can't understand why *I'm* still concerned about Damon. However, for the other thirteen hundred thirty-nine minutes in a day, I can't get your attention long enough to tell you your fly is unzipped."

"I'm sorry."

"Oh, to hell with it," Betty said. "Let's make love."

As he returned to his side of the bed, Betty spoke impetuously, "Let's do something different, Kyle."

"Like what?"

Betty sat up, pushing her pillow against the headboard. "A different position."

Kyle laughed. "I'm very partial to the ones we've always employed," he said.

"What is the most exciting thing you can think of that you've never done?" Betty questioned, her voice as intense as her expression.

"I guess I've done everything that excites me."

"That's not true and you know it," Betty countered.

"You seem very sure of that," Kyle said. He was no longer smiling, sensing more to this than met the eye.

"Kyle," Betty urged, "do you masturbate?"

"Betty, what's come over you?"

"Do you masturbate?"

Kyle's brows knitted and he twisted his mouth at the corner, as he always did when disturbed. "As a child—"

"Not as a child!" Betty snapped. "I want to know if you masturbate now."

"Look, Betty, let's forget it, all right? I'm in no mood to play analysand for an amateur psychoanalyst tonight."

Betty snorted and looked away. Her action was too near that of derision.

"I don't know what's eating you," Kyle said. "But allow me to pass." He began putting on his clothes.

"Go ahead, Kyle," Betty said, her voice low, "get dressed and run. That's generally how you end these conversations."

"This is not a conversation," Kyle said sharply, "it's a debate. I'm not sure of the resolution, but apparently it revolves around my virility, performance, or sexual compatibility."

"If that's too close to home," Betty retorted, "let's be more academic. Also, since you question my amateur status at psychoanalysis, give me your professional opinion. If a patient runs from a problem, your job is to bring him to grips with that problem and thereby effect a resolution to it, right?"

Kyle continued dressing.

"Do you think the sweven is evil?" Betty asked.

"What has that to do with anything we're discussing?"

"Are you capable of giving a straight answer, goddamn it?" Betty exploded. "This is a debate because you refuse to enter into a conversation."

Kyle turned, face red. "I think the sweven is a nonentity. Therefore, how can it be evil, per se?"

"You mean that the sweven has no body, soul, or existence as such."

"That's right."

Betty smiled, wrapping her arms around her knees. "Point one," she said. "If that is so, he must surely be Damon's alter ego."

"More than likely."

"Where does he pick up his knowledge? Damon's experiences are too limited to be the source."

"Damon picks up the thoughts and emotions of those around him and transmits, or interprets them through the sweven."

"I accept that," Betty acceded.

"That's very nice of you," Kyle said evenly.

"Point two," Betty continued. "Is everybody around Damon evil?"

"Betty, what's the matter?" Kyle asked, more gently.

"Don't pull that professional crap on me," Betty seethed. "I'm Betty and you're Kyle and this isn't a couch. Give me your opinion: are we all evil?"

"I wouldn't say so."

"Where does the sweven get evil thoughts?"

"Thoughts which are never turned to action are not generally considered evil as such," Kyle said. "We might have a fantasy in which we rape our mother, or a child, but this is an action we'll never take."

"Now we're getting somewhere," Betty gloated. "Okay, now, Kyle, this is important to me. It may be important to you. I want you to answer me and not evade the question. Do you masturbate now, as an adult?"

"Masturbation is probably the most misunderstood function of the human psyche," Kyle expounded. "People suffer guilt and apprehension over it. They assume they'll grow up one day and never do it again, thereby giving the act a tag of adolescence, which is absurd. People masturbate for as long as they live. For many people, such as the elderly, or physically deformed, or a prison inmate, it is their only means of sexual gratification."

"I assume," Betty said, "that means you do masturbate."

"This has the tenor of a fourth-grade outhouse chat," Kyle said testily.

"Now that we have given masturbation a medically acknowledged respectability," Betty continued, "let's go to point three. What do you think about when you masturbate?"

"Betty, would you mind getting to the point?"

"We're getting there," Betty said. "Please answer the question: what do you think about when you masturbate?"

"Me."

"That's an evasion," Betty declared. "Okay, so it's hard for you to discuss your fantasies. You're a psychiatrist, you know that to avoid discussing it is to elevate a fantasy to a level higher than it deserves."

"Where in God's name have you picked up your ideas on psychiatry?"

"Like the sweven," Betty said, "from everybody around me. I'll tell you what I think about when I masturbate."

"Betty, if you'd like an appointment—"

"If you wouldn't be such a smart mouth, we might get to the bottom of this!"

"All right," he yielded coldly. "I'm dying to hear about your fantasies."

"I fantasize that I'm being assaulted by several men, one of whom is black."

248

"Am I supposed to be shocked or enlightened?" Kyle asked.

"Neither. Fantasies are just fantasies. They are not important and generally they're dull if they aren't your own."

"That's the truest statement you've made thus far. Believe me, they are unimportant."

"Unless," Betty said, "we find it impossible to examine them because we harbor some Victorian attitude about the morality of thoughts. Or, unless the fantasy is so crucial to us that facing it is impossible. Then they become important, don't they?"

"That's reasonably correct."

"Final point," Betty said gently, "what do you think about when you masturbate? Tell me the deepest, darkest fantasy you have, Kyle."

"Let's see." Kyle spoke with a mock tone of acquiescence designed to let Betty know the truth was not forthcoming.

"Forget it," Betty said abruptly.

"No," Kyle insisted, "you asked and I am going to tell you."

"No you won't," Betty stated, throwing back the covers.

"You mean I won't tell the truth."

"That's right."

"Why should I?" Kyle demanded. "This is a ridiculous parlor game. It serves no constructive purpose and it has the stink of an orgy to it."

"Does an orgy stink?" Betty mused, halting at the bathroom door. "Yes, I suppose it would."

"If you can give me one good reason for pursuing this ludicrous conversation, I'll try to be more serious," Kyle said.

Betty's head reappeared at the bathroom door. "Oh, it's serious," she said. "Give me a deduction, Doctor. The patient is evasive and incapable of approaching the subject without stress."

CHAPTER 23

"I'M SCARED," Damon cried.

"Don't be," Betty said, bathing his arm with alcohol, preparing for an injection.

"I don't want to do this," Damon protested.

"It will be all right, Damon," Kyle said.

"I don't want him to come out!"

Damon's fingers dripped perspiration as Betty secured a tourniquet. "Make a fist, Damon. Open and close your hand."

Damon groaned, eyes wild. "Oh, Dr. Burnette, please—"

Damon's voice rose as Betty approached him with the needle. "Please don't let him out yet. Let's wait! Please, let's do it tomorrow!"

Pentothal entered the blood steam and Damon's words slurred, his final sentence trailing off to a mumble.

"Count backwards for me, Damon. Ten, nine, eight, seven, six—"

Dutifully, Damon began and his chest heaved a final sigh of resistance.

"Damon, how do you feel?"

"Not too good."

"You seem to be all right. What's wrong?"

"I'm afraid."

"There's no reason to be afraid. You're with friends and we're watching over you. You are comfortable and a little sleepy but everything is all right. Do you understand?"

"Yes."

"You are going to sleep, Damon," Kyle said, his voice soft and reassuring. "It will be a sleep without dreams. When you awaken, you will remember nothing, because you slept so soundly. You will feel good, when you awaken. You will be rested and refreshed. Isn't that right?"

"Yes."

"Now, Damon, as you sleep, I will ask you questions. You will answer my questions. We will talk about the sweven."

"No!"

"It's all right. Remember, we are watching over you. You are deeply asleep and will remember nothing."

"Go away, Physician!" That shockingly deep voice.

"I have no desire to speak to you," Kyle said evenly.

Damon's eyes fluttered and opened, the pupils contracting to pinpoints, face twisted.

"Get away, queer."

"Tell me what happened, Damon. Tell me about the night you had the fight with your mother."

Damon's head lifted from the pillow, rotating like a wheel on a raised axle until he was staring at the psychiatrist.

252

"Her panties had brown lace, Physician."

Kyle's voice was sharp. "I told you, I have no need to speak with you!"

"I put them on my head, the brown panties." The voice came as though expelled through liquid. It had a mocking quality.

"You are vulgar," Kyle said. "Let me speak to Damon."

"More vulgar than thee?" Taunting.

Betty had drawn away involuntarily, pressed against the back of her chair, observing. Kyle was face to face with the twisted countenance of the boy.

"Look not in my eyes for fear," the voice warned.

"I refuse to talk to you," Kyle announced.

"You are afraid to talk to me."

"I have no fear of you," Kyle responded.

"Look not in my eyes for fear—"

"Betty," Kyle said, "you may call the orderly now. I think we are through with this session."

"I am not your slave to dismiss," the voice roared.

"That's where you are wrong," Kyle rejoined mildly. "You are my prisoner."

"You are a fool!"

"You are in this boy's mind and his body is in my clinic," Kyle stated. "Tell me you are not my prisoner. I may do with you as I wish."

A long pause. Damon was sitting up now, legs over the side of the couch. His shoulders were hunched, head withdrawn, gurgling with every breath, his body tense and ominously aggressive. It was this visage that made his next statement so shocking, so serenely did the sweven speak:

"That won't work."

"What won't work?"

"Your plan to incarcerate me."

"It is working."

"I am as free as you."

"We'll see who walks out of here," Kyle said.

"Indeed!"

"You are a phantom," Kyle snapped.

"You are illiterate," the voice sneered.

253

"You are no more real than the air," Kyle said. "Like a parasite, you could not exist without the thoughts of those around you."

"Ahh, yes. Ah, yes! I am winning. It will not be long now, Dr. Kyle Burnette."

"You are defeated," Kyle corrected. "But you are right, it won't be long now."

"I put her panties on my head, Doctor."

"Betty, call the orderly, please." Kyle walked to his desk.

"My ears went through the leg holes."

"Also," Kyle continued his instructions to Betty, who was unmoving, "have someone clean Damon's room. I noticed dust on the windowsills when I was in there this morning."

"Goddamned hypocrite!" the sweven thundered.

"I must file these papers, too," Kyle said, speaking as though alone.

"Look not in my eyes for fear—" the voice warned.

Kyle looked right past the form now standing across from his desk. "Have you made plans for lunch, Betty?"

"I am winning, Physician."

"We could eat at the Regency, if you like. I know you're tired of eating at the same place."

"I *am* winning!" Damon circled the desk in a crouch, his gnomelike body postured. He took each step with a jerky, exaggerated motion like a strutting wrestler before a crowd. "I put her panties on my head, Physician. Who was there to see? She did not see. What can be wrong with that?"

"Betty, please don't just sit there. Call an orderly."

"Who do you see, queer?" the voice jeered. "Whose face do you see? Do you think you fool me, Physician? Fool!"

"Betty!" Kyle's tone was sharper. "Call the orderly."

Numbly, Betty left. A mirthless sound of laughter followed her. She stood a few seconds, back to Kyle's office door, facing the anteroom full of waiting patients. They were staring at her.

"Call an orderly for Dr. Burnette," Betty said to the receptionist.

254

Ted Drinkwater passed Betty, his hospital smock still on, but unsnapped. "How goes it, Luscious?"

"Ted!"

"Yes?"

"May I see you a moment?"

"Sure. Come in."

In Ted's office, Betty submitted to the overpowering compulsion to shiver.

"Something wrong?" Ted inquired.

"Ted, I know I'm breaching professional ethics, but I must say this."

"Shoot, Babe."

"Have you observed Kyle during abreaction with Damon recently?"

"Not in a while, no."

"Ted, Kyle is acting—strangely. I think he's getting too close to his case. Yes, that's it. He's not as objective as he needs to be anymore."

The pleasant expression on Ted's face was gone. She had said too much.

"I'm sorry," Betty said.

"Forget it."

"Thank you, Ted."

"Right, Babe."

She returned to help the orderly. Damon was lying on the couch, mumbling incoherently. Kyle was still behind his desk, shuffling papers, making busy motions.

"How about lunch?" Kyle asked, not looking up.

"I don't think so, Kyle. I'm tired. I'd better go on home and get some sleep before tonight."

"Good idea. I was thinking of skipping lunch, anyway. I've gained a few pounds recently."

Damon was on a stretcher and they lifted him to carry him to his room.

"Sleep well, Damon," Kyle said pleasantly.

As they removed the boy, Kyle pushed a button on his desk communicator. "I'm ready for my next appointment."

"You have no other patients today, Doctor."

255

"Oh?" Kyle smiled at Betty. "Thank you," he said to the receptionist.

"I guess I'll go, Kyle."

"Hold on, I'll drive you home."

"No. Really, I want to rest. I'll see you tomorrow."

Kyle stared at her quizzically, then smiled and shrugged. "As you wish," he said.

Betty drove toward the Atlanta library, her head reeling. Her hands were moist on the steering wheel. She had a queasy uneasiness in her stomach, like motion sickness. She was tempted to go to her apartment, take a scalding bath, and sleep. She could call in and get a replacement for tonight. She could. But she wouldn't.

Betty approached the librarian, a woman with a tic in her right cheek, and said, "I want the complete works of various poets. Could you help me?"

"I think so. What do you need?"

"I'm not sure, really. I'm looking for a certain poem. A quotation, actually."

"Oh, dear, dear," the librarian twitched. "That's a mite out of my line, quotations. Now, if it were Greek literature—is the quotation Greek by chance?"

"I don't think so."

"Nobody quotes Greek. Nobody. I should have majored in English, you know. Follow me, dear. English is where the quotes are. Shakespeare. They used to quote French, but that's old-fashioned now. Shakespeare hangs right in there." She smiled apologetically regarding her last statement, explaining, "Vernacular of the day: 'hangs right in there.' I try to stay abreast of idioms. They are the idiosyncrasies of the language which give it flavor and body, do they not? 'Hangs right in there,' sounds rather pleasant, doesn't it? A librarian is more than a keeper of books, you know; she's a translator of the past, a communicator for dead languages and deceased minds, all with their own special idioms, don't you see? Turn here, dear."

256

They turned down a narrow aisle and paused at a small private elevator. The librarian, twitching and talking in a professionally hushed conspiratorial tone, gave Betty a brief course in the evolutions of languages as they rode up two floors. Betty was introduced to a woman who "is our expert on the poets et al."

She could be completely wrong, Betty told herself. This might be wild supposition on her part. She was *not* a psychiatrist! Oh, please, God. Please let her be wrong.

"Whattayasay," Ted said, his head through Kyle's office door. "Still here I see."

"Yes. I had some reports to finish."

"Come in?" Ted inquired.

"Of course; want a drink?"

"Yeah," Ted said. "Why not. Jesus, what a day. Remember that guy with the *aboiement*? The one that barked like a dog? Did you ever hear him? Big guy. Pekingese bark."

"No. But you told me about him."

"Yeah, well, he's not barking anymore."

"Good."

"Good, yeah." Ted took his drink. "Thanks."

"What's on your mind?" Kyle asked.

"Oh, this and that. Do I look like something is on my mind?"

"Anytime you ask for permission to enter my office after hours, you have something on your mind," Kyle countered.

"Got me pegged."

"So, what is it?"

"Evasive action," Ted admitted. "Got a cigarette?"

The cigarette lit, Ted sat back and gazed at Kyle with a detachment both of them knew was a cover.

"How's it going with Damon?" Ted questioned

"Same as yesterday."

"Yeah. Well. Listen, Kyle—"

"Yes?"

"Can we talk business a few minutes?"

"If that's what's on your mind, Ted."

"It is, really. Have you been over the books recently?"

"No. I never do, you know. That's your department."

"Right. Well, you know, our revenue is up this year over last. It looks like we'll have the clinic paid for and we'll be a debt-free organization."

Kyle nodded, waiting.

"That's good, isn't it?" Ted said.

"Yes, it is."

"One thing's kinda bothering me, though," Ted said.

"I can see that it is, Ted."

"Well, goddamn it," Ted snapped, "I'm getting there!"

"I wish you would."

"Kyle, have you looked at your case load lately?"

"I see," Kyle said. "I'm not pulling my share."

"Man, you know you aren't," Ted replied, more gently. "You don't have but one patient, anymore."

"I see."

"Listen, Kyle, it's more than just the income factor. Matter of fact, if it were just the income, I wouldn't say a word. Jesus, I don't want to be a professional avunculate, but sometimes an outside opinion helps a guy see something he's having difficulty seeing alone. Know what I mean?"

"Go ahead, Ted."

Ted's troubled gaze dropped to his drink and he clutched the glass between both hands, as though warming it. "To hell with it," he said, softly.

"No, not to hell with it," Kyle demanded. "Get it off your chest."

"Okay, I will." Ted sat upright, leaning forward. "Kyle, you're spending a lot of time on Damon's case. Now, I'm not really bitching about the reduced income as a result. I want that clear."

"It's clear," Kyle said, his voice level.

"I know Damon is far more exciting than Mrs. Gotrocks and her compulsive obesity. I can see why you would devote so much time to Damon. Jesus, who wouldn't? If he

258

were my case, I'd probably be dwelling on it every minute, too. But, that may be the wrong approach, old pal."

Kyle's lips pulled at the corners and he held his drink unsipped.

"Maybe you're too close to it, Kyle," Ted said.

"I don't think so."

"That's important! That you don't think so. You certainly would know, better than anybody else."

"I certainly don't think so."

"Okay."

"As for the reduced income, I can't argue with that. We'll consider me on a leave of absence. I'll stop drawing my share of income out of the business. I think I have vacation time and sick leave accrued, don't I?"

Wearily, Ted nodded.

"So, there can be no gripe about my devotion to Damon's case, if we do that, right?"

"Right. But that isn't necessary. I was afraid you'd react like this and I probably shouldn't have brought it up."

"Correct me if I'm wrong," Kyle said, his voice slightly less than calm, "you're really telling me I'm slipping on this case, aren't you?"

"I don't know, Kyle. You tell me."

"I've got that sonofabitch on the run!" Kyle snapped. "I've got him right where I want him now."

"Got who?"

"The sweven, Ted! That bastard is running scared!"

Ted's eyes narrowed. "You'll have to be more explicit, Kyle. I'm not following this."

"Listen to me, Ted." Kyle rounded his desk and sat in a chair beside his associate. "Damon was uncooperative, recalcitrant, openly rebellious a few weeks back. I had reached the end of my rope. I'd tried every approach I knew to isolate this thing. Then, after what happened to his mother, I had it! Goddamn had it! Don't you see?"

"I'm afraid not."

"Damon wants to kill the bastard as much as I do," Kyle said, hands out, palms up. "It's as clear as daylight, Ted. For

259

the first time, Damon is afraid of his alter ego, if that's what it is. He *wants* to be cured. He wants to catch that elusive personality that controls him and expunge it."

"All right," Ted agreed, "we both know that's an essential move to resolve the case."

"Now," Kyle's voice lowered, "I've got him. He's caught between the boy who loathes him and me. He's my prisoner."

"Your prisoner."

"Goddamned right. My prisoner. As long as I keep Damon here, the sweven isn't going anyplace."

"How long do you think that will be, Kyle?"

"Who knows, for God's sake?"

"In your opinion, will Damon have to be institutionalized?"

"So long as his behavior is aberrant, of course."

"But shutting him up won't cure him, Kyle. It merely contains him."

"The sweven won't put up with it, though," Kyle said.

"What the hell can he do about it?" Ted questioned. "He can't pack his bags and move out in search of another body!"

"He'll have to meet me head-on, Ted."

"Kyle—" Ted rose and walked to the desk, placing his drink on a paper there. "Kyle, you are one of the most brilliant psychotherapists I know. I can't ever remember a time when I questioned your approach to a case. But I have my doubts on this one, I sure do."

"You haven't been following it," Kyle said defensively.

"That's not altogether true," Ted said. "I meet with von Ulbricht once a week. We go over Damon's charts. I monitor Damon's physical changes. Admittedly, I haven't sat in on the sessions with him, but I've been right here all along."

"You're telling me I'm wrong."

"No, I can't do that unless I know I'm right, can I?"

"Then goddamn it, what are you saying?"

"I'm saying, I think you're losing your objectivity with

this case, Kyle. You're up to your ass in cordwood and can't see the forest."

"I don't buy that."

"All right. Sorry I interfered. Like I said, sometimes a third party can see things the party of the first part and the party of the second part can't see."

"Who is the party of the second part?" Kyle demanded.

"The sweven, I suppose. It seems to be a contest between you and this id, ego, or whatever it is."

"I feel rather personal about it, I admit that."

"Too personal, perhaps?"

"I don't think so, Ted."

"That's all that counts, old buddy."

"Hey, Ted." Kyle stopped him at the door. "Thanks for understanding."

Ted laughed shortly. "I'm not really sure I do."

Kyle used his key to enter Betty's apartment. He found her sitting in bed, surrounded by books. She looked at him without greeting. Kyle lifted a thick tome and studied it.

"The complete works of Tennyson. I didn't know you liked poetry."

"Oh, yes," Betty said. "I wrote it, when I was in college. I took up nursing when I discovered poets starve by meters."

He selected a second book and leafed through the pages. "I never learned to appreciate poetry."

"That's too bad," Betty remarked, laying her book aside and getting out of bed.

"It's all so pedantically contrived," Kyle mused. "If a person can't understand it, why write it? Most of it we studied in school was a jumble of words that may or may not rhyme and with no meaning. I always liked poems that made sense, told a story."

"Such as what?" Betty asked, watching him closely.

"Oh, E. E. Cummings, for example. His stuff rhymes and it has something to say. I always considered him deeper than these people who cover their inability to rhyme with confusing stuff they excuse as 'prose.'"

261

"Can you quote any of Cummings?" Betty queried.

"No. Oh, hell no! I can't remember a single line."

"He was your favorite poet?"

"Not really," Kyle said, tossing the book back on Betty's bed. "I don't guess I have a favorite where poetry is concerned."

"You must have enjoyed somebody's work; you obviously enjoyed Cummings."

"I don't know. The stuff bores me. Listen, would you like to have dinner with me? I can get the new fellow to stand in for you at the clinic tonight."

"That's a lot of trouble, Kyle. I'll just go on in."

"No trouble. I took the liberty of calling him already. He agreed. He's approaching semester examinations and needs the enforced study, he says."

"I am exhausted," Betty acquiesced. "Fine."

As Kyle made a telephone call from the living room, Betty pawed through the books on her bed until she found one titled *Contemporary Poems*. She consulted the index and found Cummings. Two pages. She marked the selections and placed the book in her bedside table drawer to read later.

CHAPTER 24

KYLE WAS irritated. Betty had pushed him into agreeing that Damon needed a break from the confinement of the clinic. She had maneuvered him into a dinner for the three of them, at Kyle's apartment, when Kyle insisted that the boy could not be allowed the freedom of several other diversions. He had unconditionally rejected a visit to Grant's Park zoo, the Cyclorama, and the movies. Yet, he conceded that a change in surroundings and routine, no matter how brief, would probably be beneficial to the patient.

Thus, he now drove toward his apartment with Damon straddling the gearshift, wedged between Betty and himself.

"I like your car," Damon said.

"Thanks. Me too."

"Too small," Betty offered.

"It wasn't designed for family use," Kyle rebutted.

Damon laughed. Betty was riding along with her window down, having vetoed air conditioning. Unseen dust was surely covering everything.

"How fast will it go?" Damon inquired.

Kyle was surprised at the question. "Are you interested in automobiles, Damon?"

"Not really," Damon replied truthfully. Kyle mentally kicked himself. The boy was merely being sociable and, like an idiot, Kyle had terminated the conversation with a piercing query.

"I didn't buy it for speed," Kyle remarked, trying to rekindle the topic.

"I know."

Kyle sighed heavily and turned his attention to traffic. He had made a lot of stupid blunders lately and this goddamned dinner idea was one of them. He realized Damon was there and cut off the thought.

"What's for supper?" Kyle asked, raising his voice against the sound of the wind.

"Steak! What else?"

"You like steak, Damon?" Kyle asked.

"It's okay." Sullen. He'd picked up Kyle's mood.

Shit.

"I must've left my keys at the office," Kyle fumed.

"Would the house manager have a pass key?"

"Yes. But I don't need it." Kyle felt along the underside of a duct running the length of the hall and retrieved a spare key he kept for such occasions.

"Make yourselves at home," Kyle said, working at getting his mood up.

Damon entered the apartment with the sober curiosity of a high school basketball player accompanying his coach home for the first time. He strolled past the kitchen, down two steps to the sunken living room, and walked to a bookcase which covered one wall. His eyes skipped across medical and psychiatric books and periodicals. He went to the only window and gazed down at the bird's-eye view of Atlanta. When he realized Kyle was watching him, Damon

264

shrugged his shoulders and attempted a smile.

"Nice apartment," Damon said.

"Thanks."

Betty was rummaging in the kitchen, the clang of a pot and pan bespeaking the area of her activity.

"You read all those books?" Damon questioned.

"Most of them. Most of most of them. I've read a part of all of them, I guess. Research stuff for reference material more than for idle reading, most of it."

"Why did you decide on psychiatry?" Betty called, having overheard the conversation.

"Why does anybody enter any field?" Kyle countered.

"Because he likes it," Damon said.

"Not always. Not really," Kyle laughed. "I suspect most people fall into what they do. It's a rare person who plots his life and follows the plan."

"Amen, brother!" Betty hollered.

"What would you like to do, someday, Damon?" Kyle asked.

"I don't know."

"No ideas?" Kyle questioned, sitting on the sofa.

"No. I just know what I don't want to be."

"Okay," Kyle said, "what don't you want to be?"

"The usual things: fireman, policeman, stuff like that."

Betty appeared at the kitchen portal, drying her hands on a towel. "Why did you become a psychiatrist, Kyle?" she asked anew.

Noting Damon's interest, Kyle responded truthfully. "It was one of those decisions people make without really making a decision. My father was a redneck Primitive Baptist preacher. The fire and brimstone kind. He was always preaching that a person's thoughts were the mettle of the man. If you thought good thoughts, you were good. If you thought bad thoughts, you were evil. I never could agree to that. I guess that influenced me at a very impressionable age. You know how difficult it is to keep nothing but good thoughts in your brain."

Damon threw back his head and burst into laughter. Surprised at this reaction, but sympathetic to its cause,

Kyle laughed also. He had exposed a weakness to the boy. That was good. Perhaps very good, Kyle decided. He continued:

"My papa was one of those stern disciplinarians. He believed in a razor strop policy and he applied it with vengeance. He was too strict, really. I grew up confused as to what made him tick. That was another contributing factor, certainly. On the other hand, Mother was quiet, subservient, completely dominated by Papa. She seemed to exist solely for him. She dutifully made the rounds with my father, tending the sick and helping the poor. But as a child, I thought I saw brief signs of despair behind her servitude. She sang in the Sunday School choir, for example, and detested it. But she sang."

"Did you?" Damon's eyes were bright.

"I tried," Kyle laughed. "Papa thought I should and they were always missing a tenor. I didn't like it, though."

"You didn't like church at all!" Damon said.

"No," Kyle admitted. "I didn't."

"Why did you vomit?" Damon asked.

"What?"

"Why did you vomit when they took you to the river?"

Kyle jerked as though the boy had slapped him. "Damon, I'm going to have to watch you, walking around in my head like that!"

"Why did you?" Betty asked, her curiosity aroused.

"Oh, Papa was baptizing and it was my day. Naturally, they selected a chilly day when the river was cold. I didn't want to go down in the water with the congregation on the riverbank singing and watching. The little girl in front of me had her best dress on. It was pink with blue lambs on it, I remember. Her hair was carefully coiffured into long ringlets and she wore a red ribbon in the crown of her hairdo."

"Mama, I don't want to do this!"

"I told my mother I didn't want to go through with it." Kyle laughed.

"Shush, child! Do as you're told!"

"She let me know I had no choice. The little girl

266

preceding me had reddened elbows and her legs were covered with briar scratches. You know how country girls often look, even dressed up. A little bit pitiful. She was shaking, I remember that. But she marched bravely into the river where Papa stood with water creeping up his shirt as the fabric attracted it. Papa's voice was shivering and he was trembling. I never was sure whether it was from the passion of the moment or the cold water."

Damon laughed again, but Betty was not smiling. Yes, this was good for the boy, Kyle determined. It opened a wider road for them to have a mutual confessing.

"Then you vomited?" Damon asked. The child's face was intense and he had come to Kyle's knee, listening.

"Not yet!" Kyle said, grinning.

"Please, Mama! I don't want to do this!"

"The little girl grabbed her nose, just as they dunked her backward, and her cheeks poked out, holding her breath. She went down pretty, but she came up looking like a drowning chipmunk with nuts in his cheeks!"

Damon shrieked with laughter and clapped his hands. It occurred to Kyle that this was the first childlike thing he'd ever seen the boy do.

"Please, Mama, please, Mama!"

"Shut your mouth, Kyle Burnette. Don't you make a fool of your father!"

"So," Kyle continued, "I went out into that cold river, my eyes glued on that drowned chipmunk and her dress plastered to her legs and body by the water. I went, but I didn't want to go, I can tell you that!"

Damon was touching Kyle, one hand on the older man's leg, his eyes as sharp and excited as Kyle had ever seen them.

". . . in the name of the Father, and the Son and the . . ."

"I thought Papa was going to drown me. I know that was ridiculous, but it seemed like he held me under forever. He didn't, of course."

". . . Holy Ghost . . ."

"I tried to get away, to get up, and my hand slipped off my

267

nose. I strangled. I grabbed his wrist and started kicking. Still he held me under. The water was muddy."

". . . cleanse . . . evil . . ."

"When he brought me up, I was choked and I could tell by the expression on his face that I was going to catch it when we got home!" Kyle accentuated his story with lifted eyes and a mock expression of piety.

"So you vomited!"

"Yes," Kyle said, his voice softer. "Right there in front of all Papa's congregation and all over his shirt, I vomited. Let me tell you, they couldn't drag the next child into that river."

"The devil's in that vile little . . ."

"Did he spank you?"

Kyle nodded. "Wore me out."

"Please, Papa, stop! I couldn't help it, Papa!"

"Did you hate your papa?"

"Hold it!" Kyle hooted. "Let's not turn this into a Freudian feast. How far are we from supper, Betty?"

"Not far." Her voice sounded false to her own ears. "Get washed up, boys. I'll have the salad ready in a few minutes."

From the bedroom, through an open bathroom door, the sounds of water and laughter as Kyle and Damon shared the sink. This had been a good idea, Betty exulted. Excellent!

"The meal was superb!" Kyle said genuinely.

"Thank you, sir."

"I have to go to the bathroom," Damon announced.

"Then go," Betty said mildly, clearing dishes from the table.

"Shall we retire to the living room for a smoke?" Kyle asked.

"Good," Betty said. "Let me get the table cleared away. You go ahead."

Kyle was debating whether to turn on the television or risk more conversation with Damon when he became aware of the boy's presence at the bedroom door.

"What's in the trunk?" Damon asked, his voice husky.

"What were you doing in there, young man?" Kyle reprimanded.

"I was looking."

"Obviously. It isn't good manners to poke in closets and behind closed doors when you are a guest in someone's home."

"I'm sorry." Petulantly.

Kyle was looking in the bedroom, now, checking to be sure everything was in place. Absently, he said, "It's full of old odds and ends. Family things."

"About your mother and papa?"

"Yes," Kyle said, his irritation thinly masked.

"May I see it?"

"You may not."

"I wouldn't hurt anything."

"No."

Damon signaled the end of the evening by retiring to a far chair, sulking.

"Time to go," Betty acknowledged. Kyle nodded agreement.

The drive back to the clinic was devoid of idle conversation. Kyle admitted them through the side entrance and Damon went straight to bed.

"Good night," Betty whispered.

Kyle kissed her. "Thanks for supper."

"It was a good idea, wasn't it?" Betty asked.

"It appears to have been."

She kissed him and stood back, smiling. "Be careful driving home."

"See you tomorrow?" Kyle questioned.

"More than likely."

Betty watched Kyle get into his automobile, rolling up the windows, dusting the interior before starting the motor. What a moody, brooding twosome! She stood in the clinic door until Kyle disappeared out of the parking lot.

Kyle returned home by way of an all-night restaurant where he often stopped for late cups of coffee. He selected a remote rear booth and sat alone, thinking.

Papa had worn his ass out over the baptism business.

How could Damon be so frighteningly perceptive? To have dug that out of Kyle's memory! The boy had been excited about the revelations, though. This pleased Kyle. He had welded their bonds more tightly with a disclosure of something that was, painfully, so close to his heart. As a child, Kyle had often spent many agonizing hours wondering what was wrong with himself. Lord, how he struggled to make his papa proud. And how dismally he failed. Papa was a frustrated man. He yearned to be a Billy Sunday and was destined to serve in out-of-the-way, poverty-plagued parishes. The house they provided the minister was always roach-infested, drab, often with faulty plumbing and hot water problems. It was almost as though these adversities whipped Papa's religious zeal to greater frenzy, as though God were testing the man of the cloth. Papa took out his frustrations on his own son. It was a common human trait, Kyle one day learned, studying psychology. But when he was younger, before he realized that Papa could be wrong, he blamed only himself for his father's tirades. His only clue that he was not all bad came from a gentleness his mother displayed after such occurrences. She always looked at him in such a tender, compassionate manner. She lingered at his bedside at such times, wordlessly comforting him.

Having shared this piece of himself, Kyle felt sure it was a wise investment in future treatment of Damon. The boy had not missed the revealing nature of Kyle's confessions and appreciated them furthermore. Betty was right. Taking Damon to Kyle's place had been a very good idea.

Imagine that little stinker going into his closet and poking around! It was eerie the way that child could go straight to the heart of a matter.

Kyle paid for his coffee and drove home. Damn it, he'd gone back to the office and still forgot his keys! He found the hidden spare behind the duct and let himself in, carefully replacing the key for future use. He put away the dishes Betty had washed, toyed with the idea of another cup of coffee, and decided to take a bath and retire. He paused at the closet, kicking off his shoes, hanging up his jacket and trousers. He stood looking at the trunk.

It was one of those old steamers with a rounded top. Kyle wasn't sure whether you could even purchase one like it, anymore. He removed a jumble of boxes that had accumulated atop the steamer, remembering that it had to be turned on one end to get it inside the closet in the first place. He ought to dispose of most of this crap. Someday. He wrestled the trunk upend and worked it out into the bedroom.

It wasn't locked. The lock was broken, anyway. Mother used it to store her treasured mementos in the attic. The first time Kyle saw it the trunk had fascinated him. The lock was in working order, back then. He had been five. He broke the lock. God, surely he knew even at five the inevitable results of such mischief. Maybe he didn't. Kyle lifted the lid. He knew the contents well. Junk that to anybody else would be junk. He really should dispose of it all. Someday.

He lifted an old photograph of a distant relative posed beside a surrey with a young lady in the seat. Kyle had never known the names of either person. So why keep the damn thing? Still, he returned it to the drawer that covered the top half of the trunk. An inexpensive cameo brooch with a tarnished chain, a ribbon with some secret significance to Mother, faded letters relating dull family news, the drawer contained dozens of similar items. If he lifted the drawer—to hell with it. He was too tired to begin spring cleaning tonight.

He briskly reassembled the paraphernalia, pushing it back into the closet in much the same order as he found it. Someday. Not tonight.

"Easy!" Betty cautioned.

Damon's thighs pushed against her as he lifted her knees. She could feel the eruption building and she held him close. He clutched her in his ecstasy, sucking air between clenched teeth.

271

"My baby," she whispered. "My baby."

He groaned, sagging against her abdomen, his body slowly relaxing, taut muscles going tender, breathing hard from his exertion. Betty caressed his back as he lay atop her, soothing him with motion and words. One final sigh and he was asleep, arms by his sides, his cheek on her breast.

"Look not in my eyes for fear—"

Betty slipped out of Damon's bed and spent a moment smoothing the sheets, making him comfortable. She took a shower, brushed her hair, and returned to the room. She adjusted her reading light and lifted a new book of poems from a stack beside her chair and began to read. She was seeking a single phrase.

Even as she looked, she had a dread of finding it.

". . . the devil is in that boy. . . ."

"Please, Robert!" She was tearing at Papa's arm, trying to stay the vicious onslaught.

"Beat it out of him, God willing!"

"Robert! Robert! You're killing him! Our son, Robert! You're killing him!"

"Vulgar, nasty, *evil!*"

"Robert, stop it! Stop it!"

He threw her aside and she stumbled backward over the trunk. She came up, screaming, grabbing for the strap, the last he could remember, screaming. He remembered the cobwebs. They were the last conscious thing that impressed his memory. Gossamer lace filmed with attic dust stretching from joist to joist. The cobwebs and the lashing wide belt that Papa always wore. . . .

Her eyes were swollen from crying, her skin glossy like a well-polished apple. Plain. She always looked so plain. So country plain. She stood over him at the doctor's office, wincing as the medicine was applied.

"Why does he do this, Doctor?"

"God only knows, Mrs. Burnette."

"What should I do? Should I do anything?"

"I don't know. This is going to take a few stitches."

272

"He's a good man in so many ways."

"Please remain calm, Mrs. Burnette. Hysteria will be of no benefit to either of us. Hold his arm like this."

"He ministers his faith with such devotion. He has an aversion to evil things. Then—this—this has to be evil in the eyes of God. My baby. My poor baby. He was only playing."

"Mrs. Burnette, if you please! Please! I have my hands full as it is, please maintain your composure, Madam!"

"Did he say anything before he died, Reverend?"

"No, Kyle."

"Did he ask for me? Call my name?"

"Nothing."

"Not a word?"

"No."

"Please. I must know."

"There's nothing to tell. He didn't call for you or anyone else."

"Did he pray?"

"Yes."

"What did he say in his prayers?"

"To forgive his sins."

"Did he list his sins?"

"No."

"And died."

"Yes."

"Nothing more?"

"Nothing."

"Oh, God. Oh, God, I've been so bad."

"Do not condemn yourself, Kyle."

"I caused him such pain!"

"We all cause our parents pain, Kyle. It's a part of being a child. Part of being a parent. You'll see someday. Your children will do you the same way. Then you'll understand. You will forgive them."

"God rest his soul."

"Amen."

"God forgive me."

"Go back to school, Kyle."

"Poor Papa."

"Cover it over, boys. Come on, Kyle, let's not watch this. Go ahead, boys. Cover it over."

"I made him so unhappy."

"Go back to college, Kyle. Go on with your life. Stop torturing yourself. Your father was a good man. A man of God. He understands the weaknesses of man. He understood, Kyle. Someday, when you have an education and a family, you'll be more compassionate toward yourself. Toward others too, I suspect. Now, go back to school."

"Psychiatry is a highly specialized field, Mr. Burnette."

"Yes, I know. Nonetheless, that is what I elect to follow."

"It gives you nearly as many more years to go as you've spent in college already."

"I realize that."

"I feel your aptitude is more to being an internist, frankly. Personally, I never had much use for those head shrinkers. Oh, well, your decision is made, obviously. I hate to lose you from my class. You're a good student."

"Gentlemen, I have your first message in psychology. Most of you, if not all of you, are laboring under the delusion that upon graduation you will suddenly and miraculously have a keen understanding of the workings of the human mind. To this, I respond, bovine defecation!"

"Sir, are you trying to dissuade us?"

"God willing, Mr. Burnette. If I can merely enlighten you, this will dissuade you. If you truly want a study in the abnormal mind, look within. As a psychiatrist, I never knew a psychiatrist who was not in need of his own services."

Laughter.

"Good luck, gentlemen. If it should happen that you do suddenly and miraculously understand the human mind, please come back and explain it to me!"

Laughter.

274

CHAPTER 25

"HAVE YOU SEEN Larry Reirden's new book?" Betty asked.

"No." Kyle lit two cigarettes and handed her one.

"It's condensed in this month's *Cosmopolitan*."

"I wouldn't think that would be a subject that appeals to ladies."

Betty laughed. "Who said *Cosmopolitan* appealed to ladies?"

"He wrote about the same subject?"

"Damon, specifically, this time."

"Damn him," Kyle grunted, scooting farther down in the bed and pushing a pillow under his head.

"Reirden quotes Damon as saying he's a prisoner at the clinic. He says that Damon told him you intended to keep him locked up for the rest of his life."

"I suspect Damon said that."

Betty studied Kyle a few minutes as he lay staring up at the ceiling.

"Kyle?"

"Yes?"

"Damon is a prisoner, isn't he? I mean, you said so yourself—only, you said the sweven was a prisoner."

"A figure of speech," Kyle replied.

"But in fact, he is."

"I suppose, in a manner of speaking. He can't leave when he wants to, or just because he wants to. But then, not many six-year-olds can do exactly what they wish."

"How do you feel his therapy is coming along?" Betty inquired.

"We aren't losing ground."

"But are we progressing?"

"Betty," Kyle said, turning to look at her, "you've been a psychiatric nurse long enough to know that this is not an applied science, like mathematics. You don't feed in a given set of numerals and get back a given set of answers. We could be near a cure as close as tomorrow."

"Or as far away as forever?"

"Possibly, not probably."

"What would you define as a cure?"

Kyle pondered a moment, pulling on his cigarette. "If we could eliminate the sweven, certainly. And all that is attendant to the sweven, the aberrant behavior patterns, the antisocial actions. That's assuming no new factor enters the case. I think that the sweven per se is our best indication. If we could obliterate it, I feel Damon would probably go on to a relatively normal life. As normal as a genius can be, anyway."

"The other night when he was here for supper, Damon enjoyed hearing you talk about your childhood."

"I think he did, yes."

"An amazing child," Betty concluded. "Want some breakfast?"

"Coffee's good," Kyle commented.

"Mountain grown," Betty said, mimicking a television commercial.

"You know we were talking about fantasies," Kyle said.

"We were?"

"Some time ago, remember?"

"Yes."

"Do you fantasize when we're making love?" Kyle asked.

Betty contemplated Kyle's expression. "Before I cut my throat with an answer," she said, "let's swap. I asked you what your deepest darkest fantasy was and you would not answer."

"Yes, I know. I've been thinking about it."

His little finger quivered and he clamped it against the lifted coffee cup. Betty noted perspiration at the hairline of his forehead. She disguised her anticipation with busy hands, pouring more coffee for herself.

"You're right," Kyle announced. "A fantasy that is difficult to discuss becomes larger than it deserves. So, I'm going to try to tell you about it."

"Okay."

"You'll probably laugh at me."

"Us psychiatrists hear that all the time. I won't laugh."

"I fantasize that I am seducing a very young woman."

"That's a fantasy?"

"That's it."

"Oh, come on!" Betty wailed. "I'm so goddamned disappointed I may cry. Surely there's more to it than that!"

"Nope. That's it."

"I don't believe you."

"It's true."

"It's painful to tell about seducing a young woman?" Then it struck her. Kyle had given her the tools and like a psychiatrist, she must use them to dig it out of him.

"How young a woman?"

277

"Very young."

"A child?"

"Usually."

"Under ten?"

"Sometimes."

"Under eight?"

"You get the idea, why drag it out?"

Yes, she did get the idea. Betty carefully controlled her voice as she continued, "Is this young lady willing?"

"Not usually."

"Is it her first time?"

"I would imagine so."

"She is a virgin, then."

"That stands to reason."

Deliberating her questions and carefully choosing words and a tone of voice that would not drive the patient off the subject, Betty asked, "Then it's rape?"

Kyle laughed, lips twisting, eyes darting to every point except a direct glance at Betty.

"I don't know why it's so difficult to discuss a harmless fantasy," Kyle said lightly. "Everybody has them."

"Absolutely everybody," Betty acknowledged gently.

"But you know, my hands are sweating just trying to tell you about it and by God, I don't even know why I'm discussing it."

"Because we're friends and because I want to know," Betty said. "And because you discovered something the other night with Damon."

"What's that?"

"You discovered that communication is a two-way thing. A person is much more likely to bare his bones to you if he feels you have done the same thing with him."

"You know," Kyle said softly, "that's right."

"I know it's right." Betty leaned forward on the table. "Tell me how you rape her."

"Oh, come on, Betty! I don't want to talk about that. You asked for the fantasy and I've told you. I probably ruined a perfectly good fantasy in the process and will never be able to use it again."

"Do you hurt her?"

Kyle winced.

"When you enter her, it hurts her?"

"Betty, really."

Dared she go further? "Do you hurt her in any other way?"

"If you mean am I a sadist, no!"

It sounded like the murderer who indignantly denies being a thief.

"When it hurts her," Betty persisted, "does that excite you?"

"Okay!" Kyle laughed sharply. "That's enough."

"Kyle." Betty took his hand and pulled him to a standing position. "I want you to do to me exactly what you do to that young girl in your fantasy."

"Now, wait a minute!"

"I mean it! I want you to do precisely the same things. Everything, do you understand? I really want you to do it. Will you?"

She could feel the pulsating signal of an erection through his robe. "Come on," she whispered. "Come with me."

"Betty, this is going a bit far."

"It's important to me. It's exciting. Do everything, do you understand? Don't leave out anything."

Over his diminishing protests, she had lured him into it. Enticing, teasing, daring him, she pulled him into the bedroom. She played coquettish, almost childlike, and when he lifted her gown, she pushed it down with a shy smile and pulled away. This stopped him, but she could see in his eyes that she had him. She teased some more, giggling, luring him onward. His eyes had a magnificently wild glint and he was breathing through teeth gritted together with such strength that the muscles in his face were corded.

Suddenly, he shoved her down on the bed. She twisted in a gentle pretense of pulling back. He threw aside his robe and she had never seen him so large! He approached her with a tenderness that made him tremble violently, so difficult was his control. He probed gently and she tensed, both hands on his chest, her eyes wide. Deeper and she gasped, her arms shaking, holding him off her, but careful not to stop him. Deeper and she whimpered, whispering protestations. Deeper yet and she was amazed at the physical proportions he had reached in his excitement.

She did not cry aloud for fear it would snap the fragile thread of illusion. She moved with his rhythm and was shocked when he coarsely forbade it. "Lie still!" he commanded. She did so, completely unmoving. He lifted her knees, to make entry easier for her.

She now had this man at his most vulnerable moment. The pain he inflicted was not on her, because she was an adult. But had it been a child—

When he climaxed, eyes tightly shut, lips drawn back in a grimace of ecstasy, his moan rising to a cry that sounded anguished, he quivered as he held her. Playing the game, she too cried out in short accentuating sounds that heightened his moment.

When it was over, he towered over her, still in position, looking down at her. She brought him out of it slowly, correctly reading his remorse over the deed he had perpetrated.

"My baby," she soothed. "My sweet baby."

She pulled him down, rubbing his back.

"It was wonderful," Betty whispered. "Wonderful!"

"Did I hurt you?" A small voice.

"A little, but I loved it."

"I'm sorry."

"There's no reason to be sorry. It was wonderful."

Could it be? She felt him pounding erect again and with a masculine groan he urged her over onto her stomach. Betty felt him lift her into position and she struggled to keep from crying out. This time there was pain! Her act was no pantomime now. She clutched the sheets in both hands, mouth opened wide.

"Easy!" she cried. "Be easy!"

But he was not so gentle as before. His thrust was more

280

positive and she felt him driving deeper and she grabbed a pillow in her mouth to stiffle a scream. Piercing needles of heat radiated from her abdomen up her sides and down into her legs. She felt nauseated and she had a burning sensation on her shoulders of all places!

How long it took, she could not have judged. It seemed hours. She lay gasping, exhausted, eyes burning from tears, still postured when he backed away. The sheet was soaked with perspiration.

"I'm sorry." A small voice.

"It's all right."

"You won't tell anybody?"

"No. Of course not."

"Promise?"

"It—it was wonderful, my baby."

"I really am sorry."

"There's no reason to be—it was—wonderful."

She had read so many books of poems that her mind was numbed. She couldn't be sure that she hadn't read past the line she sought, letting it escape her through oversight. Finally, she gave it up and returned the books to the various libraries from which she had borrowed them.

She left her car at home so she could ride the trolley downtown. Now, with gusts of asphalt-warmed spring air sweeping Peachtree Street, she walked disconsolately past Davidson-Paxon Department Store.

She had asked for it. By God, she'd gotten it. She could blame no one but herself. It certainly wasn't Kyle's fault. He in his wisdom had tried to persuade her to drop the subject, but no, she was the big psychologist! She was going to do away with his inhibitions and make him a free man. Well, she'd succeeded. She'd gotten twice what she bargained for in the process.

He was like another person now. The scene they played out in the bedroom that morning had been repeated again and again, three times in a single day this past week. The performance seldom varied. First, in his mock rape he

281

subdued her and with tenderness took her virginity. Then, in a frenzy that was almost animal, he raped her anew.

Whoever said it got better had a big anus. Thank God she had been doing it with Damon all this time, otherwise it would have been excruciating with Kyle's size. Hell, it *was* excruciating!

Kyle had demanded that she stop staying with Damon every night. He seemed insatiable in his prurient desires. He always concluded the act with adolescent atonement and a plea not to tell.

The experience had begun to frighten her. It was as though Kyle were not Kyle for a few minutes each time. She had a horrible feeling that he was ruefully considering murder just as she reached up and pulled him down whispering, "My baby, my sweet baby."

Ridiculous, of course. It was Kyle and it was as normal as any fantasy being enacted. She had definitely asked for that, goddamn her sorry time. It was a keg of snakes she had loosed upon herself. What did she do now? Admit she had made a mistake and forfeit his companionship? That would be the ultimate result for sure.

Betty turned into a cafeteria and waited the long line through merely to get a cup of coffee. She chose a table by a window so she could watch the street traffic passing by. Her hand was trembling as she put cream and sugar into the beverage. Her hands looked old. She felt old.

She'd overplayed it, hadn't she? So goddamned sure of herself and she might have lost the game. The haunting prospect of being old, of being alone, overwhelmed her anew. She had to put the cup back into the saucer, her hand was shaking so uncontrollably.

"Okay, old girl," she counseled herself, "what's next? You have accomplished what you set out to do and now that you are holding it, what do you do with it? Let's examine a few basics."

She always talked to herself much as she would speak to someone else, or as someone would lecture her with advice, if anyone cared to do so. Which nobody did.

"Do you love this man?"

Yes. She loved him.

"Enough to marry him?"

Tomorrow, if he asked.

"Even knowing that you have made a satyr out of a dormouse?"

That was worrying her, all right. Something else, too. She was having difficulty sustaining her respect for Kyle. Yes, yes, she knew! She had respected him before the fantasy was brought out and she accepted that it was her own stupid fault. Nevertheless, and logic be damned, she was suffering cancerous doubts. She was fighting it with one rationalization after another, but this matter defied her attempts at rationale. She might as well face it, she was seeing Kyle not as the respected and dignified man she had always known him to be, but as a deviated personality under the *guise* of a respectable and dignified man. That was utterly absurd!

"Jesus, Jesus," she said aloud, "what have I done to myself?"

"Good evening, my dear."

"Ted!"

"Join you?"

"Yes!" A little too anxiously. She damn near stood up.

"Your thoughts must have consumed you," Ted observed, unloading a tray of food onto the place setting.

"I was way out there," Betty laughed.

"Have you eaten?" Ted inquired, straddling his chair and then sinking onto it.

"I'm not hungry."

"Well," he said, with a flourish of his napkin, "I'm going to go ahead and eat."

"Please do."

Here was a man who was free and easy. She was willing to bet he was the same way in his bed at night.

"Ted, may I ask you a personal question?"

"Sure."

"Do you masturbate?"

283

He spilled coffee into his mashed potatoes.

"Is this that show on TV where they hide the cameras?" Ted whispered.

"It's a serious question."

"Sure," he replied. "Do you?"

"Yes."

"Good. Pass the salt."

"Do you mind if I ask you another personal question?"

"I can scarcely wait. Maybe I should eat my dessert first. I have a feeling this meal is doomed."

"You fantasize when you masturbate, don't you?"

His eyes cut slowly to extreme left and then right, head still down and fork moving as though automated. "Yep."

"What do you fantasize about?"

Ted sipped coffee, cleared his throat, removed the napkin from his lap, and dropped it on the table.

"You know what I think?" he said, unsmiling. "I think everybody I know has gone bananas. Are you writing a thesis, or is this a liberated woman's approach to a seduction? Maybe there's a punch line somewhere along the way?"

"Actually," Betty said, reddening, "it's a serious conversation that is too personal and I owe you an apology. I realize how idiotic I must appear."

He grabbed her arm as she started to rise. "Sit down, darling. Let's start all over again. Everybody has masturbated, everybody fantasizes. Mind if I ask why you want to know?"

"I can't tell you."

"That doesn't make it easy for me to cooperate," Ted said.

"Yes. I can see that."

"Okeedoakie," Ted said, standing. "Maybe we'd better go someplace for a drink. I think I detect a damsel in distress."

Ultimately, she told him everything. Sitting at the Wit's End, surrounded by festive drinkers and ignoring the floor show, Betty began at the beginning. Ted listened, eyes

284

downcast, volunteering no reaction she could read in the dim light.

"Now, I'm scared," Betty confessed. "I'm scared of what happens when it's happening. I'm scared of the changes I'm undergoing, my attitude changes toward Kyle, I mean."

"That's unfortunate," Ted said. "Kyle is one of the finest men I know. Intelligent, dedicated, understanding, honest, one of the most brilliant psychiatrists in the business. I must congratulate you," Ted said bitterly, "you won the confidence of your patient, broke down his resistance, overcame his natural defense, and pierced his protective veil to get at the problem. Part-time psychologists and armchair doctors, God deliver me from both! A man's ego is an explosive and delicate thing. His own high opinion of himself, essential in any normal life, is ephemeral at best. He might be able to withstand abuse from an army of critics, but he can be destroyed in an instant if he doubts himself. You now have Kyle in that position, I assume you know that."

"I know." Betty cupped her mouth and nose with both hands to stop a choked sob that rose in her throat.

"You played the role of psychoanalyst and now you aren't willing to pursue the case because it's gotten sticky," Ted accused. "You managed to diagnose and expose the neurosis but you're incapable or unwilling to enter therapy to help the patient come to grips with it. Am I correct?"

Betty nodded, eyes closed.

"That's why this business isn't for amateurs," Ted said, his voice cold. "All right, let's not squander the evening with words that will damage us both. Let's see if we can work this thing out. First, I want your solemn vow that you will never tell Kyle we discussed him. That would be the final sin on the part of a psychiatrist, if he revealed a case history. I shall expect you to keep this our secret for as long as we live. I will never forgive a transgression, is that clear?"

"Yes."

"You insisted on playing psychoanalyst and you damn

well deserve this, frankly. I resent your having done it to Kyle and I doubly resent your telling me about it. However, you leave me no alternative if I want to help a friend and fellow doctor. I can't very well go in and tell Kyle what I suggest, can I? Anything done will have to be done through you."

"All right."

Ted wiggled a finger at the waiter and paid their check. Taking Betty's arm, he guided her through a maze of tables and cigarette smoke toward the exit. In his automobile, he drove toward a secluded spot in Piedmont Park where he often stopped to neck as a teen-ager during the days when he went into heat every eighteen hours.

He parked, cut the headlights, and lit a cigarette. "Now," Ted said. "Begin again and tell me absolutely everything."

CHAPTER 26

EVERYBODY LIES.
"How many miles does this automobile have on it?"
"Are the peaches fresh, Mr. Murchison?"
"When will my washing machine be delivered?"
"Honest, Mama, he didn't touch me!"
"I'll see you tonight, Damon."
"Your mother understands."
"You'll be coming home, soon."
"Your father's out of town this week."
"It will be all right."

"It won't be all right."

"All right."

"Wrong."

Damon held a book, but his eyes did not see the print. He had closed his mind to the mathematical equations working in his sitter's head as the attendant prepared a term paper.

"Oh, Kyle . . . so good . . . so good . . ."

Lies.

"Depraved . . . evil . . ."

Lies.

Damon shoved the book away and the action caught the eye of the attendant. The older man stared at Damon, waiting.

"I have to go to the bathroom."

The sitter nodded, still watching. Damon smiled weakly and walked into the toilet.

". . . kid gives me the shivers . . ."

"Assume at all times that he may not be rational. It can happen in a second. There are certain visual clues to warn you, but you must be observant . . ."

"Watch your thoughts . . . I know this is asking the impossible, but it is imperative."

"Phenomenal! Unbelievable! You want to keep testing the kid to see if he's real."

"Smart ass kid."

". . . the creeps . . ."

"I love you, Damon."

"I like you very much, Damon."

True. She did. He knew that. Betty liked him.

Where was she!

"Easy! Easy! Oh, Kyle! Please . . . easy . . ."

"My baby, my sweet baby."

"Believe me, Damon, nothing is more important to me than isolating the sweven . . . to eliminating it . . ."

Lies.

". . . like to screw that boy . . ."

". . . that girl . . ."

288

". . . his wife . . . husband . . ."

". . . her husband comes home, see . . ."

". . . ate me . . ."

". . . eat me . . ."

". . . horrible nasty people . . . no morals . . . writing things like this on public walls . . . sick . . ."

". . . blow job . . . leave time, place, date . . ."

". . . never use Lava soap, stupid! No wonder you're raw . . . when I said use soap, I thought you'd have sense enough to know it was supposed to make you slippery, not clean!"

". . . wonder if it'll hurt . . . next time, if he ever calls again . . . next time I'll let him . . ."

". . . I'm afraid you won't respect me . . ."

". . . he probably doesn't like me anymore . . ."

". . . What'll I do? I can't tell my folks . . ."

". . . he wants to divorce his wife . . . a real bitch from everything he said—"

". . . listen, he's going to San Francisco next week so the house will be empty . . ."

". . . anyway you want it, Mister. How? Ah, yeah, well. For that I'm going to have to have an extra five . . ."

". . . no girl will ever want to be touched . . . how can she want to make love to a guy with one leg . . . no, I can't let them do it . . . I'd rather be dead . . . I got to have both legs . . ."

". . . poor bastard . . . polio I think . . . wonder if he can still get it up?"

". . . sorry, honey . . . it won't cooperate . . . this happens to me sometimes and—"

". . . two chins . . . sagging breasts . . . oh, god-damn . . ."

". . . sweetest-looking ass you ever . . ."

". . . so he says, listen mother fucker . . ."

". . . hurt me . . . made me touch him with my tongue . . ."

". . . postcards with . . ."

". . . skin flicks . . . angle shots like you never . . ."

". . . Fornication Under Consent of the King . . ."

". . . like a fish market at high noon, but can she . . ."

". . . he'd rape a rock heap if he thought there was a snake in it . . . goes around sniffing girls' bicycle seats . . . you know the kind . . . Tom Dooley type, well hung . . ."

". . . look f'chrissake, it's a different world! Ten years ago they didn't allow ads on sanitary napkins, either. Or hemorrhoids! Next year, vagina sprays will sweep the market . . ."

". . . douche, see . . . new product for modern world, see . . . 'Cupid's Quiver' . . . you like that? Catchy, right? Symbolic."

"Rated X."

". . . different colored rubbers . . ."

"Once a king, always a king . . . once a knight's enough!"

". . . must've come to his knee, honest to God . . ."

". . . my luck, a beer hard and bad breath . . ."

". . . cleans up the complexion . . . it's a scientific fact . . ."

". . . he says I'm too big . . ."

". . . too loose . . ."

". . . too large . . ."

". . . small . . ."

". . . scared! Please be gentle, don't hurt me . . ."

". . . can't hear us, Melba. The door is shut; besides, he's asleep, I just checked . . ."

". . . all they think about . . . disgusting . . ."

". . . frigid . . ."

". . . horny . . ."

". . . pregnant . . . doctor can fix it . . . cost only . . ."

". . . jeezus, fella, what'd you think was in there, mint jelly? Stick it in and that's what comes out, jerk!"

". . . everything, exactly like you do to her . . . exciting . . . important to me . . . everything, understand?"

". . . panties brown, turned by time . . ."

". . . wore these on her wedding night . . . Papa pulled them down slowly, her hair came out and he looked at her . . ."

". . . there's blood!"

". . . hymen, don't you understand . . . natural. . . no reason to be alarmed . . . surprised nobody explained all this before . . ."

". . . I wanted to be gentle . . . nineteen days is a long time . . . wouldn't let me . . . started screaming, kicking . . . I mean, we are man and wife, I told her . . . hit her . . . forced her . . . mistake . . ."

"Nauseated . . . stabbing me to death . . . bit pillow . . ."

". . . she screamed and I put my hand over her mouth . . ."

". . . rape . . . so scummy . . . goddamned cops asked if I enjoyed . . ."

". . . if she hadn't wanted it to happen, it couldn't . . ."

". . . been chasing boys since she was twelve and . . ."

". . . stunt your growth, boy. Make hair grow in the palm of your hand. Go blind . . . teeth get loose . . . saps your strength . . . weakens you . . . takes calcium out of the body . . . evil . . . evil . . . God didn't mean it to be misused this way . . . unnatural . . . sick . . . evil . . . evil . . . evil . . ."

"Dr. Burnette? This is Johnny at the clinic. Listen, I hate to call you this late, but I figured I'd better not wait any longer. I was studying for my exams, like I told you I had to do. Sir? He asked to go to the toilet, Dr. Burnette, and I didn't think anything about it. I mean, he never gave me cause to think about it and, anyway, he must've taken off out the side door. No sir, no idea. About an hour ago, I guess. I did try to call you, but I spent the time looking for him. Maybe it wasn't quite an hour ago, I'm not sure. I just finished looking for him. Should I call the cops? No sir, I haven't called anybody but you, yet. No sir, I won't call anybody unless you say so. Listen, Doctor, I'm real sorry. I was studying and—"

"Kyle, it's been four hours! We must contact his father. Betty, go in there and call Mr. Daniels. Ask him to come down to the clinic. Try not to alarm him. Poor bastard. He's been through enough already without this. But we have no choice but to notify him, Kyle. Now, about the police—"

"Now lemme see here, Doc. The kid's only six years old and he shaves?"

"I really don't understand this, Dr. Burnette. I assumed you took precautions against this contingency. What's the background of this college student? Is he qualified for work of this nature? I'm not blaming you, but I do want to understand how such a thing happened. Why was Damon allowed to—"

"Hey, Earl, want something to wake you up? Get a look at this APB. Shouldn't be hard to spot this subject, right? Listen—hey, Earl, listen to this description: six years old and shaves! Under psychiatric care. Officers should use caution in handling. Genius. How'd you like a kid like that, Earl? I got enough trouble with new math without having to buy no razor blades for a six-year-old."

"Atlanta citizens are being asked to be on the lookout for six-year-old Damon Daniels. The boy, the subject of a recent best-selling book by Larry Reirden, was last seen—"

"I know it's been twenty-four hours, Doc. Our patrolmen can't give up watching banks, grocery stores, and unlighted park areas to hunt for the kid. Be patient! He'll turn up somewhere soon. Sure, sure, we'll call if we get the least inkling, okay?"

"At the conclusion of the third day, the reward total has risen to thirty-five hundred dollars with the latest offer from nationally famous author Larry Reirden, who pledged five hundred dollars. Mr. Reirden, author of a book condensed in the March issue of *Cosmopolitan* magazine, said—"

"Hey! Did you see that? Goddamned kid snatched a whole sack of hamburgers and ran. Hey! Hey! Stop that kid! Say, by God, wasn't that the kid whose picture's been on TV the last few days?"

"Investigating reports of sightings at various points around the city and as far away as Memphis . . ."

"Program note: be sure to see Larry Reirden on the *Today Show* at twenty past the hour. Mr. Reirden, author of the best-selling—"

"Fantastic mind, that boy. In my exclusive interview, which is detailed in my latest book, he told me he was being held prisoner by the doctors at—"

"In the news around the world, tonight: continued unrest in the Middle East with filmed reports on the latest conflicts. The President confronts his critics. And, in Atlanta, Georgia, the search for little Damon Daniels has been extended to cover much of the Eastern Seaboard. The FBI reports no evidence to substantiate a charge of kidnapping, contrary to earlier reports from—"

"Rape? Rape! What in God's name makes you ask that, Doc? You're not fixing to tell me the goddamned kid's got a premature dong, are ya?"

"Undergoes a metamorphosis similar to these exclusive films and photographs which appeared in my first book on this subject. Which is being reissued, incidentally. Notice the demonic expression and the facial changes that take place—"

"Publishers say the first rush printing of a hundred thousand sold out within hours and the next—"

"After Melba's death—I should've been less selfish, I know that now. I should've come by to visit more often. I just couldn't face Damon thinking, feeling, like I was. I didn't think it would be good for him, sensing the depression I felt, Doctor. I see it was a mistake. I see that now. But it took me hours to work up a front for him, you can understand that, can't you? Hours. Melba—dear God, she meant so much to me—"

". . . how d'y' spell 'fuck'? . . ."
". . . pussy . . ."
". . . climb up there, she always leaves the shades up about an inch and you can see . . ."
". . . listen, Keith, don't you ever get tired of balling? You know, morning, noon and night, Christ!"
". . . . you let Eddie have some, didn't you? He told me. Yes he did, he told me and Eddie wouldn't lie about something like that. Come on, hear? Let me have a little, okay? Come on. You let Eddie have some, didn't you? Come on . . ."
"Bird's cage full of . . ."
". . . five bucks for a quicky . . ."
". . . . she wasn't a virgin *anywhere*, know what I mean?"
". . . pickup . . ."
". . . stud . . ."
". . . talking about sex . . ."
"There you go! Always talking about something to eat!"

"Potentially dangerous—I'm not shitting! This is a goddamned medical report, so shut up and run it!"

"His mother died under tragic circumstances, a victim of her own hand. Reports from De Kalb County coroner—"

"Must be cold. Hungry. Too smart to go out by day."

"You've been here seven days, Kyle. Go home. Rest. We'll call you if there are any new reports."

"Can't believe I've made so many mistakes."

"Kyle, you're incoherent. Go home, goddamn it!"

"Come with me, Kyle," Betty urged gently.

"Need some help, Betty?"

"Yes, Ted, please. Listen, would you mind following us? I'm positive he'll fall asleep in the car and I'll never get him to his apartment alone. I wouldn't want to ask the doorman. You can imagine the talk it'll create, if I do."

"Sure. I'll be right behind you. You two go ahead."

"Come on, Kyle. Kyle, come on. Kyle! Come on, Baby, I'm taking you home."

"Better stay here."

"Kyle, for heaven's sake, be sensible. Look at yourself! You need rest. They can call you at home as well as here at the clinic. Now, damn it, get up and come on!"

"All right."

"Good boy. Come on, now."

Betty pulled into the basement parking garage and maneuvered into the space reserved with Kyle's name. True to her prediction, Kyle was snoring against the far door. She pulled him onto his side, head toward the steering wheel, and fished in his pockets for the apartment door keys. Not there. She angrily reprimanded herself for overlooking them at the office. Then she remembered the hidden key under the duct upstairs.

Ted pulled into the garage as Betty walked toward the elevator, heels echoing on concrete.

"He's asleep in the front seat, Ted. I'm going on up and unlock the door. Hold on and I'll be down to help you with him."

"Okay, Babe."

She rode the elevator to Kyle's floor and briskly covered the carpeted hall to his apartment. She felt along the duct. Nothing. Probably have to call the house manager, or worse, go back to the office for the keys. Kyle must've moved the damned key. It would be so like him to change hiding places because he'd revealed this one to Betty and Damon that night—

With a racing heart, Betty moved to the door and stood staring at it. She put a trembling hand on the knob and turned. Unlocked. She pushed it open.

Betty entered on stocking feet, leaving her shoes in the hall. She passed the kitchen door and knew immediately that Damon was here. Evidence of food consumed littered the cabinets, but no dishes. Opened cans, empty bread wrappers, an overturned jar of peanut butter could be seen in the dim light from the open hall door. She put one hand against a wall and eased herself toward the living room, barely breathing, listening, eyes wide trying to penetrate the unlighted interior of the apartment.

A gurgling rale came to her from the distance. A grunt. Like a pig in the night being nudged awake by a fellow pen mate. A sudden crash brought her up short, freezing her as she stood. She heard a new sound and for a moment had difficulty identifying it. Finally, she knew it to be urine spattering on something—it sounded like paper.

Would he run? Attack? Hurt himself? Or her? Betty rounded the corner, one shoulder striking a hanging picture which she avoided by dropping her height and sliding beneath it, her back to the wall.

There were knives in the kitchen drawers. Did Kyle own a pistol? As her eyes became more accustomed to the paucity of light, she saw the apartment was in a shambles. The couch had been shredded and cotton batting thrown everywhere. Nothing was upright, everything vandalized. The books and figurines had been raked from the shelves, the window curtain was askew, partially pulled down.

She knew approximately where he was by the consumptive breathing. She knew it was the sweven, not Damon, who stood somewhere in that bedroom.

"Cunt!"

The yell pierced her like an icepick and Betty fought to regain control of her muscles as she broke into violent shivering, biting her lip to keep from speaking, crying out.

"Do what you do to that girl, Kyle . . ." The voice was not altogether the baritone of the sweven, but lay somewhere between that resonant tone and a mocking child's voice.

"Do exactly what you do to that young girl, do you understand? It's exciting! Oh, yesssssss—"

Dear God, had he gone completely insane?

"Get thee hither, bitch!" Roaring. The reverberation of the rasping breath was louder, closer. Had she moved?

"Turn on the lights," Betty said softly.

"Oh, Kyle—my sweet baby—" The jeering inflection lifted the tone almost to contralto. "It was so nice, Kyle!"

"Damon, please turn on the lights. I can't see."

She felt before her with one hand and a foot, seeking firm and unlittered footage, dreading to give up the support of the wall. Where were the light switches? Had she never noticed before? She pushed things aside with her toe before putting her heel down on the floor.

"Anybody who says it gets better has a big—"

Betty groped for the switch and when her fingers found it, she shoved it up. The bedroom leaped at her with its illumination.

He had destroyed everything. The mattress, the seat from the toilet, an old wedding dress. Water from the smashed toilet bowl had flooded the room so that every step was a moist one. Old photographs had been torn into confetti and were like dirtied snow over the clothing Damon had thrown from the closet. A broken mirror from over the bureau caught overhead light in a hundred shards and threw reflections at odd angles onto the walls and ceiling.

Amid it all sat Damon, nude but for a single article. Upon

his head like a floppy beret was a woman's pair of brown undies with antique tatted lace bordering the legs. The garment was old and since it was weak with age it had split in the crotch, allowing some of Damon's hair to protrude garishly. A stench of ammonia pervaded the room. Damon had urinated on everything.

"Oh, there's nothing to be sorry for, Kyle." Damon's head cocked to one side like a puppy struggling to identify a strange noise.

"It was wonderful, Kyle."

Betty knew the contents of the trunk were the bulk of the litter. She correctly guessed that the underpants on Damon's head had been inside that trunk also.

"So exciting!" the thin voice exulted. It was the sweven's tortured features, but not the sweven's articulation.

Betty bumped a book with her toe and upon seeing the title, she groaned and picked it up.

"Everything just like it was with her, Kyle, please."

She looked at the naked form taunting her and sobbed. "Oh, Damon," she whispered, "oh, my poor Damon. My poor Kyle. Oh, dear God, bless them both."

The pages of the book were stuck together by moisture, yellowed with age, brittle with time. Her fingers trembling, she thumbed the sodden leaves of the book, sure already what she would find.

"Look not in my eyes for fear—"

CHAPTER 27

"WHAT THE—"

"Jesus! What's that odor?"

"Kyle, wait a minute. Kyle!"

He pawed at the living room lights and stood, legs spread, stunned by the destruction he saw. His head waggled as though knocked senseless. Kyle stumbled through the debris to the bedroom and halted, breath hissing.

"God—"

"Please, Papa"—that contemptuous contralto—"I was only playing, Papa. I didn't mean to hurt anything, Papa.

Don't whip me! Don't whip me! Don't whip me, Papa!"

Ted took it in with a glance and put a hand on Kyle's arm. "Easy," Ted said softly.

"Be *easy*, Kyle—you're hurting me—I like it!" Damon's head was postured oddly to one side, his large brown eyes turned from the normal position so that each peered in a different direction, like the victim of strabismus, yet oddly peering at Kyle. The falsetto voice came between curled lips. "Do what you did to the little girl, Kyle—*easy*, Kyle. Easy! You're hurting me!"

A sound akin to a sob escaped Kyle's throat. "Get those off your head, goddamn you!" he commanded.

"Evil!" The contralto abruptly dropped to a thundering baritone. "Evil!"

"Please, Papa," the contralto replied, "don't, Papa!"

"Get away, you bitch!" The rumbling bass.

"He was only playing, Robert."

"Look at this—cum!"

"No! No! No! I was only playing."

"What is this?"

"Blew my nose."

"On her pants?"

"Blew my nose."

"God *damn* you—evil little—"

"Please, Robert, stop. He's a child, Robert. Stop. No more, Robert! Stop! You're killing him! Robert!"

Kyle lunged at Damon and with amazing speed the boy eluded him, crouching in a far corner.

"Easy, Kyle." Ted's voice, firm.

"Get those off your head, Damon," Kyle demanded.

"Do what you did to the little girl, Kyle!" Damon taunted.

Kyle slashed out at Damon and again the child slipped away, the two of them circling like warriors seeking a vantage.

"I want to enter psychiatry to help others." Damon's voice altered to an entirely new pitch.

"Damon." Kyle was trying to speak rationally, his hand

300

quivering as he extended it. Almost pleading. "Please give those to me. Please give them to me."

"Kyle," Ted offered, "let me—"

"Shut up! Get out of here!"

Ted and Betty looked at one another, mute.

"These were things which belonged to my mama, Damon. You shouldn't have done this."

The voice climbed in pitch again, mocking, "Dirty, dirty, dirty. Fuck your mama is dirty, dirty, dirty."

"Damon, I'm losing my patience with you."

"Blew my nose!"

"On the panties?"

"Blew my nose."

"You insufferable beast!" Kyle lunged at Damon and slipped. He sprawled at the boy's feet and Damon pivoted on one heel like a matador having completed a pass.

"We are what we think, our thoughts are the fibers of the cloth that weave the man—" Sepulchral tones.

Kyle rose to one knee and looked at the cluttered room as though seeing it for the first time. He had cut his hand slightly on a piece of broken mirror. He gazed at the blood, a drop only, as though mesmerized. Damon continued, his voice alternately one character, then another.

"Forgive me, Papa, please don't die. Forgive me."

"He said nothing? Did he call my name?"

"Nothing."

"His sins—did he pray for his sins?"

"Please, Papa, I was only playing!"

Kyle's hands covered his face.

Betty took a step nearer. "Kyle, darling, I think we have the answer now." Her voice choked. "I want to read to you, Kyle. Do you hear me?"

"Get out," Kyle seethed. "Both of you, get out! I cannot do my work with you interfering."

"Kyle, let us be of assistance," Ted said.

"No, goddamn it, he's my patient. Get out of here."

"Kyle," Ted reasoned, "you're worn out from these past few days. We really want to stay and help—"

301

"I want you to leave me alone with him," Kyle demanded.

"Who are you?" the bass voice questioned.

"Look not in my eyes for fear—" Contralto.

Betty held a finger to the opened book. "There, Kyle! That's the answer, don't you see? Let me read this to you. I want you to listen and—"

"Shut up, goddamn you all, shut up!" Kyle screamed.

"Go lock the hall door, Betty," Ted commanded softly.

"You killed my mommy." Damon pointed a crooked finger at Kyle. "Not me. You!"

"Oh my God, Ted, we've got to do something!"

"Be still, Betty."

"Let me call someone."

"No. Be still."

The baritone sneered, "No better than your papa, Kyle Burnette. Why have you no progeny, Physician? I am your child!"

Kyle was on his feet again, trousers wet from the soaked floor. He advanced on Damon with a sureness he had not displayed heretofore.

"I don't want to hurt you, Damon," Kyle warned.

"Hurt me," the high-pitched taunt, "like you did the little girl, Kyle. Hurt me! So wonderful. My baby, my sweet baby."

"I want you to give me that thing off your head," Kyle ordered.

"Who are you?" the baritone queried.

"I am Dr. Burnette," Kyle replied evenly.

"Ah, Doctor! Molester, deviate, evil."

"It is you who are evil," Kyle retorted.

"Look not in my eyes for fear—"

Betty echoed the sweven's words, "Look not in my eyes for fear—"

"Ted"—Kyle's entire mood changed as he implored—"please take Nurse Snider out of here. I must have no further interruptions. Please. Do that. Please."

"Betty," Ted said, "please be silent. Let me handle this."

Betty was weeping now. "Ted, I want you to hear this. If you—"

"If you can't be quiet," Ted said sternly, "I must ask you to leave. I don't want to do that. I may need you. But I must insist, be silent!"

"You've been in that trunk again!" The grumble of the bass voice. "How many times must I beat you? Evil little—"

"Now you give me that," Kyle demanded. He worked Damon toward a corner and, like a caged animal, Damon's eyes flitted here, there, wary.

"Easy, Kyle," Ted cautioned, sanity amid madness.

"You think this hurts me?" Kyle directed at Damon. "Nobody believes you."

"Ah, Physician"—almost gentle—"you believe."

"Thoughts are not crimes," Kyle countered.

"Crime is to the beholder."

"Damon, I'm asking you nicely, take that off your head."

"To deny the thought," the sweven accused, "is to act upon it, Physician. Your actions are known by we three."

Kyle halted. "Three?"

Gloating. "Three."

Kyle turned to Betty, his lips discolored with shock. She knew. It was all over her face. Kyle's shoulders sagged and he stood with knees bent as though about to collapse.

"Kyle, let's go in the other room," Ted suggested. "We can talk this out, decide what to do. Nothing here is beyond repair or replacement. Nothing, Kyle."

"I wanted you to leave," Kyle said. "You wouldn't listen to me. I never interfered in your cases. I never did that to you."

"This is unimportant, Kyle. This is a psychiatric session, nothing more. It's the same as a clinical session. He is a hysterical patient. Nothing more."

"Lies," Damon smirked.

"You're very tired, Kyle. It's been an exhausting week. With rest you'll react differently. You'll put all this into perspective and everything will be all right."

"Lies." Amused.

"Let me take you out of here, Kyle. We'll get somebody to clean the place. I'll send a couple of orderlies from the clinic. You don't have to worry about it. I'll do it."

"Evil . . . sick . . . lies . . ."

"He's trying to destroy me," Kyle whispered, his head curiously angled, turning to stare at Damon.

"He can never destroy you," Ted soothed.

"I won't let him destroy me," Kyle said. He looked at Betty with a pained expression.

"Oh, God," she sobbed. "My babies—"

"Maybe we should handle this together," Ted suggested to Kyle.

Damon lowered his body, lips lifted, exposing his gums, eyes darting from one man to the other.

"Yes, perhaps," Kyle agreed. "He's not rational, as you can see."

"Do you think we should physically subdue him?" Ted questioned, but making no aggressive move.

"It appears we must," Kyle stated. His head was still oddly positioned.

"On the other hand," Ted proposed mildly, "possibly we should attempt to snap him out of it. You know your patient better than I, Doctor Burnette. What do you suggest? How have you brought him out of it in the past?"

"It—usually—goes away."

"Then, maybe we should ignore it. We will talk to one another and ignore it. Nothing it can say will disturb us."

A grumble from Damon, "Lies, Physician."

"You see what he's trying to do," Kyle said to Ted. "He's been in my head getting all those terrible lies to tell people."

Betty sagged against a wall, muffling her cries.

"You can see that, can't you, Ted?"

"Of course I can, old buddy."

Damon laughed. "Lies," he hissed.

"Betty, see if you can find some coffee," Ted said. "I think Kyle and I could use a cup."

She made no move.

304

"Betty." A command, now.

She tripped over an arm of the couch as she went to the kitchen. Spilled sugar gritted beneath her stockinged feet. Betty chose her steps carefully, passing through the kitchen to the hall. She opened the door to get her shoes.

"Everything all right in there, miss?" It was the guard from downstairs.

"Dr. Burnette has a patient. A boy," Betty said, struggling to assume composure and a professional bearing.

"We had some complaints about screaming. You sure everything is all right?"

"Yes, positive."

"Mind if I have a look, ma'am?"

"I'd rather you wouldn't," Betty said, blocking the partially opened door. "Dr. Burnette is a psychiatrist, you know. These moments with a patient are critical. Very critical. You understand."

"I must insist that you let me take a look."

"Wait here," Betty said, her strain now obvious even to herself. "I'll call Dr. Burnette's associate, Dr. Drinkwater. He will talk to you."

"Don't close the door, ma'am," the guard ordered, bracing it with one hand. She noticed his other hand very near a pistol on one hip.

As she stepped into the foyer, the guard pushed the door completely open, his back parallel with the wall.

"I must insist you remain there," Betty said sharply. "I'll get Dr. Drinkwater."

The man's eyes touched on the wreckage of the living room.

"Ted!"

She lifted a palm to halt the guard. "Ted, can you come here a moment?"

The pistol was out now and the guard was tense, alert.

"There's no need for that," Betty said evenly. "Ted, for God's sake!" Betty screamed.

Ted appeared at the bedroom door, red with anger. Seeing the security man, Ted heaved a sigh of resignation.

"I'm glad you're here, Guard," Ted said, softening the

305

man's offense. "I may require your assistance. I'm Dr. Drinkwater."

"What is it, Doc? Judas, what a mess!"

"I have a disturbed patient in here," Ted explained. "Wait there, if you will. Should I need you, I'll call."

"How big is he?" the guard asked.

"A child."

"A kid? Goddamned vandals."

"He's disturbed," Ted corrected curtly. Faced with obvious authority, the guard quickly put away his weapon and yielded.

"Nurse," Ted questioned, "did you do as I asked?"

"I was about to, Doctor, when I went to the door."

"Please get on it," Ted said.

"Yes, sir." Then, to the guard, Betty said, "I was looking for coffee."

"Let me help you, Miss. That floor's full of glass. Got any idea where it might be?"

"None."

"Look, I'll go down and get some at the security station. It's already made. I'll bring the pot. You reckon there's any cups not broken?"

"I'm not sure. Perhaps you could bring cups? Sugar and cream, if you can get it."

"Powdered, both of 'em."

"That's fine."

Relieved to see him exit, Betty returned to the bedroom door, outside, watching.

Kyle had been crying. He was kneeling on the floor, carefully picking up remnants of photographs, shaking water off them.

"The only pictures I had of Mama," Betty heard him say.

"We'll piece them together again," Ted said, also helping retrieve shreds of paper. "They'll shoot another shot of it and make a photo good as new."

"He shouldn't have done this," Kyle sobbed.

"Lies," Damon muttered. The boy was hunched into a corner, genitals dangling between spread legs, eyeing the

306

two men as they meticulously gathered together the torn items. Damon still wore the underpants on his head. He jabbed a forefinger of one hand into the open palm of the other hand, quick, stabbing motions designed to relieve tension, much as a person balances a leg on the ball of a foot and jiggles it for the same reason.

"Here's a piece," Kyle said, his head still tilted at the same strange angle. "He shouldn't have done this," Kyle said.

"No, he shouldn't have," Ted agreed.

Upon seeing Betty, Ted motioned her back, but she did not move.

"Those are my mama's clothes," Kyle said, identifying an article Ted lifted and dropped.

"She wore them on her wedding night," Kyle explained. He looked at Damon and suddenly screamed, "I told you to take those off your goddamned head, Damon!"

Damon bounced his weight up and down in a kneebend position that made his oversized privates flop back and forth.

When Kyle next spoke, it was the same monotone he had been using when conversing with Ted. "I guess the pressed bridal flowers are gone, too. Did you see a wedding band?"

"Not yet," Ted replied. "We'll find it, though."

"Mama never had many things to show for her life. Papa was always giving things away. She kept all this in the attic in the trunk. The lock used to work. If I had repaired the lock, maybe—"

Betty moaned, a hand over her mouth to trap the sound.

"When Papa died—" Kyle looked up at Ted. "Did you know my father was dead?"

"Yes. I knew."

"I told you?"

"Yes."

"When?"

"When it happened, I think. Oh, here's the wedding band."

"Give it to me!" Kyle snatched it away, holding it

fiercely. He looked at the ring for a long moment, then his eyes went from Ted to Betty, filled with tears. His gaze lowered slowly. Betty and Ted followed his line of vision. On his knees, sitting on his heels, Kyle's trousers were taut. Beneath the fabric they could see what was happening.

Kyle's voice was a thin wail. "I can't help it!"

"Lies," Damon rumbled.

"I can't help it, Ted! I don't know why it happens."

"It's not important, Kyle," Ted said, but his expression revealed despair.

"Oh, God!" Kyle stared at his rising penis. He then looked up at Ted and seeing his associate's face, Kyle lifted one hand in supplication, the ring in the outstretched palm.

"I can't help it, Ted!"

Kyle moved so fast, it caught them all unaware. In one fluid motion, he spun around and leaped at Damon. Surprised by the unexpected assault and hampered by his squatting position, Damon was pinned before he could escape.

Kyle snatched at the underpants. He yanked the garment off Damon's head and with it came a fistful of Damon's hair. The child screamed in pain and surprise. In the next instant, Kyle had struck the boy with a full swinging blow that knocked Damon headlong to the floor. He advanced on the fallen child as Betty and Ted scrambled to reach them. When Ted's hand touched Kyle's arm, Kyle came around and struck Ted in the face, knocking the doctor flat.

"Kyle!" Betty screamed. "Stop, Kyle!" He moved toward the boy, teeth clamped behind drawn lips; Betty saw that it was no longer the sweven they faced as Damon lifted one hand to ward off the advancing psychiatrist. "Kyle, wait!"

"You sided with him," Kyle accused.

"No, Kyle, I did not."

"Liar!" He slapped at her with a backhand and Betty barely managed to avoid being struck.

"Listen to me, Kyle."

"Get out of the way, Betty."

"I want you to hear what I have to say, Kyle." She groped

308

behind her until Damon's hand went into hers. The boy was sobbing uncontrollably. Betty circled around Kyle, moving the child toward the door.

Betty spoke softly. "Remember the poem, Kyle? *A Shropshire Lad*, by A. E. Housman. Can you remember it?"

Ted was behind Betty now; she felt Damon pulled away and then they were gone. She fell back a step. "Let's remember together, Kyle," she said, her voice trembling.

Kyle came toward her, sucking, exhaling, sucking air into a raling chest. His eyes were pinpoints, eyebrows lifted.

His head, angulated in the same disturbing manner to one side, was now held with the chin pulled inward. Although his arms were at his sides, his movements slow, he had the feel of a man bordering on aggression.

Betty fell back again, whispering, "Remember, Kyle?"

"Look not in my eyes for fear—"

CHAPTER 28

SHE MOVED toward the bathroom door, backing away from Kyle but retreating no more than necessary to remain an arm's length from him. Except for Kyle's labored breathing, the apartment seemed hushed, stilled, and ominously empty.

"The sweven was right, Kyle."

"You sided with him."

"No, my darling."

"You told him."

"No, Baby, Kyle. You told him."

She bumped the wall and sidestepped, easing out into the living room, her ankles twisting on the uncertain footing of the debris-laden floor. She kept her eyes on Kyle's face, alert for a subtle clue which might indicate his innermost emotions.

"He destroyed your property because you cherish your things so highly, Kyle. Material things, books, objects, all have a symbolic place in your life, Kyle. A man who resents people touching his belongings is a selfish man. He is selfish not only with the material things, he is selfish with his emotions, Kyle."

"You betrayed me," Kyle seethed.

"No, darling I did not."

"I trusted you."

"Damon has been systematically destroying you, Kyle. He attacked your manhood. How did he know you suffered doubts about that?"

"You told him!"

"No, baby. You told him."

She nearly tripped on an overturned chair, skirted it, still moving only so far as necessary to stay out of reach.

"He struck at the very things most precious to you, Kyle. He knew precisely where to place the dagger. Don't you see? He knew the tender spots and the tough. See, Kyle?"

Kyle's shoulders drew forward, lips aquiver.

"He knew where it hurt the most, didn't he, Kyle? He knew you fantasized about raping a child. He knew about your mother's underpants and the way her wedding ring affected you. He knew your deepest, darkest secrets. Nobody else could possibly know all that but you, and you denied them even to yourself."

"I trusted you," Kyle snorted. "Bitch!"

"You can trust me, Kyle."

"You wanted to hurt me."

"No. That's not true, Kyle. From the beginning, he knew and taunted you, remember? When you asked him, 'Who are you?' he always replied, 'That is not the question, the question is, who are you?' Kyle, don't you see what was happening?"

312

Kyle crouched, arms slightly spread, blocking escape. Jockeying for position, trapping her against the wall with the window looking down on Atlanta.

"Remember what Khan said? 'You are chasing reflections,' he said. Kyle, please listen to what I am saying. Listen to the meaning of the words. Please!"

"Bitch," Kyle hissed.

"When you are psychoanalyzing someone, Kyle, you pick at their weaknesses, exposing them. You needle the patient and maneuver him into a position of self-illumination. You put him where he can see himself. If it isn't handled properly, it may destroy him. This is what happened, Kyle. It happened to you. Because you haven't handled the information properly."

"Thou hast offended me," Kyle intoned.

"Oh, darling," Betty gasped. "Do you hear yourself?"

"Thou hast sinned!"

"Listen to your voice!"

"Bitch!"

"Listen, Kyle, listen!"

Gurgling with every inhalation, he stood between her and the exit, his legs apart, muscles taut.

"If what Damon said had not been true, it would not have hurt," Betty said, her voice husky, tremulous. "Riddled with guilt because of an adolescent sexual desire for a parent, you yielded to your father's claims of evil."

Alarmed, Betty watched Kyle's lips curl, face drawing long, contorted, eyebrows arched.

"Sweven!" Betty shouted.

He jolted.

"Sweven!" Betty accused, pointing at him. "Look at yourself. Your face is constricted, twisted, you're breathing like a tubercular patient! You're hunched, deformed. Sweven!"

He looked at his hands, shaking his head as though to cast off the transformation.

"Look not in my eyes for fear," Betty said sharply.

A shiver traced Kyle's body from top to bottom much as a puppy slings off water after a swim.

313

"He's been telling you all along, Kyle. He's been putting it right in front of you and you did not see it. Remember the poem?"

He dove at her and Betty knocked aside his hands, throwing him off balance. She jumped across an overturned chair and put it between them.

"Think, damn you, think," Betty demanded. "Your whole life depends on this moment, Kyle."

He was raging, now. A moaning wail of frustration and anger rose with each exhalation.

"Look not in my eyes for fear—"

He bounded toward her and she shoved the chair in front of him. He nearly fell. He grabbed the furniture and threw it aside with awesome strength.

> Look not in my eyes, for fear
> > They mirror true the sight I see,
> And there you find your face too clear
> > And love it and be lost like me.

Kyle had her now. Blocking her avenue to safety. Betty's lips were thinned, her voice trembling, as she recited from the depths of a memory stimulated by fear.

> One the long nights through must lie
> > Spent in star-defeated sighs,
> But why should you as well as I
> > Perish? gaze not in my eyes.

He was very close to her, fencing her with outstretched arms, his breath fetid in her face. She smelled the masculine odor of anxiety, panic, desperation.

His hand came across her face with a vicious slap that knocked her against the wall and brought blood to her mouth. She was crying, tears streaming down her face, but she continued to speak in a tremorous voice held steady by sheer determination.

"They mirror true the sight I see—"

He seized her by the hair and yanked her to her knees. His lips contorted, eyes wild, he slowly raised a closed fist. She reeled under the next blow, her head swimming, eyes glazed, and she saw blood spew from her nostrils.

"Kyle, my darling, please—"

He came down atop her, one knee in her abdomen, pinning her to the floor. He gurgled in short, heavy snorts, glaring down at her.

"I love you," she whispered. "I love you."

She saw his hands coming as though from a great distance. Moving toward her throat. She made the effort to lift an arm in defense and her hand felt leaden, too heavy to raise.

Dimly, she heard her own voice, reciting by rote, ". . . and love it . . . and be lost . . . like me . . ."

She awoke to the roar of room sounds when there are no sounds. A millennium away, somewhere at the brink of infinity, she heard a child crying. Sobbing. Her mouth tasted copperish, a brackish aftertaste similar to a morning following a night of drinking.

A bumping noise.

Betty turned, every muscle protesting, onto one side. She lay looking along the floor through a jumble of twisted, torn household belongings. Her eyes blurred and she blinked hard, fast, to clear them.

Bumping.

She focused on her own arm. Blood. Her blood. Caked, rusted scales of brown flecked her clothing, her sleeve was ripped.

Bump. Bump. Bump. Insistently. Bump. Bump.

"Betty! Kyle!"

Ted?

"Open the door!"

"Ted?"

She heard a whimpering, a sobbing. She tried to pinpoint the direction from which it came. The spare bedroom?

"Betty!"

Ted's pounding on the door rose to a frenzy.

"I'll get a crowbar." Another man's voice.

"Wait a minute. I hear something."

"Coming." Too soft. She lifted her voice. "Coming!"

Her nose was scabbed. Dried blood.

315

"Ted."

"Dear God."

"I'm all right. Please. Stay out. For a while. Give me a few more minutes."

"Are you sure?"

"I'm sure. Stay here unless I call you."

"Betty, I don't think so."

She grabbed his shirt with both hands, her teeth bared. "You stay here unless I call you!"

"Okay, Babe. I'll be here."

He checked the internal lock to be sure he could open the door from the outside, then Ted pulled it closed.

She had lost her shoes. She searched through the rubble until she found them and put them on. She teetered into the bedroom, past a small pile of salvaged photographs, across the ripped mattress. There was cotton ticking in the lavatory. She scooped it out and dropped it to the floor. The mirror was broken in here, too. She laved her face with water, a dingy brown sediment flowing from her chin to the bowl. With her tongue, she probed her teeth. Thank God they were all still there. The water seared her mouth. She spit it out.

A single towel hung neatly folded and, oddly out of place, in place. She daubed her face and eyes, wetting one corner of the terry cloth to use as a washrag.

Her ablution complete, Betty stroked her hair with the backside of one hand and stood upright, forcing tender muscles to relent, allowing her to become erect. She tested her neck, turning her head this way and that. Satisfied, sore but unbroken, she walked back into the living room.

He was in the other bedroom. On the floor, he sat flat, legs outstretched before him, his hands limp between his knees, palms up, fingers curled. His shoulders sloped forward, head down, tears and mucous dripping from the tip of his nose and chin. She stooped beside him.

"Kyle?"

She could see his mind returning from some far time and place. Tenderly, using a piece of sheet, Betty daubed his nose, cleaned his face.

316

"I'm sorry," he croaked.

Betty returned to the front door.

"We'll be down to the clinic in a while, Ted."

"Everything all right?"

"It's going to be."

"May I help?"

"No. Wait for us at the clinic, if you will. We may be a few hours, however."

"You're sure you want me to leave?"

"Positive. Go on, now."

Betty watched Ted and the security guard walk slowly down the hall.

"Ted!"

"Yes?" He turned.

"Where's Damon?"

"Downstairs. I'll take him to the clinic."

"Good."

She took a deep breath, held it, let it out slowly. Back in the bedroom, she squatted at Kyle's side, very near but not touching him.

Softly, she asked, "How do you feel?"

"Not so good." Sobs.

"That's too bad. But I think you'll feel better, soon."

"Do you still like me?"

"Like you?" Betty smiled tenderly. "I love you, Kyle."

"Are you sure?"

"Oh, yes. I'm sure." Her eyes were immensely sad.

"How can you?"

"It ain't always easy," she said gently.

The hoped-for smile did not materialize. Kyle said hoarsely, "I hurt you."

"We hurt one another."

"I'm sorry."

"It was worth it," Betty whispered. "Wasn't it?"

"I don't know." His lips twisted and he began to cry again.

"Let's get washed up, shall we?" She put a hand under his arm, guiding him as he slowly rose.

"What we both need is a bath and fresh clothing," Betty

317

said. "We can go to my place for both. I'll make some coffee and orange juice. How does that sound?"

His body was heaving with racking sobs.

She took the elevator to the subterranean garage. The keys were still in her automobile. She put him in the front seat and rounded the vehicle to get in herself.

"Everything will look better after we get cleaned up," Betty said. "The sun will begin to shine again."

They had driven to Betty's apartment in silence, Kyle sitting against the far door, looking out the window. The first order of business was a bath for them both and fresh clothing. This done, they sat in the kitchen as Betty prepared coffee. Between them they had not said ten sentences since leaving Kyle's place. Now, mute and distant, Kyle drank his coffee, avoiding Betty's gaze. Slowly, regaining a semblance of sanity, the recent hours became unreal in the prim surroundings of Betty's kitchen.

"It was my fault all along?" Kyle questioned.

"Yes."

"Why didn't I see that? I must have been blind."

"All of us are, when it's that close."

"My libido working out fantasies through that boy," Kyle said, his tone incredulous. "I wasn't fighting Damon's dissociated personality! I was fighting my own alter ego. It was me trying to destroy myself every time the sweven emerged."

"Yes, it was," Betty agreed.

He stared at her a moment. "I'm ill of course."

"Yes."

"It'll take years of analysis, probably."

"Probably."

He searched her eyes for hope. "At least I see my problem now."

"That's no small thing."

Kyle's hand went hesitantly across the table, falling short of touching her. Betty grasped his fingers and held them.

"I'm ruined," Kyle said. "My life, my career."

"That isn't true, Kyle. A statement like that refutes the premise of psychiatry. You'll get help. You'll come to grips with your problem and be a happier, more successful psychiatrist for the experience."

"They may want my resignation at the clinic."

"You know that isn't so, Kyle. You can take a leave of absence. Ted and the other doctors will be far more concerned with your health and well-being than with your absence. Ted Drinkwater is your friend first, your associate second."

"Yes," Kyle admitted, "perhaps you're right."

"I am right."

Kyle squeezed her hand and pulled away. "It'll be nice to tell Mr. Daniels we've found the key to helping Damon. By God, he deserves some good news, doesn't he?"

"Yes, he does."

"Of course, there's the glandular imbalance, still. But with the strides being made these days in endocrinology, chances are Damon will live a long and useful life."

"Sure he will." Betty smiled.

"He'll have to find another psychiatrist," Kyle said.

"Every doctor must release his patient sooner or later," Betty counseled gently. "Now is the time to release Damon from your care."

"Jesus, I'll miss that kid." Kyle stood abruptly. "Shall we go to the clinic?"

"If you're ready."

"I am. Some odds and ends to clean up. Besides, I have to talk to Ted."

"About what?"

Kyle's expression mirrored mild amazement.

"About our new patient," he said.

13/11